The Eighth Page
"A Christmas Journey"

Craig D. Lounsbrough, M.Div., LPC

For information, or to order additional copies, please contact:

Beacon Publishing Group
P.O. Box 41573 Charleston, S.C. 29423
800.817.8480| beaconpublishinggroup.com

Publisher's catalog available by request.

ISBN-13: 978-1-949472-95-0

ISBN-10: 1-949472-95-7

Publishing in 2018. New York, NY 10001.

First Edition. Printed in the USA.

Dedication

This is a book of both history and hope, for the former is the evidence of the latter. And were it not for my own history and the hope that had gifted me there, this book would not be possible. In fact, it would have been completely impossible.

Mom and dad survived a history of their own that would have extinguished the hope of most. Being the youngest in their respective families, with both of their fathers having abandoned those families in the throes of the Great Depression, life was anything but hopeful. Theirs was a story of working odd jobs for nickels and dimes while walking railroad tracks in the grip of winter to pick up coal fallen from passing trains so that they might have heat for the night.

The onset of a World War sent my dad into the Army to service radios in B-17 Flying Fortresses and B-24 Liberators. Barely a teenager, my mother picked tomatoes and did dictation to help support herself and her family. Long after the conclusion of the war they met and finally married in 1957.

They had every reason not to hope. But against all reason, their hope prevailed as indomitable. Buoyed by my mother's ever-resilient faith and my father's relentless tenacity, they built a life and raised a family. They imparted this hope to myself and my two brothers, rooting it so deeply that the onslaught of life might batter it, but it was never able to steal it away. With this indomitable hope they likewise ingrained in us both a respect for and admiration of history. We learned that history birthed the present and it never stopped speaking into it even at those times when we ignorantly turned a deaf ear to it.

Therefore, this book is dedicated to Dave and Donna Lounsbrough. Although you have both long passed, you live in the hearts and minds of many. Your history lives in our present and is relentlessly shaping our future. The words penned in this book find their inspiration in you. I hope that in some way I have made you proud.

I would also like to dedicate this book to my two remarkable children, Cheyenne and Corey. You are both a bright light in a frequently dark work, a point of inspiration when mine is waning, and the hope of the future. I believe in both of you more than you know and love you more than I thought humanly possible.

Above all, this book is dedicated to the God who inspired the concept and guided the shaping of it. Over the years that this book came together, there were innumerable moments when the right words, the perfect phrase, or an entirely fresh idea came out of nowhere. At these moments, I found myself completely cognizant of the fact that something other than myself was writing. And that 'something other' was God. I realized that I am not an author. Rather, much like my mother in the Great Depression, I was simply dictating. May God use this book in service of His Kingdom in whatever manner He deems appropriate.

Finally, my deepest thanks to the staff at Beacon Publishing Group. Their relentless partnership lent the resources necessary to bring this book to print. My heartfelt thanks to all of you.

Introduction
The Dance of History and Hope

So, what does history have to teach us? After all, it's born of another time and it died in another time. It had its run and then it fell off the precipice of time a long time ago. It might have effectively spoken to its generation. But when its words were expended with nothing left to offer in the speaking, it became history. And in no time at all, whatever it spoke to quickly followed suit.

Sadly, we possess the regrettable tendency to lock history into the ever-dimming and seemingly claustrophobic vault of the past. The heavy steel door of history grinds on massive hinges and closes with the sound of life being interred, entombing the past and firmly encasing it in the cobweb laden sarcophagus of our minds. Whatever purpose history once had, it is now expended and appropriately interred. Once buried, nothing but memory remains.

It is a great truth that history is the tomb within which the present will eventually be interred. Once buried, we have no expectation that it will ever arise from its stilled grave. Even less, it never occurs to us that it might have never really been dead in the first place.

Providentially, history seems to move backwards away from us in whatever death we ascribe to it, only to somehow and in some way circle around in front of us and visit us yet again in some form. This return reflects a sense that whatever has departed was meant to remain part of our lives. Therefore, the occasional return to things of the past can be embraced and even welcomed with a sort of soft reminiscence that soothes us against the rigors of whatever our lives have become and grants us encouragement for what will be. It comes back to give us hope.

From the backwaters of history revisited we have the opportunity to draw desperately needed resources for the future that the present doesn't afford us. These resources are handed to us as a precious preparation for what is yet to be as history is a meticulously detailed map into the future prudently written by those who were on the very same journey we are on, and who already did what we have not yet done. History is the gift of a map already written by those who authored the map in the very walking of it.

Because of this mystically circular course, we come back to whatever place we left with reams of acquired knowledge and an accumulated lineage of life experiences that have dramatically expanded us. So, we arrive at the same place, different people than when we had left it, yet entirely the same all at once. In some aspect, the place is rendered different because we are different in the returning.

But sometimes that place is the same; creating a seemingly immovable reference that shows us, by comparison, how much we've changed. Yet, in the oddity of the circular nature of life, it shows us with equal and often biting clarity how much we haven't. And out of this confluence of history revisited and life lived, change is afoot and transformations unparalleled are given birth. And here, hope is found in the very place it was never thought to exist. And the hope born of history visited is never held captive to the steel door of history shut.

Chapter 1
The Road of History
On the Byway of the Present

Time passes. Yet, it does not pass away in the passing. Although we perceive it as gone as it moves by us, it holds all things that they might be savored again and again. Time passes beyond the moment within which we stand, skirting by us to the left and to the right. Often it runs right underneath us, touching us in ways both wonderful and troubling. And without thought, we believe that once the moment has slipped by and time cascades into a forever past, the events that made the moment are gone with it.

In many ways, we wish life to be linear. We want our poor choices and the pain caused by them to always be moving away from us in some ever-widening gulf that steadily erases the choices from our memory and persistently reduces the pain in our hearts. But the sheer existence of lineage, legacy, heritage and memory do not support such a comfortable hypothesis. History captured in the elegance of penned prose or apprehended and pressed flat in faded photos suggest that this cascading is not the end of something. Rather, it is the journey of something.

They suggest that life is circular. Its route may not be perfectly so as the nuances needed to make life truly marvelous and somewhat mystical bend the shape of it along the way. But in whatever manner it does it, life turns in ways both sweeping and immediate that direct it back to a place where we thought it forever gone.

It may come back in a form somewhat different than the form within which it was packaged at its departure, leaving it to tease our minds with its vague familiarity. It may return strikingly unaltered, ripping apart the closure we had artificially imposed upon it. It may return as a longing restored, or an impossible reunion that was relegated to the impossible until life tenderly demonstrated how possible things can be.

But in whatever way it does, it comes back. So rich is this thing called 'life' that to somehow believe that it is forever lost to us once it slips past the moment seems egregious beyond excuse and irrational beyond explanation. Such a belief exemplifies the shallowness of our egos. It is our fears called out. It is our lack of faith faithfully exposed. It is the horribly stunted nature of our vision bared for all to see. Such a belief is the manifestation of everything within us that would fabricate such a pathetic rubric. Yet, the richness of time past will not be lost to a road that permits only a single passing, even if we have errantly deemed it so.

We see life as helplessly imprisoned within the indifferent parameters of time; that life is unsympathetically pinned against the yardstick of time in a manner that restricts it to being nothing more than a single journey that will not allow us to pass this way again. Life seems something of surging river rich with vitality, coursing into our lives from the future and instantly cascading over the moment in time within which we stand only to rush over the precipice of history before we can dip our fingers in it.

Errant or not, this is how we view life. This is our perception of it and the rule by which we live our lives on these roads of ours. In fact, the whole of our journey is interpreted to its demise by this spiritless perception. Because it is, time has become a road littered with magnificent treasure neglected whose golden byways are too often left abandoned, until we dare set foot upon them again or they set foot upon us.

The pristine car with its richly crafted lines, deeply mirrored polish, and voluptuous interior seemed irreversibly out of place. It appeared irksomely awkward. Flushed full of an inflated sense of superiority, it felt its cultured refinement soiled by the crude nature of this place. Somehow it found itself parked and sullen on the slightly canted berm of a dying dirt road dusty with the history of Indians, horse and heavy wagon. Its briskly tight design and clean lines projected a haughtiness of the most brazen sort. Leather appointments and rubbed wood accoutrements lent it an eminent air of aristocracy. It was superior, but superior in ignorance only.

On that frosty morning, the piercing white of its halogen headlights had effortlessly sliced the predawn darkness, surgically sweeping the road clear of pending twilight and thrusting the darkness back on retreating heels. Gliding suspension rendered the washboards of the road's dirt and gravel surface unnoticed and irrelevant. Satellite technology had reduced the world to pale streams of comatose data, calling its cold and graying shades to life with a single voice command and thereby robbing wonder of room to wonder. Radically advanced engineering cradled a rolling repository of the latest 21st century technology, setting the car perfectly within an era careening down an uncertain road quite different from the one upon which it now sat. It embodied all the strivings of the world, yet it was empty of all that is life.

The car seemed to presume that if we possess enough of the world and embrace its illusion of ingenuity and superiority, we can effortlessly course down roads whose pavement is long bled of hope. In fact, hope was deemed irrelevant, demoted to the stuff of a child's muse as technology supplanted hope by promising any solution to any problem. Hope gave way to ingenuity. Yet, even parked on a road of hope it did not understand that man's ingenuity can never manufacture hope or pave roads with it.

This place, edged with weathered stands of goldenrod, brittle stalks of black-eyed Susan's, and a scattering of chicory took no note of cars with fine lines or technological prowess. This place had no time for such superficiality. Running split rail fences hemming in yawning fields stoutly bordered on their misty horizons by muscular forests had long left such a superficiality to its own demise. The agitated calls of awakening blue jays darted in and out of the distance forest, ebbing and flowing into the forested morning. A handful of whitetail deer watched at distant wood's edge, finding sustenance in the vacant fields of a day shaking itself awake. The soft gurgling of the distant creek; the water's melody singing out of another road of the watery sort.

Here things of mankind's supposed prowess were all but invisible in a world nurtured rich by the ages and running deep with such vitality that the menial strivings of men were but horribly primitive mutations of what history had itself achieved long ago. Mankind boasts of brilliance. History is brilliant.

All around the car, light and ethereal, the spirits of history seemed to catch the waltzing tail of listless breezes and spin across fields fallen brown, cavorting through scattered barns whose hand-hewn timbers listed with a century or more of stoic vigilance. History seemed to nimbly pirouette around rusty horse-drawn implements that lay scattered at wood's edge, each royally embroidered by the golden weeds of time. Each had been gifted with a stilled retirement at the close of some distant final harvest at the turn of a century now at rest. History listlessly threaded itself in and through and around the aged split rail fences that encircled this vast expanse as if nimbly embroidering the scene and pulling life tight.

4

Muted voices of times long past effortlessly danced over the surface of this road of time, whispering in and around the whole of this place. Amidst this quiet place of farm, field, fence and road they could be heard, for the noise of men racing down other unknown roads to unknown destinations drowns them out. But here, life was 'life.' What is 'life,' we ask? The answer is quite simple. It is whatever's left over after we've extracted the meddling of men. And while such a world as farm, field, fence and road is not always silent in the limited sense that we understand silence, there is a silence of the soul. And that is the greatest silence of all.

In such a silence, the whispering voices made it clear that the remote times penned in the annals of some century long past had departed on circular roads blessed with an ending that were at the self-same moment a beginning. That in these places history is made, but it is never made history. That 'what was,' was ingeniously designed to enhance 'what will be.' And 'what was' and 'what would be' began shaping itself on this morning on this road.

In such an extraordinary alchemy, history asserted that its own roads were such that they could not be fenced in by calendars, or held captive to clocks, or be fettered by the advent of either life or death. History's essence and character knew nothing of demarcations defined by a beginning or an end. It seemed that along this road of Indians, horse and heavy wagon, history was the past utterly alive in the present, which permitted the present the wholly improbable honor of embracing the very essence from that which it was birthed.

The technology of man seems a response to mankind's misplaced fear of time.

By all accounts it seems that mankind has painted time as the rouge thief, stealing from us with every tick of the second hand. Time has long come to be viewed as always ticking down to something, rather than ticking up to something. It has become the grand adversary of our existence, for it is constantly pilfering our existence. And to our own disconcerting dismay, we have long learned that we cannot stop such atrocious thievery.

Therefore, we have seen it both as necessary and providential to create a race against time. We must wrestle it to submission not by stopping it, but by beating it. Our strategy is to maximize every second beyond what that second would wish to grant us. In essence, we attempt to elongate time by doubling up on it and doubling what we cram into it. If we can't stop time, we will beat it by forcing more out of it than it wishes to grant us. And if the roads of our lives are actually race tracks upon which we sprint against this monster we call time, we will see it as something to be beaten rather than something to be embraced. We will see it as an adversary verses comrade.

Over time, one of these two stances will settle into our souls to the degree that, in time, the one we've chosen will become utterly irreversible. And anything irreversible should be granted the 'everything' of our attention.

Hope is the gravel of all roads. It is the essence of any byway. Hope is the rationale for any road, for if there is no hope there is no reason to travel. And without a reason to travel, we have no reason to live. And the story that is now beginning to unfold gives reason to live when everything around us screams that there is none.

That hope is not birthed of competitions won, nor is it spawned of genius displayed, although we wish it were. We cannot manufacture this kind of hope by our attempts to beat time by means of our intellectual prowess or through the rigorous application of our tediously constructed paradigms (despite how marvelously shrewd they might be). We can't pen it into some philosophical prose that lends a glint to our eyes and a skip to our step. We can't carve it out of the bedrock of our existence as if the raw materials of this life were suitable material from which to craft something so grand.

Real hope, authentically sustainable hope that runs deep through the bedrock of time is found... it is never made. Ever. A journey to find something is inexplicably different than an effort to create something. Therefore, the richly appointed car and the culture that birthed it were straining to create something they could never create. The angst of failing only served to drive the effort to try. As painful as it might be, the single place in life that is absolutely void of hope is the very place where we are convinced we can create it. The technology of man that birthed a car of this sort lived ever-deeper in those places. So did the man of the car. A man who will find hope in the most unexpected of places.

History is copiously well versed in hope, for history has the singularly permanent front-row seat to life. And from that extraordinary place it has personally witnessed hope overcome impossible odds and forge down insufferable roads barely traceable. History has watched hope confidently prevail when mankind in the very midst of 'history in the making' had stood on history's road and thought 'history in the making' to be 'history in the breaking.' Yet, over and over again mankind was to find out that the march of history is never bereft of a road upon which to march even when every road appears irreparably broken. History will advance when the gravel underfoot is lost and all is abandoned to the tangled overgrowth of selfish choices. History rides on hope.

Likewise, history is not held hostage to any concept of relevancy that might attempt to define that which is valid and that which is not out of the myth that the passing of time renders roads irrelevant as it passes by. History lives unchallenged and unhidden. And in living, history evidences that its roads are never bled of hope, stripped of promise, or razed of expectation. Roads trodden underfoot might be worn to something less than attractive by the number of passages, but they are rich in the accumulation of the passages. The present leans toward referencing itself. History references everything. And it was in the middle of such a road that the car of the 21st century sat parked on a road of Indians, horse and heavy wagon, feigning the ability to travel a road leagues beyond its design.

With the passing of time, legend or history can each become fuzzy at the edges, causing them to blend in a manner that makes it difficult to discern one from the other. Roads recited and recalled can dance with history and be embellished by myth in the dancing, making fact sometimes difficult to ascertain. Such was the history of this road.

A handful of local tribes shared a common legend of a young Indian boy of poor and questionable descent. His dubious breeding was condemned by the tribe. Throughout his young and less than exemplary life, he exhibited no aptitude that was considered worthy or noble of even the most marginal status. It was held that the village spirits had mercifully spared the tribe of all bad luck and misfortune by placing such maladies entirely on this single, maligned boy.

One day, as the story goes, he had once again been run out of the village by a handful of bullying youths. Terrorized yet again, he fled to the Black Swamp, feeling that he would kill himself there as no one would ever find his body in the vegetative endlessness of the murky bog. As he slogged to the far edge of the primordial swamp preparing to slay himself and relieve himself of his torment, he happened upon a single goose egg in a tangled thatch-work of cattails and bent swamp grasses. Finding the nest abandoned, he sensed some deeply shared experience with the egg.

In those rarest of moments, we are splendidly incapacitated with something marvelous whose existence we had never comprehended. Too often we surrender to circumstance because we've surrendered to the belief that nothing exists but the circumstance. At these most desperate of moments, life effortlessly shakes itself free of such circumstance and throws itself open to reveal possibilities hitherto hidden. Unimaginably, what seemed an interminable ending turns upon itself to reveal the beginning of a beginning. And when we unexpectedly find ourselves with feet somehow planted on a road whose existence we had not imagined or known to exist, the journey from that point forward shifts with a force such that the journey forward is altogether divorced from the journey from which we stepped but a moment ago.

For the first time in the handful of years that marked his despondent existence there was birthed within this young native boy a sense that he was not alone. And herein was birthed the sense that, in fact, he was never alone. He had felt that way because while destiny of the greatest sort had always been his companion, it had been an invisible one. For to embrace the magnitude of our destiny, we must at times question its existence in order to become convinced of its presence.

Taking pity on the egg, he abandoned his own demise, gently gathered it into the soft folds of his clothing and took it home, raising the egg into a magnificent swan such as the tribe had never seen. Life, in the form of a solitary egg started the young boy's journey in the very place where he had gone to stop it.

Many years later, with the threat of attack by a local tribe looming, the tribal leaders attempted to find a path of sure retreat to save the women and children of the tribe as the village warriors were sent out to meet the threat. It is said that the boy held the swan close to him and cried out to her, lamenting to her his fear of sure and certain doom.

The swan is then said to have flown off, leading the young, outcast boy to a hitherto undiscovered pass and sure means of escape. Running back to the tribal leaders, the boy led his people to safety, being instantly turned from outcast to tribal legend. Lore and legend has it that this path eventually became the path of Indian, horse and heavy wagon. It became the path upon which a man of the 21st century had parked his car as he himself entertained stopping his life in the very place that it was about to begin.

Generations later, this enduring path had been trodden by Native Americans who held the legend close and revered it as sacred history. They took little note of the trail simply because it had embedded itself in them, becoming part of the very fabric of their lives and an unassuming conduit of their culture. They had traveled its wooded concourses and skirted its sweeping vistas for more generations than oral history could hope to hold in the telling. For them it was nothing of history, for it was a living legacy of an ever-ascending past that spilled into the robust vitality of the present and seamlessly rolled out into the anticipatory promise of the future.

Story had it that the trail had been used as a vital trade route where goods were transported from neighboring tribes to the serene village securely nestled in the bosom of the deep woods. The village was something of a story-book collection of huts tightly sprinkled amongst the hardwood behemoths. The whole tribe would gather in celebratory excitement as the assembling of goods from neighboring tribes resulted in lively days of bartering that were something of trade with a dash of sport; lasting deep into the night with both heated argument and robust laughter. The trail brought trade, holiday, camaraderie and celebration, uniting differing cultures in the common endeavor of living. The trail bonded cultures and bound families.

One mystically romantic tale told of a young, love-struck Wyandot warrior who would steal away down the trail to secretly meet the beautiful daughter of the chief of a nearby tribe. It was said that the great spirit of the forest had hewn out a secluded cove for their meetings. The story had taken on the aura of a romance of the most magical and yet forlorn kind as she was borne of privilege, while his lineage was that of a lower warrior caste.

Tragically, it was said that their secret rendezvouses were eventually discovered, resulting in the young warriors' banishment as his inferior social status forbade any love between them. Exiled, the young warrior never trod the trail again, rolling off the pages of history or myth, whichever it might have been. As incomprehensible as it might seem, his road had been devastated by love and robbed by loss.

Such tales, whether they were the stuff of history or myth added something less of history and something more of wonder to the old road. Of course, history is wonder of the greatest sort. The wonder of the road of Indians, horse and heavy wagon was rooted in the fact that myth was woven so tightly into history that it was really history embellished rather than history fabricated. This wonder granted the road a robust character, an irresistible allure and a compelling credibility that rendered it something more than a simple road threading field and forest. The road had its roots set deep in something that was little reflected in what the road now was, it's enormous majesty beautifully tucked away in its gravel loam and its mystery tastefully edged with stands of intruding weeds.

In the gaining momentum of a country outgrowing itself, vast expanses of elbow room lay westward. And in the growing pains of westward expansion, pioneers eventually stumbled upon the trail. In the stumbling, they found the path a clear and inviting access into a frontier wildly intimidating and yet untamed in a manner that dares spirited souls to wrestle it tame.

It was a thin and entirely unassuming trail (as all great trails are), skirting muscular streams, navigating precariously slight ridges and charting a sure course through behemoth hardwoods. As unassuming as it was, it led to extraordinary places far beyond the eye's horizon and the heart's most tenderly guarded imaginations. As it is with all paths to wonder, they are always preciously slight, easily unseen, and they hold their destinations close until the journey has commenced.

The pounding of horse and heavy wagon in a steady westward current widened the road, and in the widening expanded its role in the larger current of history. The flow of horse and heavy wagon carved its ruts deep, giving it all a permanence that seemed real but altogether temporal.

It was told that hearty souls heading into an ever-expanding frontier trod this path in whatever manner spirited souls on a quest might venture. Some walked this road in deep trepidation. Others rode it out of an excitement that harnessed trepidation and used its power to press through the length of an entire frontier. The shadows of myriad thousands trudging on foot, plodding on horseback and sitting atop lumbering wagons were cast on the dirt and loam of this road, eventually drifting into history as shadows do.

Some passed away along the road, resulting in a scattering of small and largely forgotten make-shift cemeteries that spoke of a road too difficult for some. Indeed, sometimes it is the death of something, despite how tragic that death might have been, that gives desperately needed meaning to a journey that would languish without it.

The years rolled on as so many wagons with the frontier retreating underfoot of advancing pioneers. The frontier eventually found itself backed to its very edges as all of its immense expanse was in some form populated, leaving nothing of the frontier remaining. It seemed that the roads to the frontier ended as the destination ceased to exist, as without a destination a road is not a road. Therefore, history is always fresh with future destinations simply because its very nature demands that it be so.

The flow of the courageous eventually slackened and thinned into a mere rivulet of adventurous humanity. In their wake were farmers and various tradesmen who had felt the need to pull in the reins of adventure, bring their westward journey to a halt and set down roots into the fertile Midwestern soils.

In time the road became theirs, becoming a by-way of mule and plow horses. Steam and gas engines followed, propelling vehicles down its dirt and gravel path until the advent of asphalt and six lane byways left the road of Indians, horse and heavy wagon obsolete. It was left abandoned and entirely alone, becoming the haunt of a few assorted farmers and the occasional city-dweller out for a drive. It was the journey of mankind abandoning the sweaty path of adventure in the pursuit of the easier causeways of leisure. Such choices are always diminishing and forever tragic.

For decades now, the old road had slowly been slipping back to something it was before the feet of Indians, horse and heavy wagon. Nature was healing the scarring of dirt, overgrowing memory with field grasses and a meadow now on a silent march of history subtly reversing itself. The wild tumult of humanity running pell-mell in search of something entirely undefined had taken to other roads that scoured other landscapes, creating six lane ribbons of asphalt to nowhere and back. History had lost its place in mankind's myopic pursuit of the future down an uncertain road, for any road not informed by the past will certainly be an uncertain one. And in that kind of journey there is no hope no matter how far we might drive.

This was a place that now appeared abandoned. Yet, appearances can be both tragically and wonderfully deceiving. Truth be told, this was a place where history and life lay deep, fertile, and entirely untouched. Indeed, it was eager to be robustly harvested by passionate hearts that would be willing to wade into silence, submerge themselves into mystery and be swept up by time. It was a place that illustrated that roads don't end, even though we are utterly convinced that they do. Neither does hope.

We all have a road underfoot. And despite the nature of it, it is a road and it is *our* road. If we commit ourselves to the road rather than foolishly focusing on the travel that it will demand of us, or if we let the nature of its surface dissuade us, it is certain to lead to places perfectly fitted to our lives. Places amply supplied with warming balm and kind words to soothe our pain. Places of perfect refuge that provide us needed respite in the midst of our grayest tumult. Places that whisper delightful messages that rain hope in the parched wasteland of our souls. Places packed tight with caches of supplies to nurture both mind and heart. Places of hope.

But, this means making certain that we're on the right road. Not a road of our creating, but a road of our calling. Not a road to feed our ego, but a road to flee from our ego. Not a highway paved dreary by cultural expectations or rendered mind-numbing by the passage of the incorrigible masses too fearful to lay claim to something remarkable. Nothing of this sort.

This means staying on the road of our calling and committing to the journey… whatever the nature or condition of that road might be. And therein lies the risk. For many of us have abandoned our roads, believing that they are paths of pain to nowhere and back rather than the circular kind such as this one.

Pensively, he stepped out of a car borne of the 21st century with history silently and expectantly circling all about him. Defying the warnings of heart and soul, he had long abandoned this road due to the nature of its demands and the state of its surface. He had believed in it at one time. It had captured a young heart and captivated a budding soul. That was the problem. That belief had been sweet. Wonderfully sweet. Despite the years that had passed, it still had some lingering essence of credibility to it which made it difficult to walk away from.

Standing, he cast a longing glance up and down this road of Indians, horse and heavy wagon while the road of his own life lay entirely decimated and wholly abandoned. This was a road of calm. The road he had created was a road of carnage. Drawing deep of the chilled November air on this early Thanksgiving morning, he pulled his coat tightly around him and cast a longing glance at the old river rock fence as everything was about to call him back to a road wonderfully familiar, entirely unknown and thick with irrepressible hope.

Chapter 2
Thanksgiving
A Road, a Fence and a Harbinger

He was nearly as much of the road as the road itself; coming home as part of a journey walked on the invisible roads of chance, destiny and intentionality. He himself would not have thought so but thinking so does not necessarily make something so. We walk many roads, and in the walking, we become something of each one. However, most of them are thinly temporal byways paved not for a robust and compelling journey. Such roads are most often a tawdry detour we have chosen because the press of pain or the push of greed drove us off the path of our calling. Oddly, this road of Indian, horse and heavy wagon was the pristine road from which he had detoured and upon which he now stood once again. This was, in fact, where his tawdry detour began. It was from here that the press of his pain and push of his greed drove him away. In a sense, this was no longer his road. Yet in a much larger sense, he still belonged to it. And in the standing, the breathtaking immensity of a road long abandoned as held against the emaciated path down which he had detoured erupted in a titanic clash within him, sending conflicting reverberations of regret and hope up both roads.

Every Thanksgiving when he returned, the road seemed to be entirely different but the same all at once, as such roads are. In coming home, we realize that we can live in many places, but there's only one place that lives in us. And it is this place that we call 'home.'

We may leave home, but it never leaves us. It is rooted within us in a manner that we must return to it, whether that be in the recollection of memory or in actually coming to that very place. Home calls us, as do many things. Yet, while some calls can be ignored or pressed to the edges of our minds, this one cannot. Home dutifully cradles all that we've forgotten. It vigilantly keeps all of those things pristine until the blend of battles fought, wounds incurred, and passions thwarted drives us back home to claim those things forgotten so that we might heal in the reclaiming. In the odd twist of life, the place we left heals us when the very place we've abandoned it for has left us. Home always waits, as do all the roads that lead home.

Home is a repository that restores to us the keen eyes of both heart and soul so that we are once again able to perceive the slightest of roads. It reminds us that hope crushed is never hope killed. It centers us long after we've lost our center. It reminds us that the thinnest path can still lead to the greatest of places despite the carnage of the path we've fallen from. Somehow home knows to collect every page and parchment, hoping that someday we will come home to retrieve that which we've so foolishly lost in our ambling journeys and disjointed detours. These pages and parchments bring us back to ourselves long after we've pawned ourselves off to a world that used us as so much chattel. History hoped that his return was less a visit and more a homecoming. Such was its agenda and so was its hope.

This primal hope for some thread of hope seemed to have been the very reality that he could never wrench himself from. The unconsciously aching need to reclaim the pages and parchments that home held drew him back again and again. He hoped to find some hope in them (although he would not have yet identified this longing in any such way).

Unconsciously, finding something in this place may have been the single thing that created the faintest tinge that maybe there was hope. That something in this place held something of his history that would explain what he could not. That something in this place could make sense of everything that laid outside of this place. And that in finding that, he might find hope since he had not found it since leaving this very road so very long ago. Despite the fact that he had attempted to tear himself from this place and transplant himself in so many other places, he never took root. The detours, as numerous and varied as they had been never ceased to be cheap byways to places that led ever further from home. In whatever direction they had gone, they had always set out away from this place. But it is foolishness to think that you can leave a place your heart never left.

He had long left the path charted by the road he now stood on in order to travel the more alluring roads of a culture going nowhere in the going. The billboards along these roads of culture purported great adventure, smooth byways, panoramic views and luxuriant destinations. Society brilliantly hawks its wares on billboards of this sort. And these innumerable billboards are liberally erected along pockmarked roads to nowhere. Standing back on the road of Indian, horse and heavy wagon, he had long learned the old saying, "buyer beware."

Something mysterious and utterly irresistible calls men home. Somewhere along the meaningless by-ways he had traveled he realized that he could never recreate home as home is not something created, rather it is something cultivated. Home is a repository beyond hope of replication. Indeed, it is utterly singular in its existence. Therefore, there is no running from home, as home can only be run to. And so, every Thanksgiving Day he came home. In his own emotional "Black Swamp," he was to find his egg. The road's dirt and gravel surface were gently bordered on each side by stalwart meadow grasses that seemed to form a perpetual sentry down its entire length. An occasional November gust roused the grasses to wave as if gesturing to passer-byers, heartily inviting them to venture further up the road. Once the invitation was extended, they fell still until the graying November skies lent another gust and extended another invitation. Down the south side of the east/west running road there ran a split-rail fence diminished by age but wholly unwavering in hedging in the field. It held the meadow back away from the road as if the road might be trod underfoot should the meadow wander onto it. The seasoned split-rail fence somehow bridged the two, creating a unifying point of connection that allowed each to live in perfect harmony with the other while granting themselves latitude to cultivate the fullest appreciation of the other. It was something of the most perfect kind of harmony one can envision, where things deemed as mutually exclusive were seamlessly interwoven into a life-giving and life-blessing camaraderie.

Hope is birthed from relationships such as these, and roads to hope are constructed when we discover that contradictions are in fact the greatest of companions. Indeed, the thin and bluntly stunted logic of men sees things as incompatible when the grand arch of history has found ample time and circumstance to blend them to perfection. And it is the alchemy of contradiction blended that paves roads and builds relationships of the most wonderful sort.

Somewhere at the onset of a spirited century that had birthed the Model T and spewed mustard gas across a European moonscape, a river-rock fence had been raised alongside the north side of the gentle road. It was no more than four feet tall, yet it was stout and muscular. It was made up of assorted boulders that fit tight as some monstrous and yet completely ingenious puzzle. A dressing of more squared stone ran along its top, granting it a bit more character and a sense of cultured refinement. An endless ocean of woods thick and wonderfully primordial lapped up against the river-rock fence in gentle eddies of trumpet creeper and American bittersweet. The river-rock fence itself seemed to stand as a muscular granite dam preventing the woods from somehow submerging the old road in a forested flood. Yet, in another kind of way the road and the rock wall seemed to engage in a partnership of sorts as well, strolling through time as steadfast comrades in the adventure of some passionate, yet undisclosed journey. At points along the fence, the woods seem to have reached out and hugged the fence with gentle vining strands of Virginia creeper and gnarled vines of wild grape. Both the road and fence had aged gentle with wisdom and the stuff of wonder that arises when one has seen enough time to understand life instead of presuming to understand it. Both rolled off each opposite horizon as if there were no such thing as a horizon at all. A horizon on the road of hope is nothing more than a starting point for the next horizon. This was his starting point to horizons unimagined.

People had always asked why the river-rock fence was ever built and what the purpose of it was. The question had come down through the last century entirely unanswered as great things are often bigger than the greatest questions we are able to ask of them. It was said that, when posed with this question, his grandfather would simply say, "Some things are done just because they are supposed to be done," …whatever that meant. It became something of the mystery of life that's only a mystery because we're too busy to pay it any mind. Words lack the capacity to explain mystery, otherwise mystery would fall prey to sentences and syntax that would kill it by stripping it naked and making it known. If we are forced to leave mystery as mystery, our only recourse is to craft some expression that speaks of the mystery without the words that would murder it. The fence seemed to be that expression; that sometimes things are not to be explained through logic, but they are to be embraced by faith. Faith is not naïve as some suppose. Rather, it is brave in its boldness and brazen in its hope. Therefore, it steps beyond logic, thereby inviting logic to something higher than itself. Hope itself is a mystery as certain as it is a reality, and in that we can have faith.

Each end of the river-rock fence rolled off the opposing horizon; something like a past with no point of origin on one end, rolling off into a perpetually endless future on the other. All of it cascaded into an emancipating endlessness in either direction. It was not about time or defining time in order to rein in time. It was about the journey that was encased in time, and the fact that time itself could not be held by any definition that would place either a beginning or ending point upon it. The road was the same. An old road and a faithful river-rock fence journeyed together, celebrating the whole of the journey and whispering in unpretentious tones that life is the robustness of the journey and much less than the terrible constriction of the moment. For it is too often the devastation of the moment which leads us to believe that the road is lost and the journey is over when the moment is but a single, minuscule point on an infinite road. Devastation is in fact the raw material from which the best journeys are forged, and the richest roads are paved. Therefore, neither are ever lost to circumstance regardless of how dire, nor are they an end in and of themselves.

The November air was edged by autumn's chill; the sultry breezes of summer long having been whittled thin by frost and chilled by a first tentative snowfall. Winter reached out to see if nature was ready for its entrance. The forest that tightly embroidered the meandering fields, that stood at attention around the adjacent meadows and pooled up against the river-rock fence had long surrendered their leaves. They now stood as drowsy sentries celebrating a season of transition in their intermittent slumber. There was something reflective hanging in the air, something of anticipation that was not stirred to any level of wild excitement but was held soft with a wise sort of patience. Sometimes, we find ourselves in places only because we know that we're supposed to be there but knowing nothing else. The reason and the rationale escape us, sometimes hinting that the purpose is grander than our rational thinking has sufficient reach to grasp. These are the places where we're supposed to be even though the recognition of why we're supposed to be there, or what this place is completely eludes us. Entirely unknowingly, we've journeyed down the road of our life to these exact places because our roads are specifically crafted to lead us where we're supposed to be, despite the fact that we don't remotely recognize where or what those places are. And at those most marvelous of times, life uses our tawdry detours in just the same way.

For you see, hope calls with a voice that we can't hear because to hear it is to risk hoping, and for some that is the greatest risk of all. Hope beckons us with a voice that only the ears of a soul still and attentive can hear. Rarely are we still and attentive, so the voice goes unheard. But when the faintest whisper of the voice of hope is captured by the ears of a longing soul, we come without recognizing why we've come or understanding what we heard that compelled us to come. If we are wise, we come. For years now, he had come. But for all those innumerable years, he was never certain as to why. Yet again, Thanksgiving morning had found him on this road of Indian, horse and heavy wagon, standing by this eternal river-rock fence. There seemed a convergence for him here; that time past and time future gave stability to the barbaric irrationality of the present. In some manner deep beyond the utterance of even the soul, he drew comfort from this place, a comfort that he could not define so that he might replicate it in some fashion someplace else. As he had discovered, replication of this sort was not possible any place else, unless of course you had hope. As with many of us, he did not.

However, stubbornness yet to be broken presumed that if he understood this comfort, he might find another place where it had taken up residence despite the failing of his best efforts to do so. Perhaps that is what drew him back here. Perhaps it was the need to wrap himself in something indefinably reassuring while attempting to define it so that he might take it with him back into the turmoil of his world. Sometimes you can have everything you want but fail to achieve anything you need because you're missing one thing. Hope is certainly 'one thing.' But as for any of us in crisis, it's the one thing that's everything. And he was on an accelerating collision course with that 'everything.'

Possibly his greatest failure was his inability to realize that. Yet, an even greater failure that compounded the first may have been his inability to comprehend that creating hope was not humanly possible in the first place. He was to learn that we cannot create hope to pave roads of our own making. Nor can we borrow it. And at those frightful moments when the road we have created has turned thin, indistinct or absent altogether, this reality becomes overwhelming to the point that we question the very existence of hope. And that is hopelessness of greatest sort. The journey to this place of awareness was to be a bit rugged and tumultuous, but he was to discover the truth that authentic hope was not made but found. In that discovery, he was also to understand that that kind of hope made any road of any kind plausible and passible. The newborn sunrise lent the first wispy mauve and golden hues to this Thanksgiving Day and this road. Indeed, this moment was a tender harbinger of a road he would shortly walk. And with the long brush of pastels engulfing the horizon, he stood among road, fence, forest and time.

He supposed that he had always chosen this point along the fence for that reason, that it seemed endless from here; vast in the way that makes ample room for things in

23

life that we don't make room for. On his eighteenth birthday, before he had left for college and the glistening vitality of cities and civilization, as it was presumed, he came here. To this point on the fence.

He had come on that Thanksgiving Day so many years ago and had etched a single hash mark on a broad, squared rock that sat on the top of the fence. Etching that first hash mark was something indisputably purposeful, yet it was perceived as entirely impulsive. It seemed that it was a newly emerging young man who felt that if he didn't leave an identifiable mark on this place, that this place would somehow forget him, or worse yet, he would forget it. Maybe it was indelibly marking a point of departure out of the fear that should he get lost in the journey he would have a clear point to return to. That somehow the hash mark tethered him to this place should his road plummet and leave him in a freefall. Whatever the motive, every Thanksgiving since he had returned, he added another hash mark next to the first. Time marked makes time three-dimensional, giving it both a character and expanse that renders us small when held against it. In time, the rock was littered with hash marks lined in perfect rows more numerous than he could imagine or wish to imagine. The total of his life as he perceived it did not match the time that he saw etched out on the rock's surface; sacrifices and investments that the hash marks detailed in glaring relief. Far too often, the rewards for our efforts seem to be mere pennies as held against the fortune of time and sacrifice spent attempting to earn them. And so, we scan our hash marks with souls marked by empty pockets.

His life was indelibly marked by deficits both gross and seemingly unredeemable; deficits that had no correlating gains to offset them even if he were to be granted an eternity of time to do so. He was briskly sharp, keenly intelligent and strategically driven. People viewed him as immaculacy manicured, sharply groomed and engaging life with a confident precision that they found themselves envious of or frequently intimidated by. He was seen as brilliant and astute in a way that makes the living of life seem entirely effortless and fluid when those around him seemed to slog through the muck and mire of it all. He possessed a steeled intelligence fired wise by the alchemy of pain and challenge. His exterior was solid, refined and sweeping.

Yet, within the groomed exterior he wrestled with the grinding angst that he had nothing to show for the collection of moss laced hash marks and the years that they so coldly catalogued on silent stone.

"Where did it all go?" he muttered, "Where?"

As he ran a gloved hand over the marks, a cresting wave of agonizing introspection washed as grief over a life that seemed squandered and harshly catalogued in the hash marks that laid silently spread before him. Those around him would never see it, but those within him could not miss it. And through circumstance and catastrophe that he would soon revisit, the only one within him was himself. The sleek car was one of the lesser monuments to his success. Yet the image of the man mirrored in the finely polished surface of the car reflected itself back to him as flat. Lifelessly flat. Success has everything to do with how we've journeyed, and nothing to do with what we've accumulated along the journey. At journey's end, empty hands mean a full heart. His was empty on both accounts.

"Where did it all go," he muttered to a stilled fence vibrating with history. "It all goes so fast. So fast," he thought shaking his head.

Taking off his gloves, he ran a now trembling hand across the hash marks as if his gloves had somehow distanced him from a past he was trying to touch.

"Where… where did it go?" His voice meandered off into the woods and dissipated in the attentive underbrush of Virginia creeper, wild grape and Queen Anne's lace.

The hash marks tenderly chronicled memories, or their accumulation, or the want of better memories. On this Thanksgiving Day, he had no ability to correlate the number of hash marks with the memories that so many marks would have suggested he should possess. Maybe he lived in denial. Maybe life is better left leaving much of it to ignorance, having fallen into the bottomless crevices of time and one's mind. Maybe it was all wasted, but wasted on what? Maybe it wasn't wasted; maybe it was lack of productivity as a result of the execution of plans that were not entirely conceived or possibly ill-conceived.

Regret spun him sideways.

"How did I get here?" he unconsciously whispered as he shook a forlorn head while running a trembling finger back and forth across the collection of hash marks. "This was not how it was supposed to be!"

Sometimes we have to pretend that we don't care in order to protect ourselves from the fact that we do. And therefore, the tersely intrusive thought, "What does it really matter anyway?" suddenly slammed its way into his thoughts. In an attempt to catch a soul plummeting into an ever-deepening distress he turned cold or tried to do so.

"Look at what you've accomplished," the effort continued. Falling into thought, his head suddenly began to inventory the sprawling list of his seemingly innumerable successes. It rapidly unrolled as if he was penning some sort of egotistical rant that quickly ran off the edges of his mind in the same way the river-rock fence ran off the edges of the horizon.

Emboldened with some redeeming sense of accomplishment, he drew a renewed breath. Then, just as quickly he helplessly watched the list of successes evaporate as nothing noted on the list made a difference in anything other than filling the list. The list could not sustain itself, much less grant meaning to life. It is far better to have wasted a life doing nothing, than having attempted to do something that turned out to be nothing. As the list vanished, the hash marks cut his soul yet again, leaving him on the verge of the very tears he thought himself too invincible to cry. Yet, invincibility is found in recognizing that we're not, nor do we need to be. Although the calendar held winter poised on the horizon of time, it had silently stepped in during the night and graced a graying landscape with a wafer-thin layer of frost. The slight predawn mauves of a world rubbing itself awake slowly revealed the artistry of winter afoot. Although delicately crystalline and bedazzling, he took no note of it, except the slight crunch that it lent as he shifted his weight from foot to foot.

Earlier that morning, the newspaper had been laid aside on the kitchen table, the front page screaming bad news in type both bold and black. Saturated to toxicity of soul, he could absorb no more of life's darkness, whether splashed across the pages of his own life, or relived in the bleak columns of the newspaper.

The news was smeared with the rotting fruit birthed of selfish actions, gluttony, power-mongering and shallow humanity on a mad mission to get whatever it could before the next guy did. To him, it seemed that the world was on was a blind quest to get as much of whatever it was that it wanted, in whatever manner it wanted to go about getting it. Ethics, morals, fairness and values of any stripe or kind seemed blithely discarded as irritating obstacles in the mad pell-mell dash of greed on a rampage. It all seemed madly accelerated by some sort of unrecognized recognition that the quest itself would destroy everything that the quest was after. Therefore, everyone had better get as much as they could as fast as they could before it all blew up in the getting. The roads and byways created by the culture as part of this maddening journey seemed to be wrecked and in irretrievable disarray with an entire culture stranded on their gravel berms. Yet, somehow in a manner completely indefinable, the pathetic events that the paper heralded did not seem to reach here, in this place of fence and forest and road. Although both the emotions and the words to describe them stood leagues outside of his reach, somehow in this place he himself was cleansed of these events, or maybe it was more that he was freed from them. Here hope somehow seemed to live intact, even though he couldn't understand how it did… or how to make it his.

As improbable as the whole thing was, time had left the farm listless and seemingly untouched by the decay that seemed to permeate everything else. It seemed that memory was interspersed with mystery that made the memory itself uncertain and the stuff of speculation. There was always the smoldering memory of the fire passed down in oral tradition, of life fallen into gray ash and charred cinder in 1928. It was said that the muscular pillars of billowing smoke could be seen a full county away. As with so much of the story, that part of the retelling was left to imagination and the aggrandizement of myth as well. Soon he would need neither myth nor imagination.

For now, it was more the stuff of story and much less the stuff of reality. It was, he supposed, his way of dealing with the fiery massacre of his past. As time draws events backward to shrinking horizons, history itself becomes indistinct and indiscernibly fuzzy around the edges. Life becomes a story gradually sterilized as something much more recited and much less lived, therefore history loses the vitality of what it was and the accelerating potency of what it can offer. For him, the fire, the farm, the death left a running thread of mystery weaving itself down to every Thanksgiving morning, including this one. In a manner rather uncanny but entirely right, this living thread somehow ran through the core of his being, reaching back into the curious shadows beyond his own origins. Such a thread left a part of himself forever a mystery to himself. The road and the river-rock fence gave him something definable when the history of the farm did not. The origin of the fire was still unknown; the question having largely abated decades ago but sometimes arising as cinders stirred in the warm coals of things curious and unknown. It was said that the death of his grandmother in the flames that December day sent his grandfather so deep into himself that a full decade passed before his found his way out. Everything stopped in the screams heard from the bowels of the flames, or so the story goes.

By 1938, his grandfather returned to the farm, drawn by some inner compulsion held at bay for ten long years to rebuild the razed farmhouse and put the screams to rest. Some dusty rumor had it that he began the project with the intent of perfectly replicating the old farmhouse that had fallen into flame and entombed his wife. Yet, the tale goes that the more the house took shape, the further his grandfather fell back into the depression that had held him captive for that long, dark decade. In mid-stride, he reinvented the house, rendering it an odd mix of something new intermingled with deeply embedded shadows and shapes that relentlessly bespoke of that December day in 1928. Because that was the case, his grandfather lived out the remainder of his years in a farmhouse that was fresh and yet always hauntingly tied to blaze and death. He never recovered, farming this land largely as a recluse, ever haunted by the fire. Apparently, the pain eventually mutated into a state of deepening delusion, or so it seemed. Trenching massive subterranean cavities within which even the deepest logic helplessly fell to its death, his grandfather appeared to have fallen into these same cavities. So deep was the fall, so the story goes, that he went to his death repeatedly asking where the pages were.

Whatever the pages might have been or not been, they were never found, leaving his grandfather in some disoriented state of mind as death closed in, stealing away whatever clues might have remained regarding the pages. However, in an odd twist of life, those at his bedside noted that moments before death a peace of unimaginable proportions came over him, causing him to smile and utter the name "David;" the name of the man of hash marks and pristine cars.

The question of the pages was assumed to be something of dementia or a mind exhausted by age. It may have been a heart haunted by the flames of 1928 until sanity had been gradually chipped away by the trauma of cinders and screams. Standing amidst the pieces strewn about by trauma, insanity was all that remained. The family ascribed nothing to it, moving on and leaving a terribly precious question buried deep in the layers of ash and history. Yet, the utterance of his own name in association with whatever the pages were remained a forever curiosity for him. Sometimes we know that something that should be, is not. We sense a deeply primal ache that speaks of a void within us that we can't voice because its identity is too insufficient to shape with words. There is quest untaken, or a calling unfilled that none of our successes address. Some summit that's awaiting an arrival that never happened. A finish line that has not witnessed a finish. Something's missing, but we can't define that 'something' so we presume it to be the stuff of mind, or the residue of pain or regret, or some fanciful dream that wasn't meant to be anything other than a dream. We fall prey to the belief that the desire for more is nothing more than a terribly misguided hope born of a desperation that's held up in some sort of heroic rebellion against a world that's often cruel. The desire for more is written off to childish dreams, irrelevant fantasies, blind heroics and the stuff of sordid myth. And so, the road to 'more' is abandoned because we don't believe it exists, or more pointedly that it should exist. And in less time than we would imagine, an abandoned road becomes a lost road.

Yet, for every life that has ever trod the earth, there's some majestic journey that has not been undertaken. And until we undertake it, life will be nothing more than a long line of fruitless hash marks that we will forever grieve. Rows of them if we're not careful. And yet, somewhere in the birthplace of our soul, we refuse to abandon all hope because our souls can't breathe without it. A life without belief in something 'more' is dead, whether it's breathing or not. We all have just enough threads of wonder woven through our beings to believe in something wonderful; something that's more than anything and everything we've experienced and come to know as life. We have hope painstakingly woven and hardily stitched within us in such a manner that it is resilient to anything and everything. And it is this hope which grates against the sense that there is none. And so, with those thin threads of hope woven within him, David came to the road of Indians, horse and heavy wagon, the river-rock fence, and the farm of 1928. And soon, all of this would come to him.

Chapter 3
A River Rock Fence
Hash Marks and Regret

We thoughtlessly and rather imprudently pass ourselves off to many things. In the passing we blithely hand off the treasure that we need for the infinitely lesser treasures that we want. And in time, with the accumulated acquisition of these lesser treasures, we assume the amalgamation of them to be the treasure we have always been in search of. It is not until we are suddenly and often mysteriously faced with real treasure that these lesser treasures are mercilessly exposed as no treasure at all. It is not that we weren't bankrupt all the time. It's that we had presumed our poverty to be wealth.

Of the many things we hand ourselves over to, fear is likely the most caustic and yet most common. Too often passion is actually flight in disguise and therefore nothing of passion at all. Through clever deception, such fraudulent passion allows us to surrender what we need for fear that what we need is simply too magnificent to exist in the manner that we need it. And if perchance what we need might in fact exist, we fear that it is far beyond the reach of our meager abilities. Subsequently, our road becomes a detour of compromise with dreams incinerated and hope turned to ash. Yet, there is an incessant magnetism that unrelentingly pulls at us regardless of the direction we have fled, or how far afield the detour has taken us in the fleeing. Many things pull us in life. Many. Yet, most of these things don't have the tenacity or the muscle to bring us back to that which we never should have left. In some instances, they might possess the tenacity and muscle, but they lack the desire. And without desire, muscle and tenacity are as if they were not.

If truth be told, many if not most of the things that pull at us are the very things that have pulled us away in the first place. They are in fact the adversary we have welcomed thinking them to be the friends we should embrace. Their nature has no resemblance to where we've come from. There is nothing shared except their differences. In fact, they are often the antitheist of the place from which we've come as in our fleeing we sought out everything that that place was *not* so as to distance ourselves from everything that that place was. Therefore, the places that we flee to will have no inclination or means by which to guide us back to the places from which we've run. Nor do they have any desire to do so. Having been pulled away by these things, we now find ourselves far down roads drawing darker and more foreboding with each step.

Yet, there is this potent and nearly parental pull; something like a loving overseer who will not be dissuaded. It's a pull that will not relent despite all that might be pulling against it. A pull this intimately coercing is such that even in those most far-flung places the pull remains just as sure and just as firm, for anything that pulls at our souls for the reclamation of our souls will only be emboldened the further that we distance ourselves from it.

All along, we know this pull to be wholly right. Yet, it is our fallen desire for lesser things that makes this pull intensely irritating. At points, the unrelenting nature of it all makes it appear a bully of sorts. When our resistance has finally been whittled thin, we realize that the irritation is in reality borne of our inability to deny the rightness of whatever pulls us. And so, in some manner of either choice or coercion, we walk this pull back to its point of origin so that we might embrace the whole of it. Once there, standing centered on this place from which this magnetic pull originates, we yet have little understanding that in this place lies everything we have longed for and yet everything we have run from.

We have long consented to a deep blindness that has darkened our ability to see the treasures now laying all about us that define all of our most desperate longings. True treasure, authentic treasure rarely takes the shape or has the form that we assumed it would have. Unbeknownst to ourselves, we shaped an image of them cast of our shallow vision and polished by our lackluster imagination. And so, we find ourselves on a hunt for what we've created and not for the treasure which seeks to create us. Indeed, we are blind to these treasures. Yielding to this blindness, we do two things far more unforgivable than simply missing the treasures strewn 'round about us. First, we forfeit the immense power that resides in them. Second, we continue to believe that the treasures we are seeking are in reality down the roads we have chosen that hold no treasures at all. And if we are not careful in this groping darkness, we will continue to pursue all of the meaningless things that we have pursued before because we can't see the far greater things that are pursuing us. Such was this road. Such was the farm. Such would be his journey.

Every Thanksgiving morning David drove to the farm, drawn back by some pressing primal pull. The pull was insistent, never remotely offset or diminished in any way by all of the other roads he had gone down. It was much like a soft but insistent parent, relentlessly calling down dark roads in order to call a wayward child home.

The many roads to 'nowhere' always hastened his need to come to this road of 'somewhere.' Diversions and detours of our grandest designs only serve to bolster our need to be in the places that we're vigorously trying to walk away from. In the perplexing oddity of life, it is in our 'running away' that the need to 'run to' finds accelerating energy. Irresistibly, each year he was drawn to the river-rock fence and gradually disappearing road of Indians, horse and heavy wagons long gone. Every year with unflinching determination the draw only intensified, increasingly backlighting all of David's efforts down other roads as futile and frustrating. Frustration is anything but sedentary. Quite the opposite. By its very nature it will gain an increasing density and an ever-expanding girth until we do not have the strength to hold it aloft. And when it comes crashing down we come crawling home. So did David.

He was looking, it seemed, for something lost that he had errantly presumed to be on the other many roads he had taken. In the insanity of our humanity, the roads we chose are typically void of the very things that prompted us to take those roads. David was incessantly searching for some pages of his life missing and never found; something akin to what his grandfather had murmured as death drew close. Some sort of script or tidbit of history that the fence and road hinted at, but something that they would not themselves disclose to him. Something that was in some way everything that he was, everything that he needed, and everything that he would be. Such a monumental search is made monumental simply because it is a search for one's soul, and if left undiscovered in the searching, it will be as if we had never lived despite all of our living. It was clear that David had yet to live. But that was to change.

At a core hidden to himself, David was looking for a history that would say there was hope even though its abysmal absence in his own century seemed to render it completely extinct or entirely fanciful at best. Was there something to offset the toxic headlines that splashed themselves across every form of media? Was there an answer to the morbid headlines that threw themselves across his past, his present, and that stood at the ready to pen his future? Was there another better story? Was there hope that such a story might be written even if the content for such a story didn't appear to exist? Was there? Or were these stories of a culture careening down roads of imminent destruction the total of all stories?

If there was an answer, had history pulled the answer so far away in time that he couldn't reach it from where he was? Or did it even exist back then so that there might be some hope of finding it today? Or is the desperation of the human condition so grave that any answer will only touch the barest periphery of the darkness, which means that in reality it is not an answer? In the vortex of his own hopelessness, David presupposed the answers as already determined in the questions.

So why ask them, he thought. *Why try?*

He came to the river-rock fence and the road of Indians, horse and heavy wagon because mystery is indomitable in its quest for answers. Therefore, you can't do anything other than ask. He came because the mystery of hope held a toxic world at bay in its promise for something more. That the whole story hasn't been told and that the rest of the story has something superbly redeeming in the telling. That somewhere there is an answer; a magnificent answer that is not the hope of hope, but the reality of hope. As improbable as it seemed, the mystery of hope seemed to possess within itself hidden answers to the world's carnage… to the carnage of his road.

There is a sense that there has to be more. There's a fuzzy premonition that life as it has played itself out on a road of rubble could not be the whole story. It simply couldn't. That unconditionally woven into this existence is a steeled thread of justice and rightness that will always pull the world tight even when the whole of it is unraveling. That life is not a nasty sham perpetrated upon a precocious humanity ill-fitted to embrace the harsh realities of this empty existence. It is wholly and cruelly improbable that our desperate need for hope is not somehow reflected by the reality of a hope that is as much a part of this existence as the darkness that it seeks to offset. Somewhere there has to be hope. Somewhere there must be answers to the mystery of how to track it down, ferret it out, grab ahold of it and hold it tight for the whole of our lives. Somewhere. Not a hope of fairytales or ancient lore or foggy mysticism. Not the hope spun in so many bedtime stories or laced through lines of rhyme penned by incorrigible poets. Not hope spouted by motivational speakers and modern-day soothsayers who peddle hope as a generic commodity. Not the bogus cures spun of words diluted to tickle ears but not challenge hearts.

Throughout a rocketing career on a trajectory to worldly greatness, David had liberally handed those pasty weak platitudes to others as some sort of cheap snake oil. He had likewise gorged himself sick on them as they were handed to him, hoping in the epidemic consumption that one of them might actually work. Hope disappointed eventually leaves one with no hope for hope. However, it's not that hope eludes death. Rather, by design it's simply not subject to it. For David, this was a lesson readied in a past that would shape his future. The grinding contradiction of it all for David was that there were many things he would just prefer to walk away from. There were seemingly innumerable things he wished to bury deep in the sands of time to be forever consumed by the sands themselves. To find these things a permanent place in the annuals of his history so that he could close the book, put it on a shelf, and then walk away from that shelf forever and ever. Hope then would be mercifully unnecessary as the existence of what which had generated the need for hope no longer existed.

Yet, he was always back to the road of Indians, horse, and heavy wagon. He always came back to a river-rock fence of hash marks and a farm that fell into flames in 1928. He always came back because they held something that he was never able to get a hold of on all the other innumerable roads that he had passionately and yet fruitlessly coursed down. We can lose hope to the point of hopeless desperation, but we are always desperate to find hope despite the enormity of our desperation. Real hope will never accede to desperation; its nature being uncompromisingly unconquerable. The tension was never abated for David, and so he was back... again.

By both nature and breeding, David was a decisive man. He could be captivated by whimsical ideas and lofty dreams if he could find enough reality in them to make them plausible. And he had come across enough of them throughout his life to draw his attention and tease his soul. It's not that he wasn't a dreamer. It was that the world had stepped up again and again out of some sort of heartless resolve to smash his dreams to the near death of his soul. Life reached out with a soulless impunity and demolished many of his dreams when there was no reason or rationale to move with such senseless brutality. It crushed them to death in a way that was something much more akin to pitiless murder than blind happenstance. Life did so in a manner that was wholly violent, entirely blind, and yet utterly malicious. Sure, his dreams were real, and his dreams were achievable. He knew he had the savvy and the resources to achieve his dreams. That was probably the most painful part of it all simply because in a world doggedly opposed to anything other than its own agenda, his dreams didn't have a chance. Against such odds, hope wasn't enough.

Therefore, David had long abandoned hope, and with the abandonment forsook every dream he had ever thought to dream. There was nothing left to dream. The vault of passion had been emptied and it had long closed upon itself. With the abandonment of passion, he likewise committed never to birth another dream because in the birthing hope would be murdered before it could draw its first breath. A man without a dream, or the hope of a dream, or the hope of hope is a man walking dead. Yet, he came back... dead or not. Sometimes what we need can conceivably come from many places. Yet, if it's going to decisively speak into our lives and not be squandered in the speaking, it can only come from one place. Sometimes the missing pages of our lives could really be delivered from anywhere, but they can only come from one place if their contents are to be truly transforming verses being simply informing. Sometimes life ardently refuses to cheapen its gifts by serendipitously tossing them out.

Rather, the gifting of the gift must transpire in a manner entirely worthy of the gift while being entirely cognizant of the need of the recipient to receive the whole of it. Nothing of such a great gift could afford to be lost in the exchange. The river-rock fence and the road could not give the gift in that manner. They could only attest to the fact that the gift existed... somewhere.

Across the road, on the sloping crest of a slightly rolling hill sat the old farmhouse of 1928. It was tucked-in and held warm by a spacious meadow in front that wrapped itself around both sides of the faded clapboard expanse. Thick woods hemmed in the back of the home and moved up into the meadow on the south side, rendering it a serene house seasoned by gentle farming and yet retaining something of a wildness not entirely tamed. Across the front of the house, a stalwart stand of sturdy white pines stood linked arm-in-arm, serving as a broad-shouldered windbreak. Dense clusters of long, tender needles handily caught the intemperate gusts that swept through field and forest on those icy December and January days, bringing them to a stilled halt before they could assail the clapboard farmhouse. Just through the woods on the south side of the house, a stones-throw or so away there ran an overgrown path. It was unpretentious and inviting, made up of two parallel ruts grown up on both sides and down its center by thin strands of switch grass interspersed with husky stalks of milkweed. Cutting a slight but sure swath through the impending woods, several yards into the forested thicket the lean path made a slight but comfortable left. Within a few scant steps of that, the forest pulled itself to a halt, divulging a modest rough-hewn barn adjoined by a shed canted by time.

Both buildings were fondly held close by thick meadow grasses on three sides. Several horse-drawn farm implements stood off to the side at wood's edge. Rusty and stilled, they settled into the landscape as something of the landscape, becoming what they had once farmed. The entire scene was granted a sense of vitality by a tranquil stream winding a watery path a few yards off on the south side of the barn. Generously sourced far upstream by a series of forest springs, the stream rippled around a course of small boulders and spun in translucent eddies under several fallen trees.

In the throes of those deep mid-western winters, the stream was ornately edged up and down it's ambling banks by crystalline sheets of paper-thin ice that reached out into the brisk current. In the thick of summer, it seemed to embrace a more leisurely course, reflectively drifting under canopies of stalwart oak and ash, or meandering through drowsy meadows. In time, it would flow out to the east, eventually joining forces with several increasingly like-minded rivers on their joint journey out to the Great Lakes and beyond. It was a road of another sort. Surrounded by such rich and enduring camaraderie, the farmhouse seemed to proudly draw up its broad, clapboard two story chest with something of humble dignity and diligent protection, overseeing the road and farm as both protector and friend. Its mortar-embossed brickwork chimneys stood as ready sentinels at each end of the farmhouse roof, widening and then descending to the ground on each side. The simple shutters stood at ramrod attention at each window, lending an air of certain vigilance. The sweeping front porch created a serene space where the slow leisure of living might join the beauty of nature in a perfect fusing of two superb existences. In and about it all, there seemed to be a nearly sacred camaraderie between everything, as if farm, fence, road, barn, meandering stream, and the long-fallowed fields were a family of sorts that dwelled in such a perfected unity that the absence of one would render all the others empty.

The sense of it all created a poignant jealousy within David, eliciting for the millionth time the longing for a grounding connection that he passionately desired. Such a connection as that had been his at one time. However, its absence (or more appropriately its loss) overtly amplified the pain. Tragically, that connection had been lost at the hands of another who viewed the sacredness of such a connection as expendable.

Marriages that are shattered break the deepest connections. It seems wholly improbable that intimacy cinched tight by covenant commitment should ever find its end. Marriages broken smash the most sacred connections that should, by any sense of universal rightness be preserved even if it cost the lives of the ones attempting the preserving. And yet, in such an indefensible shattering David was irreparably shattered. There are things that shatter us as an unfortunate but natural part of our journey in a troublesome world. 'Life happens,' as the saying goes. But then there are things so heinous in their devastation that the pieces will never be reassembled in the shattering because they no longer exist to be reassembled. Being broken and being destroyed are two very different things. And because his shattering was destruction run rampant, his life stood in the starkest contradiction to the magnificent connections he now stood amongst and around.

Connection amongst the inhabitants of the farm had run as deep furrows throughout the farm itself, tenderly accentuating the connection of farm, fence, road, barn, meandering stream, and long fallowed fields. These connections had been spun warm in the tales of a story-book love between his grandfather and grandmother. Somehow those stories cinched everything together in a manner so eternal in nature that life could not touch it.

Oral history held that they had accidently met as youngsters at a farmer's market populated by sturdy farm folk, littered with horse drawn wagons and kissed by magical tales of frontier legends like Buffalo Bill, Kit Carson and Sitting Bull. Such legends captured the adventurous minds of young boys and stirred the romantic imaginations of young girls. Brought to life in the pages of dime novels, they lent a touch of wonder to the mundane task of farming at the close of the 19th century. The stories pointed to the fact that life was more than plowing fields, rotating crops, tending to farm animals, and praying for rain to come or for rain to stop coming depending on the nature of things. During those formative years they would anticipate seeing each other at the bustling farmer's markets and yearly county fairs. And each year, neither were disappointed. Romance grew and flowered at a distance, attesting to both the reality and potency of love. The fragrant petals of their romance never faded. Neither did its blossoms wilt. It was, for once, the story of misty-eyed novelists actually come true. That fact in and of itself had always captivated David. Their romance remained strong and robust through marriage, the back-breaking rigors of farming mid-Western soils, the birth of a daughter, and finally the fire of 1928. That connection was then consumed in the flames of that fateful year as his grandmother had perished in the fury of flame and cinder.

Despite it all and because of it all, the farmhouse always struck David as a bold structure, seeming to hold itself with a timeless pride despite its timeless pain. He had always found it inviting, embracing an indescribable warmth that drew him in. Lovingly held in the embrace of a yawning front porch that drew itself around the house as a simple scarf, it was always thought to be everything a home could ever hope to be. Over the years it had been handed down to David as time had slowly diminished and then eventually called home the last of a generation who had any interest in such things as this. Yet, life draws us away from that which we desire the most or need the most. Too often, life draws us away from home and hope.

Resting a gloved hand on the river-rock fence with the car of the 21st century parked but a few steps away, David's gaze turned away from the farmhouse. With eyes tense, he squinted forward to another day that promised nothing more than the days behind. On this morning, the change of the holiday season drew his gaze beyond Thanksgiving Day and cast it out far into the holidays that beckoned not far beyond. Indeed, it was difficult enough to dread a single day. Yet to dread the coming month all at once seemed too much. His life was not as he had imagined it. The images of his future as they had enthusiastically swirled around him on the day he etched that first hash mark had soured. Completely. Over time, those images had been scorned by life. His dreams had been relegated to the inescapable death of fiction turned dark.

Yet, such disappointment and pain are relentlessly multiplied against itself when one has offered up the best of their lives and spent the entirety of their energies to construct those splendid images. To lean into life with the fullest intent, the brightest of visions and the purest of hearts, and then to have every bit of it lash back with a razor-edged impunity again and again is simply beyond human reckoning and mortal tolerance. To David, it was something like an innocent woman burned alive on that December day.

There is pain which is to some degree describable; that its common occurrence in this existence makes it reasonably explainable in word and syntax. Then, there's the pain that's wholly unleashed; mindlessly thrashing everything around it in some tyrannical rant. A savage kind of pain bent on brutality. A mindless evil untethered to anything that would restrain it. This kind of pain is so much of everything that pain unrestrained can be imagined to be that it becomes horrifically indescribable. It is a pain too great to be knit into words and then hemmed into a definition that one can hold onto. And because it is indescribable, we are left alone in it, for we cannot readily explain it enough for others to somehow join us in it… even if the joining be at some distance. David winched as he felt the weight of his heart reposition itself yet again in its attempts to find this ever-elusive place of comfort. Leaning into the river-rock fence, he bowed his head under the weight of a heart collapsing. His eyes closed in a panicked attempt to shut out the pain by shutting out life for a moment. However, despite the intensity of the effort he could not keep pain at bay. Tears edged up from a sobbing soul and traced moist edges around visionless eyes and fell in damp circles upon the river-rock fence. His breathing rapidly deepened.

In this moment of escalating pain, a pain that seemed certain to crush him with an inhuman impunity, a slight breeze drifted up and off the road. Tenderly, it brushed by him as though it were the hand of a compassionate friend showing up at a desperate moment. Catching the bottom edges of his black trench coat, it teased the hem sufficiently so that they fluttered as if they themselves were touched by something alluring and warm. The breeze was oddly tepid as if it had stepped in from some place outside of the November morning.

Glancing up at the forest's edge, every branch in the woodland maze was sullen, drowsy and hauntingly still. Of the handful of brittle yet stubborn leaves that remained on the now skeletal braces, none even so much as twitched in acknowledgment of what David had felt. The meadow grasses stood at motionless attention as if this experience was not theirs to experience. However, it was theirs to watch. Sometimes in life, at those most precious but painful of junctures, things are ours and no one else's. For at those times life gifts our pain with its fullest and most exclusive attention. Confused, David turned and scanned up the slight rise to the farmhouse. For some odd reason, the sight immediately drew him to thoughts of his grandparents and the love that they held for one another. The flames had stolen their love, leaving one ushered into an eternity where her loss would be lost in the supposed perfection of that place. It left his grandfather with a heart fallen into cinders and ash, being forced to live an empty life filled with a loss never lost.

How could life be so contradictory? David thought. *How could that be?*

It was said that his grandfather would comment on how he wished it had been him. How he wished the flames would have been his lot, so they would not have been hers. If the mere twenty feet that separated them on that fiery day had been reversed. But every time he would utter those words, he would retract them out of his recurring sense that leaving her to face the loneliness that he faced would be far more painful than being burned in the flames of farmhouse itself dying. To die is to feel pain once. To lose someone to death is to feel pain for a lifetime. David's loss occurred in the flames of a different kind. And he, like his grandfather, was himself feeling pain for a lifetime. Soon, he would find hope for eternity.

Gazing once again at the late autumn dawn of both fence and forest, he found himself distanced from it all. He wanted nothing to do with transition or celebration or anything else that autumn might presume to be. The season flooded him with memory; the kind of memory that should never be allowed to be memory as it held him captive to a past he could not reconcile and a future that he could not believe in. That irreversible juxtaposition left him stranded in the nowhere of life. Autumn marked a transition to something new; fully embracing the movement of one place to another. Autumn was a necessary death without which a resurrecting birth would be stillborn. Autumn was the womb of spring. David's life afforded him no such transition. Where do you go when the past is consumed, and the future was supposed to be paved with the hope that was lost when the past itself was consumed? He shifted his gaze to the river-rock fence running off in both directions to destinations unknown, turned a handful of meadow grasses this way and that, and fell into deep memory.

Anyone's story is complex, with nuances that send the roads of our lives spinning and sometimes peeling off in directions at times unexpected and other times entirely unwanted. It seems that an entire life can tip on the slightest event or merest circumstance. Everything can careen on a single breath that is nothing more than a thin vapor. Life can shift on the smallest decision that of itself carries no weight or substance. Life can be lived with frank honesty and forthright determination. Integrity can be the byword by which we chart our course, and we can adhere to the highest moral principles as the compass to which we ardently commit. We can do it all right, and yet it can tip at the slightest provocation and plummet into something terribly wrong.

Together the past and the present make up life, whatever and wherever it is being lived. And so, the hash marks, the etchings that chronicled his life were both a line of sorts much like the road and river rock fence. They were likewise an accumulation; life herded and gathered together at one grand point where it could be assessed as time well-spent or time misspent. Rummaging through his coat pocket David pulled out an old pocketknife. It was dutifully worn with brownish hints of rust in folded crevices. Its pearled handle had modestly yellowed with time, showing signs of age and wear. Like the farm, it had been passed down to him. However, it was a gift enfolding within itself a passage from the comfort of childhood to the difficulties of adulthood.

It had been forged by his uncle Frank in a high school metal shop class somewhere back in the 30's. It had embodied his uncle's own troubled passage. He had been forced to set aside the innocence of childhood so that he might work menial jobs earning nickels and dimes that would help feed his family during the throes of Great Depression. It never really went well for uncle Frank beyond those early years, having fallen to alcoholism and the scourge of mounting medical issues. The knife had been given to David when a combination of liver failure and cancer put a final period at the end of uncle Frank's story. Quite unexpectedly, the knife was now chronicling a life for the second time, although the correlation entirely eluded David.

Prying out a resistant blade, he turned, stepped up to the fence and laboriously etched yet another hash mark on the boulder. As he did, the prolific scattering of so many hash marks generated an anxiety in him; a sense of squandered time and life lost to time. As he etched yet another mark life replayed in front of him. It was much like the stories of someone dying when the entirety of their life rushes by in some sort of breathless, fast-forward rendering that leaves one gasping and grieving at the self-same time. The more he etched the new hash mark, the more his mind raced in a blur of time compressed and pain being compressed with it.

Memories sharp and poignant threw themselves in front of him, increasingly cascading one on top of the other. Unexplainably, each one seemed to play itself out in some sort of slow motion at the same time. The memories seemed unconnected mostly; snippets of his existence that popped and flashed through his mind. Affairs that he had no idea existed. Betrayal carried out in secret and covered with lies. Scheming to set a relationship aflame and leave him burning in the wreckage as she walked away. Stolen promises and commitments blithely discarded. A deluge of fabricated stories craftily spun to steal their two children, and in the thievery leave his life in a pile smoldering cinders and windswept ashes. The deeper he went into memory, the faster they came, and the more David spun.

Such a view of his life had never fallen together like this for him. It was an unexpected view of his existence sewn together as something so awful and yet so pathetic. Quickly, he became emotionally moribund by the indefensible reality that so much sacrifice could result in this, whatever this was. It was more akin to a scorched quilt-like patchwork that when sewn together portrayed a charred tapestry that was nothing of the sort he had dreamt of weaving when he scrawled that first mark on this very fence so many decades ago. At one time, the hash marks had been etched bursting with hope and bustling with promise until idealism fell prey to reality. After that, no amount of work or sacrifice seemed to matter. The past had been stolen, and every effort to overcome this past was stolen as soon as the effort to do so was birthed. The grossly flawed quilt-like product stitched in his head screamed failure and the futility. How can you work so hard? How could you sacrifice to the point that you've nearly abandoned yourself in the sacrificing and have it erupt in flames? In the flurry of emotions surging, the tip of his knife sheered, sending him stumbling backward, trembling and nearly infantile. Hands uncontrollably shaking, grasping his chest, he bent over, leaned against the car and attempted to catch his breath. David had experienced this before. But not like this. Nothing like this.

The morning sun had finally broached the horizon, raining the first shafts of golden brilliance through a thin frosty mist. Its lucid rays cut tight shadows throughout the forest. A sparse handful of delayed leaves pirouetted from skeletal trees as a thin breeze now rustled meadow and field. An entourage of Canadian geese, fallen far behind the hem of a summer long thrown back drew a V-shaped southern course across a Thanksgiving dawn, their haunting call rushing through wood and brush in an attempt to catch up. Soon they flew off the horizon of the day.

Yet, David was awash in an entirely different place. He'd been standing there along the river-rock fence for thirty minutes at best. Yet, it seemed a lifetime. In this place of despair, he wondered, as he had wondered a million times before, how he could love so much and yet lose so deeply? How could the willing sacrifices made be seized by life or circumstance and be turned on the one who had sacrificed so dearly? What dark thread within humanity allows people to exchange horrendous evil for endless love? What is it about those that we love that can cause them to buckle the roads of our lives and leave those roads absent of hope. Any hope. David hated any thought of being a victim. In fact, he was repulsed by it. He found such a stance a place for the weak within which they might plead their case with great vigor in order to engender some stick-sweet empathy to soothe their pain. Yet, this was history replayed for him, not a stance justified. Not a plea for anything… other than for it all to stop.

The questions ran in ever-violent circles that served only to feed every other question until they were each gorged on the others beyond his ability to entertain any one of them. He felt himself suddenly drowning in them, each being agitated by the fact that Thanksgiving was here and that it heralded the coming of a season he no longer believed in and a celebration that he would much prefer to avoid. The season was all about hope, but to hope for hope was more than he could do, because to hope and be disappointed in the hoping would be the death of him. And he was smart enough to know it.

His head spun, his heart sank, the darkness enveloped him and in the ascending fury of it all his cell phone rang. The ringing seemed terribly distant, as if coming from miles away. However, the ringing suddenly jerked his mind forward and hurled him headlong and face-first through suffocating layers of pain and memory until he found himself laying on the ground with a broken blade in front of the river-rock fence. Dropping his knife, trembling hands groped for the car. Pulling himself upright, he caught his breath, and fumbled for a cell phone lodged somewhere deep in the folds of his thick trench coat. Finally finding it, he held it to his ear and with a trembling voice said "Hello... this, this is David."

The thin voice on the other end brightly responded, "Is this Davie B?"

Chapter 4
Aunt Mabel
Dementia and Pages Lost

One of the grandest mysteries' rests buried in the fact that the truly miraculous is hidden among simple, unpretentious and entirely obscure things. The subtle genius of life is such that the mundane is perfectly designed to fully enfold the miraculous. Nothing else fits it so well. That seems to explain why so few find it, or even think to look for it. The most wondrous things in all of life are most often found tucked in the plain wrappings of things that are plain... and therefore plainly ignored. That which is plain is the palace of the astonishing.

The ringtone seemed nearly inaudible, drifting in from some impossibly distant place on the barest edge of his consciousness. It's difficult to clear your head when you're lodged in a past of pain and standing in a present of uncertainty all at once. It's difficult to clear your heart when you're searching for something deep along the river-rock fences of your soul. It's difficult to clear your soul when your knife has sheared etching the hash marks of your life in the process of marking off nothing but futility, cinders and ash. And when you can't clear head, heart or soul, you can be standing on the very road you lost and not even know it.

In the soupy fog of his ever-thickening emotions, the cellphone's impatient tone seemed to recklessly hurdle toward David. It's piercing pitch dramatically expanded until it seemed to consume every other sound of silent road, solemn forest and screaming heart.

Tersely returned to an unwanted present, David fumbled for his phone, half consciously put it to his ear and muttered "Who is this?"

No one called him "Davie B" except an aunt somewhat estranged by time, distance and the stealthy thievery of dementia. David had always found the name childish and chafingly irritating. This time was no exception.

"Davie B?" said the voice again.

Aunt Mabel had lived at least a decade longer than anyone had thought she would or maybe should. Her life and her place in the family was presumed as long expired, leaving the family to afford her an abandoned place of obscurity. It seemed that the family did little more than mill around in their lives while waiting for her to die. Too often, we thoughtlessly relegate things to the ever-dimming periphery of our lives, eventually jostling them off the edges to some ill-defined oblivion because we assume that we are done with them. The problem is, they may not be done with us.

Sometimes things seem to have been drained of their purpose. They appear expended and exhausted, yet still lingering without any identifiable purpose that would somehow justify the lingering. In some manner seemingly unfathomable, the things that are most valuable in either a person or a place are often the exact things that remain after everything else is deemed to be wholly spent and irretrievably gone. Our misshapen definition of emptiness imprudently blinds us to the reality that what appears empty is in reality brimming and entirely full.

And because we build our lives, and stake our dreams, and chart our precarious courses in the abhorrent cheapness of the superficial, the superficial is all we see or have learned to see. It's what we know. Sometimes it's all that we want to know. However, it masks everything that we need to know. When the superficial is gone and the hardy, priceless and timeless stuff of treasure is left, it's entirely invisible to us. So, we walk right past hope not even knowing it was there. David was about to walk right past aunt Mabel. And that would be to walk past hope.

"Who is this?" David asked, his voice laced with exhaustion and amplified by a twisting tension. Still spinning, he had not regained his senses sufficiently to see what he would normally see or know what he would normally know. This state of mind, or more precisely, state of heart appeared to affect him far beyond the confines of this single phone call. Much like many parts of his life, he should have known but didn't. Shortly, what he should have known he will come to know. Abruptly? Yes. Beautifully? Absolutely. Shockingly. Of course.

"You're at the farm, aren't ya?" the caller answered, not addressing David's question at all. Her voice was coarse and obviously garbled with age, but it flowed smoothly with a striking confidence. "Sometimes I just get a feeling that yer there" she continued.

"Who is this?" David repeated with a blunted sense of confusion and building irritation. *My number's unlisted*, he thought to himself, once again feeling the violation of life intruding upon him in yet another irritating and uninvited manner. Staring at the caller ID and then putting the phone back to his ear, he said, "Who is this?"

"Silly boy," the voice answered. "This is yer aunt Mabel."

To David, aunt Mabel was much more something of a fuzzy figure who seemed to always see him with an uncanny and sometimes unsettling clarity. She had been a part of his early life, back in those early years of quiet innocence. But she had been pushed off the pages as adolescence rendered her outmoded and dull. Sadly, he had let that happen. More sadly, he had let it continue. This choice had always pricked his heart and irked his conscience. Yet, the road of his choosing had led him away from her and had demanded other lesser allegiances of him. The road of Indian, horse and heavy wagon was bringing him back. It was bringing him home.

He couldn't remember how many times she would call him, as rare as those calls now were, and somehow know exactly what he was doing, or thinking, or both. At other times, she seemed to know what he was thinking before he actually thought it.

This is creepy, he thought to himself, even though some far deeper part of himself rebelled against the thought. At some indefinable level that David would likely deny he embraced the hazy notion that the call was oddly and yet potently providential.

David remembered her as always small, bent and frail, yet tough like gristle and filled with an improbable energy. At one time, she had been filled with a brimming vitality, but those were thin and now elusive memories from David's childhood. The arch of time had set them off over a horizon barely visible from the vantage point of worldly pursuits, plush cars and rogue business deals. Aunt Mabel aged as all people do, sporting gradual layers of spurious wrinkles, hair slowly washed a woolen white, and a body slowed and more thoughtful in the slowing.

Yet her eyes never aged with the rest of her. She seemed to have forcefully pulled up on the reins of time and brought those crystal blue pools to a halt in her twenties. They were always bright, lucidly clear, vividly alive and irrepressibly young. They constantly seemed to dance and to shout out loud in the dancing, revealing an emancipated soul that would not in any way be bound by the aging body within which they resided. David had always heard that the eyes were the windows to the soul, although the phrase sounded more the words of some plastic and hurried philosopher penning trite idioms. But if indeed that were actually the case, then David would be left with the singular conclusion that her soul didn't age. At all. And that truth, if it were truth, created a stinging contradiction that generated questions of why she had been relegated to far corners and shadowy recesses.

She had lived out most of her life in a simple, one-bedroom white clapboard home that was randomly attached to the back of a small general store. Out front there was a single unassuming aged gas pump; something like a stoic sentry that stood at a slight tilt surrounded by loamy Michigan dirt and the worn gravel of its reclusive byways. A solitary weathered light always painted a drab olive-green sported a transparent, bare bulb that swung overhead, being nothing more than a light casting light into obscurity. The rolling "ding" of the gas pump seemed slow and monotonous, as if the fueling of farm trucks and dusty wood-paneled station wagons was about the fuel to drive into an unhurried future.

It all was nestled on a dirt byroad in a tiny Michigan community that lay far off the map of commerce and importance. Aunt Mabel had squeezed a meager living out of pennies, nickels and quarters by running the tiny general store to which her clapboard home was attached. Her revenue was derived from small and seemingly irrelevant items such as gum, candy, sodas, a few sordid staples, mismatched canned goods, sugar sold by the pound and boxed commodities.

Yet, people always seemed to be there, in that remote store setting on the borderlands of obscurity. David often wondered where they came from, apparently emerging from nooks and crannies and far-flung farms hidden among the field and forest of the rolling Michigan landscape. It's as if they came out of 'nowhere' to be together in the 'somewhere' of the general store. As a kid, he remembered that obscurity wasn't all that bad. In fact, he found himself longing for it yet today.

As a child, David had spent part of several summers at the store, lathered in the thickness of summer's humidity, hemmed in by muscular forest, yet graced with sweeping farmlands that beckoned him to their distant horizons. And in this most improbable place, he realized that people came not to make purchases, but to cultivate friendship in exchange for a pack of gum or a pound of flour or a can of coffee. It was a gathering of community that made the concept of community something precious, alive and so vibrant that David never wanted to leave even though life demanded that he do so. Or it might have been that he demanded that life do so. He was never quite certain.

It always seemed to fill his hungering soul to unexplainable abundance just to watch the people come and go, and to touch each other's lives in the simplicity of the coming and the going. The greatest transactions that occurred in the cramped quarters of that tiny general store never involved the depositing a single coin in the aged cash register that proudly sat at the far end of the scratched glass counter. Rather, those transactions were the transactions of lives exchanged. The currency of such of a priceless exchange was time. And the item received in the exchange was an irreplaceable thing called friendship. Friendship cannot be bought, traded or bartered. You won't find it on sale, and there's never a coupon for it. Truly priceless things can only be given. That's all. Such was the case with friendship. Indeed, it was the most precious commodity ever exchanged in that simple store.

The store was filled to the tin tiled ceiling with the molasses drawl of stories real and some which were embellished enough to make you wish that they were real. The scant aisles were filled with chance meetings of earthy people who were authentic without any realization that they were, and without any effort to be so marvelously human.

Raw humanity that listlessly savored the genuineness of its very rawness seemed something so core, so blindingly pure, so in keeping with how it all should be. Yet it was something that was increasingly being lost and gradually fading into the tragic obscurity of a culture rushing down roads undefined.

Each time someone came and the tiny bell on the screen door heralded their arrival, there was a giving and a taking that left everyone with more than the total of what each person had been before the exchange. Every person, regardless of who they were or what parts they derived from left the store with more than the total of what was given and taken. Everyone left the clapboard store rooted in that great Michigan obscurity more than whatever they were when they had walked in. It was mystical and magical; something of a grand human encounter that seemed to make sense of humanity and made all the pain of living worthwhile. David remembered as a kid that he could never get enough of it; that if he could spend the whole of eternity in that store surrounded by those simple encounters he would happily do so.

The store left barely any room for aunt Mabel to live, squeezing her back into a cramped kitchen and boxy bedroom that made up the randomly attached house. Its tight confines were populated with second hand furniture and thrift shop trinkets that the treasures of time and memory had rubbed off on, rendering the clapboard house so full of wonder that it seemed to have no walls at all even though you barely had room to turn around.

David vividly remembered one entire wall strewn full of old black and white photos that hung canted in aged frames of metal and wood. Each one tenderly held their images against the thievery of time. It had seemed that history had been repeatedly caught in the act over and over, and in the catching it had been frozen in enough snapshots to give it a continuity that gave it life.

David recalled standing in front of that wall, engrossed in its pictures and swept up in the silent stories that each shouted in black and white relief. It seemed a desperate tease where history begged him to step into itself through any of these innumerable portals yet knowing all along that he could not. So many times, he had imagined that he could. Out of that magical imagination he had crafted detailed stories for each photo. Marvelous stories rich with everything that life should be rich with. But it was never to be. He could not write history. He could only pen a future. And that pen had long been snapped and broken.

His warm and enduring passion for history was given birth staring at that wall and falling into the mystical tale that each photograph spun. Although he could only stand on this side of them, they nonetheless handed his young mind a ready and irresistibly inviting passage to other times. Repeatedly he had seized those passages as a marvelous corridor through which his mind would travel even though his body could not. Each photograph offered a unique but ready road that he willingly traveled in mind and imagination since time forbade any other engagement. And travel he did.

Some were rigid tin-types; cold and inflexible. Others were yellowed, mottled and tattered at their aging edges. Some had been lightly colorized with thin pastel washes to grant them a sustaining life and vitality. Yet others were marred by inky blotches. It mattered not, for each one called forward a past long gone, and called David back to a past longed for. He never tired of walking the innumerable roads they invited him to walk. And so, the wall with the photos became a porthole to places barred by time but freely trod by imagination.

The old general store and adjoining clapboard house was one of those places that exuded a wonder that he never figured out. Never. Yet, it was that very unidentified wonder that he held him a willing hostage. David recalled endless hours sitting on the canted wooden steps that jutted out at the back of the house, listening to the muted conversations of rural folk floating in from the store while gazing out mesmerized over soft fields that swept out to the woods edge.

His young mind raced down a million roads of adventure of the wildest but safest sort. Sitting on those back steps, his heart was free to run down those roads as fast as the legs of his imagination could carry him. It was not a contrived freedom arising from some ideology about freedom that we attempt to knead into our journey. Rather, it was a real freedom that left his soul without parameters that would ever halt it.

Standing on the gravel berm of Indian, horse and heavy wagon while lost in sweet Michigan memories, David suddenly thought to himself, *What's happened to me?* Had it been up to him, he would have never left the store and the steps of field, forest and wonder. But he did. And because he did, he was different in ways that wrought disappointment of the heaviest and darkest kind. "What happened to me?" he mumbled.

Aunt Mabel navigated the tiny clapboard home as if it were expansive mansion that she was privileged to reside in. It was the home of her honeymoon, the place in which she struggled with her infertility that left her and uncle Bill childless and barren. It was the place where they built a business on spare change and the currency of prayer. It was at this home that an Army chaplain knocked on her door to inform her that uncle Bill had died somehow, somewhere in the horror of Normandy and on the bloody beaches of that June day in 1944. In the mass and confusion of the invasion, the manner of uncle Bill's death was left the stuff of mystery; the variant blanks being filled in with conjecture and imagined heroism that was probably true. It was here that she built a meager life from the ashes of a different kind of fire and lived in an odd combination of both peace and loss. Yes, this was aunt Mabel.

Yet, as life had progressed, in the living of it she had long fallen into the intermittent shadows of dementia in the same way his grandfather had. Yet, like an impenetrable fog bank momentarily moved aside by a sympathetic breeze, the dementia would lift for the briefest moments, revealing something fathomless with memory and thick with wisdom. It was easy to be missed as it was all lodged in the simplicity of her words, the apparent ease of her thoughts, and the crystal light of her eyes.

Sometimes the simplicity could be confused with dementia itself. Real wisdom, the kind of wisdom that's thick like molasses but as pure as gold refined to something glassy and nearly incandescent is a treasure so rare that it's absence makes us doubt its presence. Because of the abject shallowness of our vision, that kind of wisdom sometimes seems to brush up against the edges of insanity and co-mingle with it just enough that it becomes tainted beyond trust. Yet, aunt Mabel's brief moments of glorious lucidity were precious. David wondered, was this one such moment?

"Yer at the farm. Right at the very instance when the nurse woke me up, right then, right then and there I knew that you were at the farm. I told her that I had to call ya right now, right now. So, I'm calling" she said with an escalating intensity edged with a spritz of excitement.

"Yes," David muttered leaning against the car staring up the old road, "Yes, I'm here. *Now is not the time,* he thought to himself. *This is not the time for whatever this is or is becoming,* he mused.

What David didn't realize that there was never a good time, and because that was the case, it was the perfect time on the perfect road.

Suddenly he heard something, something indefinable. Something likely of imagination but too loud for imagination. He turned, stumbled on the soft gravel berm and dropped his phone in a stand of thick straw-like Goldenrod that edged the river-rock fence. David was a man who diligently commanded his every moment and each action that transpired within those moments. He was clean, razor-straight and unruffled. Therefore, to be startled in this moment was as uncommon as what he had just heard.

He was certain, in a manner that leaves no room for doubt, that he had heard something coming down the road. It was something of a yearning and less something tangible. Stumbling around the front of the car, he stepped onto the road's dense gravel bed to scan the road beyond the trees that edged it and the horizon that hemmed it in. Whatever the sound was it was so compelling that he expected to see something or someone. The road was empty in a way that visionless eyes perceive such roads.

The sound seemed more something like a multitude of sounds layered on and over and in each other rather than some single sound that would identify whatever it was. It was like a cacophony of voices so blended together and stacked upon each other that you simply could not tease out the threads of the individual voices.

Yet, they were voices. Somehow, he was sure of it. Generations of them, it seemed, raised in a single moment. A joyous confluence of centuries no longer barred from one another by time or the turn of some calendar. It was, it seemed, some great joint venture of humanity seamlessly linked. With the voices ebbing and flowing, David stepped further out into the road and vigorously scanned it up and down, back and forth. Yet, the road remained hauntingly vacant. His eyes failed to see what his ears could not deny. Looking yet again, he stepped into the middle of the road, convinced that he was missing something. He was.

61

Then, at that moment, the voices fell silent and a scant wind oddly warm caressed him again, spinning leaves around his feet and then sending them cavorting down the road in some secret waltz. The same breeze then silently brushed the tall grasses bordering its dirt edge on its way out to wherever it was going.

Suddenly, it seemed that there were voices again, somehow woven in the fabric of the breeze. Ebbing and flowing, not clear and distinct as if to understand what they were saying. It seemed that they weren't meant to be understood. They seemed to be words with just enough clarity to evidence that they were words and not the musings of a fall breeze playing tricks on a tired mind. It seemed a message cloaked for another time; a harbinger of what was to come. Then, all fell silent and all fell still. Again.

The line between mystery and imagination is an exceedingly thin one indeed. Mystery too often falls victim to imagination as we attribute things of great wonder to the irresponsible musings of our hungering minds. Standing in the center of a road of Indians, horse and heavy wagon, David's mind teetered between the two, listing this way and then that.

As he did, the veneer remnants of Indians, horse and heavy wagons looked back over evaporating shoulders as they spun down the road in the waltz of a warm autumn breeze. They had gracefully pirouetted by David and had gently touched him with the warmth of hope drawn from their own assorted journeys. Yet, they had not embraced him so that he might fully perceive such a great hope, for in the journey ahead of him, such an encounter would have been premature.

"That was strange," David mused, attempting in some mental angst to write something of great mystery off to happenstance, the irrelevancy of oddity, and the lack of sleep. "That was really strange."

Yet the throbbing heart of real mystery is always far, far beyond the reach of denial to render it meaningless and kill it in the rendering. Some things will always and forever defy the denial that we take up to slay them. Such was this moment. Such were others to come. In the mental wrestling wrought of such moments, David slowly walked back around the car, still looking up and down the road in befuddled confusion.

Pushing aside the husk of Goldenrod drawn silent by Fall, he reached down to pick up his phone. Brushing it off and then rubbing remnants of weed and road on his coat, he could hear the mumbling of aunt Mabel. Apparently, she had continued talking, or more likely babbling even though all the while he'd been standing in the middle of the road cavorting with history without any sense of such a magnificent engagement.

Brushing the final bits of dirt off his phone with the sleeve of his coat, he put it to his ear while he continued to scan the road.

"It's these nightmares Davie B, these awful nightmares," she continued. Talking as if in some sort of misty, post-awakened groggy state she said, "Oh, I so hate 'em. I do" she continued. "They're bad, so bad that the nurses wake me up to get me out of 'em. Yep, yep, it's the nightmares alright, the missing pages. They're everywhere. Everywhere. I try to grab 'em but they blow out of my hand every time. I can never catch 'em. They just blow away. They blow away. It's the pages Davie B."

She continued, "Davie B, the pages are the most important thing about the farm. There's seven of them. Seven. I know that yer grandfather left them somewhere, but where I don't know. I don't know where. No idea 'cause he never said. Seven of them, Davie B." Catching her breath, she paused and then lamenting with a depth that stirred David's soul itself, she continued. "Oh, I wish I knew where. I never knew. Things won't be done until ya find them. Nothing will be done until ya find them... Davie B. David B. Are ya listening?" she said, becoming a bit more forceful while fatiguing in that very forcefulness. "Our lives rest in those pages... the places they take ya... lots of places."

Shaking his head and shaking off her words, in sarcastic overtones David murmured, "I hope I never end up like this. Tell me this is not in my gene pool. Please." Wiping more dirt off the phone, he put the phone back to his ear and mumbled, "If I get like that, I'm going to give someone permission to shoot me." Turning and shaking his head as she droned on, he said a bit more forcefully, "I'm going to give them the gun too."

"What?" Aunt Mabel uttered. "What'd ya say? I didn't catch that."

"I said, yes aunt Mabel, I heard you," David responded in a patronizing manner, but in a way edged with a bit of something resiliently solemn.

For David, aunt Mabel's words sounded as if they were thick with the musings of the scourge wrought of dementia. It was like so many other calls over so many years. On some extremely rare occasions her words seemed almost divine; something mystical in a way that revealed deep and wonderful secrets for a brief moment before her mind closed in on them yet again. And in such a back and forth exchange, the line between insanity and mystery blurred unrecognizable sometimes.

His mind still held within its folds some scattered pages of memory of aunt Mabel back in the day when she was a quietly brilliant and sharply astute woman far beyond how a clapboard house and general store might define her. Back then, she had possessed an indomitable energy that had been gladly harnessed by something majestic; almost otherworldly. She seemed to have given herself over to something bigger than herself, which in turn made her infinitely bigger than all that she was. As a kid, it was mesmerizing. As the years and maturity lent a defining sharpness and clarity to who she was, David realized that she was everything he yearned for, but nothing he himself could find. Ever. Maybe that's why he had backed away from her. Standing at the river-rock fence on the road of Indian, horse and heavy wagon, he still had not found it.

"But that was then," he'd always alleged. "I was a kid."

Such a thought gave David permission to pawn it all off in trade for a stellar career, a robust portfolio, the admiration of the professional community, and roads to nowhere. Indeed, aunt Mabel's words sounded like murky lunacy and wandering madness. For years, the family had written them off as such for these characteristics seemed to have commandeered her life. They appeared to have left who she had been embedded in the annuals of history while some slight semblance of herself lived on. While aunt Mabel had apparently been lost, David had never been found.

David had no interest living his life based on myths and fictionalized stories, or to even ponder them as the stuff of amusement or curiosity. Hope had too often arisen from thin caricatures and weak tales. It never had any meat to it. And because it had arisen from such emaciated places, it was simply not sustainable, and it was certain to disappoint.

His own reality was potent enough to squash musing and gut fairytales. Life was too painful and too terribly short to entertain anything but reality, and even that was disappointing most of the time. And so, to defend himself against a world of cruelty, he had long abandoned the soft and supple stuff of child-like fervor. He had cast off the longing for something otherworldly to find him and to touch him in the finding. He had, in principle, rejected the essential essence from which dreams are spun.

To the contrary, long ago he had relegated himself to lifeless facts, for they might have been hollow, but they were safe. He had long forsaken the thoughts of a child sitting on the back steps of a general store hedged between field, forest and roads untraveled. However, hope cannot live in places where those very things are forsaken. But neither will it succumb to their absence.

"Yes, aunt Mabel, I know," said David again, "I know."

"I'm glad that ya know" she replied with a softening tone. Drawing a deep breath of profound relief, she said, "I think I can sleep now… now that ya know. Now that ya know that so many lives will never be lived until ya walk into the pages. Ya must go back there. You must… all seven…" Then all went silent. Mercifully silent.

Aunt Mabel trailed off, apparently fallen into the calm of sleep or the catacombs of dementia or something of both, whichever was most at that moment. The phone went silent and David heard the voice of a nurse helping aunt Mabel into bed. Then the phone went dead.

"I know aunt Mabel, I know," David said out loud to himself in tones thick with sarcasm. He turned off the phone and shoved it into his pocket. With an exasperated breath, he turned and looked at the river-rock fence. Then settling, he paused and softly muttered the words, "I know."

In his heart, the words seemed more of who aunt Mabel had been; that iconic woman oozing with character and flushed full of wisdom. Somehow her words refused to take up residence in the thick folds of an ever-graying dementia, thereby being personified by an advancing insanity. David fought her words, rigorously attempting to wrestle them into that place, for that was a safe place to both house them and justify the rejection of them. Yet, they were indomitable, irresistibly leaping back to the woman of days gone by; granting her words a vitality and authenticity that kept them ringing in David's head.

Catching his breath and attempting to shake off what logic could not reign in, he found himself slowly walking back to fence. There are pivotal times in this existence of ours when we are subject less to our own ruminations and caught up in something that exceeds the scope of those ruminations. Here, in these places, we follow rather than dictate. We obey without question, rather than decide without vision. We say "yes" even when there's every reason to say "no."

Stepping up to the fence, he ran a gloved hand over the hash marks once again. "Walk into the pages," David paused. "She never said that before. That's different. That's... that's real different." David was to soon find out how different that really was.

Over the years there had been a lot of talk about whatever the pages were, but never anything about walking into them. The conversations had always seemed far more casual, as if people were lightly reciting family history in some sort of joint recollection rather than attempting to investigate it. Other family members long deceased had talked about the pages as well, but nobody was certain what they were or whether they existed at all. It was unknown whether they were some sort of journal, or diary, or ledger, or a bit of poetry or writing. Maybe they were altogether fictional, lending some spice to the family history. Largely, they were altogether forgotten.

The pages were as completely mysterious as the rationale for building the river-rock fence.

Walk into the pages. Walk… into… the pages, David thought. "That's stupid. What is that anyway?" he mused outloud. "I can't walk into…"

Falling a bit into thought and then shaking himself free, with a slight slice of renewed sarcasm he said, "I've got to watch the caller ID more closely." Then pricked by a curiosity that would remain curious until he held the pages, he glanced down the road again and again.

Engulfed in something of the timeless rumination of a soul on a journey it does not yet realize it is on, he eventually rummaged for his keys. Turning, he paused and once more ran tentative fingers over the hash marks. Then, pressed by something born of the hope for more, he impulsively laid his hand flat and pressed it against the cold surface of the large boulder on top of river rock fence as if he was trying to feel some warmth or detect some sort of faint pulse. Maybe history passed was more than history lost. Desperate to feel it, or maybe repossess a bit of it, he pressed ever harder.

Somehow in his heart he knew that was exactly what he was doing, and yet he likewise knew that it wasn't as insane as one might think it to be. Sometimes we look for something more because we sense that the finality of everything around us is only the finality of appearances and not the finality of reality, or life, or our road. That something's there for the redeeming. That it hasn't fallen. That the story goes on if I can just reach out for it or reach up to it. If we stop at what we see, we stop on the thinnest horizon of a horizon-less existence. And we know somewhere within the heart of our soul that the cost of stopping there is simply too high to stop.

David permitted his mind only a few scant seconds to fall into the mystical reality of a hand seeking a pulse from river rock. For a moment he touched the aching of his soul, and in the touching, he gave it space to speak. And in the speaking, he had, for a moment, responded.

He had intended to stop by the old farm house just to see if everything was okay. Too much time there always left David feeling that the empty house had a story yet to tell, a tale breathlessly untold and in desperate need of being told. It was something akin to seeking a pulse from river rock fence or straining to hear the voices calling from the road of our lives. Sometimes we realize that something isn't finished when everything about whatever that is feels completely and entirely finished to the death of itself. Yet, to finish the story it must be told, and David was in no mood for a story.

A stiff autumn breeze carrying the frost of fall suddenly drew a razor-cold edge across his face. Reflexively he jerked back his hand and chided himself for entertaining fantasies reserved for incorrigible children and the likes of aunt Mabel. At that instant, his mind shot back to the magical obscurity of a general store sitting somewhere in a magically desolate Michigan landscape. Something about that memory resurrected a sense of renewed respect for aunt Mabel and once again called into question a conversation that seemed the fog of dementia. He wished he could wish himself back there. He quickly chided himself for the foolishness of the thought and once again allowed the adult of logic to silence the child of dreams.

David categorically wrestled the thought of the pages, whatever they were, into the file of ever-expanding dementia. Although he now thought them firmly secured there, even then they were already finding their escape. He drew himself back to farm and fence, gathered up a sheared knife, got into a car of the 21st century, took one more look down the road and headed home down a road of Indians, horse and heavy wagon very much alive. The words of aunt Mabel were likewise unexplainably alive as well. With the sun now lifting above the trees, he would postpone any visit to the old farmhouse for as long as he could tolerate the press of wonder and the hope of hope.

Chapter 5
Christmas Yet Again

Tragically, life becomes routine all too quickly and far too easily. It is not meant that way, nor is that in any respect the Designer's intent. Rather, it is our visionless meddling that slowly but deliberately pens a script of cold obscurity. Soon, obscurity becomes our story. And as we live out this life of cold obscurity (as diametrically opposed to our intrinsic thirst for passion), life becomes irreversibly hopeless. Soon we are dead without ever having died. Yet, the worse of it is that we're dead and we live fooled into thinking that we're alive.

Familiarity and routine spun of threads drawn coarse by abandoned dreams and hope discarded renders that which is terribly precious as something dreary with the magic wrung entirely out of it. Everything in all of life becomes something that just 'is' for whatever menial and irrelevant reason it 'is'. Life then becomes something to be endured as an ever-incessant battle within which we never advance, rather than a wondrous journey down a road upon which we can forever run.

A little over two weeks had passed, or blindly flown by since David's visit to the road of Indian, horse and heavy wagon. It was with this simmering hated of having to endure the festive fakeness of the holidays that David faced the onset of yet another Christmas. Christmas itself seemed the fictional combination of muse and vivid story-tellers who had no option but to create uplifting stories of hope because the reality of hope was not to be found anywhere in this life. If we have nothing to live for, we have to create something to live for. Otherwise life will become intolerable with no rationale to live it at all.

Hope is the indispensable breath without which our souls gasp and perish. Because this is so, we have no alternative but to fashion some thin facsimile of hope if in fact life does not possess it. We work diligently to mold some semblance of hope from the rancid and raw stuff of our lives. We have to somehow squeeze a drop of it out of the rock that is our existence. And yet, how is it that we can mold hope from these realities, as they are the very things that created the need for hope in the first place. Such was the insanity of Christmas. Such was the insanity of life. Such was the insanity of his life.

To David, this is exactly what Christmas was and nothing more. The holiday itself was a mechanical methodology of myths, empty legends and spurious traditions that wrapped the world in cheap tinsel, shimmering lights, thin glass bulbs and brightly wrapped packages errantly scotch taped at their ends; most of which ended up in a landfill.

Christmas was man's way of creating something that maybe should have existed in some form or fashion but did not. In fact, it may have been humanity's way of denying how sick and dysfunctional both humanity and the course of the human story had become. Christmas was, David believed, a story scribbled over and across the larger pathetic story the generations had written. Such irresponsible penmanship was a mindless and therefore fruitless attempt to blot out all the disappointment spawned of man's evil by promising some sort of improbable reclamation. For David, the indefensibly inexcusable state of mankind would far more readily provoke destruction than it would prompt redemption. The thought of redemption made the thought of Christmas itself putrid and emotionally rancid for David.

"Why we can't we just fast-forward past all of this," was a wish David had blurted out on more occasions than he could recall.

However, Christmas was somewhat fun enough despite the doleful emptiness of it all. It lent something of charm and simple magic to a world rendered dull and barren by mankind's egocentric stupidity and winter's gray chill. Christmas spiced things up a bit in the frigid doldrums of a scorned winter. If nothing else, it was a diversion as long as everyone remembered that it was just that, and nothing more. All of that was enough for him to go through the predictable motions despite the inherent emptiness of it all.

In it all, Christmas had become something less than genuinely sustaining. Sometimes it seemed real enough, as if it was actually constructed of some authentic element. Maybe there were some scattered shards and scant pieces of something real, maybe even something marvelous. Yet, even that seemed hideously fraudulent because if perchance Christmas did have something genuine in it, that genuine part of it would sustain the whole of life beyond the turn of the December calendar. If it was made up of something real, it would make complete sense that that 'something real' would hold up and hold out throughout the rest of the year regardless of how toxic the rest of life might become. It didn't. Yet even though David would fight it, this year would be different.

For David, the whole ache of Christmas was that it unashamedly promised something marvelous in a way that was breathtakingly convincing... promised. Yet promises were cheap to him, being something, someone committed to in order to manipulate a situation to whatever end would benefit the person making the promise.

Promises were merely a seductively devious vehicle crafted to achieve a selfish goal. Promises were not something forged deep in the fires of integrity and cooled to a steeled hardness in the curing waters of commitment. Promises were cheap statements of ill-intent masquerading in the clothing of something that was advertised as an unshakable pledge of one human being to another.

For David, promises promised nothing other than the fact that someone felt that they could get ahead by making a promise. So, they made one with no intent to keep the promise, for keeping it would sabotage the underlying intent. However, it was abundantly clear that whoever made the promise was most certainly committed to keeping everything that they profited from by making the promise. Promises were a charade. They were a trap.

In reality however, somewhere in some deep place of the soul he had always sensed that the promise of the holiday was not some sort of fake thing. Rather, he had an enduring sense that it had always been a genuine promise that had somehow been stolen. That time and greed distended over time had pilfered it. There was something patently authentic that had been indelibly woven into the promise of Christmas that had been whittled thin and slight as time and selfishness wore it down to nothing. In some fashion it was real, which is why humanity had killed it, or at least vigorously attempted to do so.

Indeed, was Christmas just another cruel fatality to the thievery of mankind? Had life burnt it to the ground in the flames of a culture likewise burning? Was Christmas a storehouse robbed, pillaged, left scathingly empty and then torched to its foundation? Was it a road of hope seemingly decimated beyond navigation despite the intricacy and ingenuity of the map? If so, was Christmas the victim of an abhorrent tragedy of selfish humanity on an egotistical rant that David hated so deeply. If Christmas could not endure the thievery or the fire or the decimation, and if its own promises had been stolen by the hand of the thief or incinerated in the heat of the fire, Christmas itself was nothing more than a nice idea but nothing of substance or reality. Otherwise it would and could stand against whatever might assail it.

David's life was a disillusioned compilation of things stolen. Such was the merciless and cruel nature of the thievery that the intent to steal eclipsed the theft itself. The things recklessly stolen were things of great promise, things that he had loved dearly. Things that had added to life in a manner that splendidly outweighed the total of the things themselves, sometimes outweighing them in ways entirely immeasurable in their wonder. Things that were so wonderful that they should be placed far beyond the reach of anything or anyone who might attempt to abscond with them. Things so grand by design that any shred of morality at all would make thievery entirely impossible. Christmas was the same.

His life had been stripped naked and raw in a manner that left death the single thing that remained un-stolen, for death is the only thing thieves won't steal because it's already stolen them. David's life was something of the living dead. Indeed, he was living in anticipation of death only because the anticipation of anything else had been stolen in the robbery itself.

David's life seemed the pithy, bleached skeletal remains of something that had once been tenderly complete and wholly whole. Something like what he was as a mesmerized kid in aunt Mabel's general store, surrounded by earthy farmers and people of pure stock born on furrowed Michigan farms and grown tall in deep woods… sharing the raw and wonder of life. Whatever he was supposed to be, he was that back then, along with all of those other people who were much the same.

Yet, when a spouse brutally betrayed his marriage, then rampantly stole all that was loved as part of the betrayal, promises meant nothing and thievery had no sense of any ethic. And without an ethic, thievery knew no bounds. An illicit affair had been nimbly hidden in secret rendezvous that themselves had been veiled in a web of meticulous lies. Clandestine schemes that had plotted a concealed road to the precipice of divorce. Calculated accusations constructed of toxic lies that had been designed to flee with his children and wield irreparable damage to the whole of his life, all the while cleverly cloaking her corrupt indiscretions in those very actions. Sure, he knew that he hadn't been perfect. But this... this was an evil that stepped leagues beyond anything he had done that might even remotely justify it.

Humanity becomes lost in various sorts of manifest evil of this very kind whose intent is to damage beyond hope of repair. Yet even more conniving, at its most heinous moments humanity damages to the barest edge of death itself so that life is forced to continue without the blessed relief that death would bring. David knew this kind of thing well because it had visited the whole of itself upon his life. And in the visitation, it convinced him that hope was nowhere except nowhere.

If something grounded him in the ascending turbulence created by thievery and fed by betrayal, it was the old farmhouse. At some level, he supposed that's why he journeyed there every Thanksgiving morning; a pilgrimage to the single place somehow left unscathed by the fires of present. He visited the farmhouse a number of times throughout the year, but the yearly pilgrimage on Thanksgiving Day began in earnest the year after his wife had left.

How it started David was not completely certain nor did he ponder the question, other than the history of the place always wrapped itself around him and held him centered in a way that nothing else ever did. It was a reset of sorts. He supposed that the pain of a marriage lost and a family decimated was profoundly more searing during the holidays. And so, the farmhouse braced him for the certain pain that the holidays would torrentially, and at times savagely usher into his life.

Yet, he always wondered what if anything was really there anyway. It had fallen to the flames of 1928 and risen from the fire in 1938. In some way curious beyond the reach of explanation, the farmhouse had been robbed of its very existence and then had had that existence restored. It was robbery of the worst sort; a moment where flames seized and then consumed his grandmother in the anger of an inferno enraged. The farmhouse and the memories that it held close went up in a torch of brawny flames and then fell into cinders and ash. And yet, despite the carnage the farmhouse was to be a restoration of the grandest sort, ultimately restored in its entirety and then some.

For David, it was the great anomaly of his ashen existence. It was the absolute reversal of victimization, as much as he hated that term. It was life turning out right in the face of forces that should have kept it from turning out right at all. The farmhouse was something of righteous redemption in a world that hasn't seen redemption, except in what seems accidental happenstance on a handful of scattered roads. And because the world hasn't seen it, redemption is forgotten and presumed forever lost in the fossilized strata of humanity gone wrong. Or in other cases, it's deemed something of myth and nothing of reality.

The old farmhouse sat confidently in the 21st century with its roots unashamedly anchored deep in a time marked by rattling model T's, the sheer marvel of the incandescent light bulb, and fresh-faced dough boys marching off to trench warfare on a European moonscape. Its beams were raised when steam power was heralded as the industrial force of a new century, flight was in its bi-winged infancy, and the utilization of the telephone brought distant neighbors within earshot of each other. The farmhouse was reared at a time when a young nation was raising itself up in a manner so glorious and innocent that the nation itself was oblivious to the wonder unfolding and the hand it would have in a future that would be challenging beyond comprehension.

The old farmhouse was unapologetically a house of the soil, raised firm on a rock wall foundation drawn from the strength of the soil itself. The frontier had passed over that place and down that road a scant forty years before the foundation was laid, having rolled off westward to the Great Plains and winding through the stoic Rockies on its way to a distant Pacific. Its walls were raised at a time when the restless frontier had come to maturity, having long felt the need to nestle into the woodlands, farmlands and meadows of the great mid-West, much like one might securely settle deep into the embrace of favorite chair after a long day.

The old farmhouse held its roots tenderly close, never letting go of the aura and sweet aroma of the past while standing erect and confident in a present ever accelerating toward an increasingly unclear future. Somehow the insanity of life never impaled the old farmhouse as it seemed to have done to David. Instead, history seemed to somehow grant it a firm grounding, a pure and wholly untainted basis from which the future could not only make sense but be irrefutably transformed. It seemed to hold the precious secrets lost in a world that had lost any hope that there might be some secret at all, despite how scant it might be.

David had missed Thanksgiving at the old farm house. Aunt Mabel's call, seeking an impossible and likewise implausible pulse from a river-rock fence, hash marks screaming in broad relief a life wasted, thinly transparent voices blowing down an empty road, and lost pages intrusively blown into his life by the winds of dementia… it had been too much. Far too much. The trip had not grounded him that day, as was his assumed need. Rather, it had served a far more critical role of destabilizing David. For had it not loosened his soul ever so slightly, the journey to come might not have come. And now, it was coming.

The rest of Thanksgiving Day had been one where David strove to run from pages and winds and voices that were too many and too swift for him to outrun. However bad that day had turned, he could not align his mind sufficiently to give himself permission to completely forgo a trip to the old farmhouse.

And so, fighting thoughts of the farmhouse for nearly two weeks, he tired of the battle and surrendered to the love of an old friend who sat waiting for him along a road of Indians, horse and heavy wagon. Gathering his belongings in some sort of accumulating frustration, he got in the car and headed out. The day was December 4th.

The old road was now graced with a kiss of snow. Some was newly fallen. The fresh snow gently covered the tired blankets of several prior snowfalls. Over the nearly two weeks since his visit, the landscape of Indian, horse and heavy wagon had enchantingly transitioned from the gray and mottled browns of fall to the pristine white of a glistening winter. The snow aptly illustrated an ever-present accumulation of time sandwiched into one place, yet distinct in the sandwiching. The roll of the car tires over the road's snowy surface lent a thick and throaty crunching sound to the wintry air, attesting to how hard things get when life turns frigid.

A sharp, morning chill had made it inordinately difficult for the world to rouse itself awake that day. The air seemed suspended and tightly wrapped in a thin, veneer frost that lent the woods slightly indistinct in the distance, hemming the morning in from the rest of the world. Thoughtfully driving up the road of Indians, horse and heavy wagon, the river-rock fence came alongside of him as if to guide him up the road to the farmhouse, motioning him ever forward. It remained standing as a faithful sentry formally bequeathed with a royal layer of winter's crowning snow. Driving by, David softly pondered the hash marks once again, wondering what life will have brought when Thanksgiving Day once again brings him here next year to etch yet another mark.

Slowing, he approached the winding drive to the farmhouse. The thin dirt drive was made up of two sparse tracks between which the meadow grasses had long taken hold. It was all hidden under the accumulated snow, rendering both the road and adjacent field entirely indistinguishable from the other. The wind had playfully caressed the snow into slight swells and curious rippling drifts that further confused the landscape of the road, all the while casting it beautiful.

Sometimes we've trodden a particular road so many times for so long that the indistinguishable is entirely distinguishable. Sometimes life doesn't need maps or markers or clear trails underfoot because the road is part of us, and in just the same way we are a part of it. We know where it goes, even though in some entirely beguiling way we've fooled ourselves into believing that we need some kind of precise map, or some other contrived marker to get us there.

Sometimes we feign ignorance about something because if we admit to the knowledge of the course that it takes, we are forced to once again admit the pain of the course. Yet despite the pain, feigning ignorance of our roads is forsaking the wealth that we have missed in our reckless flight from those very roads.

Despite a road seemingly hidden, the car found its way. It created a perfect pair of tracks that exposed the hidden driveway for those who might not know it, yet who in their own journeys might need to traverse it. It gently wound through sweeping pastures intermittently bordered by aged split rail sentries, some of whom had fallen under the weight of time and duty. For David it was picturesque, creating a tin-type yearning for another distant, innocent time that was in reality that very time.

David brought the car to a soft rolling stop at the foot of the yawning front porch. Gently he placed the purring engine in park, turned the key to silence, and let winter's hush inundate the plush interior of the car. Silence creates a space that's often unwanted. Space is the stuff that we fill, so sometimes we'd rather not have it because of the things that stand around the space eager to rush in and fill it to its edges. For David, space invited questions for which there were no answers. And no answers always begged more questions. Therefore, any kind of space was lethal for David.

Fumbling with uncooperative gloves and oppositional car keys, he seized a moment of intentional distraction to check his cell phone for hoped-for messages, of which there were none. With distractions terrifyingly absent, some ill-defined desperation poured into the space and welled up within him, snatching his heart wholesale and carrying it off to places of deep despondency. The emotion of the previous Thanksgiving Day thrust itself into the car. Yet, it had gained muscle and intent, for not to do so would jeopardize the journey to come.

The wrenching of mind and body to such horrid places caused him to inadvertently grab the steering wheel with an entirely irrational white-knuckled grip. His breathing accelerated to the edge of hyperventilation; the evidence of panic corroborated in the heavy frost born of each breath as the car had long filled with the hard cold of winter.

Without the slightest hint of awareness, he suddenly he found his head resting on top of the steering wheel much like an upset child beset by both the terror of fear and the onset of tantrum. David's mind blurred as a hostage shackled to his pain and simultaneously carried away by the force of it. He spun in a quickening confusion of what was happening to him, thoughts which landed him somewhere this side of nowhere. And so, he grasped the wheel ever harder.

Although he strained to hold it at bay, her image suddenly threw itself in front of him in a manner so precisely vivid that he felt he could caress the delicate lines of her supple neck. However, the image of the woman who had been his wife exuded a rank coldness. He still loved her, but he hated her all at the same confusing time. The coldness of her actions had rubbed away any softness. Anything of that nature had been rendered stiff by the coarse lies that had been relentlessly spun on the loom of her life and subsequently stitched into his.

He suddenly saw his children as they were at the moment they were stolen. Young and tender, their eyes exuded their love for him and bespoke of the terrifying confusion of it all for them. His daughter's frightened face drenched in a torrent of tears. His son's trembling arms reaching out for him. The horror that defies words so much so that it is forced to release itself in faces fallen in confusion and sobbing that ruptures the soul.

David's eyes pooled with tears that swelled to saturation, tracing shimmering rivulets of red-hot pain down cold cheeks. The raw hands of his heart reached out to both of his children, the aching vacuum desperately longing to be filled as it had longed to be a million disappointed times since they had been taken ten years before.

In a hyperventilation spawned wild by emotion, he threw the car door open, stumbled into the firm snow, drew himself erect and took a handful of forced breaths. After a few prolonged moments of impenetrable emotional duress, he cinched his coat tight as some sort of evidence that he was indeed an adult and need not be a child wrecked by emotion. Finally, he caught his breath. The frosty air that drifted around his head dissipated on the cold winds of winter much like his marriage. He stood for a moment in the solace of solitude and time unchanged.

The cold air snapped him to immediate attention, abruptly clearing his head and granting him space to retrieve his emotions. This was no new experience. Not at all. Some referred to these as panic attacks. Others more rightly attributed them to trauma. Whatever they were David had kept them to himself, rigorously shaking them off every time that they had overrun him.

He had assembled and reassembled the smoldering carnage in his mind before; carnage that had been madly incinerated and subsequently strewn to every horizon of his life. Carnage that had left nothing but carnage. Carnage that seem irretrievable and unredeemable. Out of sheer determination and a stubborn refusal to be beaten he had compartmentalized all of it in his mind before, many times before. He had wrestled to construct something marvelous out of all the ashen heaps that she had left in her wake.

Standing there, he reassembled it all yet again, for the millionth time it seemed. He did so by recounting the stellar successes that he had piecemealed and tediously erected from the ashes and smoldering cinders she had strewn across his life. When our lives lay in scorched shambles, we cannot allow our lives to take on the identity of the carnage that lies smoldering all around us. Yet, to our chagrin we often discover that we cannot assemble anything redeeming from the carnage. The carnage remains the carnage. Therefore, we must create something that irrefutably declares we are not what lies strewn at our feet. And so, we create successes that declare we are not this! Yet, the carnage remains.

Out of nowhere, David shouted, "This does not define me," as if fighting the fact that maybe it did. "This does not define me!" he said yet again in a voice surprisingly elevated, a voice that echoed over the meadow and dissipated in winter's forest. "It doesn't!" Instinctively, he drew himself back, took a reflective breath, glanced at the unshakable calm that drifted in from the distant forest, gently closed the car door, locked it, and muttered to himself "I've beaten this, I know I've beaten this," as if saying something enough times makes it so. Shaking his head in an attempt to shake the pain out of his head, he turned and headed for the front steps.

Lost in the pain that leached from his memory, suddenly, without recollection he found himself at the head of the basement stairway, shoes yet fringed in snow and the backdoor precariously open. It was as if he had warped forward in time, having stepped into the future without actually having walked there himself.

"What the…?" he stammered as if catching his balance both physically and emotionally. "I'd better pay better attention," he said as he turned and lumbered to the back door. Looking at it curiously as if it had opened itself by itself, he closed it, fiddled with the lock and firmly latched it. Turning away, he grumbled, "I'm looking more and more like aunt Mabel all the time." Pausing, he stepped back to the door and gave the knob a final tug. "Can't be too certain," he said to himself out loud. "Alright… let's get on with this."

The tight staircase that descended into the basement was roughly crafted of thick oak. It was a skeletal pathway that descended into the tepid and shadow-embossed recesses of the old farmhouse. The basement ceiling hung precariously low, cross-hatched by muscular oak beams that supported the thin clapboard flooring above. Heating ducts hung even lower, having been a later modification once the days of wood heat had passed and forced air had been born. The advent of indoor plumbing wove pipes through odd places, and the onset of electricity invited various wires to course through tiny gaps and ride naked wooden beams to their variant destinations.

The basement seemed to hold out the change of time in bold skeletal relief. It invited the passerby to witness nearly a century of transition frozen yet very much alive. The basement somehow held out the messages of the past as answers to the present, drawing precise maps through an uncertain road ahead. Yet while David saw history, he had yet to discern the maps that it penned.

The root cellar itself seemed a small, mystical hovel willingly occupying the most unobtrusive corner of an aged and forgotten basement. True wealth, the stuff of genuine riches most often comes wrapped in garments of poverty and inhabiting places of isolated obscurity. Embracing such poverty makes something truly priceless by its inaccessibility to the casual observer, for the casual observer knows nothing of observation. In some foggy past now rendered ancient and likely antiquated, David had believed that the Christmas story bespoke that truth. Mankind would contend that majesty befits majesty. That kingship should be enthroned in palaces made ornate by construct and rendered immortal by stories. That pedigree deserves privilege and bloodlines deserve power.

Yet it seemed that God would derive infinitely more pleasure and draw intimately closer to the likes of us by putting majesty squarely in a manger. God made the poverty of our existence the place of His home. He made the squalor of our surroundings the place where He settled. If there was something compelling about Christmas for David, the wonder of that choice was it.

That was a history that David found ill-suited for modern times. Those were choices that did not fit modern man in these modern times. Besides, all of that was long dead. It was history that had perished along the road of history. Yet, much like the root cellar, what was ancient was assumed as dead and declared as so. The root cellar silently declared otherwise.

True riches have no need of any frame or platform from which to be displayed simply because their value is their own witness, rending pomp and circumstance entirely cheapening. They are therefore seen only by those passionate enough to forbid cheap counterfeits, and those willing to seek riches in places where worldly logic says riches can never be found. The root cellar was such a place.

A thin dampness made heavy by the mustiness of time shuttered greeted David as he opened the root cellar door. Its hinges coarsely ground, turning on a layer of rust, dirt and inattention that sought to freeze the door closed and seal the treasures within. It granted passage, but not without testing the commitment of the person to the journey. With a series of pulls, the hinges relented, and the door granted a slow and reverent entrance to the road inside. David realized how little he came to the farmhouse, but how much less he traversed the rough oak steps down to this tiny room. It was a place that in times past held foodstuffs in its cool embrace when refrigeration was something unknown, being a convenience yet to be imagined and then invented. It was, in ages long past, a busy place, holding the sustenance of a farm family now long relegated to the cobwebs of a foggy and forgotten past. It was life-giving at one time, the literal bosom of the house. Now it was a place to store items deemed largely irrelevant and mostly forgotten.

The root cellar was set deep in the cool of the mid-western ground, hemmed in by seemingly ancient cinderblock and trimmed with rough-hewn wooden shelves. The cement floor poured thinly and somewhat unevenly over mid-western clay and loam afforded the visitor an uneven stance. It had cracked with time and shifting ground in much the same manner that David's life had shifted, subsequently sending fissures scampering in errant directions. A single, naked light bulb screwed loosely into a yellowed ceramic socket cast a tentative glow that dissipated at the edges of the room, leaving corners and cloistered recesses in an anemic stand-off between light and shadow.

It was a place of little accord; entirely bypassed by a world increasingly accelerating toward some vague goal dictated by nothing other than the magnetic ruse of success and comfort. Such a goal seems to give vagueness sufficient distinction. It stamps whatever the goal is with a veneer of legitimacy so that it is not only palatable but looks to be something that appears worthy of great sacrifice. The root cellar was forsaken, cast aside by the rumor that the past is bound entirely and wholly to the past with nothing to say beyond the confines of its own time. Such thinking assumes confines. Such assumptions are in fact confining. An anthology of boxes had been tucked and tossed into various places. Some were frayed and tattered, barely younger than the ancient contents they cradled. Others seemed new, clean and yet fairly fresh. Cryptic scrawling hastily made on their sides identified their contents.

Whatever is written is but a silent voice, unheard until it is given a voice in the reading. Even then it is entirely silent and muted unless what is read is expanded into the language of the soul and read aloud there. All of the letters that had been joined into words were more than words scrawled on boxes. They were signage pointing the way to incredible places. And somehow in the pointing, they seemed to implore that reader take up the journey to which they pointed. They were a repository of a past that was far more powerful than anything that the present could offer up. And yet, they were all just as available.

And so, it began; a process David had resisted for decades. On the surface, the process was all about cleaning out the remaining remnants of the farmhouse. Over the years, much of the house had been cleared out, at least sufficiently so. A sufficient smattering of furniture and décor had been left to lend some warmth and imbue the house with a bit of character. The root cellar was all that remained. Yet, this was not a remedial cleaning and sorting. David had avoided it all of these years for that reason. Something in his soul spoke that the task would be substantially more than that, even though there was no rational or logical basis to believe that to be so. Sometimes wonder is held hostage to fear. Sometimes the conviction of a better road is less than the desire to travel one. Sometimes the call of adventure falls to the complacency of comfort. Sometimes we pass on wonder because we wonder what would come to pass if we didn't. Sometimes we leave hope in boxes. Such things kept David out of this tiny hovel. Until this day.

History in the root cellar was a door unlocked in invitation, a latch freed in preparation, and a knob begging for a slight tug of anticipation. History held clear answers to daunting questions. It paved unobstructed pathways to mysterious people whose own history held the map to a future that the future itself had assumed as dead. History held keys to rusty doors long locked, granting with a single turn access to vast places centuries removed that stood just a doorway away. Clues and answers alike were there, carefully shelved in the hovel of the old root cellar.

Yet, David embraced a fear of history. He loved it, being entranced by it those many days staring at the photos hanging on the wall in aunt Mabel's clapboard home. However, he had infused it with a sense of irrelevance. That had granted him wholesale permission to leave history the stuff of history.

However, the messages of the past can be so undeniably relevant that they completely alter the realities of the present and brilliantly recalibrate every dream for the future. History makes devastated roads feasible. Albeit entirely contradictory, roads paved with hope embodied a reality that haunted David, for what if such a road was actually the impoverished farce he presumed it to be? Hope scorned is a heart torn. Slowly, unbeknownst to himself, David moved forward into hope anyway. David stepped down the single step into this most reverent sanctum of cinderblock and rough wooden shelves. Scanning the musty confines of history rousing, he was slightly brushed by something that radiated warmth in the passing. It was the touch of something that left a bit of itself in the touching.

What, what was that? David thought turning around in a complete circle and then turning back a second time.

Something or someone passed him, as implausible as that seemed when held against the logic that so strictly defined David's life. It was not a happenstance passing of lives brushing past each other on their separate journeys. Rather, it was much more an intersection of the most intentional sort. It did not possess the force of a collision. However, it was certainly thoughtful in its intentionality. Strikingly, it was much the same as what David had experienced out on the road two weeks before. That encounter had left his soul wondering. So, did this one.

Whatever it was, it seemed alive in a place which was not. Yet odd as it was, at the self-same time it was unexplainably soothing in a manner that puts the whole of a restless man's soul entirely to rest. It was a stranger who was only a stranger because it was a friendship either forgotten or in the making. In this momentary and yet odd conjunction, David was about to learn that it is in the grand contradictions of the deepest soul that great moments of life are afoot. *Stupid,* David thought looking around. *Stupid.*

But for a desperate man, even stupidity is worth a second look.

Drawn to the edge of curiosity, suddenly a strange blurring of his mind moved in him and then rolled out all around him. It was as if David's entire existence was blurring and becoming completely indistinct. As it did, another entirely separate existence seemed to be attempting to take form and shape all around him. David squinted in confusion. As it took shape, David's reality began to slip away. Everything he knew drew off at an ever-greater distance as something else was slipping into the space now being left increasingly vacant.

Halting for a moment in its progression as if to readjust itself, it then strengthened with a gentle but resolute intensity. As the blurring inside of him and outside of him accelerated, David was overcome by a disorienting sense that he somehow stood in more than one place at one time. It was completely irrational. Yet, it fit in some way unexplainably rational. That this was a transition, or so it seemed. A relocation. To what or where was a complete mystery to the rational rubrics that his mind repeatedly attempted to affix to whatever was happening. It was as if he was somehow divided. Split. Dissected. As it intensified, he was made both dizzy and nauseous in the dissecting.

Clearly, it was an aberrant sort of experience arising from humanity's stubborn refusal to be any place other than where we have decided to be. Consequently, when we step into some other experience our equilibrium is lost for our lack of mastery of this side of life.

David was tenderly cradled and then lovingly spun by a disorientation wholly surreal, yet indescribably authentic. Words of logic failed a heart now stirring. In whatever was happening, it was best explained by the emergence of a barrier that was irresistibly inviting while appearing irresistibly impenetrable in the allure. It was a barrier that some part of him had stepped into quite by accident, rendering him divided in a surreal sort of way. Had he known that it was coming, he would have not had stepped there out of the belief it did not exist. Yet, there he stood, believing while fighting not to. Suddenly his legs became rubbery and found themselves unable to entirely bear the weight of his body. Somehow this divided existence demanded more energy of him than living in one existence afforded him.

He stood, shifting his weight and trying to find some stability. He placed trembling hands against the cool cinderblock in an effort to steady himself, all the while wondering why he was here in the first place. His head demanded that he leave, seemingly screaming the demand out of the fear that it would not be heard. His heart spoke in softer, but more powerful tones that were exceedingly more compelling. His head fled from whatever this was. His heart ran to it. And it was this wrenching contradiction that embodied the entirety of his life.

Passion unleashed will overcome fear despite how dictatorial that fear might become. For the first time in a longtime David felt an eruption of passion he could completely identify with, but a passion he could not identify at all. He would not let whatever this was get the better of him.

With some sort of unidentified reflex born of the stubbornness of survivors, he forced strength into weakened legs, braced himself against the cinderblock wall, and in the blur, he reached for a box.

Chapter 6
A Chest and a Cache of Time

Life is anything but flagrant. It's too wise for that. Rather, flagrance is an attribute born of men who attempt to create greatness rather than live it. Quite the opposite, in this thing we call 'life,' things of utmost value are cloaked and concealed in things obscure. This leaves their treasures only for the eyes and hearts of seekers not dissuaded by the search or fooled by the transient rubrics of society. As we have noted, true riches do not need the stuff of pomp and circumstance to stage them as their inherent value is stage enough.

The root cellar was dense with a musky dampness; horribly dreary, heavy and emotionally claustrophobic. It was less a place, for being solely a place diminished it in ways blatantly unforgivable. In reality, it was an experience. And as an experience, it was one of immense contradiction. It was one of those rare yet precious places where we must visit if we are to live, yet the power that it emanates is far too immense to endure beyond a precarious handful of moments. David's attitude sat worlds away from the world he was entering when he flicked the switch and set the bare bulb ablaze. Light leapt from the bulb, throwing back the darkness and drawing in a sense of expansiveness beyond the pressing confines and tattered contents of the room itself. Sometimes things are simple and trite which means we grant them little accord. And yet, in contrast to their simplicity, these things embody an incarnate essence; something that was always within them that we always missed. Something that was terribly grand and astonishingly glorious. And yet despite such splendid grandness, it was always concealed in such a way that these things are paid no mind. It is something of glory hidden in plain sight. And the potency of this truth is such that the limits of these things are always infinitely greater than the confines within which we find them.

The concept of simplicity holding the glorious was odd to David, something to be resisted for the simple reason that it was odd. It was something to be denied outright because on this side of things it made no sense. Maybe it was something to be hated so that it could be denied by the hating, for denial grants us permission to ignore that which upsets our comfortable rubrics. Yet, despite the deliberation of wordsmiths and poets alike, ignorance is not bliss. Ignorance is glory missed.

At times we want permission to hate life, to see it as cruel, wicked and irreversibly unfair. We want to lump it all into one horrific category, point at it all with venomous disgust and tell both ourselves and the world that we are justified in our hatred of it. We want permission to believe that it's all no good, that there is nothing of any redemptive merit anywhere and therefore our hopelessness is soundly justified by the reality of it all.

David lived exactly that way. He etched out his life on principles not designed to embrace the sweep of life but justify the rejection of it. All of it. You love your wife. You love all the wonderful things as well as the things not so wonderful that are softened and wholly absorbed in the enormity of all that is good. You love your children, their soft innocence and their wide-eyed wonder. You love a world of hugs, magical bedtime stories, the full-bodied laughter of tickle fights, first steps, training wheels, sparkling holidays, and the satisfaction of a day well lived, and a family well loved.

You love all those indescribable things and the way in which they meld together into something that is everything good and right and true. You work for it, sacrifice for it, nurture it, speak into it, and think it's flowering because you're pouring all of these things into it.

You bask in it; revel in it even. And in doing so it becomes something of the norm. Not something normative, as that would be too diminishing. But a wonderful norm that embodies all that life should be. Because it is, we've granted it a sturdy longevity. It's the place where we settle forever. It's an impenetrable place in the whole of this grand existence. It's the providential residence that we were shaped for because it was shaped for us. It's the long-sought place within which we've been destined to live out the whole of our lives. We exhausted ourselves in our search of it, and we spent eons creating it. It's where we belong. It's home in the most indescribable way. And because it's all of these things, it will always be there. Permanently; to the point that we never have reason or suspicion to believe it won't be. Because it's this kind of place, it will always throwback whatever darkness might roll up against it, much like the bare bulb in the root cellar. Always. In essence, we will die here. And when death comes in this place, the place itself makes death safe and right.

But unexpectedly, the darkness pitches forward like a foul tsunami committed to drowning everything that it can engulf in its lewd darkness. And in the accelerating lunacy of death on the march, the darkness only finds its appetite aggravated in the feeding. Such aggravation sends it on a mad hunt for anything it can gorge itself on. The brutality of the hunt is escalated to the point that it has no consideration for whatever it finds itself hunting.

And for the first time in our lives, despite our anxious waiting, and all our desperate hoping, and all the ornate prayers we can muster in the desolation of sleepless nights, the tsunami does not subside, and the darkness is not thrown back. This place of home, destiny and comfort falls. Irretrievably. Unnecessarily. Often viciously. And there is no recourse simply because the falling is not from without, for if that were the case any darkness could be handily rebuffed. Rather, it is perpetrated from within.

Within us there rests a deeply instinctual sense of justice that is stitched in the heart of the soul. And in that sanctum, there rests a conviction that evil must abide by some kind of restraint, even if that evil comes from within. Once the shock of justice thwarted begins to abate, we are left with the sobering reality that the darkness will never be thrown back because there is no sense of justice to constrain it. People change. Unexpectedly and often without any forewarning that would bespeak of the approaching carnage, they change. There's something vulnerable about the human condition, where people can transmute into something so astonishingly altered that whatever is left is wholly unrecognizable. It doesn't matter how hard one might squint and how doggedly you might attempt to see something of what you once knew in their words, their gestures and their features. All these efforts don't matter because what we're seeking no longer exists to be found. And it's gone with such an irrevocability finality that it's difficult to fathom that it was ever there even though we possess reams of memory that painfully evidence that it was.

And when people change in this manner, they set about the task of rewriting history as a means of editing out who they were and editing in who they've now chosen to be. Such editing demands a catastrophic rewrite as its goal is to evidence that whatever this is, this is who the person always was. The implications for such a rewrite are unfathomable.

Histories are reconstructed in a radically revisionist fashion, taking the pen of liberality in hand and making history whatever history needs to be in order to support selfish agendas and justify caustic choices. Selfishness blinds us to the fact that the present is constructed from the raw material of our history. It drives us to ignore the reality that the trajectory of our future is forecast by the path of the past and the events of the present. And when we take it upon ourselves to rewrite our history to suit our agendas, the present and the future of spouses and children fall into an irretrievable oblivion. All is lost, and the stricken people who happen to be around the revisionist are lost in the loss.

There are those dangerous moments when integrity is cast off as something burdensome verses being something blessed. In its absence, truth is contorted in order to force-fit it into twisted plans that are an unrecognizable departure from every commitment that had once been loved and held. Yes, there are times when the world turns upside down, logic becomes subject to the muse of reckless interpretation, truth becomes the bed-child of selfish goals, and people are off on a wild course that bludgeons everyone they once loved or anyone who gets in the way of what they now purport to love.

Most often, these new agendas are nurtured in secrecy while the manifestation of everything needed to support them occurs in broad daylight, leaving spouses confused, disoriented, spun and increasingly frightened. When the agendas are finally strutted out onto the stage of life in full view, everything suddenly makes harrowing sense. The resulting devastation of these agendas is flatly denied, resolutely ignored and brutally written off.

Out of the ashes of the carnage that now lays strewn everywhere, it's brazenly advocated that everything will work out, that it will all be fine, that the kids will be okay and that she should have left right after the wedding a decade and a half ago. Such words run entirely counter to the indelible lineage of history, they smudge the reality of fact, and they rub cold the warm memories held by everyone else. Such are the disparaging devices employed and then deployed by selfishness and greed. Such is the murder of a relationship.

Any good that was woven through the marriage is abolished and relegated to the place of 'never-been' when in fact it had 'always-been.' Historical revision never stops once its initial goals are achieved. Instead, it continues to be relentlessly rampant and ruthless, erratically writing out a history that is mind-boggling. That history is nothing of anything recorded in cards given, poems written, successes achieved, the warmth of holidays shared, and photos snapped along the way.

As it evolves in the flux of its own evil, character assassination is tediously scripted out. Once the script is completed to satisfaction, it's liberally broadcast, making that which was good suddenly appear appallingly evil. Everything is spun so that a spouse is deemed worthy of being discarded as a natural consequence of the evil that they never embodied. Monsters are created from fiction gone dark. These are followed by the repeated sightings of such a fictional monster. Such fraudulent caricature justifies flight from the marriage in whatever way one must flee.

For David, the finality of it all was played out in chronic scheming, composite distortions, and carefully laid out lies that resulted in the loss of the marriage and the far greater loss of two innocent children. It was an orchestrated betrayal of the greatest sort, where the betrayer justifies the betrayal at the expense of the one being betrayed. It all turns in a manner entirely sadistic. And now, a spouse that had sacrificed for family is sacrificed for the agendas of selfishness and carelessly discarded along the road of humanity. Time is then left to do to the emotional corpse whatever the scavengers of time deem appropriate.

Humanity is capable of horrific things. Terrible things. Inhuman things. David knew that because he had lived them. But sometimes things move beyond even that which humanity is capable of. Some things defy explanation as even human cruelty seems to have some sort of boundary. It has some place that all of its accumulated cruelty is spent and exhausted, leaving it no resource to go any further. At the point that human cruelty somehow, someway crosses that particular line, it could have only done so because some external evil gave it the power and resource to do so. Such was David's experience of it anyway. Subsequently, his road had been decimated, and hope had become a myth. And when you have no road and no hope, what do you have?

Arousing himself from the emotion of memory and the scourge of it all, he suddenly found himself sitting on the hard root cellar floor, arms firmly wrapped around folded legs drawn tight to a throbbing chest; something like a lost child in inescapable distress. Tears had traced an array of lines down his shirt.

"What the...?" David mumbled wiping them away with trembling fingers. He thought the disorienting feelings of a moment ago to be the torrential sweep of emotions and nothing of a transition. They were now gone. Subsequently he wrote the feelings off accordingly.

Pulling himself up, he chided himself for somehow losing himself. He was a man of three-piece poise with spit-polished shoes and an ever-steady acumen. He was razor-sharp in the most daunting crisis. His words were strategically concise, his vocabulary sharply mirrored the precision of his acumen. Yet, here he was something entirely different, but entirely himself. And this is what he would soon become more of.

Trembling and noticeably sweaty, he brushed the back of his pants, wiped swollen eyes, and said with a rather familiar sarcastic tone that "It's time to put your big boy pants on David."

Clearing his throat, he turned and inadvertently scanned the root cellar once again; her memory fading until another time.

Forgotten boxes proliferated. They seemed stacked without any real regard for the fact that in whatever manner they were stacked they would remain so for decades. It was as if someone had amassed them thinking that they would be back to retrieve them shortly, so any real order would not be necessary. And yet, 'shortly' never came, rendering the boxes captive to the abyss of time and the tragedy of forgetfulness.

David scanned the scrawling's on the boxes, gathered his strength and randomly reached for them, breaking the bonds of time and self by sorting and moving the brittle boxes. Oddly, this time there was no sapping of strength. No blurring. No ethereal sense of anything or anyone. It was as if whatever the purpose of whatever that was had been entirely served by the recollection of betrayal. The groundwork had been laid.

As he moved time packed in brittle boxes, in the deeply graying and cobwebbed shadows of a far corner David suddenly spied the old chest. It was fine in every respect; elegant, proud and meticulously crafted. Generous cedar boards still sweet and aromatic made up the body of the chest. It had been entirely covered with a single layer of rich, rubbed leather that was pulled tight and seamless all around. Ornate metalwork ran down every edge and met at each corner, drawing around both the bottom and the top. The metalwork accented the chest with a subtle touch of pristine royalty. Its massive lid was aptly secured by a muscular lock the size of David's fist. Thick leather handles on each side stood ready to be grasped and lifted into yet another journey of which the chest had seen many.

David had always thought it beautiful but outmoded. It was the relic of another time that marked that particular time quite well. However, concurrently it had no ability to mark his own. He felt that it had spoken into its time and that it had expended its words in the speaking.

Blithely, he turned his glance away from it and continued parting the sea of brittle boxes.

It is true that when we seek great things we most often never find them, for we have created a sense of what great things look like, what the nature of them is, and in what manner they should arrive. And what we discover is that we are typically wrong on all accounts. Therefore, when genuine greatness shows up (and in the showing brushes right by us), we miss it because it was not what we were looking for even though it was looking for us.

Dust rose in thin scant wisps that hung in the air as there was no breeze to dissipate them. Scents of various kinds drifted out of boxes jostled and awakened. All was stale and thick. Brittle newspaper gently folded and tucked around objects both fragile and tender lent a musky odor when moved.

A shelf of brilliant crystal vases cried out for fresh-cut flowers harvested from the meadows outside. Their job seemed to be over, but not completed. Directly below that, two other shelves of canning jars lined up in regimented rows stood coated with a foggy haze of time and dust. Yet despite draw of time, they remained at full attention and at the ready. Lining an upper shelf, a handful of ceramic caricatures seemed to have gathered. They sported the gaiety of an era that they did not seem to know had passed. Glancing at them, they oddly appeared as some sort of small entourage of fellow travelers leaning into another journey that was about to commence. Assorted urns that had held the foodstuffs drawn from the fields and farm of a generation long past seemed to anticipate the privilege of holding sustenance once again. What was done didn't seem done.

In the midst of such animated richness, rummaging through the boxes something inaudible suddenly and mysteriously met David's ears; something that would not go unheard. It was both invitation and demand. Although it was difficult to tell, it sounded as if it arose from some great and inestimable distance so far away that the distance itself should have kept the sound from ever being heard at all.

It drew directly toward David until it was nearly upon him. In the rush, David stepped back until the cinderblock wall blocked his retreat. Suddenly the commotion turned away from him and lodged itself in the chest a few feet away. The cacophony of voices filled the chest so completely and robustly that it was almost as if the chest had somehow called out to him; as if it had a single voice that was in reality many voices melded together. That the whole of whatever this was simply could not be contained in such a small place and therefore both begged and demanded release.

There are times when some truth is so unalterably profound that a million voices are seamlessly unified by it in a manner so complete that they sound as one. Truth is as irresistible as it is unifying. We're all drawn to truth although at some point we all rail against it. Yet, it is unifying beyond imagination. And at these seminal moments of millions unified we know that we have encountered something so utterly rare that the whole of our existence will hinge on what we do, or do not do with it.

This voice of many voices was silent to the ear, but sufficiently loud and altogether familiar to the soul. David reflexively jerked back yet again. The wall gave him no means of retreat. Neither would the weeks ahead. He realized that he had heard something, but that he had not. That something audible had spoken to his soul or his heart or something that doesn't hear in words but hears in the far more convincing and compelling language of the soul. In the emotional mobbing that assailed David, it suddenly came to him that this was the same voice he had heard out on the road two weeks ago. Same breeze. Same voice.

Whatever was here was what he had never defined out there.

It was not as if this single voice of many voices had called his out name, but it seemed to have called to something in David's core that was more core to him than a name could ever possibly define. It called in some sort of name that wasn't a name at all but was something that spoke to everything that David was and every emotion he had ever experienced. It spoke to every shred of his being and left nothing out of the calling, making it infinitely more expansive than a simple name. And in the calling, it called him forward to something that he had never defined as forward. There was an invitation in it all that he couldn't even define as an invitation except that he knew it to be so.

The call of life never calls us by name, for the call of life is a call to the deep soul. This place of the deep soul can never be confined by the limits of a single name that we might place upon it. That call is forever a call forward despite the fact that we are forever retreating from it. A call forward with no means of retreat is likely the most petrifying thing of all. Yet, it is the most exhilarating.

It was the same exact feeling that he had experienced out on the road back on Thanksgiving Day. It was the same message, but different messengers. It was a repeat of something he never thought would or could be repeated. It was a call beyond the confines of our beyond. How he perceived that and knew it he did not know only that it was one of those truths you don't need to know in order to know it to be truth. Sometimes life intersects us without explanation, for life on the move needs none even though we often demand one of it.

You are hearing what you just saw, something said. It was something said in his head. Something not his own, but something that resonated with him as if it were. It was so clean and clear that it was as if he had heard it out loud.

Somehow these were the voices of the images he had seen moments ago. The voices had trailed sufficiently behind the images to give David ample space to fall back into the memory of his divorce, as it is the pain of our past that lays the groundwork for the victories in our future. Such preparation is so monumental that we are wholly expended in the course of it, which means that we are now open to the course of it. That is why, left to our own devices, we avoid it. David no longer possessed such power.

David stumbled, spun from the kind of disorientation that happens when some hitherto hidden veil is thrown back and for the first time we see something that's too big to absorb and too vast to conceptualize. Pain did its work, but it exhausted him in the doing. Reaching for the door, he stumbled out of the root cellar and into the basement.

"I am not crazy, I am not crazy, I am not crazy…," he said out loud with a forced authority he hoped would convince him that he wasn't. Turning, he slammed the door closed. Stumbling forward, his breathing was sporadic and crazed. Reaching for the wall, he steadied himself. But leaning on a wall won't steady the soul.

There are those terrifying moments when our lucidity is challenged. Life opens some door to the impossible and invites us in. Our assumptions are challenged, and our sanity is questioned in the challenging. We reflexively declare our sanity for fear that we are not. Yet, at the self-same time events declare with absolute authority that we simply cannot be for such wonder is just too impossible.

At times, life vast beyond our understanding careens and then collides headlong with the scrawny limitations of our understanding in an all-out brawl that will dictate whether we stay stunted or whether we rise liberated. It is here, at these sacred convergences that our lives swing. It is here that we need to move away from our futile attempts to reconcile what is happening and let life be bigger than our ability to imagine it.

"I gotta quit talking to aunt Mabel, David grumbled. "Maybe it's work, maybe it's all that stress. Maybe it's the Henderson deal. If they pull that off…" He continued, "Then there's the Folmer buyout. Ugh. That's been way too complicated. It's small enough. There's minimal risk, but it's shaking up a few key investors." Pausing, he attempted to catch his breath said, "That's it. That's gotta be it." Calming himself in-between frantic breaths he said, "It's all been stressful… I just need to sleep… I'll be fine… yea, some sleep will help, sleep will help."

Reopening the door, he reached in from outside of the root cellar and turned off the light. Gently drawing the door closed as if he didn't want to disturb anyone he hurried himself up the basement stairs. Yet, his pace slowed as if he was drawn down by some inestimable force that drained him of the energy to run from great things. Slowly, he stopped at the landing just before reaching the kitchen. He stood there rubbing his forehead and staring out the side door of the old farmhouse.

There are times in this journey of ours when we are torn to the essential core of our beings. We find ourselves pulled in entirely opposing directions by two entirely equal forces that leave us no place of compromise. We find ourselves forced to make a decision that we don't want to make, knowing that if we don't make it we'll be torn to the very foundations of ourselves with a regret we'll never be able to shake.

He had been callously rammed by a runaway divorce that held massive parts of him a captive to a history within which he never found his feet, nor another road upon which to place them. And now it seemed that he was confronted with a voice that unexplainably invited him to something right at the point when he couldn't get out of his own 'something.' The contradiction of this completely unexpected and unwanted convergence seemed to grip two sides of him and slowly rip him in two.

Sometimes life brilliantly intersects us. In the intersecting, it grants us the briefest opportunity to shatter the past and break open the future. It suddenly points to a road where we had never seen one. It lasts but a moment. But if we seize such a road, it will seize us forever. And when these rarest of moments pass our way, we would be as foolish as foolish can be to ignore the opportunity even though the full weight of our logic screams that we do exactly that.

Here, in these places of conflicted opportunity, we are forced to rally ourselves from some deep and nearly primordial place. Here, we must summon up all of the inherent power of our God-given humanity and tap into some bit of the infinite that God has placed within us. These are the extraordinary moments that convince us of the infinite. For although opportunity stands a mere step away, and although we might wish with all of our hearts to take that step, we realize that such a simple step is beyond the strength of all of our accumulated resources. At times such as these, the most difficult thing is not the belief in the infinite. No. The most difficult thing of all is to believe that the infinite would be so grand and gracious as to reside in the smallness of us. That is what requires the greatest faith.

If we can believe that, we then take that bit of infinite within us, hold it up against the forces that assail us and go wherever that bit of God tells us to go in the strength that it gives us to go there. We find ourselves compelled to obey something infinite because in those moments all our finiteness stands as terribly inadequate and wholly paralyzed. And in that moment with logic exhausted by pain, David reached down, grabbed that bit of God within him, shook himself free, turned around and headed back down the basement stairs. From here forward, he would never be the same.

Timelessly regal and ever stout, the chest was deeply aged. In some sort of exacting communion with the old farmhouse, it likewise had retained every bit of its character and held its sense of pride. It exuded a seasoned age and a nimble youth at the same time. Such an implausible contradiction made it entirely captivating. Although nearly hidden, the chest stood out from the plain wrap cardboard boxes and their scrawling's, exuding something of prominence and commanding stature. And the voices appeared to have gone to it, and now appeared to come from it.

"I wonder…," David mused. "I wonder."

The chest was a root cellar within a root cellar of sorts; something precious set and lodged within something precious. Life is something like innumerable layers, leaving us wrongly assuming that the first or even the second layer is the essence of the thing. Yet, life is many layers. It is something of endless layers actually, wholly worth probing and relentlessly peeling back until some priceless nugget is exposed in some layer we never thought to exist.

The old chest was assumed to be empty; a spin of fiction that over time became a spin on reality. And the assumed reality left the chest something inexcusably obscure; lost to time and the sympathetic shadows of the root cellar. It was never an object to be explored because the exploration would yield nothing due to the obvious fact that there was nothing within it. Assumption is pompous and careless, causing us to miss life's greatest treasures in the arrogance that embodies assumptions. In David's mind, fact completely yielded itself to assumption, which was quite vexing for a man of fact. And once a man of three-piece polish and raw logic is vexed, assumption will eventually give up ground to curiosity. He turned and went back down the steps.

With the confusion creating slight rivulets through which fear began to seep, David entered the root cellar and flicked on the light. Tentatively, he extended trembling fingers toward an old chest of age and youth. This presence of fear, at least this type of fear, was unknown to David. His fear was not birthed of the presence of fear, for fear was nothing but a very old adversary with which he had jousted innumerable times. He had learned its character, deciphered its strategies, and had become practiced at corralling it. Rather, this seeping fear was birthed of the fact that fear had now made him fearful.

The chest seemed curious as all else were boxes, assorted flax bags that once contained seed for planting, clay jars and ceramic figurines. The chest was unusual. Completely displaced, as was David. It seemed superior, as if it were more resplendent and something of royalty sitting among the boxes and bags of commonality.

Sometimes it's extraordinarily difficult to discern the difference between the simple musing of a playful mind, and a voice arising from the rumblings of the soul. It seemed that the chest had been intentionally left, as if patiently waiting for him. For David. For today. For this moment in time; in his time. It had a gripping magnetism about it that made David want to ignore it so as not fall to its devices. Yet, he wanted to engage it because it seemed so much humbler than that. His road led to here. To the root cellar. To treasure. Yet, a road so clear was not yet obvious to him.

It seemed that whatever the voices were, they had stirred curiosity to the point that curiosity was now sufficient. And so, with their task completed, the voices melted away. All was suddenly silent while curiosity was screaming, and passion was pulling.

With curiosity surging and passion churning, David pondered the chest for what seemed an eternity with a pondering that answered nothing about the chest and revealed nothing of the chest. It became clear that discerning the chest while safely outside of it failed to discern it at all. Sometimes we find that responsibly discerning something from a distance is nothing more than cowardice creating an excuse to keep our distance from that which we fear. And when that's the case, life will shut down our discernment so that we are left with no option but to engage what we would otherwise run from. Curiosity may have killed the cat, but it can open vast roads for us.

In another sense, we intuitively know that some actions take us forward in manner that we can never go back to wherever it was before we took that action. We gain whatever's ahead at the cost of whatever's behind. The trade-off is something we ponder. This would not be the last time that David would face this dilemma.

David slowly reached out for the chest. As he did, he felt his breath being sucked out of him. It was not a weakness as before. It was the inability to breath. The further he reached, the more he found himself gasping for breath. The more he gasped, the harder he forced each breath. Yet, he kept reaching as sometimes sacrifice is far outweighed by the rewards of the sacrifice.

As he reached forward through fear and accelerating breathlessness, his vision blurred again. This time, the root cellar fell into an unidentifiable fog that seemed much more the place of something else, someplace else. It shifted to something unknown yet concurrently known. Squinting into the murky confusion, he was suddenly presented with the shadow of some figure that coalesced but somehow could not take any form identifiable or consistent. The shadow came to him, becoming more defined and then falling back into something indefinable as if it felt some urgent need to connect but could not do so of its own accord.

David was a man of logic and reason. This event fit within the parameters of neither. Yet, logic and reason postulates that if we press into that which is illogical and unreasonable with enough force, logic and reason will at some point bring perfect clarity. To surrender to anything less is to undermine one's faith in logic and reason. And so David pressed against whatever this was.

The shadow itself seemed to be profoundly struggling to become whatever it was; to become something that it seemed to have been yearning to be for decades, maybe centuries, maybe more. Sometimes we yearn with desperation both silent and screaming to be who we are, to coalesce into whatever life or God intended us to be. There's a frantic passion in it all. There's some yearning that speaks to the very essence of life, of existence, of all that is and all that we are. That somehow if we don't achieve it we'll reach the end of our days in a desperation that will make death welcomed because of the relief that it will provide us. But we fear death because it affords us no opportunity to try again. We fear dying indefinable shadows that have lived out a murky existence of no importance.

David's mind, more his heart, became enraptured with the shadowy image as if it were familiar, maybe more familiar than anything he could possibly be familiar with. The feeling of dizziness set in, yet it was superseded by an increasing curiosity. Leaning forward, he found it captivatingly strange that he seemed to know something that he didn't know, much like meeting a stranger that you've known all of your life. It all struck him as odd, yet oddity that layered itself into a thickening confusion.

Fear and passion find common ground at life's most critical points, throwing us both forward and backward simultaneously. The contradiction saps our strength, leaving us excited and debilitated all at once. Most often, we chose neither to move toward or away from that which calls us. Rather we escape in some direction defined by neither. David finally pulled back, felt his knees weaken, stumbled out of the root cellar and collapsed on the basement floor.

Often determination is born of defeat. David was a durable kind of man, profoundly wounded and emotionally tender in some subterranean place that lay fathoms below the strata that he presented to the world. Pain makes one formidable either out of the sweat of working through it, or the emotional muscle developed in the denial of it. That muscle drew him to his feet and threw him back to the threshold of the root cellar door. It was strength ill-used.

Facing the old chest out of a sense of curiosity tinged with an obstinate touch of adversarial determination, he wiped his hands on his shirt and reentered the root cellar. Slowly he reached out to the chest yet again. Nothing happened, nothing at all. Not this time. Just as in reaching for the boxes, whatever it was came and went indefinably and without explanation. Yet, explanation is not critical to discovery, unless we think it to be so. If we think it so, we will limit discovery to that which we can explain. And hemmed in by the confines of our intellect, discovery will go undiscovered.

Pensively, David grabbed a leather handle. Nothing happened. Gently he sandwiched the chest between a gauntlet of brittle boxes and drew it to the edge of the recessed root cellar. Turning it to face him, he backed away out of the uncertainty that having gotten the chest this far without incident would not necessarily mean that he would get it to the floor without incident. Yet, standing there, still nothing happened. He thought through the voices on the road, the feelings he had experienced in the root cellar, and this shadowy figure. Logically none of it made sense. Yet, logically there had to be a connection. Some linking path between all of these experiences must exist. But when it comes to things of great stature, the things that rock our lives to new heights, the road refuses to be revealed until we take it.

Carefully, he grabbed both leather handles, pulled the chest outward and gently placed it on the uneven concrete floor poured over mid-Western clay and loam. Canting it slightly, he nudged it up the single step out of the root cellar and placed it just outside the root cellar door. Standing up, he backed away, wondering if some contrived intelligence somehow inhabited the chest and was waiting to catch David off-guard. It's not often that we tediously strategize the opening of a simple chest, but he quickly realized that that was exactly what he was doing.

"How stupid is this?" David murmured.

Slowly and surely, he reached for the tarnished fist-sized latch, the only barrier between himself and the contents of the old chest. To his surprise, nothing occurred. Nothing at all. Backing away and reaching out a second time as a sort of self-assuring test, he found that again nothing happened. Catching his breath, he wrote the previous episode off as one of those things that happens in the course of life and the throes of stress.

Oddly, such a rationale for a man of logic and reason was somehow sufficient for him when it would have never met such a litmus test in any other situation. And here began the unrecognized transformation. Here it would begin, although a row of hash marks and an old road had given it all a slight push. Here everything that put him here would begin its own end. It would be a calculated journey of single steps, but it began here. Putting logic squarely behind him, he manipulated the latch, gently drew it back, and opened the chest.

It relented with squeaky hinges and the resistance of age embedding stiffness in its joints. It was as musty as the root cellar itself. Yet, it was tainted with some slight aromatic scent. The mixing of the various scents was irreconcilably odd. There emanated the musty odor of time having passed in massive volume; of age that only time can concoct. However, the aromatic smell also held something new, fresh and as current in time as this day itself. Past and present in the same place. Peering inside, it was unexpectedly full of mementos.

Somehow the chest seemed to embody a century and a half or more. Yet, some scent seemed to have been released from some bottle of pure essence only a moment ago. The past and the present mingled in the chest in a manner entirely confusing. David pondered it only for a moment, losing the strangeness of it all in all the other accumulating oddities that seemed to be intersecting his otherwise stoic, cookie-cutter existence.

The chest was a relic of the Civil War. It had held the personal belongings of his great-grandmother through the upheaval of the Civil War. How close it had come to actual musket shot and cannon fire had been an ongoing question of debate. Some said his great-grandmother lived within earshot of Gettysburg as that epic battle moved through Little Roundtop, Seminary Ridge and on into American history, leaving farm fields bloodied, fallow and forever sacred. It was rumored that his great-grandmother had actually met President Lincoln following his now infamous Gettysburg address. She had reportedly pulled off the feat by being an adamant eight-year-old whose persistence garnered a muscular handshake and an engulfing hug from a tired and war-worn President. Who knows? Such pondering was even fuzzier than the fire of 1928.

Apparently, the chest had held pieces and parts of history for a century and a half. Most of it came and went;

something like the coming and going of life. Yet, there were some artifacts that had pulled up in their journey through time and had settled in the chest; something like the 19th century pioneers pulling up to settle in the fertile Midwest. Family had thought them lost. But what was presumed lost was simply waiting, as is so much of life. It was those things that caught David's eye and began sparking his imagination.

There was an assortment of things lying dormant in the old chest. A potpourri of life, of a journey and pieces of a life lived. There was enough in the old chest to construct an essential framework of whatever that life had been and the roads that it had walked. Assorted mismatched jewelry, yellowed papers rendered brittle by time, a pair of elegant gloves worn thin on the palms, a tattered silk scarf, a stack of letters loosely bound by a faded red ribbon, several novels whose stories had grown old in the telling of their stories, a tattered photo album, and several scattered glass bottles that had long forgotten what ointment or perfume or liquid they had once held.

Among the precious things, there was one thing that was more precious than the rest. It was a family Bible. Leather bound with gold edging, it was dated 1854. It was here, at this doorway that determination was to fail him and the road away from the chest was chosen. But that choice would not last.

Chapter 7
Aunt Mabel and Back Again

Life is full of running. The key to a life lived or an existence tolerated is held in the single decision as to the direction in which we will run. Roads permit us to run in either direction. It's typically our perception, our deeply held belief that we spend most of it running 'toward' something. We reach for lofty goals that incessantly demand the best of everything that we are; goals that press us beyond ourselves to intentionally demand more so that we might discover in the press that in reality we are more.

We pursue deeply held dreams fashioned in some place of the secret soul. We ascend toward fond aspirations that capture the entirety of our imagination in the net of dreams and enflame our passion by touching the match of possibilities to the kindling of those dreams. We hold out great challenges for ourselves that are framed and constructed on all the things we feel we can't overcome in order to force ourselves to overcome them anyway. This is what we run toward.

Yet, for everything we run 'towards,' there seems to be an equal if not greater number of things that we run 'from.' It would seem that the things that we run from are the very things that are irrevocably foundational to achieving the things that we're running to. Indeed, they are imperative in the achieving of grand goals, of harnessing the ability to draw dreams squarely into the realm of reality, of laying hold of aspirations that are so marvelous in scope and form that we fear they will be nothing more than aspirations. And finally, they are irreplaceable in realizing our ability to finally summit the challenges of our lives, stunned that we are actually able to stand in that place. We can ill afford to run from the things that make these achievements possible. Yet, we run. We run pell-mell in any direction that's in the other direction. And we run at terrible cost to ourselves.

To do great things, it's much more about intentionally running to everything that we are by nature inclined to run away from. It would seem that the biggest thing that we must overcome in order to achieve the things we're running 'to' is to intentionally embrace the very things we'd prefer to run from; to seize that which seizes us with great fear. To understand that the sanity of God seems insanity to men, and to purge our sanity so that ours might be His. The road that we trod affords travel in either direction. Choosing to run, David contacted a real estate agent.

The chest had been left on the basement floor. Its contents were left where they had been. The angst had become too much. There had been no more feelings of disarray of dizziness. Those had been replaced by something far more frightening. There was a sense that everything in David's life had somehow led up to everything that had happened in the secret confines of the old root cellar that day. And the fact that such a notion held nothing of logic but held everything that David was made it intolerable. Faced with a seminal moment that was beyond David as all seminal moments are, he fled deep into the night of the soul.

But most of all, the fleeing was centered on the family Bible. It had held too many promises that had been broken in the play of his life. It promised what Christmas did. What wedding vows did. What the smile of a simple child tucked into bed seemed to have promised. What a world of hugs, magical bedtime stories, the full-bodied laughter of tickle fights, first steps, training wheels, and the satisfaction of a day well lived, and a family well loved appeared to have promised at some time long ago.

This 'God' purported the depositing of good things and the administration of divine protection, all of which never came off the pages of that Bible to be delivered into David's life. His life evidenced in acute chronological detail one broken promise after another. The road of his life was mordantly littered along the whole of its course with promises less broken and more shattered. And David would have none of it. And so, with hope shattered by promises broken and faced with a seminal moment around it all, he left.

The drive home that night was fuzzy and entirely murky as if he was sobering up from a night of hard drinking. The night was dark both inside and out which creates the darkest darkness imaginable. His focus wasn't focused anywhere. The combination of fatigue and confusion wouldn't allow him to line up anything in a head that was tilting in full-bore disarray. What little energy he had was directed to getting a good distance away from whatever it was that had just happened, particularly the family Bible and its failed promises. The accumulated sum total of his mental energies were woefully inadequate in sorting it all out; not because they were fatigued or less than adequate. Rather, it was because they were expended in running 'from' instead of running 'to.'

Snow had started to fall; the kind of gentle snow that's more about listless beauty and less about the inconvenience of slushy roads turned slick. It was the type of snow that was intentionally listless; the kind of snow that has a mind to lend a magical trim to the accelerating excitement of the pending holiday. More than excitement, it lent something austere and reverent to the tinny and incessant rush of bargain shopping, party planning, gift wrapping, candy-cane stories of a distant North Pole and all the assorted things that seemed to cheapen everything about Christmas.

As he navigated the city streets on his way home, it seemed that he was encased in a perfect snow globe that lovingly held within its glassy expanse a perfect world; a world where Christmas suddenly fit and made sense. The snow seemed to pirouette past street lights that illuminated the dance in a spotlight erected at ground zero of a world falling apart. The snow drifted past stoplights, allowing their red, green and yellow lights to illuminate them, bringing a vibrancy and a hint of color to the season. It lent a misty charm down long streets whose stale asphalt concourses now seemed to be magically transformed by something vastly more wonderful that would stay wonderful because it was too grand to be caged or tamed by any kind of explanation. In some way, it all became what that family Bible said it could be. But, snow would melt.

Finally pulling up his long driveway, the pine trees around the front of his home were being dressed in a delicate, flawlessly white icing spun by some otherworldly confectioner whose handiwork was nothing other than perfect. Times like this caused David wonder if maybe, just maybe life was more than the evil and crassness that seemed to paint it black.

The large maples and muscular oaks along the street were graced with a kiss of white that gave a gracious holiday dressing to naked limbs. It seemed as if the trees were astonished by the noble dressing with which they were clothed, and that something of their genuine majesty was now seen in the dressing. Stepping out of his car into magic, the night was entirely still beyond what David thought stillness could ever possibly be.

This stillness, unlike the stillness that David often feared, invited the pondering of wonderment and gave room for nothing else. It was a stillness that gestured to him, inviting him out to entertain the idea of the marvelous and to touch it in order to entertain the idea that it might actually be real. Was this a glimpse of what it all should be? Was this a moment to savor what it would be? Was this God afoot in a world that had cast Him underfoot? Was this God on a silent march of redemption in the same way that He was on that Christmas night so many years ago? Captivated and mesmerized, ushered to the precipice of hope that it might all be true, David stepped down the driveway into the middle of this marvelous snow globe moment and let it inundate him.

Standing there in the deep of that winter's night, life suddenly became much more than David had ever allowed it to be. Something was enlarged beyond anything he had lived, thrusting out his walls in every direction to the point that he was lost in the sudden space within which he now stood; a space infinitely expanded within himself. It was engulfing, far larger than anything he had known even before the betrayal and the loss of all things loved. As the listless snow drifted from hushed skies and the trees reverently held out expectant limbs to be graced by the glory of it all, David found himself unexplainably enlarged. A chest, a Bible and a snowfall rubbed their magic into his soul.

We all have those moments when something reveals to us just how constricted we've lived our lives or how impossible we've seen our roads as being. Our life experience is exponentially expanded and in the expansion, we become convinced of the larger life being revealed to us. And in the ascending conviction, we become entranced by the sense that there's even more life beyond that. At those magical moments our lives are left ever and forever changed. David stood out in the middle of it until he could absorb it no more.

Suddenly, his cell phone rang harsh and demanding. Jarred, he leapt up from a rumpled lounge chair. The lights in the living room were on and a half empty cup of tea sat cold on the end table next to him with the tea bag limp at its bottom. Rummaging through a discarded coat, he found the phone. However, it had gone to voicemail before he could reach it. Peering at the mantel clock, it read 1:13 a.m. He leaned back in his chair and it all went misty again.

It was early morning before David was able to fully collect himself. He remembered being home, a snow globe moment and a phone call. Yet, just like his drive home from the farmhouse, he had no idea when or how he had fallen asleep in the chair, much less how he got there. He thought the whole episode in the root cellar to be a dream, finding some calm and relief in the fact that it was all a mind asleep rather than a life awake. Whatever the night of snow had done to him, he had pulled the boundaries of his walls back in, rendering his world confined and tight yet again. We have the power to kill wonder and the ability to constrict a wide-open journey even when we've been exposed to snippets of both. David did exactly that. Life would not permit him space to do that for long.

The irritated cell phone vibrated, informing him that he had an assemblage of waiting messages that demanded his immediate attention. Finally, as the sun began pushing the night off to a retreating western horizon he reached for the phone. Groping for it, he scrolled through an array of mixed messages, most heralding the demands of innumerable clients requesting assorted deadlines, or questioning product delivery, or wishing to adjust contracts. In a slowly clearing head he checked off each one, proactively preparing a clean and tightly professional response to each before placing the call. Pausing in the scrolling, one stood out… or rather leapt out. One that he didn't want to hear, but one that could not go unheard. One that would not let him go. And so, he retrieved the message.

It was aunt Mabel… again.

"Davie B, Davie B?" the voice said. Her voice became softly distant as if she'd moved away from the phone. In the distance, she mumbled as if talking to someone else in her room, "I don't know what this is… I think it's his phone's recording," she said to someone. After a confused pause as if determining how to talk to an inhuman voicemail, she returned to the phone and said, "Davie B, you were at the farmhouse today. You were so close, you were so close, I could tell. Why didn't you do it? The pages Davie. Seven of them. You were so close. I know that he saw you. Davie B? Oh… " and it all drew away to muffled sounds. A series of indistinct mumbles trailed off to silence and the message ended.

Shaking himself to crystalline clarity, David sat up and fumbled with the thoughts of the root cellar, gradually realizing that it was a reality. The evening, the episode in the root cellar whatever that was, a blurry drive home, snow globes and a kind of fatigue he had never experienced; something like being drained to the point that it seemed that he had no energy left at all. The closest way he could explain it to himself was that he was dead but somehow alive at the same time, which was worrisome.

I'm done, he thought to himself as his emotions frantically ricocheted all over his head. *I'm selling the place. I'm ending whatever this is, and I'm done.*

David ran from wonder because the magnitude of it all is sometimes too much and the road too vast. Here he took a lesser path that, thankfully, would not grant him passage.

The week rolled on. The typical routine of work and home, the stuff of the mundane within which we all hide, peering out on occasion in order to see if life is still out there prowling about. Life calls us out. Somewhere from horizons both far and distant, life constantly calls us out. We might not hear the call because of the distances we intentionally put between ourselves and those horizons. We fear the call of the road because to answer the call we must be willing to move beyond ourselves, out beyond our comfort zones and all that is known. We must be willing to transcend ourselves and all of the fears that seem to be so much of who we are, and to strike out on the shaken belief that such a risk is warranted, worthy and of inestimable value.

And so, it plagued him, as do great things when we choose to run from them. He spent a week running... running with all his might and all of the strength of his ingenuity. He ran by means of justification, rationalization and all the things that give us permission to run from the very road that we were built for and that were built for us. He ran into his career, his calendar, empty meetings, threaded emails and terse voicemails. He ran into mergers and deals simple and complex. He ran because a road bled of hope is an impossible road, as is a life bled of the same thing. He ran. But the direction of his running would soon change.

In his running, he had called a real estate agent. Tediously, he prepared to list the old farmhouse which was something akin to intentionally abandoning an old friend and saying no to the road and no to hope at the same time. She had been a reference from a friend. Bypassing his normal researching, as that would only draw out time, he simply made an appointment. The call, the appointment, the decision to sell never sat well with him despite his efforts to sit on it. The solemn compilation of it all haunted him until it amassed a heaviness that his heart had to ignore for otherwise it would die.

Worse, it was abandoning farmhouse, road and hope unnecessarily. The selling process extended the cruelty of it all by drawing out the abandonment over time. David knew such abandonment well, which drew the pain deep within him. He knew exactly what it was to be abandoned when there was no justification for the abandonment. And he knew full well that abandonment without justification is cruelty of the most heinous sort. Yet, here he was doing what had been perpetrated upon him.

He adamantly railed against these feelings, calling on the tenacity and strength that loss had granted him. David took the gifts afforded by loss and turned them against the very challenges they had been forged to fight. He was to find out that working against what we know to be true, despite how proficient we are at doing it, is choosing the cowardice of flight. What he didn't realize was that we can never flee far enough. Neither could he.

The real estate agent seemed professional enough, well groomed, articulate and finely concise. It was clear that Ms. Scott knew her business well. Her knowledge and acumen were refined to a near razors edge. She was, in many ways, the female manifestation of himself. He found those attributes deeply reassuring but oddly perplexing at the same time.

Even she could not remotely fathom the rationale for selling the old farmhouse. Although she could not put her finger on it, the decision seemed an odd mix of fear, irrational thinking and some unidentified anger.

Several times during the walk-through she paused, looked intently at David and asked, "Are you confident in your decision to sell, Mr. Morris?"

With a bubbling anger held in check by his own professionalism he replied rather curtly, "Ms. Scott, let's just list it, if that's okay with you."

With a brief nod, she resumed her notations and entered data into her laptop.

The walk-through itself went well enough until the real estate agent asked to see the basement.

"Umm, I would prefer that you look at it yourself," David stammered. "I mean... I don't want to bias your opinion of it... if you don't mind."

"Of course," she said politely, finding the request a bit odd but reasonable enough. Oddity in her business was not an entirely unknown commodity, so she wrote it off to oddity and descended the rough-hewn oak steps.

As she walked down the basement stairs David could hear her methodically going through the basement, stopping likely to make various notations. In a few moments she walked up the basement stairs, her pen vigorously finalizing her notes.

"Needs to be cleaned up a bit," she said. "Particularly the root cellar and that empty chest. You might want to put it somewhere or move it out if it has some sentimental value to you," she said as she walked over the kitchen counter to continue her note taking.

Empty? David thought.

Walking over to her in something of more a meandering gait, clearing his throat he said, "Excuse me, do you mean the large chest, the one sitting outside the root cellar there?"

"Yes Mr. Morris, that's the only one I saw," she replied while vigorously making further notations on her laptop.

"It was empty; you say?" David said. "Completely empty."

"Yes" she said still flipping pages and making notations.

Clearing his throat and his mind yet again, he said, "You mean... there was nothing in it... that's what you mean right?" he said.

Pausing and casting a curious glance at David, she said, "Yes, that old chest outside the root cellar. I'd get it out of there."

Scanning the recesses of his mind while mindlessly scanning the ground, he suddenly said, "Excuse me. I'll… I'll be right back." Hurriedly turning, he descended the stairs with panicked steps. Eyeing the chest at some safe distance determined by both confusion and fear, he slowly walked over, extended his head ahead of his body, and peered in. Oddly, he found it full of the very same items that had been in it before. Very full. Completely full. *She must be mistaken*, he thought to himself shaking his head.

"This is exactly why I'm selling this place," he said to himself in some sort of reassuring tone that bolstered his sense of escalating confusion.

It was odd that the intensity of David's conviction to sell the old farmhouse was completed countered by a single, core feeling that selling it was entirely wrong. How often hope calls us to a road that, out of fear or apprehension we refuse to travel even though everything within us shouts that we should travel it. With every justification he could muster, that gnawing internal sense of some gross and inexcusable error only grew, entirely offsetting the very evidences that he so desperately sought out and rampantly collected. However, they were falling ever short and ever more inadequate.

He ascended the basement stairs to find the real estate agent with laptop in hand performing a flurry of final calculations.

"Excuse me again," David said. "You meant the chest sitting in front of the root cellar, right?"

"Yes" she replied with some sort of curious irritation, "The one that's got the ripped fabric in the bottom of it."

What? David thought.

Trying to sort out what he should and shouldn't do, David wanted to go back into the basement to look again, but he figured it would look strangely odd if he excused himself again. *She thinks I'm weird already*, he thought to himself.

After she had completed her calculations she said, "I'll get this all consolidated so that we can go over the figures this week. I'll give you a call tomorrow and we can set something up." Shaking his hand, David escorted her out the door and onto the sweeping front porch border by a row of sweeping white pines.

Unexpectedly she paused at the edge of the porch, caught in a transition of her own. Whatever parts of him that she shared seemed to coalesce and abruptly emerged with a brisk but passionate subtly. There was a dynamic shift within her, a clear movement away from the business of selling a home to the far superior business of living.

The landscape spread out like a majestic tapestry, rolling out from the foot of the front porch, moving out beyond the pines and spilling out to distant forests that found themselves engulfed by infinite sky-blue horizons beyond.

Surveying it with the tender heart of appreciation, she contemplatively said, "You ever get the feeling there's something alive about this place?"

David smiled oddly, momentarily lost in her words as it correlated with his own heart. Shaking himself free of it, he cleared his throat and said, "Unfortunately, some things you just have to do." She nodded and descended the steps to her car.

As she opened her car door she paused, looked up and said, "Please forgive me, but are you certain about this decision Mr. Morris?"

"Ms. Scott, I'll see you this week," David replied curtly. With a hesitant nod, she got in her car, started the engine and drove out to a road of Indians, horse and heavy wagon.

Watching her car roll out of sight, he turned and hurried to the basement and the old chest. The fear of anything happening again was overridden by the greater fear of not understanding what was happening. Frantically searching the basement, he grabbed on old broom handle. Gently putting an end of it into the chest as if touching the chest wrongly might result in something terrible, he methodically moved the items to each side. As he did, underneath he found the fabric in the bottom torn just as the real agent had said.

"She didn't see this stuff… how could, how could she not see it?" Frantically pulling out the broom handle, stepping back and dropping the handle to the floor, David was left with questions that he had no energy to answer.

"I just hope it sells quickly" he said as he scurried up the basement steps, looking back as if something might be following him. For in fact something was. And that something was his destiny hidden in the pages of history.

Within a few days, for the first time in its history, the old farmhouse stood with a 'For Sale' sign at the foot of its lengthy drive, about to be abandoned to the hands of others and in the process losing the richness of a history accessible to one and only one person. Hope was being bartered away for hopelessness and a cashier's check. It would be the priceless sold for a bowl of pottage.

David buried himself in any place he could to bury the sale of the farmhouse. Yet, for all his determination to bury himself deep in life and work and the pursuit of leisure (which was actually work in clever disguise), the farm called to him in a voice not louder than everything else that called out to him, but in a voice more compelling than all the other voices. It's not the volume of that which calls us. It's the vastness. David wrestled with whatever it was that called him, hoping that the farm would sell so that he could squash this annoying inner voice. Repeated, sometimes frantic calls were made to Ms. Scott.

Each time, she gently answered the same.

"Mr. Morris, farms are a tough sell," she would say. "Typically, they sit on the market for a while. Unfortunately, your property sits too far out from the city limits to generate any interest from a developer. The zoning is also complicated. So, we'll have to find someone who is either retired or wants to farm. Unfortunately, the city's not projected to grow in that direction for at least a decade. I would encourage you to give it a month or two to see how the market's going to respond to it," she recommended with a sterile professionalism. "We can re-evaluate it then."

"I hate life," David said.

"I'm sorry?" Ms. Scott responded to David. "I didn't hear what you said."

"Not a big deal," David replied. "Keep me posted. Have a great day. We'll be in touch," he said. Then he hung up and dropped the phone on the table with a resignation hot in a bath of anger.

Sometimes our lives seem to steer themselves all by themselves, something like life grabbing the steering wheel of our lives resulting in a sharp and entirely unexpected turn that takes us down a road that we prefer not to go down. All of our efforts to wrest the wheel away and set our course down the roads of denial fail. Sometimes we're just along for the ride. Such was this moment.

Driving home from a frustrating day at work, the steering wheel of David's life exercised a mind of its own. In no time, he once again found himself driving down a road of Indians, horse and heavy wagon, past a river-rock fence and up the long driveway. The short winter's day had begun pushing the night into the afternoon, so it seemed.

The snow remained. However, it seemed slightly tired. An ivory half-moon in a waning gibbous and a crystal-clear night combined to draw a thin, veneered layer of silky white across the vast landscape. It seemed kissed with something that lent a bit of magic and timelessness to the night. Everything seemed tenderly suspended in a soothing and completely appropriate kind of limbo. There was a pause in life; a generous moment when everything stops and gives us a reprieve from everything that we need a reprieve from. It almost seemed that an invitation had been extended; that hope was calling out from somewhere, that a moment had been staged.

The car rolled up to the old farmhouse with the sound of gravel crunching beneath muscular tires. The house was inky dark inside with a milky layer of silky white spun from an observant moon white-washing the house in wonder. The black blankness of the numerous wavy glass windows seemed starkly accentuated against the moonlight, bespeaking a house that seemed to be without a soul and a structure without a pulse; something vigorously contrary to the comments of the real estate agent… something vigorously and entirely contrary to David's life-long experience of it.

"I hate this place," David mumbled in complete denial of his love for every inch of it. "Why am I straddled with this cancerous relic?" Grumbling with a biting edge, he emerged from the car, slammed the car door closed and then walked up to the front steps with anger dripping off his every step. "But," he paused, becoming painfully honest with himself, "I love this place. I hate it and I love it," he said, wrenched with the kind of grinding contradiction that readies a man's heart for great things. As he turned, he glanced down at the basement windows to see that the basement lights were on. *I could have sworn…* he thought. *Oh well.*

Making his way into the house, he walked through the kitchen to the basement door. Opening the basement door, he found that the lights were off. Yet, there was a soft glow coming from a far corner of the basement. Descending the steps, he turned the corner and saw that the bare light bulb in the root cellar was lit, warm and glowing. There was something subtly inviting about that light; not a boisterous invitation that would sweep someone into the room, but a gentle calling. In every way, it was a sort of soft gesturing that bade him come into the root cellar. It was a calling he didn't extend; a light he hadn't left on… rather it had left itself on for him.

His vision immediately went to the old chest patiently sitting outside the root cellar. Something in him locked on it and penetrated it. Shedding his trench coat and rolling up his dress sleeves, he turned on the basement light and reached for the old chest. Immediately, the air seemed sucked out of the room. He continued to reach for the chest, sweat instantly cresting his forehead and beading in innumerable droplets. This time, whatever this was it hit hard and it hit fast. Extending trembling hands into the chest his vision blurred like before but without any shadowy figure.

He was a man not offset by challenges, and this had been challenging enough. Driving through breathlessness and blurred vision, he reached further into the bowels of mystery, barely touching the old family Bible. The breathlessness and dizziness proved too much. He passed out and dropped to the floor. In essence, he dropped into history, or it into him.

How much time had passed was uncertain, as time is funny about being reined in to our definitions of time. Rousing himself from the murky fog of a mind floating in time, he instantly sat up and scanned the basement. Rubbing a cold hand on a throbbing forehead, he slowly realized where he was; quickly recalling the moment of passing out and reassembling the events prior to that as some sort of puzzle whose pieces had been thoughtfully scattered.

With the puzzle largely completed, he then turned his attention to the more pressing agenda of what had happened afterwards, as that was far more difficult to ascertain. In the blacking out something had said something to him, so it seemed. It was not just a fall into darkness. It was a fall into something that he couldn't identify. Sure, we all have dreams that give us a recollection of our sleep. But this, this was a visitation from something, or a visitation to something. It was not a mind liberated in the throes of slumber. It was not an imagination untethered by sleep. This was not of himself. Whatever it was, it was indefinable.

Finding his balance and slowly standing, he again stepped toward the chest with a sense of fear offset by a growing sense of defiance. It might be said that when it came to 'fight verses flight' as the old adage goes, David was clearly a fighter. Anyone who knew him would readily attest to that. Yet the paradoxical oddity of it all rested in the reality that the fighter in him was driven by the fear of flight. It might be said that the embarrassment and unadulterated shame born of fleeing drove him to fight when everything else in him drove him to run. In essence, the brave exterior was goaded into action by a terribly fearful interior.

Some things must be pursued, or they may in fact pursue us. We are caught either way. Therefore, we might be wise to surrender by pursuing. With real fear pounding at his chest, David reached into the old chest and prayed. Nothing occurred this time, as was the same each time he had engaged things a second time. He pulled back a bit and tentatively reached in again. Nothing happened. Nothing at all. Turning in frustration, David grabbed his keys, headed up the steps, slammed the door behind him and headed home. But that was soon to change.

Chapter 8
A Whisper

The world is an enormous cache of muted whispers, drifting silently but not sullenly all around us. Sadly, they seem all too absent or we see them as the stuff of vivid imaginations driven by escapist ruminations. The world indeed is thick with the very things that give us life and sustenance in a manner that is always sufficient and ever adequate despite our inadequacy to believe in them.

Hope waits to be discovered, begging it seems that we believe in its existence sufficiently to pursue it in order to find it to be real in the pursuing. However, we don't see it, leaving us to believe in the totality of its absence and therefore living out shrunken lives based on such an errant premise. Yet, whispers not apprehended leave the reality of those whispers entirely unaltered.

It seems that of all places, a forgotten root cellar is entirely absent of any voices at all, much less those spoken in muted whispers. It seemed to be the place of perpetually emptying silence, with any whispers having been spoken long ago and irrevocably concluded the moment that they were uttered. The root cellar seemed to be a place that stored the dead, broken and disjointed shards of yesterday, rendering it a vacant mausoleum permeated by the death of what was and nothing more.

David preferred that it remain just that… a mausoleum. His ascending fear generated by all the many bizarre events of the past several weeks was the fear that what was dead might jump to life if it be engaged yet again. That some muted whisper of something past might actually be heard. Some things are better left stone-cold dead and evermore locked in the dank catacombs of the past rather than retrieved and thrust brazenly alive into the present.

He knew that when Thanksgiving turned and headed toward the Christmas season. His dread was embracing a holiday that appeared to be outwardly bright. Because it was, he feared that he might begin to believe that it might actually be bright, only to find that the brightness was darkness in cruel disguise. Such was the story of 'his' life, and therefore it was assumed that such was the story 'of' life.

Life had turned for him in manner that suggested that it was all dark all the time. 'Good,' as he had defined it, lived it and presumed it to be had shown itself as nothing more than an ideal and anything but a reality. 'Good' was nothing more than a wily fictional concept crafted solely by the panicked need to believe that evil was not the single and sole option of our existence. The concept of 'good' was certainly admirable and actually rather ingenious. However, naively assuming 'good' as a reality that would actually have the breath of life breathed into it if it was acted upon proved to be nothing of the sort. In the end, 'good' never took a breath despite David's efforts to breathe life into it. And if 'good' never breathes on its own, hope had to be a concept just as lifeless.

Life, it seemed, was an empty assortment of ideals and hopes that duped people into thinking that it was all worthwhile. Christmas seemed to be one of those things. Sprightly brilliant, it teased the onlooker by feigning of the hope of hope. But David found it to be just that… a tease.

We are fearful people, and fear erects imposing obstacles against opportunity, regardless of how grand the opportunity might be. Rather, we relegate life to the lifeless notions borne of our inherent pessimism and fed fat by fear. David's pessimism was not borne of anything other than reality. He had deliberately invested in all that was good believing that all that was good would handily offset all that was bad. He had loved another out of the greatest good he could conceive, only to see that 'good' was not good enough. Ideals perish in the face of realities. Ethics are wantonly expendable. Values vanish. Selfish agendas implode marriages in plumes of asphyxiating ash and leave families wandering lost among the cinders. David saw hope in just such a way.

All the mementoes of this questionable good and this spurious hope lay in the root cellar, boxed and silent. They were connected to dreams dashed and relationships lost. They screamed that what he thought love could do, in reality it could not do. That what life should have been, wasn't. That in the end, even hope was not enough. Far from it. And so, they all laid buried in this dank mausoleum.

The mementos however were not mementos of his life. They were the various shards and thin slivers of his kin; of ancestors mostly unknown to him. These people now laid in various cemeteries in places where their journeys had pulled in the reins and ended.

One particular cemetery down in Belpre nudged up to a small white church adorned with a pristine steeple and hemmed in by a short diminutive fence. Another over in Elyria had fallen to time and inattention, itself having aged in unison with the headstones that littered its uneven rows. Several others rested in a sweeping cemetery whose manicured vistas rolled off to a forested edge that tip-toed along the border between Michigan and Ohio. Headstones in each were moss-embossed, canted by the press of time, and sporting dates of an era unrecognizable from the vantage point of the 21st century.

The remnants of these kin long past sat collected in a damp root cellar. Each artifact had been present at some living event now long past. They had beautifully and rather marvelously attached that time and those events to themselves, carrying something of that time and those events undiminished across time. They lay packed in the present full of something of the past. The old root cellar was a storehouse, which is quite the opposite of a cemetery.

As a storehouse, it tenderly held the mementos of someone else, someplace else. Yet, sometimes things that are not ours are in reality a part of us as much as anything might be. Nothing in the root cellar was of David, yet it was everything of David.

He wished not to stir any of the boxes or their contents any more, particularly the old chest or its contents. The outcome of doing that before was anything but good. The exact fear of such an action was entirely unidentifiable to him other than the fear was embarrassingly real. David was not typically a fearful man, yet for all his efforts to do so, fear of this place was a fear he could not calm. And when we cannot calm fear despite the heroics of mind and heart to do so, we will press through despite the fear, or we will flee from it. David was caught in a colossal pull between the two. Calls like the one from aunt Mabel stirred those fears even more, sometimes raising them to a frenzy and rubbing him up against the edge of panic itself.

Yet something whispered to him out of that place of dead and decaying memories. Something that held out something more than black memories smeared in the cold pain of loss. Something said that there was something more. David had stood facing the boxes and heard a voice of sorts, the kind of voice that's completely undefinable, yet entirely familiar. A voice that we doubt with the fullest of our fears, but yet believe with the fullest of our hopes. In such a terse conundrum, we are tantalized by the very hope that we doubt. And our lives turn on the choices we make at just such moments.

Indeed, once upon a time David had been a dreamer; a vitally expansive and explosive dreamer filled with robust ideas and a hope that seemed at times irreverent in the way that they challenged life. The whispers reminded him of that because at one time, in a place now far away he had responded to them without question, thought or fear. Those earliest hash marks scrawled on the old river-rock fence just across the road were marks of a hardy journey infused with ravenous hope. He had been bursting with hope in those early days to the point that he was gladly swept up and swept away in it. But no more. That part of him had died in the flames of a divorce and a family fallen into cinders and ash.

Pondering this inner prompting, he recalled a gentler time when such voices would have seized his imagination and sent him on a journey seeking out the voices. Without question, he would have set off running after them in wild pursuit of whatever crumpled boxes they might have been hidden in. As the memories burst open from some hidden spring within him and filled the expanse of his entire being he found himself passionately longing for what he used to be. What he thought he was. What he wanted to be again. The longing itself reached a manic-like intensity that, for the first time since his wife walked away with distraught children in tow, he found himself willing to once again risk that life might be good.

For the first time there was in it all a violent grieving that ignited a fiery desire to return to the something and someone of hope, adventure and challenge. His soul had gone gray. His heart had become listless. He had devolved into a netherworld where all was black and deathly still, causing him to become the same. He stood realizing that his heart had altogether stopped beating a decade ago, and his lungs were filled with the stale air of a breath not taken in ten long years.

Over the years, the root cellar seemed to develop a voice of its own. There had always been something. It had called him over and over, or so it seemed as he now pondered it all. Up until this point, such musing had been written off to imagination or the manifestation of grief. Only now however had he heard something of its voice, a tattered phrase, a fragmented sentence. And laced in it all he heard something of his own voice from long ago mixed in the calling.

The root cellar had been the one place that he was desperate to avoid, yet it became the one place that began to become irresistible. He was nothing of a weak man, yet he was caught in the bottomless chasm between the man he once was, and the man he had become. Each of those two people responded entirely differently to the voices emanating from the root cellar. One part of him found himself desperately desperate to believe that something more existed to which the voices spoke. The other part of him mercilessly chided himself for believing in such nonsense and setting himself up to be disappointed in hope and fooled by love.

One of the reasons he had never moved into the old farmhouse was the root cellar, as immature as he thought that sounded. Instead, he had opted for a comfortable home in a tidy neighborhood on the outskirts of the city. If he were to be vulnerably honest with himself, David would have confessed that the root cellar was the single reason he had made that choice. Sure, living in the old farmhouse would have represented a rather long commute, but that excuse was always insufficient. The house itself was largely empty; having a few sordid remnants of discarded furniture and wall decor hanging canted and dusty. Bits of wallpaper hung faded, peeling and curled at various edges. It always seemed a place entirely abandoned, but entirely alive in some way that defied logic or explanation. With some tender loving care, it could have been a marvelous home and David knew it. But to know something and to be assaulted by fear in the knowing leaves 'doing' abandoned.

The root cellar was the single room, something like a sacred catacomb that had remained intact and untouched over the sprawling decades. Most everything else had at some point been moved out or sold or rearranged. Yet the root cellar went oddly unnoticed and unaltered. If we leave something alone it is either out of a deep reverence or paralyzing fear. There are things that adamantly refuse to touch our lives without transforming us in the touching. David knew that the root cellar was full of just such things. And so, he avoided it out of the ever-accelerating fear that passion might someday rise sufficiently to offset fear. And with fear abated, he knew that he could no longer avoid touching and being touched in the touching. And that day was coalescing at that very moment.

Aside from the deep dust of inattention, it was exactly as it had been at the very moment his grandfather had been moved from the farmhouse to the nursing home on that December morning in 1957. What David was to learn was that sometimes in life things fall into a shrouded state of inattention so that their treasures might be held in the fullest state of preservation for another time.

Suddenly David's cell phone angrily vibrated yet again, demanding his immediate attention. Yanking it out of his pocket he read the caller ID.

"Aunt Mabel again," he muttered.

The date read December 11th.

"That's going to voicemail," he said with a voice laced tight with irritation. "I'm not in the mood for another 'pages' conversation, whatever that is. Why don't they medicate her for that?" As soon as the thought passed through his head he felt a tug of regret that was instantly followed by a swell of regret. *Ugh,* he thought. *I'll call her back in a minute.*

David found himself increasingly conflicted, ever angrier, and yet ever more curious at the same time, all of which was projected onto aunt Mabel and her call. For it was not the call of aunt Mabel. It was, in fact, the call of life. The ascending anxiety within him was accelerated by the guilt of hurting her as she had no part in the feelings that churned within him. Suddenly, pain rendered him soft instead of casting him hard.

As with so many moments that thrust us out of the smallest of ourselves into the greatness of great things, he found himself driven to a restored softness that tenderized him sufficiently around the edges. Yet, such tenderness stood against the whole of his will. David battled with himself for the entire hour it took to drive back to the old farm. He found himself engaged in a draining seesaw battle of being grounded by all things practical but being unable to shun the voice of something greater that invited him to places that the practical would never dare to tread or think to exist. And so, he once again returned to the farm of fence, field and forest, driving the road of Indians, horse and heavy wagon after a long day at work.

Entering the engulfing vacancy of the farmhouse, he reflexively stopped, turned and walked back out onto the yawning front porch. Standing on its vast expanse, he scanned the rolling vista of slumbering fields and quietly napping forest as darkness began pulling a veil over the day. Piecemeal flocks of birds rose and dropped into the field's growth of winter stubble. The shrill call of mischievous blue-jays rolled out from dense stands of maple and ash. Far down the field a handful of deer skirted wood's edge, feeding on a bounty of acorns dropped from the muscular oaks that flanked the woods. Sporadically the deer anxiously scanned the open fields, fearing to wander too far from the safety of the wood's primitive tangle. A lone hawk circled high on generous updrafts, soon joined by a second as both danced on the wings of the wind.

Sighing, David took a step to the railing, put his hands on its wooden surface, leaned forward and drew in a breath of sweet country air. And suddenly, this battle began to lift. Everything began to orient itself alive with color, wildly fragrant scents and the soothing sound of a world at peace with itself. Nature sets things right when the nature of our minds throws them into disarray.

At some point every person who has ever lived has a moment when everything that they are suddenly comes face to face with everything that they should be. Every person has a seminal moment when this gentle collision leaves them aghast with who they've been, fearful of how much they've missed, and cautiously electrified with what they could be. Decisions made at these moments will soundly dictate every other moment that will transpire for every moment of life that one has yet to live.

It suddenly dawned on David that he had relegated the farm to a lifeless piece of stale real estate, and he therefore had inhumanly compartmentalized it as a sterilized commodity. He had thoughtlessly ripped the beating heart of history out of it, except for a few piecemeal stories whose origins and authenticity he had seen as fictionalized to the point that fact was entirely indiscernible. All of that was about to change.

Again, standing on the very precipice of transformation, he froze as he realized that he had done the same to himself. And it was here that the change that had begun in the old root cellar began to crystalize. Tentatively, but surely. David was far too hurt and interminably too wounded to be transformed in this single moment, or any single moment. Yet, drawing in the quiet glory of field and forest it began in a manner sufficiently strong that it would not be stopped. He drew another breath, and in the breath realized that something was changing and that he need not yet understand the change for it do to its work. He then turned and stepped into the farmhouse.

Closing and thoughtfully latching the door behind him, he walked across the kitchen and descended the rough-hewn oak stairs to the basement. Apparently, the root cellar light had been left on again, extending an invitation to a moment beyond the moment. Turning, he walked up to the old chest and stood in front of it. This was for him the ridiculousness of it all. It was a chest. Just a chest. An inanimate object. The logical side of himself that he had so meticulously constructed after the divorce had kept him emotionally safe and sufficiently distant from every calamity and injustice that had been perpetrated on him since. It had even shielded him from the barbs and attacks that populated the divorce.

But here, in front of an antique chest, everything logical within him went completely limp. The change that had been put into gentle forward momentum in the root cellar and was roused on the front porch finally, and quite mercifully, gave all of this a meaning that logic could not and need not make reasonable. He had faced far more than this on roads both personal and professional, but here he stood trembling and afraid in front of a chest full of relics.

We certainly feel some element of fear when life attacks us. But real fear is felt when life calls us out beyond our safe confines and points us to great things that don't feel all that safe. That's when we feel real fear. So, with real fear pounding at his chest, David reached into the old chest and prayed.

Nothing occurred this time, as was the same each time he had engaged things a second time. He pulled back a bit and tentatively reached in again. Nothing happened. Nothing at all. No passing out. No blurring. Nothing. With the logical side of himself being gradually reassured that this was simply a mismatched collection of relics and nothing more, he reached into the chest.

As he did, he was drawn to the old family Bible. It had a coal black leather cover that was cracked along its curling edges. The words "Holy Bible" were imprinted in a simple flowing script across the upper third of the front cover. It was a bit stiff all about. Its binding appeared stiff as well, with its pages having been embossed by a gold trim that was slightly faded at points and places. It was thick and robust, much like the message inside. Someone had applied a touch of glue on the binding at the top of the book and had run a slight bead down a fraying edge. Pulling it out, he turned it back and forth as if determining how he was going to engage it or how it might engage him.

As he did, he found six crisp, new pages that had obviously been tucked in its pages at some point in history.

"Pages," David blurted. "What?" He counted them. Six. "Oh my… are these…? Are these?" David's mind spun. *Are you kidding*, he thought. *This can't be… can it?* Holding the Bible at arm's length and canting his head as if in some sort of catatonic disbelief, he said, "There are pages. There actually are pages. They're for real. Really real."

He drew the Bible to himself, took out the pages and counted them again. Six. Recalling, he remembered that aunt Mabel had said seven. She was adamant about that number for some reason. Very adamant. But, dementia does strange things. It messes with minds and it screws up numbers. So, it didn't much matter… until it would. But for now, there were pages. Six of them.

With curiosity consuming him, he pulled out the first page. Squinting, he walked under one of the bare bulbs just outside the root cellar. It appeared that the writing had been done in pencil and was somewhat crude. Yet, it seemed entirely fresh, as if it had only been written but a moment ago. Its message was short, something more like the meandering of someone who was waxing a bit philosophical or trying to figure oneself out in the writing. Taking it and holding it under the light, it read:

"The fire burnt down the farmhouse ten years ago today. Seems that it was only yesterday, but time does that to you. It always amazed me that it takes a man so long to face his fires, much less believe that he can rebuild something out of them. I went back to the farm today. I've driven by it here and there over the past ten years out a kind of itching curiosity, but I never drove up the driveway."

"Hmm. Sounds like me," David mused. "Just like me."

He continued:

"Never walked through what was left of the farmhouse. Couldn't bring myself to do that. I couldn't because all I saw was destruction and ash and cinders and such. Couldn't see nothing good rising out of any of it. Just thought that when something is destroyed, it's destroyed for good. Move on is what I thought. So, after ten years I came back and spent most of the day today just walking around it. Looking at it and thinking about it and praying some. Remembering that day for the first time in a long time. Thinking about Nellie and frozen pumps and all."

This must be my grandfather, David thought, finding himself irresistibly drawn into the emotions of an event long past and a man long dead. "This is him!" David blurted out loud. Immediately, he started reading again. However, the writing was slightly different, as if his grandfather had paused or written the last part of the letter after some subtle shift in thought, much like David's shift. It read:

"But something's come over me, telling me that it's not over, only if I want it to be. It's burnt down, but it isn't done. Something says I need to rebuild it. Raise it back up. Make it kind of a symbol that genuine hope will withstand any fire, and in the middle of the cinders and ashes hope always has the power to make all things new. Hope says things aren't done. What got burnt up don't need to be lost, even though we think it's gone. It don't need to be gone. Fires don't kill hope. Hope's fireproof. I'm not sure why, but I believe that hope can redeem anything, so I'm gonna start right here with this house.

David Morris

December 12, 1938"

"This was after the fire," David mumbled. "Ten years after. This is when he decided to come back here and rebuild it," he muttered looking up at the flooring overhead and scanning the basement. *This is what made him do all of this,* he thought. David was completely unfamiliar with the kind of hope that would allow a single man to take on such a daunting task. *Wouldn't it just be easier to walk away,* he thought to himself.

David's mind suddenly stepped outside itself into a space entirely unknown. His mind began to fashion the emerging reality that false hope, regardless of how craftily it might be constructed, could not have the power or force to compel a man to give himself over to his ashes in order to rise above those ashes. So, this must be…

His cell phone suddenly buzzed. As he reflexively reached it for, the page slipped out of the Bible and fell toward the floor. David turned and quickly reached for it, grabbing it in its spiraled descent. As he did, he fell to the floor… again.

Suddenly David came to, finding himself sitting on the basement floor in front of the old chest with page in hand.

"Again?" he said. "Again?" he said a second time, chiding himself a bit while rubbing his forehead.

Drawing himself up from the root cellar floor and summarily collecting himself, he turned to see a young man standing in the doorway of the old root cellar.

"Howdy," the man said staring directly at him with a clear softness and a hint of tease.

Squinting, David sharply said, "Who or what are you? And what are you doing in my house?" Looking beyond the young man, sunshine poured into the basement windows, pulling his attention away from the young man to embrace night having instantly turned to day. *Wasn't it night,* he thought to himself.

In the pause of the conversation he thought he heard the soft neighing of horses off in the distance, and the more pronounced sound of chickens that seemed somewhat closer although they were a bit off as well. The sounds completely disoriented him as they were never part of the farm as he had known it. Clearly, the presence of the young man became secondary to all the misplaced things that David was hearing and seeing and even smelling.

Suddenly, upstairs he could hear the soft sound of someone walking.

"Who you takin' to?" came a voice from upstairs.

"Just talking to myself Nel," the young man shouted at the basement ceiling, "You know full well that I do that quite a bit."

"Well, pumps froze again," came a delicate but strong female voice. "Can't do supper without water," she continued.

"Things do tend to get froze in December, don't they?" the young man replied, casting a winking eye toward David. "Be right up," he said, projecting his voice toward the stairway. With that, the footsteps walked away from the door.

Nel? David thought, *Who's Nel? There's two of them in my house!*

The young man's attention turned back to David, scanning him up and down rather quizzically. "I always wondered how this moment would go," he said with an air of curiosity mingled with an electric tingle of excitement. "Always wondered, but wondering's over 'cause, well here we are. Here you are! Come on over here," the young man motioned vigorously as David stood to confused feet and weak knees.

He could not have been much more than thirty, maybe thirty-five if that. His features were sharply chiseled with his skin seasoned deep and rubbed golden by the Mid-Western sun. His clothes were simple, earthy and not pretentious in any way. He sported a worn pair of hardworking overalls and a stained t-shirt that bespoke the labor and life of simple farm-folk. Leather work boots caked with dried mud and framed with meaty soles peered out from under turned up denim cuffs that themselves sported threadbare holes in variant places. His clothing had been worn thin by the kind of full-bodied labor that grants a man a stalwart sense of purpose, while filling him with the unalterable peace that the day was well lived instead of wholly squandered.

Light blue eyes were set as deep pools against his richly tanned skin. Locks of tussled brown hair fell in short, uncombed clusters across the breadth of his forehead. His hands were broad and sturdy. Thick callouses lent a sense of adversity overcome by leaning into the hardships of life and bending them backwards against themselves.

He had a slow, drawl-like mannerism about him that outwardly seemed a lot like stupidity and slog of mental slowness. Yet the more David watched him the more it seemed that the slowness was about a fallowed maturity and a seasoned wisdom that allowed this young man to simply be comfortable just being. It was something that had eluded David all of his life, yet this simple person has grasped it in a way most masterful.

Collecting himself as much as he could, David said, "What are you doing in my house?" He found himself caught between looking around the basement in order to orient himself to something that was not quite his basement, while confronting what he thought be an intruder.

"Funny thing 'bout that," the young man replied, "Life sometimes doesn't go like we think it should or like it's always gone before. Seems to me that sometimes life kinda interrupts and, well, we don't know what to do with the interruption 'cause we didn't plan for it. But I'll tell ya what, I've learned that if life interrupts us, it's 'cause it's got somethin' good and right to say to us."

"What? What does that mean?" David responded critically, not really knowing what to say, but having to say something. Still looking around he said, "Look, I don't need a lesson in philosophy or pop-psychology. Who are you and what are you doing in my house?" David again asserted. "Are you one of the neighbors, or some sort of homeless person… or who are you?" he said. With a pause that was the continuation of David's attempt collect himself, he then said, "And who's that upstairs?" pointing upward.

The young man's calm comfort and molasses ease was uncanny, as if he were home and David was not.

"Well, which one of those questions to you want me to answer first?" the young man replied. "That a passel of 'em fer sure. But, they make sense… given where ya've come from."

Pulling a rag out of his back pocket and contemplatively wiping something off his hands, he held up the rag as if to lend weight to his words and said, "Well, here, let me answer 'em in the best order. Sometimes you youngsters don't really understand the order of things," he said while tucking the rag back into his back pocket. "I suppose you couldn't in this situation anyway. Most folks couldn't." Shaking his head, with a bit of a drawl and looking back up at David he said, "I reckon I couldn't if I was in yer shoes either."

Youngster? David thought, *I've got this guy by at least twenty years, at least! Probably more.* "What did you mean by that?" David shot back in a mix of anger and confusion. "Are you one of those mental patients or something?" he said stammering and now evermore lost.

"Let me see… let's start with what am I doin' in your house and see where we go from there," the young man replied stepping back, leaning against the basement wall and completely ignoring David's last comment.

Looking at the man, David's attention was suddenly drawn away from the young man as he realized that there was supposed to be a utility sink on the wall to the young man's right, with an old, black sump pump to his left. Neither was there. Turning to his left, he saw that the steps were there in the right place, and the windows were where they were supposed to be. But the washer and dryer were gone, as was the large gray fuse box that was supposed to be above the dryer. Spinning around, the furnace was likewise gone with something that looked cast iron coal burner of some sort sitting in its place. For some illogical reason that David couldn't understand things weren't in their right place, or they weren't there at all. It all just wasn't…

The young man silently watched David's confusion mount, doing so with an entirely assured calm that gave rise to the notion that somehow, the events were entirely known to him. Sometimes we anticipate something for so long that when it actually happens it's strikingly different than we could have ever imagined it to be. At other times, particularly when life is afoot, it's everything that we thought and more. Such was the young man's experience.

"Well," said the young man, interrupting David's accelerating thoughts, "Some things are darn right easy to explain and fer a farmer like me, some things ain't quite as easy... kind of like plowing a field straight. Sometimes you get the furrow a little crooked, you know. Kinda depends on you and kinda depends on the horses... its working as a team." Pausing and casting a rather longing glance out of the basement window next to David, he said, "Seems to me that great things in life happen 'cause there's a team that's working together and sacrificin' together. Ya know, cuttin' the furrows together. Makes great things happen, ya know. Like plowin' a field or plowin' a future." He looked down and wiped his hands on the rag once again.

"Okay," David said now trying to be calm, "I have no interest in mind games or philosophical mush or home-spun farm stories." With his voice developing a bit of an edge, he said, "What are you doing in my house," half asking the question and half looking around trying to make sense of things missing and things out of place and things different.

"David," the young man said with a striking softness and a tenderness, something like a gentle father, "This ain't your house... not yet, but in half a century or there bout's it'll be yours; not this house exactly, but one a whole lot like it." Waving his arm across the basement while scanning it, he said "This here is about a day away from burnin' down. All of this right here, where you and I are standin'. And it's about another ten years from being rebuilt... a long ten years. Mighty long." Pausing, the young continued, "That there's the fact of the matter."

"What?" David bumbled.

The young man replied, "Let me answer the second question," he said as he pushed himself off the wall and stepped toward David. The young man stared at the floor as if formulating something unthinkably profound. He then shifted his gazed directly into David's eyes. Drawing in a deep breath he said, "David... David, what day is it... today, what day is this?"

"It's Tuesday" David snapped.

"Let me rephrase that," the young man said. "What's the date?"

"December 11th," David replied.

"Yup" said the young man, pausing as if something life-altering was about to happen. "Yup, yer got that right. But here's the next question that's worth some ponderin'. What year is this?" the young man asked, "what year son?"

With anger and confusion building simultaneously within him, David said, "I'm calling the sheriff!" With that he thrust his hand into his pocket to retrieve his cell phone. He found his pocket empty of everything but a bit of fluffy lint. Rummaging through his pocket, he frantically began going through all of his other pockets. "I don't have my phone," he said out loud. "My wallet, that's gone too!" he said with a mixture of confusion and anger. "What's this about?" he said looking at the young man and left going back to rummage through his pockets. "You've stolen my wallet and phone!"

The young man said, "Well David, ya don't have any such contraption 'cause, well, how do I say this right... ya don't exist yet. Neither does the stuff that yer scratching 'round in yer pockets for. It'll be invented, created and all, but not fer a while."

"Of course I exist," David retorted while continuing to rummage through his pockets with a mounting anxiety and somewhat comical confusion.

Snapping out of some sort of fog, David became erect and said, "Wait. How did you know my name? How did you know that? Did you get that from my wallet?" Continuing to frantically look around to see if he might

150

have dropped his wallet, he then blurted out, "Did you go through my phone?"

Pausing, the young man repeated, "What year is it?"

"I don't know! What year is it? You tell me" David said out of escalating anger and a developing sarcasm while continuing to rummage through his pockets and repeatedly checking the ground around him.

At times we're faced with realities that are genuine realities but are realities that far too great for us to embrace. We would be wise to live life cognizant of life's realities, but we'd be even wiser to be equally cognizant that sometimes greater realities exist that shun our logic and circumvent the best of our mind. Such openness gives life ample space to work out wondrous things. Such openness creates room for hope.

Staring David in the eyes, the young man said, "David, its 1928. December 11th, 1928."

Chapter 9
Grandpa and 1928

"David," a delicate but stout female voice called from the basement door a second time. "David, do I need to come down there; who ya talkin' to?"

"Jest muttering to myself honey" the young man shouted up the stairs. "Jest a conversation in my head," he said, winking at David. "No need to come down, I'll be up shortly."

"Days a wastin' and pumps still froze solid as can be," came the female voice as David heard footsteps move away from the basement door and out the back of the house.

Not that recent events weren't more than enough to thrust one's mind to some improbable precipice of insanity. Yet, the voice from upstairs abruptly pressed David further toward the cliff's edge. Confounded, he pensively asked, "Is your name David?" looking directly at the young man. "My name's David," he muttered to himself. "And… your name's David," he said pointing a quivering finger at the young man.

David stepped back and walked aimless circles in the basement as the young man resumed his position leaning against the wall. "1928, or so you say anyway. Your name is David. Her name is… Nel. Nellie? The sink's not there, and the sump pump is missing, and this isn't our furnace, I'm not even certain what this is," David continued as he did a mental inventorying of what was there and what was not. "And farm animals… out there," he said pointing. "Chickens. Horses, I think. Daylight when it should be night. What is all of this?" Abruptly turning to his left, he rushed to the basement window that faced the driveway, pulled his chin up to the sill and peered out. Rapidly scanning back and forth, there was no garage; no garage where it should have been. No car parked. "Am I looking out the right window?" David thought looking around the basement, attempting to reorient himself to whatever all of this was. "Is this the right window? Or…"

Obstructing his view was a horse-drawn plow unhitched, caked with black mid-Western loam which sat patiently and somewhat sleepily as it awaited the turn to spring. To the right of that at some distance there stood an old, tired wagon sitting somewhat canted on a slight berm. Despite the weariness of its frame, it seemed doggedly ready for a call to duty. Horses milling about in a sweeping pasture out beyond the wagon peacefully meandered about in December's tranquil white. It seemed as if they drew in the gentle solitude that enfolded itself upon them, somehow liberally exuding it back into the scene through the power of their calm.

"Those things weren't there when I drove up" David thought to himself out loud. "Those things aren't there at all. They've never been there… at all," he half mumbled, staring at the ground and then back up and out the window. "At all."

"No, they weren't there when ya drove up, but ninety or so years before ya drove up they were there, right there where they are right now." Despite his seemingly simple appearance, the young man seemed intimately acquainted with the ways of the earth. And it seemed that farming the earth had forged a deep camaraderie within which he had come to understand the ways of life as well. However, the words to enfold such a rich understanding and deliver it to another were slight and meager. But, great things lie in the poverty of a few scant words.

Pausing, the young man formulated his meager choice of words and said, "It's 1928 David. That's what this is," he said slowly motioning back and forth. "At least, that's what part of this is," the young man said. "1928, and, well, you ain't born yet, but yer here anyway, if that makes any kinda sense."

Pointing upstairs, he said, "That woman upstairs… that woman up there, that's your Grandma." he said, choking on some unexpected surge of emotion. "You, you never met her, never had the chance, I know. Sad, but ya won't get the chance this time 'round either, even though she's right up there. That's fer another time, in another kinda way. Purpose of her in all of this fer ya isn't for now." He paused, stared out the window and continued. "But I think ya know, 'cause ya know the history, ya know, ya know that she's gonna die David," the young man said with an increasing catch in his voice.

Clearing his throat, he paused and drew a breath that went soul deep and said, "Tomorrow she's going die in a fire that's gonna happen right here," pointing all around him. With a troubling pause the young man said, "David, ya know about the fire, the stories of the smoke and all, it's all history for you; like some sad story that's so long ago it doesn't much matter anymore. For you it's just a story, like some kinda distant fable that yer not even sure about. Somethin' ya heard told by family members over holiday dinners and card games and such. That kinda sterilizes it ya know. But it's the future for her and for me," he said pointing upstairs. "Jest a day in the future… that's all. Jest a day."

Pausing again and falling into thought, the young man resumed, "After the fire, I got ten years of bein' lost… real lost. The kinda lost that ya think is what yer gonna be forever. But it won't be, even though it seems so. And then I'll come back and rebuild this whole thing," he said, motioning around the basement. "Not quite like this yer seeing here, like it is right here, right now," he said running his hands over the support beams overhead, "Brought back too many bad memories, too much darkness to recreate jest like this. But close enough to keep me close but keep me

154

distant at the same time. What I won't be able to recreate is that fine young woman upstairs. No rebuildin' that. People… they're once in a lifetime. Ya get that once in this life. That's it. So, enjoy 'em while ya got 'em, 'cause ya don't realize what a gift they are until they ain't there."

Reflexively, David's logical orientation clamped down once again. He shouted, "That's crazy. That's just crazy. You sound like aunt Mabel! You sound just like her."

With a contemplative look that belied the weight of the situation, the young man replied, "Yeah, well yer aunt Mabel isn't born just yet either, but let me tell ya, she's going to be quite a woman." Pausing, he said, "She kinda reminded me of your Grandmother upstairs, you know, strong and improbable, but kinda gristle like. Your aunt Mabel, yup… yup," he said nodding his head soft and gentle. "She had your Grandma in her for certain." With tears welling up in his eyes, he continued, "Some great things got passed on into her fer certain. Great things mind ya."

Rubbing his hands together and staring off the nothingness born of pain and contemplation, the young man straightened himself, canted his head and said, "In my years I found out that sometimes what seems crazy is more real than anything else, it just looks crazy, that's all. Lookin' like somethin' doesn't mean that's what it is. Crazy is just something that we tag onto the truth when we're not strong enough to face the truth or when we don't want to understand it 'cause it's uncomfortable and all. If we don't wanna hear it, or it just ain't to our likin' we call it crazy 'cause then we don't have to pay it no mind." Thinking a bit, he said, "Just a piece of advice for ya, ya'd be smart to listen to aunt Mabel when that time comes David. When it comes."

"Okay, enough," David yelled. Holding his head in his hands then looking up and pointing a finger directly at the young man he said, "I don't know what this is, but whatever it is, it's not what you're telling me. It can't be. This is, this is… like a bad joke or a concussion or a hangover or a really bad dream or a really 'bad' hangover, but it's not what you're telling me," he said with a depth and intensity, attempting to ward off truth as we too often do. "This is not that! It can't be! It just can't."

There are those acutely perplexing moments when a man is unexpectedly thrust to the end of himself. From there, he's pushed out beyond himself. It is here, in that frightening place that a man fears the collapse of himself in a manner so complete that this may be the end of who or what he is, or what he thinks he is.

While we have all witnessed life end in a myriad of ways, we have done so from a safe and somewhat distant distance. Facing the appearance of our end means that we will experience that which we have only witnessed. Fortunate as it seemed to be, some bit of the transformation that had happened on the front porch only moments ago or would happen ninety years from now or whatever it was, was seasoning David's rigid mind soft again.

The young man leaned forward, turned toward the door of the root cellar and drew the old chest into the middle of the basement. Turning the chest toward David so that he had a full-frontal view of it, the young man looked up and said, "Look at this, David. Look here," he said pointing at the chest. "Recognize this?"

David took his head out of his hands, turned, and stared at the old chest. His gazed penetrated the chest, causing his hands to fall to his sides as he stumbled toward it. With his mouth gaping open he walked up to it, bent slightly and ran a trembling hand over it.

He gazed back and forth across it with a dizzyingly surreal amazement; the kind of amazement that briskly wipes the head clear so that the miraculous has sufficient room to start running. The chest was strikingly new; not brand new, but much newer. Remarkably newer. Unmistakably newer. Indeed, it was the same chest, the very same chest with a whole lot of years peeled off of it. It was the chest in reverse. Time, as we've come to know it, only goes forward. We can look back, but nothing goes back. Ever. Nothing gets new. It just doesn't work that way. With a little time and some practiced craftsmanship things can be made to look new, but that's only the old in redress. Not the old in reverse.

For David the chest was time in radical reverse, which is potentially or maybe providentially a reversal of everything; of the way we think, or the way we thought things to be, or the way we thought ourselves to be, or how we conceptualized everything. We can only imagine and subsequently understand things methodically moving forward toward some future place of death or decay. But to suddenly throw the hands of time in reverse and to reverse decay in that action was for David to invert the whole of existence and throw it all backwards.

And if that was true, if that was possible, if this was in fact 1928, it all suggested that anything, literally anything could be reversed. Anything. That what our limp imaginations and lifeless faith hold as an insurmountable reality may actually be completely surmountable, or more pointedly, may not be reality at all. And if that is so, then life is a journey of unimagined possibilities.

Snapping David back, with a calm air of reverent sadness the young man said, "It was my mother's. My grandfather gave it to her way back when she was jest a child, to keep her keepsakes and important things in. Ya know," he said with an air of warmed reminiscing, "She had this at Gettysburg when she was about eight or so.

Somethin' like that. That old chest right there," he said pointing, "that old chest was within earshot of that battle. Yup, it heard it all they say. It heard men dying David. It heard cannon shot and the shout of battle on them rolling hills. Always seemed to me that it kept those memories close, real close, like it could almost talk." With a slight and wistful pause, he said, "Wish it could. Really wish it could. That'd be fascinatin' wouldn't it?" Running his hand across the leather and oak lid he said, "I wonder what it would say if it could talk? But I guess it does, kinda… talk."

David found his mind pummeled by the whole of the experience, helplessly free-falling into some gyrating emotional abyss from which no bottom seemed to exist. He was spinning, wandering, attempting to pull it all into some cohesive whole that would make sense of the senselessness and would give him permission to believe that he was not insane. He wanted to believe everything that was happening in front of him, but to believe would mean a blatantly militant readjustment of his whole life, his entire thinking, and the way he looked at everything.

As David pondered everything that was transpiring, or supposedly transpiring, he began to rapidly realize that this would not be merely an adjustment as such. This would mean altering the whole of his existence, for something this massive and incomprehensible would leave nothing untouched; nothing unaltered. Nothing. Even if this were some sort of aberration of stress or, God forbid, early onset dementia or something else, this singular moment in and of itself would change everything for evermore. The monumental nature of such a shift left him immobilized.

Sometimes life abruptly opens up in ways so vast that it engulfs all of our constructs and theories and beliefs in the swiftness of that single moment. At times such as these, life does nothing less than demand a brutally exacting reconstruction of everything that we've expended the raw essence of our lives constructing. Much like the farmhouse that tomorrow would fall into ashes and blown cinder, such is the course of our lives in such moments. And at these moments we are left wondering if we have the passion or compassion to rebuild on foundations now razed. And so, David fought believing what he wanted to believe.

When life is about to do something great, it often sneaks up on us in order that the element of surprise might enhance every part of what it's about to do. There has been a grand withholding of sorts that makes the culmination of the moment as sweeping and momentous as the change that life is about to birth and the road that it is about to pave.

And then it dawned on him, kind of like a slow dawn that reveals the new day gradually but surely, like that Thanksgiving morning two weeks ago, or in reality that morning that will happen ninety or so years from now. David turned, pointed at the young man, but the words he had escaped him. Then he pointed at the chest, and then back again to the young man with no ability to access any words or craft any syntax that could deliver the emotions spinning within him.

Suddenly, the sound of chickens floated into the basement, followed by the neighing of distant horses. The woman called again from the top of the basement steps causing David to jump.

"David, the well needs to be unfroze and primed again. Can you get to that? I got clothes to launder and dinner to fix; the days getting' on."

"Be right there," the young man replied, returning his gaze to David. "David, I gotta go. But there's something we need to talk about."

With his mind now finally shaking itself loose, David turned to the young man and muttered, "You're… you're my grandfather? Is that, is that what you're saying?

159

You're my grandfather... grandfather David? Is that, is that possible?" he stammered. "You're the guy I'm named after? You're him, you're him, the guy in all the stories? The pictures? But, but, you're dead, a long time ago... and you're certainly not young, or you shouldn't be, you can't be, and..." his words trailed off.

"David," the young man said stepping up and putting a hand on David's shoulder, "Yup, I'm yer grandfather," he said with an odd smile that bespoke the oddity and sheer unbelievability of it all. "I know," he said. "I know." With a depth that comes from great age and painful experience, he said, "I've gotta tell ya, it's a privilege to meet ya. A great privilege. I mean it. I've been lookin' forward to this." With a pause he said, "I for sure have."

With another pause to catch his breath and reign in the swell of emotion, his grandpa said, "Our lives never crossed ya know, we lived in different times. That's the way God set it up so it can't be anything but right and fittin'. But ah, things change. Time's done a good thing for us David. A gracious thing. It's gone and overlapped for us... it's overlapped for these few minutes anyway." Staring into David's eyes his grandfather said, "I'm glad for that. Mighty glad. But it's overlapped because there's somethin' ya gotta do David. None of the rest of us can do it, 'cause sometimes great things are reserved for great people, and yer that person, David. Yer him."

"Great? Great?!" David quipped. "Are you kidding me? I'm not great" he said pointing at himself. "I barely survive. All the success and the career and all that... that's, that's just a cover for my failures. For, for all my inadequacies," he said, throwing his arms wide. Pointing at his chest he said, "The way she left me," he said, "that says it all. Just look at that. Just look at me! You know what I'm great at?" David said leaning forward. "I'm great at pretending, but that's all I'm great at. You don't know me. I'm not great at all."

Giving the moment some space, his grandfather said, "Ya have just said who ya think ya are. Which means you have yet to find who ya really are. And that, well that's comin'. No David, I don't know who ye are, but I know what yer goin' be 'cause I met ya on the other side of all the meetings." Before David could ask what in the world that meant his grandfather turned and said, "I want to give you somethin'."

Kneeling down, his grandfather opened the chest and tenderly sorted through various objects as if he was handling something sacred. After a few moments he pulled out an old Bible. Turning to David he said, "Seen this before?" Indeed, David had seen this before. Indeed! Absolutely. Yet, much the same as the old chest, it too was once much older. The years had somehow fallen off the old Bible, rendering it newer yet still old; the reversal sent David careening again.

Cradling it in his hands, his grandfather said, "This was my mother's, your great-grandmother. It was a gift from her father… my grandfather. I know that this was passed down to ya 'cause that's how I wanted it. It'll be a whole lot older when ya get it, but some things aren't changed by time no matter how much time passes. Age don't diminish important things. It ain't that powerful. You know David, those things that really matter, that stuff that's real valuable… time don't change that kinda stuff. It can't. It don't want to anyway."

With a bit more seriousness, he continued, "David, some things go on forever 'cause they're supposed to and 'cause what they give people isn't limited to one time or one place. Some things are eternal; worth holdin' onto cause nothin' can replace 'em. And things are eternal David 'cause there's a part of us that's eternal. This life ain't wide enough or long enough ya know. Not nearly. There ain't near enough runnin' room for us to live out all that we are in one life. Nope. Only eternity has that kind of space. Only eternity. I need ya to remember that."

Opening the Bible, he pulled out the six pieces of paper that were just as crisp, new and clean as they were when David would hold them over ninety years from now, or when he held them only a moment ago, whichever was most true as it seemed that both were true. The pages were everything in reverse. They should have aged, but they did not. Everything else showed the wear of time, whether time was forward or time was backward. But the pages seemed to defy both. Like before, they were exactly the same when nothing else was the same at all. They had that uncanny steadiness about them, that they stood above time whether it was going forward or backward. Any maybe that was a characteristic of hope. Consistency. Stability. Steadiness. Invincibility. The stuff of hope.

Each page had something written on them. The top page was different, written in words that were a bit crude, basic and almost cryptic in script and form. In scanning the pages more thoroughly than he had had the chance to previously, David noted that others were something more like scrawling, some were quite ornamental, and yet others had some degree of regal penmanship.

Handing them to David, his grandfather said, "This top page here is nearly fifty years old David. Fifty years from here. I know ya wouldn't know it lookin' at it, but, well it is. Don't reckon I know about the others, but they's important for sure. They's all important. Real important. My mom wrote this one sometime just after the Civil War. Sometime after all of that settled."

Pausing, he continued, "I guess war makes ya think about a whole lot of things. She never wanted to talk about the war; never did... guess it was all too bloody, kind of like mankind killing itself thinkin' that there was anything that would justify killin' in the first place." Thinking for a moment, he continued, "Ya know, it made her stronger. Ya think you'd see stuff like that and you couldn't help but be convinced that there weren't no hope. Never happened to her. Nope. Never. Not mom."

Raising himself as if he was about to tell a story, he said, "You know, she said she snuck off to the battlefield one evening a couple a days after the battle was over. Some of the bodies had been buried and such… not all, but some. But she said there was enough of them left to paint a picture that changed her forever. Something like a photo snapped in yer head that ya can't get rid of, much as you try. So, you gotta figure out what you're gonna do with it; whether you're gonna let it tear ya down or build you up, 'cause mom said we always have the choice ya know."

With his mannerisms picking up a bit of energy, he said, "She said that one kindly soldier, some young boy really, found her wanderin', took her aside and said, 'Ya know what? These men got to get to heaven a little early. I bet they're kinda likin' that about now, walkin' around heaven and all. No war. No dying. Just real livin'. They're good men. God'll treat 'em real well.' And then he walked her home, all the while chatting about home and hearth. When she got home her parents were mighty angry, but the young soldier requested that they treat her kindly so that the memory of death might become something that she would use to bring life."

"Guess it all forced her to look at the good in life 'cause if ya don't… well, if ya don't it just all becomes too much I guess. Life becomes what we focus on David, so pick carefully what ya focus on. Sides, there's always good no matter how bad it gets. Always. Even after tomorrow, they'll be good. The fire won't change that either. Nope, nope it won't," he said. Pulling himself emotionally back for a moment he said, "Enough of the reminiscing."

David looked at the pages, sorting through them over and over. "They all look new, they look like they're totally new," he said. "They were new before I came back here or did whatever this is or was or whatever… so they stayed new when everything else didn't."

"Well, that's because they are David," his grandfather replied, as if that fact was rather obvious and that David was somehow remiss for not understanding it. Yet for its bit of sarcasm, there was much, much more that lay hidden behind his answer.

Looking down as David held all six in his hand, his grandfather said, "I'm a simple farmer David, I'm what they call a 'man of the earth,' so all I know is that time hasn't touched any of 'em, but I don't exactly know why nor do I wanna ponder all that. Pretty much the first one here's fifty years old or there abouts', but at the same time all of 'em look like they were just written, just like they were written today despite the fact they weren't. Nope. They ain't aged at all, not a one of 'em. David, they haven't aged 'cause they've been waiting for ya. Yup, they've been waiting for ya; plumb pulled up and out of the progression of time and all the while waitin' for ya. All except one."

David's mind continued to spin. Despite all of the mental prowess he possessed, he could not correlate what he heard, what he held in his hand, and what was going on all around him. In the midst of mental and emotional vortex that ceaselessly spun him, suddenly a thought flew out of the sordid mess. Mentally picking it up off the floor of his mind, they were the words of his aunt Mabel. With stunning clarity, he heard her words perfectly in his head, "Davie B, the pages are the most important thing about the farm. I know that yer grandfather left them somewhere, but where I don't know. I don't know where. Oh, I wish I knew where. Things won't be done until you find them. Nothing will be done until you find them…"

"Yup, yer aunt Mabel was right, David," his grandfather said, invading David's thoughts and causing aunt Mabel's words to shatter like broken glass, falling to the floor all around him. "What? What do you mean… how do you know what I'm thinking? How did you know about that conversation?" David responded with a sense of impending lost-ness.

"Well, David, let me explain, or try anyway" his grandfather said. "I lived a long-life David," he said having taken the pages back and sorting through them with deeply calloused hands. "I got married young 'cause I was in love. Darn good reason to marry. Right reason. Ain't no better reason. Saw that girl upstairs at farmer's markets and some fairs and never fell out of love after that. Love hooked me good. I farmed all that land out there," he said, holding out his left arm in some sweeping motion. "And did pretty darn good. Takes it outta a man to farm a piece a ground like that, but ya put yer life in it, jest like ya put your life into yer marriage and yer family. All yer life, no matter what," his grandfather said, speaking from the heart of a fellow sojourner who had likewise traveled down roads bled of hope.

"You know, didn't matter how hard I worked 'cause I watched this house burn down anyway, jest like it will again tomorrow. And I watched my wife upstairs die in the flames, like I will again tomorrow. Sometimes the best man ya can be isn't good enough to save those ya love… ya know, to keep 'em from leavin'. People leave David. There's a million ways they do it, but they leave. People leave one way or another even though ya do yer best. Can't keep people leashed ya know. Ya do good by 'em 'cause that's the right thing. But ya gotta let them make their own choices." Pausing and staring squarely at David, his grandfather said, "Ya know that son. I know that ya know that."

Picking up the old Bible and tenderly thumbing through it, his grandfather continued, "After ten years of sadness that jest about killed me, I came back here and rebuilt this house. This house right here," he said pointing around himself. "I couldn't bring your grandmother back, but I could bring back a piece of what we shared… this place and farmin' and such," he said continuing to gesture around the basement. "I did that 'cause I gave up, and then in the givin' up I learned enough to know that I needed to give up givin' up." Looking up at David his grandfather said, "Ya following me?"

"Yes, I believe I am," David said slowly and reflectively.

"I needed to have it back. Ya know, I needed to farm again, jest didn't know that at first is all. Pick life back up and do it again. Yup, some things you just have to come back to 'cause they're too much of who ya are. Can't run away from those sorts of things. If ya don't come back and hold onto the good things," he paused and continued, "'cause there's always good things David, ya'll get really bitter and I don't think life's supposed to be like that. Not at all."

It seemed as if his grandfather drifted off into some warm thought or haunting emotion or fear of some future event. Catching himself he drew back, cleared his throat, looked up and said, "I'm sorry, that was not right of me."

Drawing a deep breath, he said, "I never farmed quite like I did before; somethin' just was never quite there and I couldn't get it back. Not all of it. But I farmed anyway. I farmed in seclusion you know, pretty much by myself; staying to myself. Your Mom was here of course; she was… but when she turned eighteen she went off to college. I thought that was a fine idea, mighty fine and much needed. Ya know, I kind of figured that the 20th century and these new times would demand that of 'er, everything seemed to be moving so fast and all. She did the right thing, moving on ya know. So... I farmed right up to 1957. That's when they took me to the nursing home David."

Gathering himself as recounting the span of a life yet to come caught him, he continued, "Now that's twenty-nine years from now, so I've got another twenty-nine years of doing it all over again, but it's worth it. I reckoned it was worth it a long time ago."

"What's worth it?" David asked with a voice lathed thick in curiosity. "What do mean, it's worth it? What's worth it? What?" David's question emerged from a biting sense that there was nothing in life worth going through all that again; that there was barely enough value in life to live it at all. So if something was worth it, really actually worth it, he wanted to know. Desperately.

Turning and walking to the basement window, his grandfather looked out and with a voice cracking in emotion he said, "Our family has had a lot of pain David. Yep. A lot. A whole lot. A lot of us have lost a lot of things along the road ya know. Some died in fires and some died in war... a war that hasn't been had yet, but it's a comin', ya can be sure of that. Like on the horizon of history. Some died deep inside, kinda like you David, which I reckon is the hardest kind of death. Some died in their minds, the strange things that the mind does. And some died just because they let it happen."

Turning back to David his grandfather continued, "But life's a whole lot more than that. There's good in it David, real good. There's something good in it that ya just can't beat." Pausing, he continued. "It gets lost and all, sometimes so lost that you can't see it anymore so ya think it ain't there to be found, but there's a good, a kind of eternal good that's always bigger than everything that's bad, and 'cause it's bigger there's always hope. The only thing that can kill hope is you 'cause life ain't big enough to kill it, but you are, so ya better be real careful."

With a pointedness is his voice, he grandfather said, "Ya need to remind us of that David. That's yer job. Remindin' us is remindin' yerself, 'cause you need that too. So, yer job's to remind all of us of an eternal good, ya know, of hope that's always right there even though we can't see it in spite of the fact that it's sittin' right next to us; like right on top of us." Pausing, he continued, "And it goes beyond us; family I mean, 'cause there's a world out there, particularly your world that needs to know that too. For certain, it's mighty desperate to know that."

Wiping a bit of smudge off the window with his sleeve, he continued. "Yep, kinda wipin' yer vision clean so you can wipe ours too. And there's folks that are willin' to relive their lives just to give ya the one chance to do that. There's people who's gonna go through that pain again, 'cept knowing what it is 'cause they did it once already. 'Cause the message of hope, I mean the God kind of hope, well that's a message worth dying for again."

Canting his head slightly as if in that deep kind of thought, he said, "I been thinkin' that makes what they're doing easier, but there's another part of me that's thinkin' it's harder and such 'cause ya know what's comin'. Don't know. But, that's why yer here, and that's what these here pages are about, and that what's these folks are sacrificing for."

David heard the sound of a back door close firm and footsteps above heading for the basement door. "David, David Allen, is you coming up or do I need to come down and rustle you up these steps?"

"I'm on my way," his grandfather shouted. "I'm coming right this second Nell."

"So, here ya go" his grandfather said, handing David the Bible, "one page at a time David; one trip at a time. I got them in the order my Mom gave them to me, so do them just like that. In this order right here."

"Do what like that?" David said with a voice now weak and mired in confusion. "Do what? In what order? What am I supposed to do?" he pleaded. "What?"

David had lived out the better part of his life based on meticulous plans that tediously mapped out every step. He was a man of carefully calculated action, mostly to avoid any more pain. Yet, he stood in a basement supposedly ninety years or so in the past with history in front of him instead of behind him. No amount of logic or reasoning could hand him even the thinnest thread of reason from which he could weave even the most primitive map. What he was yet to realize was that the miraculous tethered to the crude cord of logic and reason was always strangled in the restraining. And once dead, it leaves a corpse of dreams forever unrealized and hope forsaken in the loss of those dreams.

Pausing, he looked deep into David's eyes and beyond them into the depths of his soul. "Help us David; help us to see good 'cause there's been so much bad. Lots of folks are counting on ya. They're waiting for ya, but they can't do it for ya. Help us find hope in all this mess. Help the world out there find it."

Tucking the pages in the old Bible, his grandfather casually knelt and reached into the chest. Turning back the first page of an old photo album that lay in the chest, he pulled out a faded and mottled black and white photograph almost as if such an action had been rehearsed many times before. He handed it to David without looking at it as if he knew all too well the image emblazoned on it in vacillating shades of gray on an ornate patchwork of black and white. Taking the photo in yet trembling hands, David said, "I hadn't seen this in here before."

"Well David," his grandfather said, "I reckon that means ya weren't ready to see it before now," as truly great things will only reveal themselves when we are ready in both heart and soul to see them, which is why we see 'em so rarely.

Unexplainably caught in the photo, David held it out a bit, squinted his eyes and asked, "Who is this?" canting it back and forth. It seemed to be a photograph of some unidentified child, more of an infant that could have been any one of a million infants.

"Look closely," his grandfather said, "Look real close. David squinted and looked deeper, beyond shades and gray to something of the soul of the photo. Although small, the child had an oddly commandeering face of confidence. It seemed a newborn with an aged sort of soul that eclipsed whatever age the infant appeared to be. It was something of the 'old soul' in the greatest relief David had ever seen.

Gently taking it from David's hand, his grandfather took the photo, turned it, stared at it for a moment with some sort of compassion borne of the deep soul and said, "Hope grows David. It ain't somethin' that we just have ya know. Nope, it grows as we grow, if we let it. So, you might hold onto this picture 'cause it's gonna be part of yer growth."

Handing it back to David, he turned it and gazed at it again. Yet, it was no longer the infant that stared back at him in black, white and gray relief. Rather, it was now a child, three maybe four years of age. Looking closer, David realized it was the same child only grown older. "What? How?" he stammered.

Sometimes words only diminish the magnificence of a moment because the moment begs the silence needed to most effectively savor it. And so, before David could say anything, his grandfather reverently inserted the photo back into the Bible and gently closed it.

"Wait," David said, "I don't…"

"Knowin' will come David, it'll come," his grandfather said taking David's hand and tenderly grasping it. "It'll come sure as tomorrow, sure as my promise to ya that it'll come." His grandfather then turned David's hand and held it palm down over the leather cover. The woman's voice from upstairs said, "I'm coming down there to rustle you up."

With footsteps descending the basement stairs, his grandfather looked into David's eyes with something of both deep longing and profound pain; like a forever farewell that's bigger than our ability to accept it or express it. Then he pressed David's palm squarely against the Bible. "Goodbye David, God-speed on yer journey."

Suddenly it all blurred; the image of his grandfather fell into the same indistinct shadow as before. The shadow slowly drew away into some sort of grainy mist. As it did, a second shadow approached the first, and then everything fell away as if it was sucked out from reality and thrown out of a past that drew backward beyond reach. Yet, history would soon come forward again.

Chapter 10
Questions

Insanity and wonder are divided by a terribly thin line. It is, in fact a line so untraceably thin at times that it quietly renders itself imperceptible, particularly when our vision is tight to the point that vision is lost. We too often sentence wonder to the prison of insanity, relegating it there largely out of the fear that wonder might just be wonder and therefore too wonderful. We are prone to wonder if wonder can be real; which is really that tiny bit of hope within us that yet refuses not to hope.

Can wonder exist, and can it be squarely grounded in reality and suspended above it at the same time, working in and around and through everything? Is wonder the very thing, maybe the single thing that redefines the whole of reality? Could it be the thing that shakes the very pillars of our understanding by unabashedly declaring that wonder in fact defines reality as something exquisitely expansive, entirely welcoming and wildly liberating?

In a curious mix of compassionate friend and unrelenting mentor, real wonder must invite and demand that we step outside of our comfortable confines, for one cannot do so without the other. Wonder beckons us to chivalrous adventure that reality too frequently declines and kills in the declining. Despite its immense power, wonder recognizes that its very survival is dependent upon the willingness of humanity to allow wonder to be liberated from the chains of our mental confines in order to valiantly redefine life as we know it. As with all great things, their influence lives or dies by our permission, leaving great things at the hapless mercy of the fearful beings that we are. Wonder is no different. For wonder to survive then, wonder must force us to wonder if the cost of reason is the price of wonder. And if so, are we willing to pay such an exorbitant price?

Wonder recognizes that it falls to each of us to decide where we will live out our lives, whether that be in the heights ascribed by wonder, or the cavernous depths excavated by the instruments of fear. Wonder hopes that we recognize that we have been entrusted with the improbable power to reject the majesty that wonder ushers into our lives. Wonder is too unfathomable for the menial lives that we've misinterpreted as marvelous. So, we pull up, (if we ever journeyed at all), and settle into the mundane as it can be tediously mapped and predictably plotted. Wonder goes wanting, fading into some blurry emotional distance; calling out a muted invitation out of the hope that it might be permitted a place to transform the very life that's walking away from it. And when we walk away from wonder, we walk away from hope. And that is a 'walk' we dare not take.

The blur went to a listlessly free-falling blackout that seemed instant but elongated at the same time. There are times in our lives that time itself cannot measure as the nature of these moments places them squarely outside of the rubric of time. Wonder cannot be measured in increments of any kind, despite our desire to draw the lines and erect the barriers. And so, for David time had been entirely breached in a manner that made time timeless.

Apparently, David had fallen to the floor, although he had no recollection that he had done so. The chilled cement roused him, being the first thing that gave him a gradually emerging sense of reality that pressed into the shrouding mist of unreality. Grappling with the dark gap in events, he pulled himself into a disheveled sitting position, drew up his legs, leaned a heavy head on shaking knees, took several deep breaths and allowed the fog to gradually abate. As the fog slowly dissipated, his mind began to throb with a mix of indistinct thoughts that moved in and out of reality as he knew it; refusing to be neatly sorted into mental boxes so that he could explain it all.

After a moment, David pressed a palm against his forehead and canted his head slightly. The interminable pounding in his head seemed to send pulsating shock waves throughout his entire body; a throbbing that happens when the soul is touched in places made sacred by rawness. Shaking himself from the mist that enshrouded his mind, he agonizingly looked up to see the old chest exactly where his grandfather had put it only several moments, or maybe ninety year ago, or maybe where he had put it. The Bible with the pages had somehow remained in his hands with the first page lying on top. David pulled out the first page and held it against the other six. It was now aged, yellowed and tattered at the corners. The others remained unexplainably new. Sorting back and forth through them, he said, "I could have sworn…"

Gazing up past the chest he was caught with the reality that the utility sink and sump pump were there… again. Leaping to his feet and catching himself as lightheadedness cause him to list, he stumbled to the basement window, pressed his face against the glass and peered out to the see the garage standing where it should be, and his car parked in the snow, lightly iced with a wafer-thin layer of winter's white kiss.

It was dark, as it was supposed to be, or as it was, or has it should have been… or something. No farm machinery. No sound of animals. Day had gone back to night. No voices were calling from upstairs. David stood in a silence that was screaming what he had just witnessed, witnessing to its reality before it would fade into unreality. Taking the disheveled shards of whatever it was that he had just experienced, he attempted to force-fit them into something that made sense. He stood in the middle of the basement, diligently working to find a rational line of logic that would compartmentalize it all sufficiently to say,

"Okay, that's what that was." Nothing did that … quite enough.

What little energy he had left abruptly vaporized, disseminating into the air around him. Suddenly he was rendered as limp as a damp cloth with the understanding of life now largely rung out of it. Collapsing to trembling hands and knees he crawled up to the old chest with anticipating palms pressed on the cold cement floor. Dream or reality? Destiny or dementia? Delusion or something else much more real? The choice that we make at such terribly delicate junctures has the power to break life open, demolishing every barrier to every road in the opening. Or, they have the power raise the barriers to unassailable heights and forever strand us on whatever road we've chosen to live on. And so, the two opponents vied as bloodied combatants for a place of prominence in a mind still misty.

David eyed the chest out of an ascending fear that was offset just enough by the sense that he had stood before that chest nearly a century ago and watched a grandfather anoint its contents as good, making them redemptive in the anointing. It was old again, having aged in what appeared to be a blur of seconds. David realized that it was not some vivid imagination that aged it because it was all too perfect to have been the muse of imagination. Yet, the logic within his mind took up arms against the realities that were in his heart. And so the battle for the soul of a man raged on a cold basement floor.

Life sometimes tip-toes up on us at intentionally undisclosed times with surprises sufficiently strong to fully pry open that which we've completely shut down. Things that we blithely relegated to the confines of the irrelevant are unexpectedly resuscitated in our minds, granting them a value we had never ascribed them before. We stand stunned that something we've held, something we've estimated as holding no value, something we've relegated to the pit of

175

the irrelevant is now suddenly raised and seen as priceless. That sense of being stunned by riches missed is geometrically multiplied as we realize what we forfeited along the way, what such forfeiting says about who we are, and what would have happened had we continued to have missed them.

The old chest was aged again, as it had been before whatever it was that happened, had happened. David pulled himself up to it, daring to believe his eyes for a moment, and then calling them into question. He roiled and rolled between belief and disbelief. Utterly helpless, he gyrated back and forth between the two, unable to affix himself to either.

Slowly he ran his hands around the chest's proud, quiet frame as if tenderly engaging a gentle friend once again now ninety years later; trying to create an intimate camaraderie with this most strange object. He found himself unexplainably compelled to touch it, running finger-tips over its ornate buckles and rich wood; daring to look for something with the eyes of his soul verses the single dimension of wounded eyes that turn rational for their own protection. David found himself driven by some raging passion to believe that what had happened was indeed as true as it was rich.

Standing up and reaching for the Bible, he stumbled underneath a basement light, allowed the dimness of the bulb to illuminate its cover and peered at the Bible. It too had aged or re-aged, returning to a leather cover cracked, worn and tired as he had always remembered it. Gently opening it he looked at the pages that his grandfather had handed him, attempting to make sense of one page aged and five impossibly new.

Taking the page that his grandfather had placed in his hands and putting it on the top of the others, he studied the first page again. *This can't be the same page*, David thought. Thumbing through the old Bible and then looking around the floor, David felt that maybe this was another page; a different page, a page he had missed. Maybe the original, bright and new had fallen somewhere. But you can't find something that isn't lost. Sometimes we think things to be lost only because we are lost and we have transferred such a sense onto them. At times such as those, we are the ones needing to be found.

Giving up the search and surrendering to the reality laying in his hands, he stared at the page, attempting to decipher what this was. The aging the page had become brittle, yellowed and terribly faded; irreconcilably different than all the other pages. He had clearly and unmistakably recalled it as clean and as new as the others; that was how his grandfather had put it in his hand and pressed him palm against it. But now, for whatever unexplainable reason it was old like some sort of aged parchment. Same page, but aged in an instant, so it seemed. It was worn around the edges, stained in several places and no longer supple or snowy white; all of which seemed entirely appropriate somehow.

Underneath the page was photo with the image that had aged or appeared to have aged. Holding it under the light, his mind met the photo with the memory of the infant and then the toddler. Instead, he now saw a child, eight maybe nine. And in the seeing, he remembered that it had aged before. Holding the photo at a distance and then bringing it close yet again, he peered and indeed the child had aged yet again. The photo remained old and exactly the same in every respect except the child had grown into what appeared to be a shy and tentative preteen.

In a panic that was likely something more of surprise than panic, David dropped the Bible and the papers, sending the pages floating to the floor and the photo pirouetting as well. Confused but simultaneously aghast at such an irreverent action, he begged the forgiveness of a grandfather who had stood there only a moment ago nearly a century ago, as terribly confusing as that was for David.

"I'm, I'm sorry... I'm sorry" he said stepping forward. *There's no one here,* David suddenly thought, feeling that some apology was warranted but to who or what?

Everything had irreparably unraveled, demolishing every piece of David's life in the unraveling. Nothing fit into the sturdy and safe rubric that David had tediously constructed to protect himself and deal with his pain. All of the rubrics and intricate frameworks that had propped up a world incinerated by a divorce bent and collapsed. The trustworthy benchmarks that had always provided a sure and certain orientation in the most turbulent storms had been toppled. Their absence left David desperately wishing them back, yet simultaneously wondering why and how they had fallen so easily.

For life to afford us a truly new road, particularly a road of wonder and hope, we must have any remnants of the old road removed lest we are tempted to take them up yet again. And if they cannot be removed, they must be made so undesirable that nothing would behoove us to ever take them.

At times, we are left at crossroads that pave innumerable roads off to every conceivable horizon. At this bewildering juncture, our rubrics no longer fit and our trustworthy benchmarks are gone. All of the resources that we have used to choose our roads suddenly provide no direction. And it is in this place of utter helplessness and confusion that we have yet to realize that we are at the same time free of anything that might prompt us to pick up old roads to nowhere. Sometimes life has to strip us in order to save us. Sometimes it's less about making the right decision and more about not making the wrong one. And sometimes, it's possessing the faith that something bigger than us is preparing to do something bigger in us.

David stood at a juncture that seemed to send roads off in a bewildering array of directions. With trembling fingers, he stooped and picked up the pages, neatly putting them in the order that his grandfather had put them. Once arranged to his satisfaction, he took the next one. Bringing it back to the light, David squinted and tried to read the words. In ornate handwritten script now faded, he read:

"The great war of this troubled union rolled by our home. It laid the terrible sounds of gunfire and men dying at the threshold of our tiny front porch. The great sin of man was unleashed on these hallowed fields. The world was engulfed in Armageddon. How could there be anything after the horrible carnage that lay in these fields and on these hills? How can life rise up from flesh and blood violently slaughtered and strewn in hatred of one brother for another? We must believe that something exists beyond the stench of death. With all earnestness we must believe that each battle builds the character of eternity into the fabric of men. Battles build hope. Send him home my son to find it."

It all went black again, effortlessly and without any sort of forewarning at all.

Some scant furniture had been left in the old farmhouse. Part of the abandonment was that no one really wanted the stuff. The other part of it was the feeling that stripping the farmhouse entirely would be tantamount to some sort of inexcusable thievery. Such an action would have been a blatant disregard for all the memory that made the place what it was. Even death did not warrant that all of one's possessions should be removed as if death had some sort of finality about it, particularly in this place. Death did not, David had found.

David was stirred awake to the sound of a lone, diesel pick-up truck rumbling down the road of Indians, horse and heavy wagon. The sun had just begun to paint gentle mauve and pink pastels on a wintery eastern horizon, albeit while competing with a mottled masking of gathering gray skies. Hurtling out of his drowsy state, he shot up, finding himself sitting on the old sofa that had been left in the front family room. It had somehow held its color and its sense of purpose for the decades it had sat waiting and patiently anticipating. Catching his breath, David firmly planted his hands on the cushions on each of side of himself, leaned forward and drew himself out of the deep mental mist that had encircled his brain.

Next to him his cell phone vibrated, demanding that he give attention to what seemed a million messages reminding him of various meetings, pending deals to be closed, appointments to be rescheduled, shareholders to be calmed, and the ceaseless rearranging of a horrid array of conferences, most of which seemed irrelevant and uneventful. He realized that his phone was back, if it had ever really been gone. Squinting at the screen, the display read 6:12 a.m., Wednesday, December 12th.

Exhausted to numbness, he rose to his feet, stroked back his hair and attempted to shake himself loose from whatever had just happened. Slowly, it all began to fall into the various slots in his mind, recreating a fuzzy time-line of bizarre events and impossible happenings. Clarity only brought confusion as wonder defined and corralled by definition is not wonder; therefore, it will remain what it is… undefined. And yet, he easily ascribed it all to assorted dreams stimulated by whatever life crisis he thought himself to be in. It was not about fear or the impossibility of such happenings. Rather, logic rendered the impossible possible and even reasonable… to the point it could.

The world out the window seemed the same, something that he was entirely grateful for. Yet, there was a hint of disappointment that the wonderful imaginings of the previous night might be just imaginings. A dream that seemed real, but a dream nonetheless. His world had spun to heights of what seemed insanity, yet at the same improbable time it also felt wonderful. He desperately wanted to find something to ground him, to pull him back to some sense of normality. Normality might be bland and flat and entirely un-compelling, but it's familiar.

The world outside was just as he had left it the night before. What had transpired in-between then and now was unclear and begging for some explanation that David figured he'd try to avoid. Yes, a dream it was. Maybe if it was avoided and labeled as a dream born of a mind stressed to breaking it would disappear, giving David a desperately need 'out.' Maybe it was a mind driven by stress to some strange edge that could easily be abated by a little rest. And so for David, an explanation of dreams borne of life transitions and fed by stress worked well enough. It was indeed a dream. That's all. And for the moment, the explanation of the experience was settled.

With the previous night's events sufficiently explained and categorized, David sat back down on the sofa. Confidently at ease, he picked up his cell phone. Rapidly scrolling through the many messages, he attempted to reassemble a life terribly disjointed by reviewing his calendar and letting the meetings of the upcoming day reorient him to some sort of focus.

Apparently, the buy-out had hit a glitch. Again. The market had taken an unanticipated dip, although it appeared to be on the path of recovery. The COO was in tizzy about getting a contract firmed-up, although this was how he always responded to such matters. The attorney said that the changes to the buyout were legit, which was calming for David. "Nothing new there," he pondered. A client indicated that he didn't have the funds he had purported to have had which meant that the agreement that had eaten up so much of David's time had to be modified yet again.

"Busy day," he mumbled, "busy day… why does it always have to be so busy… so stupid busy?"

In his tone there was a chilled thread of meaninglessness; the kind of meaninglessness that shakes a man's soul to the core and strips his life of any meaning at all. The kind of meaninglessness that hits us entirely unexpectedly and renders the whole of our life's existence as a script played out to an end that's bankrupt. And somehow, despite the crafty denial, we know the ending to be exactly that.

This seemed to be the kind of meaningless that was so strikingly opposite of what his grandfather had said to him, or supposedly said to him in last night's dream. Even though he had relegated it to a dream, it possessed power nonetheless. A dream it might have been, but it remained worthy of contemplation. That bit of hope drawn from his grandfather's words now collided head-on with a deluge of hopelessness returned. And sitting in a 20th century farmhouse facing the hopelessness of the 21st century, David found himself caught in the horrible angst of it all. The night had been categorized as a dream, rendering it as nothing more than the muse of a tired mind. Therefore, nothing had changed although everything had changed. Everything will continue to change.

Shaking the thought out of his head, David again centered on his schedule, attempting to cull meaning out of the innumerable meetings, phone conferences and deadlines that populated his day. For the first time, he could draw no meaning out of them. None. Sorting, resorting and recalibrating it to mental oblivion he could not resuscitate any meaning from the cold corpse of his schedule and the inert life that it defined. We are a stubborn people at times, having collided with greatness, yet finding ourselves attempting to revive all the dead things that had gratefully and mercifully perished in the colliding. We relegate wonderful things to the infantile musing of dreams gone sour.

Whatever had been said to him the night before, whether it was real, imagined or a mind skirting the precipice of insanity, life would never be the same although he presumed it would be. Never. When truth arrives, despite the manner of its arrival, it is simply too visceral not to permeate everything it touches, leaving us less concerned regarding its arrival and more caught up in the fact that it came.

It shakes a man to his core when what gave him a purpose for living is suddenly empty, leaving the whole of his life constructed on a foundation of sand. It's particularly devastating when everything that had given him purpose before had been stripped from him in a blur of selfish choices, flagrant lies and the deceit of another that strips a man so thinly raw that life beyond that point seems wholly improbable. It is when we are pillaged of things that we thought untouchable that we are left in the paralysis of shock. When someone sets out to steal that which is sacred, some sort of inexcusable line gets crossed that we presumed to be impregnable. And at the point that we realize that even the sacred can be stolen, our vulnerability becomes total.

We then attempt to replace all that was lost with the thin veneers of success and achievement. We gather up whatever charred pieces that remain and we attempt to arrange them in some sort of composite that represents something of that which is no longer there. And so, we live a life that's not a life. The most dangerous part of that was that it actually worked for a bit or had the appearance of working. And then to have these veneers consumed by the words of a grandfather ninety years ago, or a night ago, or a dream ago, or whatever it had been was unimaginable.

183

Suddenly, for the first time since his wife's abandonment there was nothing to his life. Despite the exasperating mental exercises to reconstruct something from the cinders and ash, he could not. The life of escape he had effectively designed was now, for some inexplicable reason, wholly ineffective. David could not make it what it had been. Sitting on the worn sofa of a 20th century farmhouse after a nine-decade journey back and forward through time (whether that journey was a dream or not), the thought processes that had saved him now failed him. By now, the phone read 6:52 a.m. It took David a mere forty minutes to realize that the life he had created over a decade was gone. Irretrievably gone.

Gathering himself, he headed out the farmhouse door into the sharp chill of a curious December morning, somehow forgetting the night before in the impending rush of the impending day. Sometimes rushing into our day is in fact running away from our past. And when we run in that manner, all of our energy is consumed in the running with little focus on the destination to which we are running.

David headed for the car, woke a sleepy engine to the cold of the day, turned around, headed down the expectant driveway, pulled out onto the road of Indians, horse and heavy wagon, and drove into a world of meaninglessness.

The old family Bible, the pages, and an aging photo was left lying on the old sofa, waiting in silent anticipation for another journey.

The office seemed sickeningly flat and vain; a pointedly disturbing feeling that David thought would dissipate once he arrived. He assumed that he would seamlessly step back into that which he had stepped out of. That life is always a process of picking up where we left off, even when where we 'left off' should be 'left behind.' And where David was 'left' after a grandfather and nine decades was some place where everything would be 'left behind.'

The office was irreconcilable for David, much like he was someplace else entirely. As the minutes droned on, the creeping realization that whatever it used to be, whether in imagination or reality, it would never be that again. Sitting at his muscular oak desk with its well-appointed decor, the office was now thinly one-dimensional; flat and stale and empty of color or a pulse. The hearty plants tastefully placed about his office, original paintings that adorned cream-colored walls, various awards and trophies strategically displayed to evidence attainment, plush leather chairs that greeted visitors and hosted meetings... it meant nothing.

Standing at the immense windows that framed two walls of his expansive office, David peered out over a cityscape of glistening skyscrapers, concrete sidewalks, asphalt byways and canyons borne of buildings squeezed into tight city blocks. Innumerable cars and a sprinkling of pedestrians far below hurried off to destinations unknown to David and likely unknown to those doing the traveling. Streets and small parks were adorned with a sprinkling of trees and shrubbery asleep in winter's embrace. While he had made this very existence his everything, suddenly it was nothing.

This very office had been robust and filled with improbable energy. It had flooded his life with purpose when purpose had been scandalized in the flames of an unwanted divorce. His career had saved him, but only for this moment.

Now, nothing held anything of value anymore. The contracts, the marketing, the meetings, employee development, hard-won bonuses, career advancement... all the stuff that had energized his depleted life and gave meaning to his own meaninglessness was suddenly empty and entirely void. He seemed to sit there at his broad desk, grabbing his job by the throat in an attempt to bring it back to life. Taking it by the collar and shaking it in his mind, he tried to shake it alive. Yet despite the incessant shaking, it remained a corpse; cold and lifeless and void of everything that David desperately needed it to be. It would not be revived. What David hadn't realized was that it had never been alive in the first place. And what he had yet to realize was that you can't resurrect that which never lived.

We naively invest in a life that is not a life, the whole while thinking it to be the best sort of life. What we invest in can look the part, seeming to hold a robust vitality and a sustaining meaning that grants it a perceived richness worth investing in and living for and even dying for. Yet, in time the fraudulent becomes depleted, and in the depletion it becomes startlingly exposed. When it finally becomes exposed, we typically rush with great vigor to prop it up and rigorously breathe life back into it. Our lives become entirely focused on the resuscitation of our lives where we desperately pledge a renewed allegiance to it, hoping that such dedicated action will revive what was always dead.

Yet, all that we're doing is expending ourselves in the attempt to breathe life into something that is not life and therefore never had the breath of life in the first place. Such an endeavor will result in the maintaining of a limply contrived life which is not capable of being anything but contrived. We see a heroic sort of boldness in the effort of resuscitation, but we think resuscitation to be life when it is the false perpetuation of something much less. Once we hear the voice of a grandfather in our heads, nothing is ever the same.

"Dave, Dave, are you... okay?" Steve asked tentatively. "You alright?" Out of nowhere, Steve was suddenly standing at the head of David's desk. For Steve, the environment never defined him. He had always stood above it; his authenticity defining his environment instead

186

of it defining him. Steve was 'enough' in a manner that anything that might define him would end up being defined by him instead. All of that was something David could never quite define. Sometimes we can't quite put our finger on something because we're not quite ready to stake our lives on it. Yet, despite the lack of definition it was something that he had always admired and had often wished for himself.

In addition to all of that, Steve was an astute administrator with a heart sensitive and attuned; sharply shrewd and yet softly wise all at once. Steve possessed a balance forged of balancing the living of life, instead of balancing an avoidance of life. David always appreciated those qualities. Out of that appreciation they had formed a deep friendship both inside and outside of work.

David had few friends because few people could be trusted in a soul-baring kind of way. A life of isolation, despite the sequestered depth of aloneness was indisputably preferred to a life of vulnerability and risk. Work had become his trusted companion. Survival had become his sole goal. And forever outdistancing a past that frustratingly kept pace with him was his motivation. Friendships of any kind did not fit in any of these places. Except Steve.

Steve had been born with cerebral palsy, rendering his life a challenge prematurely robbed by his disability. His disability had never granted him permission to fake life. Therefore, he had lived his life engaging life as he had no other choice. It is our handicaps, whatever the nature of them might be that steel us against the shallowness of the world and keep us transparently authentic. As such, we should wish for more of them, rather than deny those which we have. Steve stood as starkly authentic as compared to David who had built a life starkly contrived into to survive.

"Dave, are you okay?" Steve asked again.

David had been robbed along the way, having had something only to lose it. Steve knew a kind of reverse robbery where something was stolen without it ever being experienced in the first place. Indeed, he had been robbed without ever having experienced the enjoyment of that which had been robbed. It made him a unique kind of person, embodying great loss with the tenacity that brought great success and fostered great hope.

"You okay?" Steve asked again with a quizzical tone in his voice.

"Yeah, yeah," David replied in a long and drawn out tone. "No… I guess I don't know," he said spinning his chair toward Steve and looking past him out the office window to the cityscape below. "I don't know." Taking a deep breath, his eyes aimlessly meandered around the office and then fixed themselves on Steve. "What do you do when everything you've worked for, all the stuff you've poured yourself into for, for years, suddenly seems meaningless?"

Staring back out the window with a heavy, lingering pause he continued, "Ever have that happen, like the purpose is all gone, like life loses a heart… and it slowly dawns on you that there wasn't probably any purpose ever, in the first place?"

Pausing and shaking his head, he continued. "It's like you face something you don't want to face, but you don't really know what it is. Maybe, maybe it's like facing yourself, you know. Or facing that you've settled in life and whatever the settling is has cost you. Only you don't realize that until some… something happens. I don't know," he said shaking his head again. "It's just, it's just like I've gone down a really long road that I chose to go down, and I never doubted it to be the right road, and I'm wondering if it was ever the right road. Maybe it wasn't even a road." Pausing, he stared down at the floor and said, "And all of that might just be fanciful musing of a guy that's just really tired."

Leaning introspectively on his cane as he so often did, Steve said, "You know, sometimes everything we've worked for was only to take us to the next thing. Sometimes it doesn't look like the right road because it was just a road to the next road, even though we thought it was more than that. I wonder," he said while leaning against David's desk, "If life's not about trying to get us to the very place we don't want to go because that's the very place that we're supposed to go. Like we want to stay on whatever road we're on because the next one might take us to places we should be going, but don't want to go. I think that might be true," Steve said with a slight nod of the head.

After a pause where he seemed to be sorting out what he just said, Steve said, "I'm not certain why I'm telling you that, other than it just feels right to say."

David smiled for first time in a long time, looked up at Steve and replied, "How do you know this stuff? What'd you do, major in philosophy in college or something?"

"No, no, I get it," David continued. "I get it. Sometimes life's too busy for us to think about the important stuff. Stuff like what you just said," he said pointing at Steve. "Time, well time just moves too fast you know." Pausing, he continued, "I need to think about this… yeah, think about it. A lot."

Standing up, he laid his hand on Steve's shoulder and said, "Can you handle the Bowen merger, at least for today? It's just getting the buyers to review the conditions of the sale, that's all. It should be pretty clean. I'll pick it up tomorrow."

"Sure," Steve replied heartedly.

"Okay. I'm out for the day. See you tomorrow." Grabbing his coat, David turned toward Steve and with a smile born of a softening heart said, "Thank you. I really mean it you know. Probably in a way that you don't understand. Thank you." Then he turned and headed into a history that would build his future.

Chapter 11
Verifying Wonder

Sometimes it appears that we are journeying to destinations that are clear. Yet, the apparent reality is that life never quite permits us the certainty that we impose upon it. Therefore, most of the time we journey trying to find a destination, discovering in the effort that the real destination of the journey is the attempt to find a destination to journey to. For whether we prefer to admit it or not, we all need a destination. And while we prefer to craft and chart the destination, there is something deep within us that would much prefer that something far greater than us tell us what that destination is.

If life graces us sufficiently to reveal our destination, or more correctly, if we allow it to, often we find ourselves fleeing in the opposite direction out of the fear that the destination is too big for us. So, life is a journey of both finding our destination and fearing it all at same glorious time, for such a vigorous juxtaposition suggests the glory of the destination. And if we succumb to fear, the destination will never be anything other than a destination and it never be anything of experience.

Shutting down his computer, David arranged his desk into some kind of order that was nothing more than a futile effort to regain a sense of order. Yet, despite the arranging and rearranging, the order he was seeking had nothing to do with categorizing the sweeping desk in front of him. If anything, Steve's words began the process of ordering both his mind and his heart.

At times we are quite meticulous in organizing our lives for purposes of efficiency and ease. And at other times, that organization is a vexingly unnerving effort to grant our lives the organization that we know they do not have. These are often times of alarming desperation where what needs to be organized is agonizingly beyond our ability to organize. And in the incapacitating impossibility of it all, we find ourselves soothing ourselves by organizing all other lesser things, hoping that some slight thread of sanity might find room to weave itself through the rest of our lives. The tedium that David found himself in around his office was exactly that. Life could not and would not come together that easily because, at times like these, it would be entirely egregious to do so.

On the face of it, David began to realize that the exercise of organization was not organization… at all. It was, in fact, a panicked effort to resuscitate 'what was' by means of rampant organization simply because he feared the unknown of 'what was to be.' There is a heavy turn at these points, a jostling realignment where we come to understand what now is. This sense of this 'new normal' is straightaway joined by the alarming anticipation of what this will result in and how far it will be from where we've been headed to up to this point. These moments are not about reclamation or anything even closely approximating a salvage operation of a past now past. They are a reorientation borne of surrender.

Stopping mid-stride in this futile attempt at organization, he paused, dropped his head, embraced the realization of what he was doing without yet understanding why he was doing it. After being enlightened yet again by Steve's sage words, David grabbed his coat.

Exiting his office, he walked down the florescent bathed hallway. As he did, he extended casual and rather routine greetings to various employees bound in the confines of what he had affectionately, or not so affectionately come to call 'the cube-farm.' It seemed that it was not that easy to compartmentalize life, although his associates had fully fallen for the sick joke. It was all too irreligious to heartlessly mark off cubicles as defining the sum total of one's life, and to then exile that life from everything outside the cubicle. But that was always the sense he derived from the 'cube-farm.'

In the insanity of the cube we feel safe within its confines, yet the insanity is believing that confines equate to safety. Safe or not, our heart dies in the confines. Therefore, we might ask, "How safe is it?" In reality, most things we deem as safe are not. Parameters simply imply limits, but we cannot be assured that those limits are sufficiently sturdy to grant us safety. They are, in fact, products of our cowardice. And if something is a product of our cowardice, it is anything but safe.

The cube is force-fitting simplicity onto the majesty of life based on the absurd assumption that such an action can actually be achieved in the first place. It is a mindless life. It is an automaton mentality where we regiment the life out of life. It is laying boundaries in places that are not designed for boundaries. The cube is death being invited to show up long before death had scheduled itself to show up. And yet, here were dozens of David's co-workers living an early death in just such a manner. And for a moment, just a moment, he craved their naiveté.

David stopped half-way down the long aisle that parsed the sea of cubicles and scanned the length of them. The florescent lights lent a pasty sterile glow to it all, further de-humanizing the scene. *How could this have been what I defined as my life?* he thought. *How was this life?* He wondered how a person could possibly define something as life that was nothing of life, yet he had done exactly that. How could one's perception of his existence be relegated to something so pathetic and so unpardonably comatose? How could he have been so ignorant, but what insanity would cause him to want all of that back?

David wondered what had changed in him, or what had snapped, or what was different. What kind of line is it that becomes a wall behind you the moment that you step over it? How could he be in the very existence that gave him so much satisfaction and suddenly see that it was an existence-less existence with no satisfaction? The realization of such an unexplainable reality struck him in a full-force manner that sent him reeling so far out of his existence that there would be no coming back… ever. Somewhere, David knew that. Somehow, it was okay. However, the far greater question was what had the power to do that, for whatever it was it was greater than any power David had ever thought to exist.

David opened the watermarked glass door, stepped outside of the sea of cubes and headed down the long hallway to an awaiting elevator. He uttered a whispered, "Good morning" to a neatly dressed woman who had arrived several steps after he did. Pressing the 'down' button, it cordially lit in the acknowledgement of a call sent to a distant elevator.

Looking around in the nothingness that we find ourselves in when waiting on things to arrive, his eye brushed past the number '28' above the elevator door. Reflexively turning back to it, he said it over in his head. *28,* David thought. *1928.*

"That's what's different," he blurted out.

"Excuse me?" the kindly woman said.

"Oh… sorry." David said. "Just an old memory." Pausing, he continued, "A really old memory."

"Oh," the woman replied. "It's a good one I hope."

"It was," David said. Filled with a warming rush of the memory of his grandfather he said, "I really enjoyed my time there." With the elevator door opening, the woman cast a quizzical glance toward David. "I mean, the memory, it is a great one," David said stumbling around his words as his heart stumbled around his emotions.

The elevator was populated by a handful of various people, each sporting the uniqueness of humanity gathered. They were all different, but at the selfsame time, they were people of the cube. They were dead in their own right. They were lifeless; breathing but only so that they might come from some place to go to another. Yet, there were dead in the traversing. It was the coming and the going that gave their lives the semblance of life. But the semblance of something does not mean the existence of something.

The road of their lives had terminated in the cubes of their lives. If you don't have hope, the cube makes all the sense in the world. Of course you live in a cube because it's the only place you can go. You don't need hope to live in a cube because there's nothing to hope for. You don't need a road because the cube is both the beginning and end of itself. Nothing leaves the cube so you don't need a road.

When you traverse ninety years, when you see life before the flames and yet you lived to see that life exist after them, you begin to see the utter lunacy of the cubes. Dream or not, the lesson remained for David. And if the cubes are shattered by the lessons of nine decades, what of the entire existence of humanity? What about that? What about the hope of knowing that ashes are only a precursor to that which is destined rise from them? What about a tomorrow that's about ashes reborn, not ashes revisited? How many cubes would that smash? And it is here that we see both the wonder of the road, but we also see the unarguable reality of it. Cubes are our imaginations used in the service of our denial. There never were cubes. There are only roads upon which we huddled up and holed up. But thank God they remained roads despite what we did while on them.

When we grasp the steadiness of that truth, it doesn't matter if the surface of our road is rough, broken, littered with fissures, or so demolished that it's difficult to trace. It doesn't matter because we know that there's a place that we've come from, and the certain promise of a place to go to. The state of our roads can't deny either, nor can them impede either.

And that kind of hope makes any road entirely traversable. Any road at all. Even David's road of sordid lies, calculated betrayal, heartless abandonment, the death of divorce and the death of the family within it… even this road was passable. The elevator opened to the first floor, and the first time in longer than memory could recall, David was on a road of hope.

David drove out of the office through the metropolitan chaos of concrete, asphalt and tightly knit traffic to a road of Indians, horse and heavy wagon. It was now a journey from one world to another, from one existence to a completely different existence. He had never really thought about the transition before; about life being so very different. He supposed that he never considered the contradictions because he viewed them as incompatible. Maybe more, he didn't believe them to exist at all because it wasn't until a chance meeting with a long-lost grandfather that he actually began to believe them to be.

This world of concrete and asphalt was, for better or for worse, the reality of modern life. It was indeed the sole and singular reality. These roads were laid as a path from one point to another and back again. They were bleakly utilitarian in nature and nothing of adventure. Utterly practical but nothing magical. In contrast, the road of Indian, horse and heavy wagon had been nothing more than a dusty reminder of something forever passed into a forever past. David had unconsciously likened it to a museum that entombed an existence now held forever mummified in the sarcophagus of time. It now seemed to be something more.

It seemed to be a place on the loose. David slowly realized that it had always seemed something more.

As that thought took shape, David found himself disappointed that great things live, die and are then relegated to shadowy corners death and obscurity. And in visualizing the seasoned face, reflective touch and thoughtful voice of his grandfather, (whether those were dream or reality), he found the doors of his mind turning on rusty hinges that gave way to impossibility possibilities. It was as if his mind had crept out to the outskirts of logic and had begun to run playful fingers outside the fence. It seemed that he finally dared to step over the fence to walk in and through and around impossible impossibilities to see if in the play some part of something dead within him might be reignited.

With time having been lost in the thoughts of roads and such, he suddenly realized that he was approaching the fleeting edge of suburbia. He traversed past developments cross-stitched with cookie-cutter homes populated by people living out cookie-cutter lives. David had often thought of the gray mundaneness of it all. It seemed to him that culture or life or society had penned a script of compromise and uniformity that squashed the human spirit to death. Too often it all seemed robotic and contrived, leaving something of the indefinable grandeur of the human spirit to languish in the pathology of conformity. Something precious had been lost, and in the loss mankind had opted for the mediocrity of uniformity; of cubes, cookie-cutter lives and roads forsaken.

Somewhere we give up ourselves. Subsequently, we give up 'on' ourselves. And in the sacrifice we lose ourselves. As he fell into thought, he realized that he had done the same. The exact same. He had become everything that he was now finding as repulsive. When we finally stand fully exposed before what we've been, as held in contradiction to what we told ourselves we were, the contradiction is so enormous that it will either crush us with insufferable regret, or it will thrust us entirely out of that place.

With both hands gripping the steering wheel, David mused, or more accurately contemplated that the lesson here was the same as the one that had sideswiped him in the office and chased him down the elevator. That if indeed there were so many different vessels dispensing the very same lesson, there must be something securely credible about it all. Logic would say, "pay it no mind." Yet the heart would say, "to pay it no mind would be to pay too much." The process of softening continued as the road passed under him.

Broaching the edge of the sprawling development, David began to cross some nearly invisible boundary into the ever-expanding fields and farms. Forever fences and bouncing hedgerows ran alongside the car as if attempting to add impetus to some yet unidentified journey. There seemed to be a developing urgency for something not yet identified, yet something desperately critical despite its vagueness. More often than not, the degree of urgency tells of the importance of the destination. And urgency was escalating in manner that swept David up in some sort of illogical and yet entirely wonderful anticipation.

Winter lent a few slight hours of sunlight for the trip. As the road began to break free of the grip of concrete and traffic his cell phone rang. It seemed to pull him back to what he had just broken free of, snapping him back into a world that he was leaving; a world of cubes and cookie-cutter developments.

If there was a point of grinding irritation for David, it was that he never put his cell phone in the same place. His life was inordinately orderly, right down to the most basic things like placing paperclips in the same small box, dollar bills all facing forward in his wallet in numerical order, files having layers of organization within layers of organization such that David could put his finger on any piece of information as fast as he could get his finger there, and using his GPS even though he knew exactly where he was going. His life was orchestrated down to the clutter of minutia. But the stupid phone; it was everywhere and anywhere. It seemed odd that he permitted one thing, this one thing to be unorganized and free of constraints despite the irritation that it brought him. It was, he thought, a rebellion against everything that gave him identity.

The call was from Steve. *Odd,* David thought as he tapped his touch screen and ushered the world into his car.

"Hello?" he said.

"Dave, not to bother you, but I just got this odd feeling that you were going to do some traveling... maybe out of town. Is that true?"

David smiled, turned to scan the skeletal trees that were now running a foot race with his car and said, "Naw, not unless you mean heading out *into* the country. That's about as far as I'm going. I'll be in the office tomorrow morning, don't sweat it. I'll keep the place running" David said.

"Yeah," Steve replied, "No worries about that. I know you. I'm worried about keeping you running buddy. You looked a little ragged today. Look, if you need anything, call me... okay?"

"Thanks man," David said with a sense of deep appreciation. "Listen Steve, I mean, well... just thanks for being a great friend. Right now that means... that means a lot. A lot more than you know. Okay?"

"You bet," came the reply.

At that moment David's caller ID lit up. "Listen, I've got another call Steve, I'll see you early in the morning. Have the coffee on. Remember, six scoops of coffee for ten cups of water, right? Don't screw that up.

There's nothing worse than starting the day with bad coffee."

"I know," Steve said with a firm but casual tone of deep friendship, "I know I'm the poster child for bad coffee. I'll eventually get it right. See you then."

By now the road had turned to gravel, the stuff of Indians, horse and heavy wagon. The second call had gone to voicemail. Clicking over on his touchscreen he listened to the message. At first there was a pause with the clutter of unidentified sounds deep in the background. Then a familiar voice:

"Davie B, Davie B?" It took aunt Mabel a few seconds to orient herself to the fact that she had reached David's voicemail and how that was going to change what she was going to say. She never seemed to get used to voicemail.

"Davie B, what was he like? I remember him sort of, but I can't pull out any real memories of him out anymore. My mind can't reach that far anymore. Did he look good? He was a strapping young man back then, just like the old photos. Remember the one by the tractor?" she said and then paused.

As always, aunt Mabel wandered to wherever wandering took her. David always found himself attempting to figure out what in world she was trying to say; to attempt to trace the untraceable wanderings of dementia. He always found himself working to decipher the tangled and cryptic messages, finding such an effort as blatantly exhausting. It was something akin to the secret code of dementia that had to be decoded every time. And every time, the decoding was different. For David, it was enormously exhausting in a way that bred some level of frustration. "Why can't it be easy?" he would always say.

Indeed, it was, for in making sense of that which is wonderful we miss that which is wonderful. Many times life is not about deciphering life as that's most often our attempts to make life what we want it to be. We have the diminishing bent to force life to fit within our primitive rubrics; our cubes so to speak. Wonder will always call us outside of ourselves, for that is what makes it wonderful. And so, it won't necessarily speak our language, which doesn't mean that it's not speaking a language. In fact, more often than not the language of wonder is far, far superior to our own. And therefore, we would be wise not to drag it down to the baser place where our syntax and grammar grovel to articulate our primitive notions. David had yet to figure out that this is what he was doing.

She continued, "That one... that one right there was a classic for sure. Do you remember that one? No, no of course you wouldn't... but it was one that always seemed to capture who he was. Some pictures do that you know."

There was pause where aunt Mabel seemed to find some bit of enthusiasm that reinvigorated her and she said, "It's really not about that anyway Davie B, it's about the pages. I am so glad that they've been found, I'm so glad that you have them. Now you know what to do." Suddenly in the background David heard the gentle but firm voice of a nurse saying something about medications and her weekly bingo. "Okay," aunt Mabel said to the attending nurse, "I'll be by. I love bingo Davie B, have to go. Love you." And then it went dead.

By the time the voice mail had ended David had parked at the front of the old farmhouse.

"How does this woman know this stuff?" David said as he turned off his phone, tucked it in his pocket and put the car in park. It was something of a phenomenon that he struggled attributing to someone walking ever deeper into the lacey shadows of dementia. Rather sarcastically he blurted out, "I think my car's bugged. No, I think my life's bugged," he said shaking his head. Rummaging for his gloves, he mumbled, "That's creepy, and I hate bingo." Softening around the edges, his face traced a slight smile that lent a wisp of something light. Opening the car door, he said, "But I'm glad that she knows, however she does that."

Sitting in front of the old farmhouse, in the winter stillness that now invaded his car and his heart, he leaned on the front of the car and thought for a moment. "The photo of grandpa and the tractor… seems I've, maybe I've seen that one somewhere." Suddenly his mind was inundated with an assembling barrage of memories from the night before. Dream was becoming reality despite David's fight against such a transition.

He had somehow unconsciously and rather convincingly worked to attribute the memories to dreams or the sort of fantasy thinking that we do in the drowsy, pre-sleep state when reality becomes something of mush and imagination. Yet, he could not corral them there. He could not keep it as a dream, although that was far more comfortable and certainly more sensible. At some level, he was okay with that for some part of himself long discarded wished the experience as real.

On their own, the memories of that evening began to coalesce in a rapidly sharpening series of snapshots that flashed through his mind in a relentless series of images, one after the other after the other. Sure he had thought about them throughout the day. How could he not? But now they rolled by in his head in some sort of escalating fashion to the point that they moved so fast that he could no longer see their individual images.

Slowly, they began to merge into a continuous mental image that ran as something more like a movie and less like a dream. It started as something somewhat fuzzy, filled flat in cloudy grays, splotches of black and smearing of whites. As if finding its focus, the images started to come into sharp relief, granting them character and a hint of vitality. Slowly, they gained a wash of color that possessed a richness and vitality that David had never realized or possibly permitted. Within moments, something more real than his own life was playing through his head and handily displacing his own reality, leaving his existence colorless by comparison. What it all real? Had it been real?

Startled as to how he had so easily relegated these images of the night before to imagination, the memories rushed forward in a flood of convincing faces and voices and emotions and confusion. The images and the feelings raced across the forefront of his mind in vivid display, wiping out the receding afternoon of farm fields, distant forests and dirt road. They played until they bunched up into some sort of ill-defined but perfectly synced collage, throwing him back into the reality of the car, farm fields, distant forests and dirt road.

After it had all blown by him, all that was left of the wild fast-forward play were the words of aunt Mabel. "He was a strapping young man back then, just the old photos. Remember the one by the tractor?" Aunt Mabel had said. "A strapping young man back then, just the old photos," David pondered. "Remember the one by the tractor... the one by the..."

The album? David suddenly thought. *The album.* There had been many things in the old chest, from yellowed letters to a pair of worn gloves to the old family Bible. But for some reason David had not granted the old photo album any real importance. More than that, it had somehow not even been catalogued in his own head as being a part of the old chest. For reasons unknown to David, it had been rendered entirely non-existent. Maybe the photo was there. Maybe.

It is indeed odd that we have this daunting proclivity to render invisible the very things that would render our lives unimaginably wonderful. We are far too practical, and in our practicality we far too often forget that what is practical is far too limited to open the door to the impossible.

Leaping from the car and running up the steps, he threw open the front door, ran through the kitchen and surged down the basement steps as a child racing down the stairs on Christmas morning. Throwing on the root cellar light, he ran to the old chest, and immediately spied the album. "Oh my," David thought. "It's here! It's here!"

Gently reaching into the chest he picked up the album, slowly drew it out, and gently set it on the floor. There were no odd feelings as before, even though David's excitement was such that the thought had not even crossed his mind. To become engrossed in wonder is to overcome our fear of it. David would need to do exactly that for what lay ahead.

The photos were somehow familiar, but most of them were entirely unknown. There were some obvious people, but most were not. It's as if they'd been somewhere that he had not been, but somehow might go. Something like life preparing us for where we're going by giving us access to where we've never been before we actually get there. Maybe the road forward is paved by the road behind us, even if at times it wasn't our road. Maybe old roads are harbingers to the road home. Maybe they are the road home. Whatever the case, there was something familiar in the proliferation of black and white collages.

David could not find the photo. He desperately thumbed through the albums stiff pages, but the photo was not there. Leaning back, David caught his breath and thought, *I guess it was a dream.*

Sometimes we stand caught between reality and fantasy. Such is the intensity of fantasy at moments like these that we can't separate it from reality for it seems real itself. Likewise, sometimes reality seems so terribly improbable that we can't be certain if it's actually fantasy. And then sometimes we have within our grasp some shred of evidence that will conclusively tell us which is which.

We arrive breathless at those times and places, sometimes wanting all of it to be reality, and at other times hoping it was all fantasy. Either way, we know that there is some large and very precious part of our lives that will be precariously at stake depending on which way it all falls. The picture of the child from the night before had made fantasy something of reality unlike anything David had ever experienced. And so, with the weight of that kind of moment teetering in the balance, David began sorting through the pages of the album yet again. Yet, there was an enhanced intensity and applied acumen as his eyes searched out the nuances of each image.

They were a compilation of pictures and faces and places. Mostly black and white, they had frozen people and moments in time, holding them fast in the confines of their many varied borders; time halted as if the gears of time themselves seized up and froze at the snap of the camera. One page after another yielded nothing of tremendous import. They were simply snapshots of history that seemed to be the recitation of similar events playing themselves out in various momentary poses.

David flipped to the last page. Nothing. However, reality shows up in the most unexpected places at the most unexpected times. It can be tempestuous when it need be, letting us know that it is not entirely prone to predictability if the cause demand it not be.

Suddenly, David remembered the single photo. The photo that had aged, or seemed to have aged, or looked different under different light. *Is it…?* he thought, *is that the child who had aged?* He hadn't put it in the album. He hadn't even recalled it. It had been put in the family Bible. Turning, he grabbed the album and ran back up the basement steps to the family room with the old sofa patiently awaiting his return. Dropping down on the sofa, he picked up the Bible, gently opened its pages and pulled out the old photo.

It had aged again; now leaping from a preteen to a young man. A familiar young man. Strikingly familiar. David found himself falling into the image, searching every slight nuance of the face and the photo itself.

It was a photo of his grandfather; his grandfather now standing by a tractor, however that had happened. Leaning against it soiled and seemingly sweaty, there was an air of indomitable pride etched across his face. There seemed to be an invitation in his grandfather's face, daring the impossible to show up if it would dare to do so. Daring David, it seemed, to believe that the night before had been nearly a century before. The photo seemed to possess a life, as if it were actually living and breathing and moving within its stilled confines. The photo spoke a million words that brought that still-life moment to life for David.

It was the very same man he had met the night before whether in dream or something else. It was the very same man. Even the mannerisms in the photo were exactly the same. Same clothes, it seemed. Same shoes. Same tussled hair. Same smile. Same relaxed posture. It was as if David had seen this yesterday; this man in this place in time. It was entirely fresh with the aging of the photo seeming to be faked as time simply could not move that fast.

If David could not be convinced of the reality of this single meeting with his grandfather, he would question everything that was about to come. The outcome of the journeys that remained would fall into question and then fall to skepticism and then fall to their death. And that would kill the whole of the adventure. Therefore, this photo of albums and general store walls would play a most critical role.

A date had somehow appeared at the bottom of the brittle and aged photo. December, 1928. "I met him… I met him within days of this being taken; ninety years ago… but only a night ago. But…" Turning this way and that, pacing back and forth, looking at the photo and then looking away. Thinking. Contemplating. Rationalizing. Yet the sense of it all was that he could not make sense of it all, leaving the impossible as the only thing that was possible. David's mind trailed off. His life would surge forward.

Chapter 12
A Uniform and Normandy

Can the past be worn much like a garment or piece of clothing? Can we dress ourselves in the marvelous and sometimes painful lessons of the past? Can our lives be robed in the resplendence of history while lived out in the center of the present at the same time? And can those garments communicate to us the riches of the past that not only elevate us above the carnage of the present, but make the present impossibly good and the future entirely worthy?

David had returned to the basement, planning on rummaging through the other items in the old chest. Running down the rough-hewn oaks steps, David turned the corner at the bottom only to spy the old armoire. It was oaken; somewhat ornate but entirely non-assuming. Gently muscular, it was a sentry of sorts, tasked with protecting the contents that had been its trust. Two broad doors hinged on each side closed in the center, holding history in its wooden embrace.

Pulling up at the bottom of the oaken steps, David felt a slight tug. It was nothing compelling really. It was something of a gentle call that is much more an invitation and much less a demand. It was history afoot, whispering as it went.

By now, these illogical feelings had been given space within David. Somehow, in light of current events, what felt completely improbable had found a slight permissive foothold; something akin to who and where he had been when he etched that very first hash on the river rock fence so many years ago. David knew something was afoot, and that if were to be denied or written off to muse and fancy it would haunt him nonetheless. A repressed part of himself once subjugated to the fury of his own pain was being given fresh space once again. A part of himself that had fled inward seeking protection from everything that was outward was now tentatively peering out from the confines of a decade or more. And so, he walked to the oak armoire, taking in its clean lines and deep finish.

Reaching out with both hands, he invited himself in. The hinges relented much easier than those of the old root cellar; smooth but firm. The mid-western humidity had expanded them a bit with both doors slightly pinched against each other. Nonetheless, with a slight tug they opened.

Pulling back both doors in opposite directions as if drawing back curtains on some grand stage, he was met with the musty scent of history exhaling. Hanging inside David discovered a mix of old clothing. Most of it was from David's own adolescence, being a mismatched collection of winter coats, several shirts and a pair of fishing waders from back when David found both solace and majesty in the various streams and adjacent lakes that generously populated the landscape.

To the left of this menagerie of discarded clothing, David's eyes came to a halt upon the old uniform. It was clean, pressed by time and without a single wrinkle. Its pleats were sharp and crisp. Folded with tight corners, it had a few scant medals that ran a single line across the top of the left pocket. A solitary stripe was stitched on each shoulder suggesting that common people fight for uncommon freedoms. It was entirely simple but marvelously regal, being a memento of what had reverentially come to be described as the "greatest generation." It had once been worn by a simple man who, unknown to himself had been in the process of creating that generation. Simple men do great things simply because they do not purport to see anything great in their efforts.

They only see the responsibility of living life in keeping with the gift that it is. And so they do.

Often we wear symbols of sacrifice. Those things we stand for are emblazoned on us either in ways that are subtle or distinct, but emblazed nonetheless. If we stand for nothing we will likely become nothing and subsequently achieve nothing, for nothing can only breed more of itself. That was part of the issue for David... what did he stand for? Sitting in his office several hours earlier, all of the things that he had antagonistically erected and subsequently stood for suddenly became achingly hollow of meaning. His life was sucked of content. His soul emptied. Meaning is not something created, for despite our most rigorous efforts we cannot create a calling. We can only respond to one. The uniform embodied all of that.

Gently sliding it off the hanger and holding the uniform, he began asking the questions that its symbolism stirred him to ask. Questions of symbolism had become an entirely fresh and an entirely unexpected line of questions for David. Yet, such questions would bear answers that only questions of this nature could bear. And his journey would demand them.

Standing for something implies an allegiance based on a conviction or a belief. Ultimately, it means that we believe in something as a 'good' that will better our existence on this globe. It's an odd thing that if we stand for nothing, it may be that we believe in nothing. And it may be that believing in nothing is the worst kind of believing of all.

David often wondered what called people off to war, other than the draft? He was passionate... at one time. But passion was too often replaced by reality and realism. To David, passion was what happened when people doted upon nice ideas that would eventually seize their imaginations and ultimately run away with them. Passion became equated with idealism run amuck. It was a set-up for disappointment. Passion was a dream that you had while you were awake that was too soft for the steeled realities of life. Passion was disappointment in the making, or so David saw it. "Enough of pain and disappointment," he mused. "But…"

He admired those who had a passion, though he had lost most of his own. He wouldn't acknowledge that to others. That's what made the whole thing more difficult. It seemed that life was big enough to have ample room for a passion or a vision or a dream… or something like that that was bigger than everything around him or in him. But just because something should be, or justifiably could be didn't mean that it was so. The far less risky option of survival seemed the better alternative.

Turning back to the uniform he turned it this way and that. "I wonder how often he wore this?" David mused out loud. "Hmm. It seems kind of small," he said. "Not my size."

Slipping it on, he turned and jostled his shoulders to get a tight fit. Pulling it down tight, it almost seemed to expand and mold itself to him as if to shape it to his body as well as his heart. He pulled down on the sleeves, buttoned several brass buttons and gazed at himself. "Bigger than I thought." Turning as he was admiring himself, he spied the old Bible and the pages. Walking over to it, he picked it up as some precious relic. Succumbing to curiosity yet again, he began thumbing through the pages. As he did, his mind completely slipped out of the coat while his body remained.

He sorted through pages yet again, this time coming to the second of six. It remained crisp and new, which made him once again think about the first page and how it had unexplainably aged. The thought left him rather quickly as happens when we're met with a mix of emotions all vigorously vying for their place. He meandered to a nearby window and allowed the remnants of the setting sun to illuminate the page sufficiently to read. The words penned in a rather tight script packed on the page read:

"Tomorrow's the big day. It seems like the whole U.S. Army is here, and the Navy's out there too. Never seen so many people in one place at the same time. No one here tonight is talking about death, but I know for certain that everyone is thinking about it. People just don't want that kind of talk tonight.

"Everyone here on the eve of this invasion is here because life kind of turned in a way that put a dictator out there and caused a lot of bad things to happen. People are living in darkness over there. Like a black cloud just fell over all of Europe so it's dark even during the day. Some folks talk about it being an invasion of evil that's got all of these people enslaved. It seems that what people need here in England and over there in Europe right now is an invasion of hope. Sure, lots of troops are going to hit those beaches tomorrow, I'm sure that it's going to be a sight to see. But its hope that's the best weapon. Not ships and guns and such. We got lots of those. But an invasion of hope. I think that's the most needed kind of invasion that could ever be launched. And that's part of what's gonna happen tomorrow. An invasion of hope right into whatever all that evil is over on the other side of the channel.

Makes me think about my own life some because most of us tonight are thinking about things like that. There's a lot of pondering going on, as it should be I suppose. There's some dark in me too, in all of us I think. Seems we all have some pretty dark places in our lives and it occurred to me sitting here that hope is like an invasion in those places in me. I'm just thinking that I need my own invasion too. Wouldn't mind letting hope liberate me some.
William Bauman

June 5, 1944"

Uncle Bill was a bit of a mystery, having died on D-Day on the beaches of Normandy. Beyond dying in the invasion, no one seemed to know the manner of his death or anything about his involvement in the war. The few scant photos David had seen suggested a mild-mannered man who possessed a commitment to all things right. He apparently had enlisted a week after the bombing of Pearl Harbor, leaving aunt Mabel alone to tend the general store in the backwaters of the quite Michigan landscape. He never returned.

Tears welled up in David's eyes. He found it odd to cry for someone that he met only in hand-me-down stories recounted over card games and lazy summer-time barbeques. Reflectively pressing a gentle palm on his uncle's words he suddenly felt his body thrown backward as if some terrific force had seized him in some unrelenting suction and was reeling him ever backward. His body became weightless, being lifted off the floor and suspended by nothing except the overpowering force that propelled him backward. He seemed to float but to fly at the self-same time.

It was entirely odd, but not necessarily terrifying. He never felt a loss of balance or a feeling of great confusion; simply a sense of phenomenal speed hurdling him backwards without any sort of wind or physical sense of speed that would seem a natural part of such momentum. It was all silent to the body, but turbulent to the soul. Not a sound, but incredibly loud at the same time. Turning his body around and facing the blur that now ran at him and by him at such a great speed, it suddenly slowed and then coalesced into something of men milling about.

The speed stopped entirely, giving David a sudden and unexpected sense of standing completely still. It all remained entirely silent. Entirely silent. Hushed if you will.

213

The scene around him sharpened, taking shadow and blotches of color and giving them body, focus and an ever-extending sense of depth. It continued all around him until it became perfectly clear and distinct. Yet it remained without a sound, being deathly silent.

Before David had time to figure of what this place was, a voice behind him broken the silence and said "So, might I ask, what are you doing in my uniform?"

Spinning around, David saw a young man sitting on a simple bunk with hands holding a pad of paper and a pencil. A quizzical expression almost humorous was drawn across his face. At that instant, other sounds washed into the silence on some auditory wave, immediately filling the scene full of voices and banter.

Forgetting the young man and looking around, David suddenly realized that he was in something like a barracks. Endless rows of metal bunk beds, their thin mattresses bespeaking the discomfort of war. Each perfectly lined row rolled off to distant walls on both sides of him with small high sets of windows and rotating exhaust fans perched at each end. Bare incandescent light bulbs hung in regimented rows, casting a pallor-like glow.

Innumerable conversations enfolded upon each other to the point that it all became blended together into a rolling sort of hum. The scene suggested the presence of some goliath-like challenge that demanded a corporate strength to stand against it.

"I said, what are ya doing in my uniform?" the young man repeated again with a touch of humor yet remaining in his tone.

Turning back to the young man, David stammered for words; any words. Despite being a man of words, he found none. An uncomfortable but wholly appropriate pause ensued. "Ah..." David muttered.

"It doesn't much matter," the young man said leaning back against his bedpost and filling in the void. "I won't be needing it much after tomorrow; at all really." With that, he returned to writing.

Turning to his left and then his right and then back again, David momentarily brought his attention to bear on the young man. "Who are you... who are you and what is this place?" David asked, still continuing to look back and forth again and again in some kind of disorienting stupor. He attempted to step out of the way of several uniformed young men who looked to be nothing but teenagers. As they walked by, they passed through him as if he was a ghostly apparition of some sort. Perplexed, he stared at the men as they passed. As they sauntered down the aisle, David placed hands on his own body to guarantee its firmness. Pondering the situation further, he then touched his own hands together to see if they would pass through each other. Not convinced of whatever he needed convincing of, he then he pressed his hands against his chest yet again. Finally, he reached out to touch the bunk behind him to insure his existence or his sanity or both.

The young man looked up, took in the scene, smiled in amusement at David's gestures, shook his head and returned to his writing.

"Well," said the young man sitting back up on the edge of his bed and interrupting David's little exercise in reality, "It's a place we'd all prefer not to be, 'specially tonight. Probably any night really. Ya get caught up in the flow of things you know, of events bigger than us. And then ya end up here," he said pointing around the barracks, or whatever this was.

Pulling a tiny photo off the bedpost, he held it and said, "I would have preferred just to stay back in Michigan with my new wife. Runnin' a general store, well, that isn't much for most people, but it was more than enough for me.

It was magic. Ya know, the woods and the meadows and just livin' a life where ya got room to breathe. And then… well… yer loved. That tops it all off. That makes any place a place worth being whether ya got woods or not."

While the awareness regarding who his grandfather was had taken a bit of time the other night, it rather quickly began to dawn on David who this was…*This is uncle Bill,* he thought. *This is… this is uncle Bill. 'The' uncle Bill.*

Suddenly waving his hand in some disgusted gesture the young man blurted out, "Then some dictator decides he's gonna rule the world and a lot of people that had nothing to do with it at all are called up to tell him that he can't do that. They say that fighting for the greatest good is the highest principal," he said looking up at David and pointing at him, "But the fight ain't always fair." Pausing, the young man thoughtfully said, "But I don't think it's about fairness." With some sort of conviction rising up within him, he said, "I think it's about doing right no matter what the consequences are 'cause doing right is good enough all by itself."

"Who you talking to?" came a voice from the top bunk. Rolling over, a quizzical head appeared over the edge of the bed. He too couldn't have been more than eighteen, maybe nineteen at best. His face was generously sprinkled in freckles that sat atop a light milky complexion. His hair was red with a slight curl despite the short length of it. His face had an innocence about it that seemed ill-suited to the show of strength all about David.

"Who you talking to Billy?" he said again.

Turning to the young man hanging over the top bunk, he said, "Jest myself. Thinkin' through life and all of that. Seems that might be a good idea 'cause I don't know if I'll have the chance to think it all through tomorrow. So now's the time I reckon. Don't want to meet my Maker not having really thought about His creation and life all that kinda stuff."

Pausing, the young man stared as if caught up in the idea and then said, "Never really thought about that. Never thought about that like you're thinking about it." After a pause, he said, "I think I'll think on that myself a bit." And with that, he turned, adjusted his pillow and laid back in his bunk.

At that instant, the deep-throated sound of muscular engines aloft drew in from a distance, building, deepening and then rising to something of a man-made thunder that passed directly over the barracks, shaking them in the thunderous passing. David's attention immediately turned upwards. Columns of heavy aircraft droned overhead, the column in front barely passing before the next lumbered in behind it. It seemed to be the raw muscle of man's technology drawn together in a mighty collaboration and jointly flying off to some grand crusade.

This feeling of raw power somehow coursed through David's bones, coalesced in his heart and took captive the concourses of his soul. For an instant he knew what it was to live with a purpose that fired every thread of his imagination and lit the seams of his soul. And for that instant he understood what it was to be willing to fling oneself into a cause without any thought of what the cost might be. For David it was a revival of everything that he had once lived for, and of everything that he had now lost. It was who he had been those many years ago along the river-rock fence, decades of hash marks ago. For a moment he was ignited with hope, and at the same time he was summarily lost in it.

With the aircraft having passed, David resumed his looking about. Half hearing what the young man was continuing to say, David knew enough to say, "This is England. Right?" Remembering his encounter with his grandfather and wishing to confirm what his heart seemed at some level to know, he stammered, "This, this, ah… this is going to sound a little crazy, or maybe a lot crazy so please forgive me in advance, okay… but what year is this?" David inherently knew that this was his uncle Bill, or at least he thought he knew. Yet his question regarding the year side-stepped what his heart really wanted to know.

Continuing to write without looking up, the young man said, "I don't know that that's the right question, ya probably should've asked the first one you had on yer mind. But since you didn't ask it…" David twitched, having felt again that these journeys, whatever they were or weren't, rendered him transparent in whatever manner they did that. That was both somehow affirming, yet at the same time it was horrifying. Aunt Mabel kinda did the same thing, in a different sort of way.

Pausing, the young man let out a breath and replied, "Oh well." Smiling, he reached over the bunk next to his, grabbed a lonely and wrinkled newspaper and handed it to David. Across the top in bold print it read, News Chronicle. Underneath the heading in small print, it read June 5th, 1944.

Effortlessly moving on, the young man said, "Now, about my coat," putting the photo back onto the bedpost and setting down his pencil and paper.

Staring at the newspaper, David looked up, interrupted the flow of the moment and said, "Your name is… Bill? That guy, that guy up there," he said pointing to the bunk above the young man's, "that guy called you Billy. Are you… Bill?" David asked. "You are Bill, aren't you?"

The young man turned to David with a sense of seriousness that was held fast by a serene calmness, bypassed David's question entirely and said, "David, do ya know what day tomorrow is?"

"Yes, I know," David replied softly, "But I don't know how it's possible... not what tomorrow is I mean, but how it's tomorrow. Tomorrow is, tomorrow's D-Day. But I don't know how it can be." Gesturing with his hands, he said, "I've read about it and watched the films over and over." Reminiscing about history yet to happen, he said, "You have no idea how many documentaries there are about tomorrow." Holding the paper and attempting to catch his breath, he said, "... and if tomorrow's D-Day then, you're my uncle Bill... right? It has to be you; it has to be... as weird as that all is." David's reply possessed enough confidence, and yet enough uncertainty to make his question slightly tentative should he be wrong.

Standing up the young man said, "Ya can keep the coat. Fits ya better anyway." Quizzically he said, "Somehow it looks too big for me." Standing in front of David and placing a finger on the row of ribbons on the breast of the coat, uncle Bill cited what each one meant. "This one right here, they call that one the toilet seat. It was for marksmanship. Really, all ya had to do was hit the target and they pinned that on ya." Pausing, he pointed and said, "And that one, that one's for completing boot camp. That was an interestin' time fer sure. More times than I remember I stood there wishin' they'd booted me out." Moving his finger, he said, "And that one, that one there's fer good conduct. Often thought, what else would I do but conduct myself good?" Caught in reminiscence himself, he paused, shook himself from the warm webs of memory, patted David on the chest and then said, "Yep, yep, ya keep it."

Shifting out of a place of soft nostalgia, he continued. "Nice to finally meet ya. Yeah, well, as odd as life can get sometimes, I'm yer uncle Bill" he said extending his hand to shake David's. "It's all a bit odd for me too, on my end I mean," he said as he grasped David's hand. Firmly taking David's hand in the midst of David's own disorientation, his uncle Bill said, "I know. Kinda formal for family and all, and I ain't much at all for formalities; neither is yer aunt Mabel." Staring off into the barracks, he said, "We're just common folk. Good Michigan people ya know. Simple. That's how we like it. Simple. In fact, I just finished a letter for her."

Taking up the paper, he handed it to David. It looked oddly familiar. Staring at it, David realized that it was the same letter that he pulled from the family Bible along with the others. The same. Exactly the same. The very one, penned moments ago, not seventy years ago.

"Yup," said his uncle Bill, "I know. That's the letter that brought ya here, in your hand right there," he said pointing at David's hand. "I know that ya got it in the future, whatever the future looks like. Yep. Jest finished it jest now and jest as I do, you showed up. Real timely and all. Right in front of me, with that letter. This letter," he said pointing at the letter he just completed. "The one I was jest writing. Funny how life is," he said taking his letter back from David. "There's a timing to this that we don't understand, at least I don't. I don't think most people do. And I don't need to understand it fer it to be perfect. Painful sometimes, maybe confusing, but perfect."

With a drawn out pause that was about the abruptly change the entire course of the conversation, uncle Bill cleared his throat, looked into David's eyes with an intensity fired by love and said, "Did she… did she go on to live a good life David?" The question seemed to be asked with a touch of fear that it might not be so. It was the past asking about the future, knowing that the future had already happened, but that it was waiting to happen again. It was wanting something for someone else that he would never have. It was love in words.

"She did," David said as he nodded. Looking directly at his uncle Bill, he paused and continued. "She did. She did. She was a big part of my life growing up, a big part," David said falling into his own reflections. "My days at the store with her were the best," he said. "Those times were my favorites. I mean, they shaped me... a lot." Pausing, David said, "What I saw in that store was about the closest thing to life, to real living that I've ever had. Fact is, she had," David said, (pausing to correlate his statements as spoken in 1944), "I mean she did have, and she will have some pictures of you hanging on this big old wall of hers. I caught her glancing at them every time she passed by. Pretty much every time. She would reach out and touch them every now and then too. That kind of touch that's got a lot of love in it." Pausing, David continued, "Now that I think about it, you were never gone for her. Not really. Not like you might think. You were always in her heart. All the time. Fact is, you still are."

Tears welled in uncle Bill's eyes and coursed glistening trails down his cheeks. Lifting up his arm, he wiped his tears on a sleeve that was about to face the horror of mankind gone insane. "Good, that's real good... real good," Uncle Bill said, sorting out the emotion in his head and heart, "that's...good, real good."

Wiping his face on his sleeve yet again, he said, "That was supposed to be a marriage for a lifetime, not jest a short-time. That was a forever kind of relationship... if ya know what I mean. You don't have many of those kinds of relationships. Not like that one," he said, now staring off into the distance. "But... sometimes life calls us to things that are greater than our things. You know. Greater than our wants." Pausing, he turned and pointed, "That's why all these boys are here. They're here fer somethin' great than them."

With tears now coursing down his own face, David replied, "It *was* a lifetime for her. She got that lifetime. She got it. I just want you to know that."

Shaking himself free from the emotion and clearing his throat a second time, his uncle Bill pointed around the room and said, "What ya see here," he said, continuing to wipe tears from his eyes, "What ya see here, all of this is shadows of the past. The journey you're on is gonna be full of shadows, David, yer gonna see that. But for me, well they're, they're my present. Past for you. Present for me. Shadows for you. Reality for me."

Turning to fold some t-shirts sitting on his bed, his uncle Bill continued in an almost matter of fact manner, "Tomorrow I'll hit Omaha beach with these guys, all of these guys," he said swinging his arm around in some sort of inclusive gesture. "These guys, they're a proud part of the 1st Division. They're all scared. Some will tell you that. Others won't. But it don't matter much. War is scary business and they all know it. All these guys left what they want to preserve something greater."

His thoughts interrupted, a group of three men in uniform walked by, caught in a lively conversation about the Brooklyn Dodgers and the feeling that 1944 wasn't going to be a winning year. That Mickey Owen needed to pick up the pace, and Howie Schultz was getting the most at bats because he could "hit 'em out of the park" and that he was racking up the RBI's. David stepped back, invisible as before. Yet, nothing was invisible to him.

"You see," his uncle interrupted as they walked past, "Men deal with things real different. These guys," he said looking up and down the barracks, "these guys aren't really all that interested in baseball. Not like that anyway. Not like they're talkin'. It's their way of celebratin' something good. And if they die tomorrow, or sometime before this god-awful war is over, their death kept the good goin'. 1945 and 1946 and all the years after that, the Mickey Owen's and Howie Schultz's and all the other guys will run out onto those baseball diamonds and play the game because these guys, these guys all around these barracks," he motioned, "these guys stepped up knowin' that good will always overcome the bad. Good will go on even if we don't 'cause God is good and He always goes on. And all of us here have the privilege of being part of keeping the good goin'. And that's a privilege... a real privilege." Gesturing toward David, he said, "It'll do ya good to hold onto that."

Continuing without skipping a beat, uncle Bill turned the conversation and said, "At three o'clock in the morning, about nine hours from now, our ship will pull up about ten miles off the coast of France," he said, gesturing out beyond David to some rendezvous with history. "From there it'll be Higgins boats to the beaches; that'll be rougher than drivin' some of those Michigan roads back home. Especially in the weather that's out there right now; incoming storm and all."

With a reflective intonation, he continued, "It's gonna be so rough most of these guys, me included, are gonna get real sick; real sick. Sea sick, ya know." Pausing, he said, "I've been on Lake Erie in some bad storms in my day, but Lake Erie ain't no ocean. No it ain't." Running off on a slight tangent, he said, "Nice guy and all, no doubt his intents were the best, but Eishenhower's first mistake was givin' us such a big breakfast, figurin' it might be our last. It was good and all, but a bit heavy. Them potatoes sure stuck with me, 'till I got sick."

Smiling and shaking his head with a bit levity, he said, "But, oh well. Anyway, back to what I was sayin', there's gonna be thirty-one guys in my boat. Only seven of 'em will make it. Just seven. That's all. I'm darn sure glad that those seven did. Says something about resilience and all. Gives me hope realizin' that when we're called to great things we have great things inside of us to do it. Ya know, we can step up like we never thought and keep going despite the cost."

Uncle Bill paused with tears welling up yet again. Clearing his throat, he continued. "We hit the beach about six-thirty in the morning." With his voice picking up, he said, "Ya know, I always loved the morning, my favorite time of the day, reflective and all. Morning leaves a space for you to think about things before the day fills that space right up so much so that ya can't think at all. The birds are fresh so they're singing up a storm, and the air's clean ya know." Pausing to shift his thinking to a very different kind of morning, he said, "But that morning, well, that one was different... I mean that it will be different."

"Never heard so much noise", he continued. "It was deafenin'. Kind of noise that goes right through you, like it's more than noise. Like it's life comin' at ya with enough force to knock ya flat." Shaking his head, he said, "If hell has a sound, that would be it. That would most certainly be it. Mankind on a rampage of the evilest sort. That's what it sounds like."

Motioning, he said, "The tall guy standing over there and the two guys to his right... see 'em?" "Yes," David replied. "They'll get hit before they ever get off the landing craft. The really young guy down there with the stack of magazines will have his left arm blown off and he'll drown; watched it and I couldn't do nothing' about it. The other guy folding his laundry on the bottom bunk round the back side there, that guy, that guy will take a whole bunch of shrapnel directly in the chest. What he won't live to know is that he saved the lives of three other guys by doing that," he said as his voice began to waver. Pausing, he said, "Too many stories for me to tell ya, David. Jest too many. Can't do it. Can't." "I understand," David replied in a sullen tone born of the realities that he could only once imagine, but realities that he could now actually see.

Cradling the letter in his hand and staring deep into it, he said, "Ya know... I won't be on the beach long, but for however long I was there, I heard no complainin'. Not a word of it. These guys, these guys right here, every one of these good old American boys," he said pointing around the barracks, "These guys, they just knew what their job was… and they did it. With those German MG's and 38's cutting up everything, they kept moving. Not certain I believed in humanity a whole bunch at most times in my life. But when I watched these guys, my belief in humanity got restored. But, as I think about it, it's more my belief in humanity when humanity hopes. Hope invades any kind of beach. These guys did it… we all did it."

With a lingering pause, uncle Bill looked up and said, "Do ya want me to go on, David?" David found himself wiping several errant tears from his face. You read about history and it reads kind of flat because over time it's become a story instead of an event. It's telling a story about humanity, but not humanity that's telling a story. We lose the life of it in the reciting. And every time we recite it, it loses a little more life. David wondered how many great events had only become stories for him; flat and gray. A string of words sewn together to spin a lively tale, for life is too big to be held in the pages of a tale. And how much had he lost because of that.

"No." David replied, "No, no you don't need to."

Turning around and sitting down, he motioned for David to take a seat on the bunk across the narrow walkway. David backed up, continuing to look around the barracks in puzzlement and disbelief and then slowly sat down. Several other soldiers walked by, passing through him as before. *That's interesting*, he thought. However, he quickly turned and fixed his focus on his uncle.

Leaning over with his hands clasped in his lap still holding the letter, he said, "David, David… back home no one knows how I died, tomorrow I mean. I wish it were heroic or something like that. I'd be the first to say that it wasn't." Fiddling with his fingers, he looked down and said, "There was one guy, just after we hit the beach… that was really wounded. Didn't know him. But I did pull him behind a tank barrier. I thought that was pretty heroic given that all hell seemed to have broken loose. Sure never seen anything like that in Michigan," he said with a slight laugh as if attempting to offset the pain and fear of facing another D-Day. Turning somber again, he said, "I didn't realize it, but he was already dead so, I guess the intent was good."

"About halfway up the beach I got hit right here, in the left shoulder with some shrapnel. I was kinda happy, figuring that was all that was gonna happen to me, that I'd gotten whatever I was gonna get. I can remember thinking 'This ain't so bad.' Then I just remember turning around, and as I did I felt like I got slugged right in the chest, right here," he said pointing to the center of his upper chest. "Except it was real hot like… knocked the breath plum out of me. I remember dropping to my knees thinking I just needed to rest a bit and I'd be alright. I really thought that. Maybe I didn't want to admit that that was it. I didn't feel ready for life to be over, ya know. Too much that I wanted to do. Then it all went black."

Uncle Bill paused, leaving a vacuum that David was now leaning into, irrepressibly drawn into; mesmerized and hanging on every word that uncle Bill spoke. The waiting seemed completely intolerable and so David said, "What else uncle Bill, what else?"

Drawing himself up and breathing deep, uncle Bill said, "David, I'm going to go through all of that again tomorrow. That was part of the deal. The noise, ah the noise, the mortars that just kept coming kinda like a bad rain, a downpour, except ya died in this kind rain. It was raining metal… everywhere up and down that beach. Ya wondered where it all came from, machine gun fire, artillery… nobody has that much ammunition… can't imagine," he said shaking his head. Pausing, he continued,

"Didn't know that people wanted to kill other people that badly. But they do."

Turning to the photo again, he said "Most people die just once. I'm gonna die twice. I suppose there's comfort in knowin' how it's gonna happen and I know where I'm goin', so all that's settled and all. Don't have to guess about that one like most people do. Gives me a bunch of comfort sittin' here; a real deep kinda comfort." Shaking his head while searching the floor for words, he said "But, gonna do it again."

Leaning forward and putting a hand on David's knee, uncle Bill's hand did not pass through him as the other men had. Confused, David said, "These guys pass through me and you... you don't because this is real isn't it? I mean, this is shadow, you said, all of this is shadow. But you and me... this is real."

Uncle Bill looked deep into David's eyes in a manner that brought all of David's thought to an immediate halt. He drew a weighty breath and said, "I want ya to understand, life is good David, no matter what happens, life is good... I need ya to remember that, 'cause that's real. Real as you and me."

Drawing in a deep breath, he continued. "David, things get taken from us, everyone gets robbed somehow. Some way. It jest happens. It's unfair, lots of times it's real unfair. But life's bigger than all that David; a whole lot bigger. Life can never get all swallowed up in all of that, no matter how unfair; life's too big to get swallowed up in that. Neither can you." With a decisively firmer tone, he said, "Neither will you. There's purpose in all of this," uncle Bill said motioning around the room. "Good purpose. Worthy purpose. Even when it all looks crazy-like and outta control just like it will tomorrow on Omaha."

Pausing to let the words sink in, his voice took on a more sage-like tone thick with wisdom. "God is good

David. It's evil and the selfish stuff that mankind does that's the bad stuff. Don't attribute that to God 'cause that ain't Him," uncle Bill said with vigor in his tone. "Ya got to look beyond it David. Ya got to. 'Cause if ya don't all yer gonna see is the bad and you'll miss all the good, which is always more than all the bad combined. I'm not a man who talks real well and sometimes I just can't stir up the words, but David, most these guys are gonna die tomorrow and so am I. But even in death I will not, I will not surrender the belief that life is good; never. Won't do it. And neither can you."

"This," he said, adamantly pointing around the room, "This invasion is an invasion of hope, David." With a voice of gathering conviction, he pointed directly at David and said, "Don't really matter how evil and dark it all is, 'cause hope can invade all of that no matter." Leaning further forward, uncle Bill continued, "This world of ours needs an invasion of hope. The world that you're going back to needs it. Heck, you need that yerself, probably more than most."

Pulling back and sitting up straight on the edge of the bed, he looked down the small aisle, pulled back a bit and said, "Never was much for lectures, but I reckon that I just gave ya one. Hope ya remember it when you get back home. Maybe share some with yer aunt Mabel if ya get the chance."

Taking a deep breath and collecting his thoughts, he rung his hands and looked up at David and softly said, "I gonna die again. Yeah... again. Same way. But, I chose that because that was the only way I could tell you what I just told ya. Figured that you wouldn't hear it lessen I told you this way. Makes it heavy-like ya know; important and all. I'm guessin' this all lends some weight to my words so they sink in ya and carry ya 'cause they sunk in. Same with your grandpa in the basement, when you met him I mean. He had to watch your grandma die a second time; then all his depression after that. Ten long years. Tough stuff for sure. I truly love that man. Love 'em will all my heart."

David found himself lost, suddenly attempting to grapple with two incredible, unexplainable experiences that were now being woven together with the simple words of a long-lost uncle. No one would believe any of it; not a word of it. David wasn't certain that he believed it all either. Sometimes the unbelievable is in reality the most believable thing of all because it holds within it something of the eternal. And that gives the unbelievable credibility.

"David," said uncle Bill, interrupting David's thoughts. "People are choosing to relive the most horrific experiences in their lives to give ya this message." Pointing directly at David, he said, "That's how important it is."

David stammered, "What's the message... what am I supposed to know? Please, what am I supposed to know that caused all of these people to do whatever they're doing and all of this to happen?" he said gesturing around the room. "For you and grandpa to do this... what's the message?"

Uncle Bill shot back with a mix of passion and deep love, "That life is always good no matter what happens, no matter. Ya hear that? There's always hope, and life's good, and we have what we need to face it no matter what comes. David, look, life is always bigger than anything that happens to us. God set it up that way. There's a whole lot'a evil in life David, there just is; shouldn't be surprised by that. But there's a whole lot'a good, a lot more good. Good goes on forever. Evil, well that's limited and because it is, hope can invade it and hope can beat it dead."

Leaning further toward David, he continued, "Kinda reminds me of all the folks that would come in the store; just good people, a kinda good that's bigger than all the bad 'cause God's bigger David... always bigger. Some people can't see God 'cause they don't want to. Seeing God asks too much of them so they don't want to see Him, so they don't. But ya don't need to see God directly, like face-to-face 'cause ya can see Him plenty well in those good, simple people. In simple things. In fields and forests and deer that run through them fields like they're walkin' on air. In those farmers, and harvesting corn in the fall, and swapping stories. God 'is', and 'cause He is there's always hope David. Always. Believe in hope. Let hope invade yer life... yer soul... all of you." After a pause, he said, "That's the message... that's what we all lived for and died for, and we'd do it again... we are doin' it again."

Pausing, he continued, "Now the kinda hope I'm talking about yer not gonna get by just experiencing this," he said gesturing around the room, "even though this is pretty powerful I know. Would be for me if I came back from where you came from and was watchin' all this." With a firm tone, he said, "I'm talking about the kinda hope that's beyond what most of us know. Rare kind of hope, but hope that's there for the takin'."

Standing up uncle Bill said, "Let me see that Bible of yers." Taking it from David's hand he said, "I remember this, your grandfather always had it layin' on the end table in the living room of the old farmhouse; right by that big front window with all the panes in it. Ya know what I'm talk about?" "I do," David replied. Pausing for a moment, uncle Bill looked up said "The farmhouse still there?"

Conflicted by the fact it was presently for sale, or would be in the future, David said, "Yeah, looks pretty much the same as you probably remember it."

"That's good," his uncle replied. "That's real good." Without missing a beat, he said, "Needs to stay that way."

It would.

Chapter 13
Great-Grandma and Gettysburg

There are times when we feel that we've got it; that some principal or idea is firmly in our grasp and we understand whole of it. We believe that we see whatever it is that we're supposed to see, and that we possess a full and rather commanding understanding of it. Such a feeling gives us both a sense that we need not know any more, and that we're fully equipped to step up and step out into whatever part of life this is because we're amply prepared to do so. We move forward, lulled into a sense of inflated confidence and pithy knowledge.

However, life itself is infinitely bigger than the entire breadth of our thin vision or the stifling parameters of our constrained minds. When we think we understand something it's really that we've forced-fit it into some confining and conforming framework that gives us a sense of control over it rather than leaving us breathless by the breadth of it.

Sometimes life allows us to pull up and stop. Sometimes... at the right times. Sometimes it allows us to surrender wonder and hope to our suffocating frameworks so that in the surrender we might actually become appallingly aware of our pathetic frameworks. At other times life realizes that the magnificence of what lays in front of us is far too priceless to surrender it to those frameworks despite how much we might learn. It is then that incredible things happen.

"Let's take a walk," uncle Bill said soberly. Getting up, uncle Bill proceeded through a maze of bunks and men, turning this way and that. He extending greetings, patted a few on the back, and smiled a country smile at each one. There exists a deep brotherhood in times of deep crisis. Indeed, there is a deep melding of our humanity around a shared experience, and in that melding we find profound comfort knowing that we are not alone in the experience of it. Even though David passed through them, he nonetheless dodged them as well, extending a greeting that he knew couldn't be seen. At times, it's not that what we do is seen by others. It's that what we've done is seen by ourselves.

Past men they went. Hundreds of them it seemed. Young. Just teens. Kids really. Barely shaven. Pimple faced. Barely skirting the arriving cusp of adulthood. They were called out to face a giant that had forced these teens to forever displace adolescence and abruptly step into adulthood. David had always known these men in their later years as fathers of his own friends, going to work, raising families, fixing cars, and painting houses. With time, there came receding hairlines edged with advancing grays. Weakening eyes and stiffening backs followed. And then the funerals came with folded flags and the flagging hearts of forlorn families.

Therefore, David had correlated their experience in war the same as he had seen them in his life. Older. More mature. As men, going off to war. But they were not men, not on this day, although that would change by day's end. Most of them were mere teens called out on a man's errand… called out to save the world.

Sometimes we look past people because they're just people and we've seen plenty of them. We begin to peg them with the commonalities that we all share, or we label them with the prejudices that jade us to their uniqueness, making those things the whole of their stories. We make them what fits our rubrics in order to tame them and keep them common so that we are not frustrated with our own commonness. We relegate them to the stale of the mundane, thinking to ourselves, "Yeah, I've heard that one

232

before," so that we don't find our worlds shaken by the fact that we haven't heard that one before.

At other times, such as this one, we realize that people are far more than simply people. We come to understand that each person has a story; a profound story. Whether it be a story of pain or pleasure. Riveting success or demoralizing failure. Love found or love never found or love unfounded. It's a story that's so wonderful that it simply could not be humanly authored; that there is divine story-teller generously unfolding millions of wondrously penned stories for the reading. And in the spinning of the tale, this divine author crafts stories that send these mundane humans on journeys that are bold, spectacular, daring, fringed in wonder and saturated with the improbable. Suddenly we find ourselves desperately wanting to read all the stories; held in some kind of rapture that enlarges us in the hearing.

As they milled about him, David wanted to hear them all. Every one of them. And into the pages of all of the thousands of stories that stood around him, the story of D-Day and Omaha Beach would be penned tomorrow. That story would be different for each. For many it would be the concluding chapter; the period at the end of the final sentence. For others, it would carry punctuations that would not end the story, but most certainly effect the telling of the rest of their stories for the rest of their lives. Many of these boys would carry those stories past the 'tomorrow' that stood in front of them, carrying them out beyond going to work, raising their families, fixing cars, and painting houses to folded flags set on coffins fashioned of maple and oak.

Whatever the case might be, the books were open, the pages laid bare, and the pens were readied. The writing would commence within nine short hours. Before this moment, the entirety of David's understanding of this inconceivable day was solely the product of those pages and the grand summary of them; all of which were compiled after the unfolding of events. It would be the news reels that played out in spotty black and white hues. Photos of history frozen and forever held suspended in time. Men who in their later years would talk about the day, or refuse to talk about it depending upon their experience of it and how it had left them.

Today, he saw these stories on the eve of being written. Pen has yet to be laid to paper. Film was yet fresh in cameras, not yet having caught the scene and imprinted it on its 16mm reels. To have heard the stories over and over, and then to be present to watch the writing of those stories was to know history before it became history. And in that singular experience, history came to embrace a sacredness that David had never contemplated. To reverence it before it happened. And then to touch the lives of those who made it happen before they ever realized that they would make it happen was astounding.

History is appreciated after it is history, not before. Such a juxtaposition was indescribable, yet it was marvelous in a way that rendered all of David's pain a mute, nearly invisible point on the map of his life. He had never felt so alive.

Uncle Bill led David to a large door guarded by an MP sentry. Saluting, uncle Bill showed him his papers and said that he just wanted to step out into the night air for a moment.

"Confined to barracks at nineteen hundred hours private. That's in fifteen minutes."

"Yes sir," uncle Bill replied, motioning David out the door, entirely unseen by the MP, leaving David again fascinated. "Don't worry about that," uncle Bill said. "It's not important that yer invisible to him. What's important is that all of this is not invisible to you. And most important, when yer journeys complete and yer done travelin', yer not invisible to you," he said pointing at David's heart and then his head.

Standing in a slight open area under an overhang between the barracks, the weather was heavy, wet and gray. The dampness was warm, yet penetrating. In a large open space between the barracks David spied two M3 Half Tracks sitting next to a group of Jeep Willys MB 4x4's. Off to their left he saw three Crusader Gun Tractors parked neatly in a row. They all seemed to be sitting somehow holding their breaths in anticipation of the invasion to come. Their counterparts had long departed for the shores of Normandy, leaving these behind should events unfold in such a way that their services might be necessary on this side of the channel.

The stillness of the evening was gradually imposed upon by what seemed a sustained thunder; something like the deep-throated roll of thunder that just kept rolling on without interruption. "More B-17's," his uncle said. "They've been rolling out of here all afternoon, softenin' up the beaches. Problem is, they don't hit much of the beaches, getting' turned around in this weather and all. Good boys those flyboys... but the weather's got the better of 'em. They'll drop their sticks all over creation, but not on them beaches."

Standing in front of his uncle Bill with his grandfather's Bible in his hand, his uncle Bill nodded his head and said, "Let me see that." Taking the Bible, he pulled out the third page and held it out in front of David. "Guessin' this is yer next one," he said.

"Next what... where?" David said. David fully anticipated some sort of journey through time as such travel was becoming less of a surprise for David, but no less a mystery. However, he had assumed that he understood the whole of what had been laid before him by his grandfather and now his uncle. That he got it. That he understood it.

235

Yet, if we somehow think ourselves to have understood life, we are still living in the dank confines of what we've made life to be, not what life wants to make us to be. David's world had most certainly been shaken, but not sufficiently so.

Nonetheless, David assumed that whatever this trip was that he was about to take, it would take him home… back to the root cellar, in his time. He had no point of reference for an experience like this. No one had. Where do you read about something like this? Who do you call? Where in history has someone traveled through history and can therefore tell you how to do it? Nowhere. So far, time had not afforded him the space or place to figure this out; if it could be figured out at all. Home would permit that. There he could figure out what to do with all that he'd learned. There could try to make sense of it. He could collect it and categorize it as was his way of handling things. Yet where we wish for a period, most often life adds a comma.

His uncle Bill motioned him to look up at the handful of stars that peaked out between the clouds and said, "That's infinite out there David, it just goes on and on. Life's just like that. So is opportunity. So is hope. There's always the next thing if you're wantin' it… whatever happens here on this ole' earth is gonna all be swallowed up by everythin' out there. That out there is gonna invade all of this right here someday real soon. It's already on its way. So, I'm not livin' for this," he said pointing around. "I'm living for that," he said pointing up.

The contradiction was consuming for David. Bombers and escort aircraft, thousands of them plied the skies, headed out for a conflict created by men who did not understand the exquisiteness of life shared with others. Why did it need to come to control instead of cooperation? Why are others sacrificed in the toxicity of people playing out their greed? Why should anyone have to die to insure the privilege of living? Why should any of this ever happen? David had died in a similar fashion. He had perished at the hands of greed being played out by a wife committed to betrayal for no reason other than selfishness gone blind.

Yet out beyond these waves of aircraft, peeking out between various clouds was something of eternity. The planes that droned by seemed to pay it no mind as they were focused on earthly pursuits at the cost of eternal ones. Looking up, the temporal and the eternal stood side by side with the temporal suddenly appearing so small, shallow and insignificant. The plans of men tediously crafted for selfish gain and the unrelenting purpose of God for great good were in that moment held up side by side in the boldest relief. Bombers and stars both vying for the lives of men.

Suddenly David's attention was drawn back to his uncle Bill who was holding the old family Bible and the third page. It was clean and crisp as the others had been. Walking under a light hanging off the front of a barracks he said, "I slipped my letter into the Bible David. Last time it got to the future through another route, bein' handed down which was fine. This time, I want you to take it there yerself. You becomin' part of history. I would be honored, really honored if ye'd do that fer me."

"Of course," David replied, "it would be, well, an honor beyond what I understand or what I'm worthy of for sure. But I'll take it."

Taking the third page, his uncle Bill handed it to David and said, "read this," he said. David began:

"War. What is this beastly thing that men throw themselves into for country or for cause? Wretched it seems to me. Till I happened upon a Union soldier who embarked on his journey home after a leg wound rendered him incapable of fighting further for this most noble cause. Mama offered him some food and drink as he walked past our home on his precipitous journey back to the Ohio country. He said many things during his brief visit, stories of war and such, of home and hearth missed.

"As he thanked Mama for her generosity he said, 'This war's brother against brother, like the heart and soul of this nation has been torn right in two. Somethin' that got divided that shouldn't have. Ya sit there awaitin' for battle and ya wonder how you can heal something that's been torn so bad, with so much hated and bloodshed and all. Some things get so torn apart that it seems they can't be stitched back together ever,' he said. 'But some things are meant to be together, like this country for instance. It's just supposed to be so. Watching men die I learned that there's nothing torn in two that hope can't weaved into one again. Seems to me that hope can make things whole again jest like they'd never been torn apart at all.' Mama never forget his words. Neither have I.

Donna Fosnaugh

November 16th, 1863"

"Yer Great-Grandmother wrote that," uncle Bill said. "I never met her, but I understood her to be a fine woman, a great woman really. One of those women you don't have to make stories up about because the real things plenty good all by itself." Taking David's hand, his uncle Bill turned it palm down and said, "Goodbye David, many are countin' on you. I'm countin' you. Yer a good man to count on," he said. With that he pressed David's palm to the paper.

Immediately the clouds dissipated; instantly, although uncle Bill and the barracks remained for a moment. Then they themselves were gone. With the clouds removed, the stars began to hurdle across the sky, oddly moving backward with accelerating speed from west to east. Eventually they created a blur of thread-like lines arching across the black velvet of space. The moon came and went with accelerating flurry, moving through the various phases faster than David could watch it. No sun. All night.

"It's all going backwards," David realized, peering up into life walking backwards, or running as was the case. It was odd that it went from night to night without the sun ever showing itself, something like a life lived shuttered in a forever dark. In the midst of it, David did not seem to be moving at all. This experience seemed to be less about sensing some monumental shift and more about observing it. To be at the epicenter of some unfolding journey, but to be insulated in a way that we can take in the essence of it. For too often we feel the energy spent by the journey, but we have nothing to show for the expenditure. This time this journey demanded nothing of David, allowing him to trade energy for anticipation, and that would give David everything to show for this journey.

The stars slowed and then gradually surrendered to a lightening sky. It all slowed to a soft stop. As it did, everything fell deathly quiet. It was all vacant as if there were plenty of space to set a grand stage. Everything was hushed as if something grand was indeed approaching or being assembled as the case might be. All around him deeper grays with lighter shadows began to appear and then dissipate over and over: touching and then retreating from the silence. Moving in and moving out as if they were attempting to find a footing. David turned this way and that, scanning, squinting, and anticipating.

It seemed that in the midst of the grays he could slowly begin to hear what seemed to be a thousand muted whispers, or more. Although fuzzy and garbled, they rose. Sometimes we have a sense about things that is nothing more than a sense. These things refute our examination of them. Rather, they demand our wholesale acceptance of them without the evidence that would legitimize them. And so, rather than analyze them in order to explain them,

David found himself in the odd but freeing position of letting life explain itself.

Whatever they were, they appeared to have been voices once hushed that were once again finding their voice. Clearing their throats after centuries of silence it seemed. They had become muted. Not silenced, but muted. Too often we mistake silence for the absence of something when in reality it is the preparation for something. And when life's ready, life's no longer muted. This was that moment.

Slowly they teased David's ear: becoming slightly audible then pulling away it seemed. They came and went, delicately ebbing and flowing. Each was indistinguishable from the other; entirely indiscernible but clearly alive. There was a robust energy about them; a generous vitality that gave them a life and a pulse. They were strangers but friends as well; soft and unpretentious.

It seemed that they were voices of people lost to time; echoes of lives long past that died a physical death. Yet, despite that death they continued to live in some place that's out of the reach of an ending; of any ending. There seemed to be a soft vigor about that rendered them eagerly alive. They seemed far more alive in the place that death had passed them onto than anything remotely close to the life that they had come from. Apparently, there was something beyond broken marriages, broken families and a broken existence. And here it was… all around him. Coming to him and speaking as they came.

There was not a hint of brokenness about them. Nothing dark or tainted. Indeed, they were far more alive than anything that David had ever experienced even during the best days of his own life. Those warm days in the old farmhouse. Early morning walks on the road of Indian, horse, and heavy wagon. Hash marks on a river-rock fence. Aunt Mabel and the soft summers of earthy people and listless Michigan farms. Whatever this was that was coalescing all around him, it was all of those things a hundred times over; maybe more.

Wholly enraptured by the vitality of all of the voices ebbing and flowing all around him, David did not recognize the light. But the light dawned, very slowly illuminating a broad area largely treeless that sat cradled on a gently rolling slope. It was as if the light was reverently pulling back a mammoth curtain on an extraordinarily sacred place. Sacredness is that rare moment when we finally take part in what we were meant to be. We don't create these moments because they aren't made. They simply are. These moments are obvious because in them, we are complete in a way that brilliantly highlights our incompleteness.

Off in a listless distance, rows of naked tree lines slowly took shape. Tangled and thick, they seemed primordial and glorious. As they took shape, David realized that they embroidered farm fields, much like those back by the old farmhouse. Watching as the scene coalesced, he realized rather quickly that this was not the farmhouse, and despite his premonition to the contrary, he had not been sent home. With that realization setting in, curiosity followed close on its heels and set in right behind it.

The tenor and tone of whatever day and place that this was began to creep in, feeling somewhat cold and barren. Yet, it was filled with an electricity which is found when humanity gathers in great droves for great things. As the sun continued to brighten, the thin and misty apparitions of people began to sporadically coalesce on the rolling slope at various spots; some singularly and others in larger groupings.

At first it seemed that there were separate pockets of them. Then the holes began to fill in, creating a crowd of people largely solid with small handfuls of people scattered on the rolling periphery. They seemed as ghostly apparitions; more of memory than living.

Horses slowly appeared in columns scattered through the heart of the crowd, while hundreds of them dotted the edges in sordid bands, tails swaying and manes dancing with a slight breeze. Wagons and carriages of several sorts materialized; parked in odd places with awaiting horses hitched and patient. Concorde and Stanhope carriages sat about. Conestoga and Bain wagons lumbered in. For all the emerging activity it remained ghastly silent as if it were nothing but shadows without life; something akin to a massive Matthew Brady tin-type photo set in motion.

Slowly, an oddly warm breeze listed through the cold air, loosening the scene and breathing a bit of life into it. Sounds of voices sporadically took a more precise shape, appearing to be swept in on the wind and given a swelling crispness. Individual voices sharpened and stepped into the scene, moving from soft and indistinct to clear and present. David began to hear children running, being scolded by parents caught in whatever spectacle this was. Greetings were exchanged. Talk of infestations and thin soybean crops. Poor corn prices. Stuart's raid on Chambersburg October a year ago. The Pennsylvania Reserves and two cousins who currently served. The rebel sharpshooter's body who was found just over there in 'Devil's Den.'

None of this history was known to David. These were the silent sidebars of larger historical happenings; important to the assemblage of common-folk, but irrelevant to the larger sweep of history. It seemed that these people were drawn into something grand while being forced to attend to the mundane chores of life.

Conversations of adults floated in with greater intensity and clarity. They were an odd mix of recollections of warfare that was nothing of history, but everything of experience. There were discussions of various regiments, conversations of mutual friends serving and the latest stories that seemed fact with a touch of fiction in places. It was homey; the conversation of relationships shared and battles lived. These were intermixed with conversations of horse-trading, the sharp rise in the cost of cotton, a flurry of illnesses that sounded much like the common cold, and when will this "blasted thing be over."

There were conversations that seemed sharply political, discussing matters entirely alien to David but brisk enough to elevate voices and set an edge to conversations. Conversely, there were those a bit more subdued who spoke of pillaging, death and fear with words that could only be crafted by those who lived those very words and cried those very thoughts.

As if coming up from behind and surrounding these myriad individual conversations, the throaty blend of a thousand voices talking slowly rolled in, surrounding the scene and adding an auditory depth to the visual that stood before him. David turned and saw lines of others coming down a wide, dirt road; their voices coming with them with a sense of anticipation spiriting them along. It was life being lived in expectation of some great but entirely unidentified event.

As David scanned the scene, color tentatively emerged in light pastel wisps and thin washes, gradually growing in intensity until the scene was brilliant and throbbing in color. The woods were skeletal, sleeping in the embrace of fall or winter, whichever this might be. Turning this way and that, he saw men with silky top hats and rounded derbies. Women walked about with flowing dresses that seemed to draw behind them in some manner wholly obedient; their hair bound in chenille hair nets.

Most however appeared more casual with the clothing of a farmer, or possibly a tradesman of some sort.

Children had button up boots, bonnets, suspenders and high collar coats; something of another era, but entirely timely and fresh in this place. Soldiers proliferated with various uniforms; some clean and pressed while others seemed to bear the haunting weariness of battle in their worn threads and errant patches. Many held what appeared to be muskets that were long and graceful. Others had side arms or various sorts, while others seemed much more leisure but no less regal, bearing no weaponry at all.

Whatever this place was and wherever it was, this was certainly another time, yet a time David could not ascertain with any degree of precision. In his mind, David affixed the time as the late 19th century, although what and where were entirely unclear. He assumed it to be history unfolding, yet it was not history at all, but the present being lived in history.

There was no confusion this time. No fear. Rather, it was as if David wanted it to be the events of their present verses the shadows of his past. It seemed that that yearning was rooted in his desire to fully participate in whatever excitement was building and to be a part of life instead of a distant observer of it. For the first time in whatever these travels were, David developed an ever-ascending desperation to live the past before it became the past yet again. After decades of emotional death, he was finally a child again, waiting with boundless anticipation for the wonder of the day to unfold in whatever way it might unfold.

Each of the two times he had gone through time before, someone had met him; some vintage character from his past had shown up. Yet, not this time. That made this different. Nobody showed up or showed themselves to him. He had never been alone in history before, but why should he expect otherwise? There was no guide through this place or these events or to whatever destination this was all to result in. As David pondered the thought he abruptly realized that that's how he'd chosen to live his life. He had chosen to live alone. He was used to this. *So what did it matter,* he thought, *if I face the past or present alone. Either way, I'm alone.*

Shaking himself free of the thought, as much as he could, he said, "Well, let's see what all the fuss is about." Moving into the crowd that had now fully coalesced, he attempted to weave through the gyrating masses, excusing himself as he went. *Rude,* he thought as people appeared to snub his gentle courtesies. *Guess I'm odd, at least in this era.*

Suddenly two shabbily dressed men and a bouncing child suddenly stepped in front of him. As they did, he effortlessly passed through them; making what seemed starkly real to be more things of shadow and of no consciousness. *Oh yeah,* he thought. *Shadows. Uncle Bill told me already.* He found it saddening, that somehow he could not participate; being relegated solely to watching from a distant sideline, or shoreline, or in this case… timeline.

Despite his apparent ability to pass through these images or people or whatever they actually were, he continued to navigate the crowd as if he might bump into someone; seemingly needing to believe that whatever this was, it was more real than not. He could hear the voices, smell the smells, feel the breeze and sense the ambience of the moment flowing through every part of him. It was as alive and real as anything he could imagine, or ever had imagined.

Surprisingly, his senses drew in every slight nuance of the scene, granting it a reality that was liberatingly superior and briskly sharper than anything David experienced in the nominal life that he had stooped to. His senses were nimbly keen beyond anything he had ever known, even during those wondrous moments at the river-rock fence as a young man, or those glorious times with his wife and children before the death of all of that. The clothing of these people. The unfamiliar accents that lent a magical air to the most mundane conversations. Topics long relegated to history books that were now alive as alive ever was or ever could be. To imagine something (as much as one is capable of imagining it), and then to have it actually stand in front of you and walk all around you and through you as the case was. To breath it in and have it breath into you. To do this and in the doing have your imagination gladly fall to a reality that your imagination could never grasp, much less create. Oh, the wonder of it all!

I must really be here, he thought. *I don't have this kind of imagination. I'm not that good.* "This can't be anything other than real," he yelled out loud. Closing he eyes, he drew in history alive and he alive in history.

Casting a quick glance at the ground, he realized that despite the fact that he walked through the loamy dirt, he left no footprints. Coming to a halt, he raised his foot and pounded it on the ground. Yet, no print emerged nor was any dust stirred. He twisted his foot back and forth. He could feel the ground, but still, no print. Kneeling, he removed the old knife from his pocket and attempted to draw hash marks in the soil as he did on the river rock fence. The dirt would not relent. He was here, but he was not here. He stood there, but somehow he stood a century or more away at the same time.

Standing back up, he gently put his knife back into his pocket. As he did, he began to leave the notions of insanity and oddity further behind, replacing them instead with a growing sense of awe and privilege. He could not make a hash mark here because sometimes life doesn't want us to chronicle our own existence by leaving something behind in life. Rather, life simply invites us to a partnership where something is left behind in us. He continued walking, turning this way and that, watching the ground to see if he might yet leave a print.

As he made his way through the jostling crowd of top hats, farms folks and romping children, he spied a stage of sorts, hastily constructed around which people were gathering. It was a platform really; plain and quite simple. The front was edged in antiquated American flags. Not those with fifty stars. On the platform were several individuals, entirely indistinct from where he was. They seemed to be milling about and conversing with each other, find both humor and some element of consternation in the apparently chivalrous and energetic dialogue.

As he attempted to peer over the crowd of spectators, a man to his left lazily rummaged through the pages of a newspaper.

What day is this, David wondered. *What place is this?*

Leaning over, he attempted to scan the pages to determine what date this might be; to ground himself in wherever he was. Frustratingly, the man moved away while reading. Irritated, David followed, repeatedly attempting to look over the man's shoulder.

"Excuse me sir," David blurted out, "excuse me," suddenly realizing that his irritation had gotten the best of him and had played him the fool. Like the rest, the man obviously couldn't see David. "I'll get this figured out eventually," he mumbled. As the man folded the paper and tucked it under his arm, David was able to lean down and make out the date... November 19, 1863.

1863? David thought. "1944 to 1863?" he said turning and taking in the scene. Turning back and forth, he scanned the assembling spectacle. "So, this is what 1863 actually looks like. This is what it looks like," he murmured. "Wow," he said. "But what happened in November, 1863? What's going on here?" he said to himself. Scanning the crowd, with a slight sigh he said, "I wish I'd paid more attention in Mr. Trubell's history class."

"Well," he said, settling himself a bit now that at least he knew the year. "Now what? Who do I know here? Where is here anyway?" he said turning in complete circles hoping to catch a glimpse of something that would tell him where he was. 1863… yes. But where in 1863? At what event?

As the thought cartwheeled through his mind, someone abruptly took hold of his left arm and pulled him forward.

"This way," came a tiny and diminutive female voice. Looking down with a stammering sort of gaze he saw a petite little girl, eight, maybe nine years of age with a softly smile sweet and an expression that held something far beyond her years. She was dressed in a finely tailored blue dress with a thin white trim; simple but orderly. Her collar was trimmed in lace and her bonnet was held secure by a slight silk ribbon.

She did not pass through him or him through her like everyone else here. This was a characteristic of all the people he met in his travels. *I'm supposed to meet a kid?* he thought.

"Who are you," he said. But before he could complete the sentence, they were off. Pulling on his sleeve, David found himself following her at a rather quick pace, not certain why he followed other than he did. The little girl navigated the throng, gingerly skirting the gathering crowd while he passed through everyone with ease.

Sometimes our first questions are a product of our impulse rather than an expression of our thoughts. Sometimes we want to find out too fast that which life would prefer we discover in slower steps as part of the larger journey down the road. Sometimes a journey forced is a journey wrecked. At some moments in life, the best questions are those never asked.

As he was being pulled along, the little girl waved and shouted, "Hello Mr. Clemon's," a brisk smile on her face. "Good morning to you sir!" She kept moving. A moment later she said, "Yes Mr. Granger, my father's right over there. Thank you for asking!"

Attempting to keep with this vigorous youngster, over the noise of the crowd David shouted, "Who exactly are you? And, and how old are you?" The questions had now become more something of curiosity and less of fear.

David pulled her to a stop. Without the first two answered, David said, "I think I might know this already, but why, why it is you don't pass through me like the rest of these people?"

"Because I can see you" she said sprightly and with great vigor. "You're right there!" she said pointing directly at him.

"That's rather apparent," David said tilting his head with a touch of twenty-first century sarcasm. "But…"

Before David could say anything else, she said, "Come this way." Without missing a step in her gait she again dragged David toward the distant stage.

Caught in this sudden forward momentum, David stammered, "Okay, fine, but who are you?"

As if she had never heard his question at all, the little girl abruptly said, "That's an odd uniform. What state do you fight with?" David had entirely forgotten that he still was wearing his uncle Bill's military coat.

"Well," he paused, "I'm not sure, but I think it's from a war hasn't been fought yet… I think."

"Men will always be at battle," the little girl said with an uncanny maturity. With her stride unbroken, she continued "Whether that battle is on a battlefield like this one, or on the most difficult battlefield of the heart and mind. It really doesn't matter all that much, men will battle." Perplexed by the rather astute answer, David found her acumen clear and her maturity shocking.

Continuing to pull David forward, she said, "It seems to me that it's not about the battle at all, but about how a man engages the battle, most particularly when he's wounded, or worse yet, when he loses the battle."

Stunned, David stopped, looked down and said, "Who or what are you?"

With a curious smile curling around the entirety of her lucid face she motioned for him to lean his ear down toward her. Cupping her hand by his ear, she whispered, "I am your great-grandmother." With a smile and a wink, she once again yanked him forward toward the platform, almost tripping David in the momentum of lives merging.

In our lives we live in one of three places. We can be on the other side of personal devastation with it having passed us and fallen into history. We can live right in the middle of personal devastation as its transpiring. Or we can scan the horizon of our lives and circumstances, nervously anticipating its arrival. Each place is uniquely different and entirely exclusive unto itself, providing us a different prism through which to view whatever the nature of our devastation might be. Yet, that's the beauty we can find in the horror. We are privileged to have three different but equally valid views of the devastation in our lives. With the blessing of perspective, devastation becomes insight. Insight lays the groundwork for growth. And out of growth grows hope.

Lost in what this little girl had just said, before he knew it David had been escorted near the stage.

"Papa," the little girl shouted to an older, rather rotund gentleman. Before David could turn and see to whom the greeting was directed, he heard a gravely, rather throaty male voice say,

"Umm… and where have you been Donna?"

"Oh father, I had to find my friend," she said with that bubbly sort of voice. "He's come a long way."

"I see," said the man with a slight draw in his voice. "So then, did you find him?" he said making room for a child's apparent imagination.

"Yes Papa, he's right here!" she said gesturing to David with a smile as big as history itself.

It was clear that whoever this older man was, he was a bit polished, refined and cleanly austere. He had an authenticity about him; something that bespoke of an earthly kind of mentality with the clean-edged refinement born of culture and cultivated by education. It seemed that he might have been a man of means as he was clothed in manner that seemed a bit more formal that most of the people there that milled about. His frock coat and wide elaborate cravats lent him a polished air of distinction.

His face was edged with a tight, trim beard that had grayed to maturity with a few salt and pepper highlights. His vivid blue eyes stood out against a milky white complexion, with each cheek having been dusted with a slight rosy hue. He appeared to exude a tender but firm confidence, embellished with a language and prose that was smooth but to the point.

"This must be my great-great-grandfather," David thought out loud as he attempted to assemble the myriad of people and places that he had encountered over the past several days.

"Quite right," the little girl whispered, playfully nudging David. Staring at the man, David explored his features, attempting to discern in his features anything that he might have seen in the genetics of later family members, or in himself.

So, David thought. *You're where I come from.*

The puzzle that David found himself in the middle of seemed onerously enormous, as are many of the circumstances in which we find ourselves. He neurotically attempted to fill in the puzzle with pieces that might have been doable if they had been more than bits of faded history. The study of history is one-dimensional. We assimilate it in a kind of cut and paste effort where we attempt to assemble mementos and relics that have been saved and passed down. We tediously piece these aged shards together in a primitive mosaic that reads easy from the comfortable armchair existence of our present.

Yet, this was history come alive. This was nothing of shards, but everything of living, breathing people living out history in the currency of the now. David was standing in a full-faced encounter with it, feeling the very breath of history pass across his heart and soul as the present itself. When our soul engages history at the point that it is nothing of history but everything of the present, it tastes succulent and fresh, not aged and decayed as we have always known it to taste.

When that happens, everything is restored to the priceless reality that history was before the winds of time threw its sands in a million different directions and rubbed it gray. Pulling those kinds of pieces together is nearly insurmountable; tantamount to anything anyone in all of history had ever had the privilege of doing. And this, this was David's dilemma as much as it was his privilege.

The gentleman standing before him extended his hand to David. Shocked, David had thought himself to be invisible, to most anyway. He turned to his great-grandmother who simply gave him an affirming nod of the head. Turning, he slowly he reached out to grasp the hand of his own history, to touch someone four generations removed, to feel the embrace of someone without which David himself would not exist.

He reached out in an exhilarating expectation of meeting his lineage in the flesh, with all the wonder of time and the mystery of family rushing through his head. To feel the connection of heritage with an intimacy deemed impossible. But heritage was reaching a very real hand out to him. As he reached, the man's hand passed through his own.

What? David thought.

"Very nice to meet you, sir," the man said with a slight bow as if he actually saw David. Confused, David looked at his great-grandmother and then back at the hand held out to him. He repeatedly reached for the man's hand, grabbing and waving his hand in and through his great-great-grandfather's. "I've heard much about you," he said. David stopped and looked back up. "Indeed, it is a pleasure to be graced with your presence," he continued. Yet, looking into the man's eyes, he could see that he was not looking at him. Rather, he was looking through him, as if staring into blank space. David's heart sank and his eyes swelled with tears wrought of reunion disappointed.

"He can't see you," whispered his great-grandmother with some sort of knowing and fun-seeking tone. "He loves me enough to humor me," she said, directing the comment both to David and his great, great-grandfather. David found himself smiling, looking up and seeing his great, great-grandfather with the identical smile on his face that David himself saw in his own mirror. *That's me, that's my smile. Must be family,* David thought. *Must be.* Suddenly, David felt at home in a manner that he hadn't known for years.

"Our place has been reserved at the front of the stage," his great-great grandfather interrupted, suddenly altering the direction of the conversation. "It would not be preferable to be late. Shall we," he said motioning them forward.

Chapter 14
Lincoln
A Handshake in History

If we're willing to walk the precipice of risk, we can find ourselves in wonderfully improbable places with wonderfully improbable opportunities being held out in front of us for the taking. Life can be terribly gracious, affording us the privilege of walking roads that we thought were reserved for an elite class of people whose ranks we felt to be eternally beyond us. These roads often seem to be a concoction of our fondest fantasies and boldest dreams. Therefore, they seem entirely unreasonable and something less than tangible reality. Yet, they are not.

After clearing a bit of the fog from his head, David quickly realized where he was, or thought he was.

This is Gettysburg, or so he thought. *It must be.*

Instinctively and quite without thought, he reached for his phone, thinking he could access the internet to determine the date to see if it matched the newspaper he had seen the gentleman carrying.

Sometimes when life takes us to other places, we remain in the place from which we've come. We find ourselves tied to it in a way that often diminishes where we now are now. Without question, the 'now' in our life might be a by-product of the 'then' in our life. Yet, while one can build on the other, if not allowed to be separate they can also diminish the other. His phone was not there. Neither was the internet, as it was invention at least one hundred and twenty-six years in the future, give or take a year.

Still checking his pockets as if he was unable to breech the gulf of time and habit, David thought, *But, how could this be Gettysburg?* All seemed elation and madness at the self-same time.

There was something almost mythical about Gettysburg. Something sanctified. 1928. D-Day. Sure. If he was really even there anymore than he was really even here. Yet it was as if the legendary nature of Gettysburg rendered that day and that moment as unrepeatable and unreachable. Some things are so sacred that they seem ordained to step on the stage of eternity for a single moment and then exit into history without return.

Could it be, he thought vigorously scanning the scene. *Could this...? If so,* David suddenly realized who would be here. "Lincoln... Abraham Lincoln himself is, is around here...somewhere!" he said, nearly shouting it out loud. His eight or nine-year-old great-grandmother (however old she was or wasn't) looked up and lent a knowing smile far beyond her years.

David's head was sent reeling. If by some wildly improbable set of circumstances Lincoln was here, actually here, what was about to happen was the Gettysburg address. That explained the stage, the people, the electricity of the moment, and this sprawling tin-type rendering come alive. It was something lodged flat and one-dimensional in those tin-type photos and romanticized in artistic renderings. It had been analyzed, memorized and memorialized more than just about any other moment in American history. Yet, if David recalled history sufficiently, Lincoln had walked this place the night before, a scant few hours ago, drawing into himself the sacredness of this hallowed ground. He had reflected on the gallant deaths of three thousand brave men, while embracing the loss of his own friend, General Reynolds who likewise sacrificed himself here...on this ground a mere four months ago.

David searched the misty archives of his memory.

"Yes, right, he was so touched by this, this place right here," David said out loud while making a broad sweep with his arms. Pondering, he continued, "After that, he went back to his quarters and revised the speech." David found himself in the extraordinary position of reporting on history not yet written. With an elongated pause of thought and emotion gathering, David said out loud, "He's going to give that speech again!" David, nearly panicked in the thought of it all stood on tip-toe, frantically looked back and forth, eagerly scanning the crowd and the stage looking for that looming figure that was Lincoln.

Wait, wait a minute. She'll know, David's mind abruptly screamed. Suddenly, leaning down and tugging on the little girl who embodied his great-grandmother, he asked a question layered in heavily tentative tones. At certain crossroads we desperately want something to be true because if it is, it sets a course for our lives that no other course could hope to match. If it's not, we feel an engulfing loss of disappointment unleashed. So the questions become terribly risky.

With his thoughts spinning in a wild vortex, David asked, "Is this Gettysburg? Is… is this… is this…?" he said pointing back and forth. "Is he, I mean Lincoln, he is really going to give the Gettysburg address again?" Taking David's hands gently in hers, his great-grandmother looked at him with eyes far beyond the tender face within which they were set and said, "No, David. No, he's not going to give the speech 'again.' No. No he's not," she said thoughtfully.

A rush of disappointment coursed through David and left him weak. "No?" David asked, his voice seeping the ashen gray of deep disappointment. "No?"

"No David," she said. "Not again. For him David, it will be the 'first time' he ever gave it." It was the disorientation of understanding that people separated by over one hundred and fifty years somehow stood in the exact same place at the exact same time. And that meant that their experience of the moment unfolding would be inconceivably different in every way conceivable. Such thinking would be a nearly impossible stretch for anyone. "Okay. Of course, of course. I get that. I think I get that," he said. Quickly David rose and lent a broad smile in ecstatic expectation of what was to come.

"Yes, David, this place is Gettysburg." Lifting a tender arm and pointing out to the horizon she continued, "And today, out there, this nation is torn completely in two. Badly torn." Sinking into a dark sadness of her own, she continued, "Four days from now, down south from here, they'll fight the Battle of Chattanooga. Over eleven hundred men, men who right now, right now as we speak are writing letters home to loved ones, or warming themselves around a campfire, or staring at some picture of their wives, or are thinking about home, or all of the things that men do on the eve of battle... they're going to die."

Tightening her hold on David's hand, her eyes sliced through the gathering crowd and fixed themselves out somewhere beyond the carnage of those eleven hundred bloodied bodies. Collecting her words and steeling her delicate voice, she continued. "Two days after Chattanooga, just two short days later eight hundred and sixty boys are going to die down south in Knoxville. They'll call it the Battle of Fort Sanders, that's what they'll call it eventually. They're already there. Nothing's happening yet. They're waiting for reinforcements right now, sitting in the cold and waiting. Sitting in mud and cold and fear and all such things. Getting things right with their Maker just in case. Warming themselves by some fire. I can only imagine what those boys are thinking, wishing, fearing.

"It's going to be terribly ill-planned. Terribly. Not thought it out at all. That isn't like him, typically, but

Longstreet's not thinking. Just isn't," she said shaking her head. "Lots of men are going to get shot up for nothing. Union soldiers will say it was something more akin to an all-out slaughter than an honorable battle... if there is such a thing."

Turning toward David, she said, "After that, they'll be more boys who won't be going home. More than you can count. Mass graves will be filled right to the brim." Pausing as if reflecting on some deep thought she said, "You look into those silent faces all still and such, like the ones I saw here back in July, I mean you squint and really look and you realize this isn't right. They shouldn't be dead. There was still life in them. Lots of life. It's backwards. It's mankind turning God's plan backwards. Killing life instead of creating it. Stopping it short instead of nurturing it long.

"These boys that died here should be standing ramrod straight and going on about their families, or what they're planning for their futures, or sharing stories of friends, or talking about that special girl. They should have that brightness in their eyes; that energy in their voices, you know, I mean really alive. But they don't because the life's gone out of them. Shot or stabbed or blown out of them." Looking around, she said, "There's a lot of death ahead of what's happening here today. Too much." After a slight pause, scanning off into nothingness, she said, "This nation's torn in two."

After a lingering pause she gathered herself, drew herself up and said, "But today you're going to watch a man believe that it can be healed. Made whole when nothing is whole. Listen to what people are sayin', David. They're standing all around you. You'll hear it. Not many believe in that kind of healing anymore. But he does." Pausing, she pointed at David's heart and said, "It's ripped apart David, just like your heart. Just like you are right in here. It's all backwards. It's not what God intended. And

259

just because we've made a mess of it doesn't mean that God still doesn't intend to make a miracle out of it. He always working things out to do that." Intently staring into his eyes, she leveled her voice and said, "Difference between you and him is that he believes and most times you don't." Lingering a moment, with a shift in her tone she smiled said, "Maybe that'll change today. Maybe it will."

Pummeling into thought regarding his own heart and this place and the commonality of life regardless of what time in history it is being lived, he randomly said, "I've read this speech, probably a hundred times. This is stuff that's taught in school. How can you hear it and not have hope?" Turning to his great-grandmother held close in the tiny eight-year-old body he said, "Do you know that this is considered... or, I mean will be considered... it's one of the greatest speeches in American history... I had to memorize this... do you know that?"

Suddenly stopping, his great, great-grandfather gestured, "Here's our place."

Even though he passed through everyone, there was an actual space for David to stand; something he found rather odd indeed, particularly given the packed nature of the place and the close quarters of people gathered to find hope.

Settling in, his great-grandmother turned to David and said, "The President will ride up on a gray horse. It will be rather strange as the horse will be a small stallion in stature. Why they chose such a small animal, I don't know. And because of its demure size, the President's legs will nearly touch the ground." Pausing in recollection, she continued, "I recall him as looking pained and forlorn. I suppose it was the weight of war. War does that. All kinds of war. We all have war and we all have the weight of war. The President's is this clash of brothers, that they'll come to call it." Pausing and resuming, she said, "When he speaks, it will direct and quietly passionate. In listening to the words, don't miss the weight of them or the pain that crafted them. This isn't pen put to paper. This is his soul lifted to heaven. You'll hear it in his voice. I think that many around here admire him for his gentle strength; tender but rather steeled at the same time. David, you will see that today."

"Then, you've been here before. Wait, wait a minute," David said collecting himself. "This is history for you too, even though it's not for them?" he asked with an air of accelerating confusion. "That will come later," his great-grandmother responded softly. "That will be for later."

With a tenderly reflective pause as if drawing into herself and then bringing the riches of memory back out, she went on, "This is one of the times in my life that I remember most fondly. It was a painful time filled with about as much uncertainty as a human being can withstand. But that has never robbed it of the fondness I have held for it. It's one of those precious moments that can never be explained, so you find yourself living alone in the wonder of it." Lost in the deep thought that made her residence in an eight-year-old body nearly incongruent for David, she looked up, took David's hand and squeezed it, saying, "It is a blessing indeed that I do not need to be alone in this any longer."

Grasping part of what she said, David realized that she lived in the past, but had lived out the entirety of her life prior to her return to this place... just like his grandfather and his uncle had. She knew that what was about to happen would be etched in the annuals of history because she had been in the future to see that unfold. But she had come back here as well... come back to relive her own pain. Suddenly, it fell in place. She was would die again to deliver this message as well.

"You came back… didn't you? You came back too," David said softly, holding her tiny hand and staring into her eyes. "You came back too… right?"

"As I said, that conversation is for another time my dear David," she said. "For now, be here with me."

"My dearest daughter," his great, great-grandfather blurted into the conversation, "You are such a creative young woman. It is my hope that you never forsake your invisible friend and your imagination that makes him so real to you. He means far too much to you I can see."

"Yes Papa, he means so very much to me," she said squeezing David's hand." Everything."

Suddenly, while squeezing David's hand tightly she pointed with the other and said, "Look!" His great-grandmother suddenly seemed filled with the excitement and irrepressible energy of an eight-year-old girl. "Look David, its Mr. Lincoln. It's the President. It's him!" Her eyes were gently held captive in the privilege of a magical moment relived. His great-grandmother was about to re-experience magic twice when most of us live it once, if we're lucky. If we relive a magical moment a second time, most times it's only in memory. Therefore, we would be quite wise not to miss magical moments the first time around, for that may be the last time around.

Lost in her as she was lost in the event, David was convinced as to where he was. Despite the flagrant impossibility of it all, he had accepted that he was here, at Gettysburg. It was all too elaborate to be a ruse of the mind or a theatrical re-creation. Most often we can embrace the improbable. We can even skirt the fringes of the impossible, kind of toying with it in our heads. Yet, despite our ability to rise to great heights, sometimes there are things we seem unable to fathom and realities whose boundaries we appear entirely unable to cross despite our madly desperate desire to do so. We want to believe, and we want to embrace the full extent of what we want to believe. Yet, whether it be emotional paralysis, or reason gone rogue, or logic gone captor, we simply can't. This was one of those moments for David.

Suddenly, from the side of the stage there strode a lean, tall gentleman dressed in a full suit and garnished in a top hat, tie and shining boots. He seemed tired and fatigued... teetering on the verge of illness, so it seemed. David had seen endless re-creations of this man. Actors had portrayed him in movies. Artists had painted limitless renderings of him. His image had been sculpted in marble, cast in bronze, and imprinted on coppers coins and five dollar bills. Those re-creations had become this man to David; surrendering the reality of the actual individual to the images that had been made to reflect the individual. Yet, here was the real thing, the reality that so many had attempted to replicate. And in the face of seeing him, it was clear that the renderings had failed. Miserably.

The moment that he saw him, David realized that all of the attempts to replicate this man had fallen dreadfully short. They had spun sideways, blatantly missing the mark. He supposed that no one really understood that because no one else had the point of comparison that David now was privileged to have. It seemed that everyone after this era lived out a deteriorating diminishment of this man and this moment. Yet there was something of majesty wrapped in humility that couldn't possibly be replicated even by the most talented actors or practiced artists. In the awe of it all, David stood with mouth open, soul stilled and heart entirely enraptured.

The events spun by David. The two-hour discourse of Edward Everett was filled with phrases and words that moved David at times, and at others had left him mired in flowery verbiage. He realized that he did not have the assembled acumen acquired from having lived in this period of time. Therefore, he heard the words as an outsider; parsing them through a life lived in the 20th and 21st century, as ineffectual and diminishing as that now seemed to be. Yet, he was an orator of immense quality and a figure powerful in character. In his words there was enough of shared humanity despite the gaping chasm of culture and time to glean something of great value from his words. It was moving.

The crowd listened in breathless silence, listing on his every word. He was entirely masterful and eloquent; those attributes emerging again and again throughout the discourse. The crowd was at times moved to tears, hearing intimate descriptions of the battle for the first time. He passionately spoke of the reunification of the North and South, stating the Gettysburg made that hope much more possible.

As compelling and energized as the speech was, David could not remove his eyes from Lincoln. Two hours were not enough to feed his mind on the image of the man who sat not fifty feet in front of him, verses standing a century and a half behind him. David watched his every move, charted his every gesture, noted each expression regardless of how subtle it seemed to everyone else. He watched Lincoln sort through his notes, grant the courtesy of his attention to Everett, scan the crowd and scratch his beard.

What struck David was Lincoln's humanity; that history had rendered him bigger than life and larger than history. This man was caught in the titanic upheaval of a nation torn. And he was doing little more than expending himself, with all of his limitations, in order to restore it to wholeness. Yet, history was made by this simple and entirely human Illinois lawyer who had no idea that he would shape history in the manner and fashion that he would. Particularly today. He had no inkling whatsoever as to the monuments that would be erected and the stories that would be spun of who he was and what he said, particularly what he would say in just a few moments; all two hundred and seventy-two words. He was, at that very moment, a man desperately caught up in the angst of attempting to save a nation, not a man attempting to write a script that would live in history.

David seemed to drink in every mannerism so as to bring this man of history alive in a manner, that for David, would stay alive forever. In a nearly fanatical sort of way, he pleaded that the moment would never end. That this would not fall to the dank catacombs of history and flat tin-types. He knew that the next page was coming, that another journey was about to transpire sending him on a trajectory to some other time. What time he didn't know, other than it would be somewhere. That this most glorious moment would helplessly fall backwards into a moment gone. Forever gone. So he consumed every word, every action, every move so that it would never be gone.

Suddenly he felt an incessant tug on his coat. It was his great grandmother once again speaking wisdom from an eight-year-old body. Setting the stage for David in a manner that no history book could, she said, "Mr. Lincoln is here to dedicate this cemetery David. I cannot help but think that his heart is heavy with the knowledge that as the President of this Union, he sent these men to their deaths. All three thousand of them. They're not going home because he sent them out. I have often thought that in honoring them here today he was, or is somehow purging the toxins of guilt and remorse from his own heart."

Pausing and briefly contemplating the war years yet ahead, she continued, "The war will wear on him David. Wear on him badly. The truth of it is, he's in the early stages of small pox right now, right as he sits right there," she said pointing. "He won't know that until he's on the train back to Washington tonight, but he already knows he's not well."

Looking at the stage with a deep longing borne of a soul torn, she said, "The Union will win the war, but he doesn't know that yet... not entirely. Not with a conviction that gives him any real comfort. He tells everyone he's confident of victory, but doubt haunts him like it haunts all of us. Tonight on that long train back to Washington he'll ponder Gettysburg and in the months to come he will continue to walk through this nightmarish war where brother kills brother."

Letting a moment pass, she continued, "Mr. Lincoln will suffer great loss, even his life in Ford's Theatre. He already suspects that he might well be assassinated by some southern patriot or sympathizer. Somewhere, he knows. I could be very wrong, but sometimes I wonder at the moment when he signed the Emancipation Proclamation back in January, right when he put the pen down, I wonder if he knew he'd signed away his life. I think he might have known that as some speculate he did, but he signed it anyway."

Ascending into deep thought, his great-grandmother stared at the stage and said, "Great sacrifice David at great cost. You're about to watch that... not just ponder it as some lofty and grand idea that people think about but never do 'cause that's easy. No... you're about to see sacrifice; to see it right on that platform. And there will be a most worthy outcome because the nation will be sewn back together, real seamless like."

As if pulling together a great thought of great magnitude, she continued, "Sometimes our pain bespeaks of a great outcome that we can't see while we're feeling the pain. But pain can herald the coming of great things. It sets the stage for it; nice and open and wide. So David, we keep moving believing in great things we can't see. That's called hope."

A sudden applause broke into the conversation, suggesting a transition to something possibly grand and likely memorable. It began with arousing greetings and lavish salutations being offered in preparation of the President's speech. The people around David anticipated a speech by the President, but they were more focused on the President than whatever he might say. The crowd assumed a speech, but not one that will have a monumental history built around it. Everyone here was about to be part of history, yet no one suspected it at all. Not a bit. It was a special day, but just another day for them. David stood alone with his great-grandmother, knowing the nature of the speech and how it would ripple through a nation finding itself and at other times losing itself.

Yes, David knew that this was history in the making. He knew the place that this speech and this man would have on and in history itself. He was about to live the moment and yet have a knowledge of what this moment will mean, not from a distant historical vantage point... but standing in the present of this moment while having already lived the recollection of it in the future. This was a raw and revered moment in American history. Aside from his great-grandmother, David was the only one of thousands there that day to have any inkling of such.

So often we blithely assume the events of the past to be spent, emptied of their energy, vitality and meaning. We graciously and often patronizingly afford them their place in history as meaningful and appropriate in their time and for their time. If we cherish them, we cherish them for what they were, not what they continue to be. We fall prey to the belief that their lessons were most effectively expressed at the time that the events occurred.

We perceive a thinning as they are rubbed against the sands of time passing. However, while worn thin by time, we often feel that some sliver of their essence might remain a bit worthwhile; something like finding a penny on the ground that won't buy you much, but having enough value for us to stoop down and pick it up. Regardless of any latent value, we are prone to assign these lessons a relevance applicable to their distant niche in history. In short, it is history relegated to the confines of history.

Suddenly David realized that life was unimaginably more than the tight swath and precariously knit swatches within which he lived out his life. Life was so terribly expansive and irreparably wide; far too expansive to be blocked by the contrivances of men or thwarted by their schemes regardless of how ingenious they might appear. Everything that seemed so vitally important to David shrunk to near non-importance; some to things of no importance at all. His life had been wasted in the minutia of people, events and circumstances. It had been strangled by betrayal, but more accurately, it had been strangled by David's focus on the betrayal. David realized that real life was much broader, infinitely broader than the terribly small frames and suffocatingly90- tight reliefs within which he had jammed it.

His thoughts became interrupted by a growing hush that moved out through the crowd, much like a wave gathering momentum as it ebbed to the periphery of history in the making. It was a sort of mystical hush that anticipates something grand while earnestly hoping that such a space will grace that moment and all other moments to come with something terribly precious and inescapably hopeful.

David began conjecturing; realizing that the people standing here had had a brush with the incivility of what was called the Civil War. This was nothing of history for these people; of tin-type photos and silver-surfaced daguerreotypes. They had not even thought of it as history in any sense, as it was their present, and a cruelly vicious one at that. He doubted that anyone had really thought out how this would play out in the future because the entire focus of everyone was on nothing more and nothing less than surviving this colossal catastrophe that had brushed by their homes. The heroic thoughts of ending the scourge of slavery was not something reflected in any of the faces around David. This was not about nobility or bravery or some sacrificial stance taken against the tyranny of slavery or all the other things that war was said to stand for. Somewhere underneath the carnage, it did stand for those things. Yet, this was human savagery; raw and bloody and traumatic. This was about the desperate hope and most earnest yearning that it all might be coming to an end.

And so, this was not a seminal moment for these people. It was just another moment in a long series of bloody moments, the next of which was a mere four days away. This was a commentary about a war that had cost them loved ones either through death or alienation; that had put their entire existence in jeopardy and had called the future of their nation and their security into total question. It was an upheaval that had left them walking traumatized by the horror of what had just swept by the front porches of their lives. These people, these gathered people were desperate for some word that would suggest that their lives might actually go on and that there might be a future somewhere out there.

Appomattox Courthouse was a year and a half away. They did not have the comfort of knowing that. From this place in history there was no end in sight for these people, other than the sight of no end. This was not history. This was the desperation of the present facing the uncertainty of the future. This was the brutality of the human existence played out in a thousand hopeful, yet drawn faces, none of which seemed to be embedded with the brutality of it more than the President.

With the obligatory salutations completed, Mr. Lincoln extended a nod, rose to his feet, and slowly walked to the front of the platform. His features didn't seem like those focused on the delivery of a speech. His eyes were far

269

deeper than that, seeming to suggest that sometimes things are beyond words and carefully crafted speeches; that sometimes it's the sharing of one human being with another, or thousands of others. It seemed much more of a desire to connect with these people out of what seemed to be an aching loneliness within himself. He seemed forlorn, isolated and standing abjectly alone as great times in history often demand that great leaders stand in great loneliness.

Collecting himself and briefly clearing his throat, he drew a breath and began… "Four score and seven years ago…," projecting what seemed to be a fatigued voice to desperate listeners. The words were real for David, not the flat stuff of history repeatedly embellished to near oblivion by historians and moviemakers. The words weren't some tedious homework assignment to be memorized when you'd rather be doing something else with your friends. They weren't the cold words etched in cold granite on so many cold memorials. This was an utterly exhausted human being carrying the weight of a nation in such desperate loneliness that his words were dripping with an odd mix of pain, desperation, loneliness and some impossibly irrepressible hope.

"Do you see the pain in his heart?" his great, great-grandfather whispered to his great-grandmother. "This is a man of history, a man born for this time," he continued. "He knows more of pain than you or I will ever know, yet he stands and he forges forward. He believes Donna. With his entire soul, he believes that this nation can be healed while many of these standing here today have long abandoned that belief." Leaning down, he said, "Remember what a person of stature does with pain, my dear daughter. And remember Mr. Lincoln as a picture of hope. Do you see him, Donna? Do you really see him? Because if you do, you see hope."

David wondered if his great, great-grandfather's words were for his great-grandmother, or might they have been for him? Or, were they for both of them. Or more likely, were they actually for the desperate people in his own 21st century that would need them on the many broken and abandoned roads; first and foremost, his own.

The speech proceeded, entirely familiar as David had heard it a hundred times before. Yet, hearing it spoken by Lincoln himself made it entirely unfamiliar at the very same time. The thoughtful inflexions, the reflective pauses, the words penned directly from the heart of his soul breathed vigorous life into every word. David desperately wished that those there that day had his perspective as it would magnify his words in their minds many times over. Yet, in pondering that thought he realized that their experience needed to be unique to them; to their pain, their experiences and their time.

It all ended far sooner than he thought it should; that great moments are typically brief snippets of wisdom displayed at critical junctures. True greatness does not flaunt itself in long displays. Rather, it comes in the briefest moments to quickly appear and then submerge itself to shape the tides of time from deep places. In two minutes the speech was over.

Applause followed; the kind of applause that suggested an appreciation for what had been said, while not fully understanding the importance of what had been said. No one knew, really knew the precipice of history that would turn the arch of history from this point forward. Scanning the crowd, there were those who clearly had been moved by Lincoln's words. Others that seemed occupied by the President himself, or with restless children, or the impending cold of the November day. The larger crowd seemed pleased, but seemed to have missed the entire weight of his words in the foreboding complexities of their own existence and a war that had just rolled precariously close to their lives.

Five days from that day, in the November 24th, 1863 edition of The Harrison Patriot and Union Newspaper, the paper would state that Lincoln's speech was filled with "silly remarks" that deserved a "veil of oblivion." Often true greatness is beyond the vision of the average man or the average times. With a humble gesture toward the crowd, Mr. Lincoln made his way back to his chair and remained standing. After a few short remarks the events concluded.

David turned to his great-grandmother and said, "What am I supposed to take away from this? What he said," David indicated pointing to the stage. "What's happening here. Hope, or how to hope in hope? What...?"

"I wonder," his great-grandmother replied as she turned toward David, "If people in your time move far too fast and miss far too much because they do. Waiting can be most rewarding David. So I suggest that you wait."

Some element of anger rose up within David, consuming his attention from greater things afoot for which he must wait. It might have been that the strife involved in 'hoping' for an answer would forge a 'hope' within David capable of handily overcoming any kind of strife that would set itself against him, or the people in a distant future who will be waiting for him.

Working through the crowd, Lincoln made his way off the platform and was lost in the sea of people swirling around him. David stretched to see and stood on tip-toe out of the hope that he might catch one final, fleeting glimpse of this man of sorrow and history. The mass was so thick that any such effort was entirely hopeless. Even Lincoln's great height was lost in the dense sea of swarming people.

David presumed that Lincoln had been shuttled off to his horse and an awaiting train. Turning the cogs of his

272

mind inward, he repeatedly ran the scene over and over and over in order to root it so that recollection of it would forever be clear and not fall tragic victim to some tin-type memory. Turning deep in thought, he stared at the ground and let the events roll through his mind. David was always a man who thought deeply, except in those times when such thought was too painful. Sadly, he had abandoned the depth of his thinking and had long decided it better to stay on the surface as it was less painful. Far less painful. But these trips through time had shaken him back to the core of himself; so he returned to depths abandoned.

As he did, voices in front of him became elevated and increasingly entangled. Yet, they were insufficient to draw him up from the deep strata of thought and wonder that he had returned to. Although they clamored for his attention, they were relegated to the far recesses of a mind amazed and revitalized. And so, they remained muted and indistinct until there was a tug on his coat.

As if swimming up from some deep and murky depth, David abruptly broke the surface of his thoughts and broke into the light of his surroundings. Looking up, Lincoln, the man of stature, height and history stood in directly front of him, poised and commanding, yet soft and gentle. He was exchanging kind words and handshakes with the milling throngs along the way. The man of myth, legend and history whose face was carved on endless edifices stood little more than an arm's length away. David felt his knees weaken and his hands shake.

A tug on his sleeve and his great-grandmother whispered, "It'll be just fine David, don't you worry about a thing. It'll be just fine."

Turning to David's great-grandmother, Lincoln bowed and said, "Young lady, indeed I am in receipt of your many letters. They have moved me and given me great comfort in these most difficult times. Your penmanship and wisdom are far beyond your tender years. Thank you for your kind thoughts."

With a slight curtsy, she said, "You are welcome, Mr. President. The pleasure is mine sir, all mine."

At that point her father interrupted and carried on a brief dialogue with the President; something that sounded like a mix of thanks and encouragement.

When they had concluded, the President lifted his stovepipe hat to his head and leaned forward as if to take a departing step.

"Mr. President," his great-grandmother interrupted, "Mr. President, sir, if you don't mind, I would like you to meet someone before you leave." Turning to David, she slightly gestured and said, "Mr. President, this is my friend David."

"Ah hem," he said clearing his throat. Turning slightly toward David, he said, "Of course, it is indeed a pleasure to meet you David."

David found himself shocked but comfortable knowing that this was an image in time that had no consciousness of him as did all the rest of the people around him. Nonetheless, it was magnificent.

His great, great-grandfather found little amusement in the situation, bearing on his face a somewhat tolerate but wholly uncomfortable smile. Mr. Lincoln removed his hat and gently extended his hand to David. David turned to his great-grandmother, smiled a sort of silly smile and reached toward the President's hand. Suddenly his hand was squeezed tight in the vice of a huge, bony hand. David froze, looked at the hand in disbelief, and then up into the eyes of the President, and then back at the hand of an Illinois lawyer who held his hand impossibly tight.

Returning to the President's face, he leaned forward ever so slightly and intently scanned Lincoln's eyes. They did not pass through David. Instead, they set themselves squarely on David's eyes and seemed to go beyond them to rest themselves in David's very soul. David blinked, squinted and canted his head in confusion. Lincoln followed his every move, smiling at this most confused and uncomfortable man of another century.

"David," the President interrupted, "It is indeed a pleasure to meet you. And I might add, it is always a privilege to meet a man in uniform, though this, I believe is one of another war." Pausing, Lincoln continued, "We only have a moment as my train is waiting as are other pressing matters of state and war." Leaning toward David he said in a subdued voice, "Hope David. You must always hope as the weight of history rests on the shoulders of those who hope. Hope will not fail you. Only you will fail you, and I do not believe that that will be your lot."

With an apparent tear welling in his eye, he stared directly into David's eyes, shifted his comments and continued, "David, you must understand that the most difficult person to extend forgiveness to is ourselves. The second most difficult people to forgive are those who have stolen hope from us in whatever manner that they have performed that most grievous act. Forgive both, and you will discover great hope. Forgive both and in whatever manner things have been torn in two, much like this nation and much like your heart," he said pointing to David's chest, "they can be brought back together." Staring into David's very soul, Lincoln paused, thoughtfully placed his hat on his head, smiled, turned and made his way through the crowd. David stood there aghast, paralyzed and wrapped in a wonderment of the greatest sort.

"Papa," his great-grandmother blurted, "may I have a moment with my friend before we leave?"

"Of course," his great, great-grandfather replied. "I would not want to interrupt such a special friendship."

Taking him aside, his great-grandmother led David out to the edges of the dissipating crowd. His mind was entirely numb, catatonic nearly, but wholly moved, constantly looking back as his great-grandmother gently pulled him forward. Scanning the crowd and attempting to catch a fleeting glimpse of Lincoln and his great-great-grandfather, he stumbled along in a daze of amazement. Finding himself entirely lost in the few minutes of what had just transpired, his great-grandmother led him like a little child swept up in the arms wonder from which he could not come down.

Once they were sufficiently set apart, standing on the edge of wood and field she turned and said, "You are more than I assumed you to be David. You have not disappointed me. Not in any way at all. Rather, you have made me proud." With a reflective pause, she said, "It gives me immeasurable comfort to know that part of me lives in a man as great as you, and that my legacy lives far into what is the future for me, but the present for you."

Squeezing her tiny hand, David said, "Thank you… thank you so much for this, for… for this experience and for what you said and for, for, for all of this," he said looking around. "Thank you so much."

"David," his great-grandmother said, "it's time for you to go. It's time for me to go."

Staring into his great-grandmother's tiny eight-year-old eyes, his eyes turned to the departing crowd disbursing from this monumental moment in history. "Do they know," he muttered.

"Know what, David?" his great-grandmother replied. "That they've just witnessed history. That they've just seen what millions of people would give everything to have seen? Do they know that?"

Turning back to her, she had suddenly and shockingly transformed into a stately woman, aged and graying, but stately. She was sixty, seventy maybe. She was debonair and cultured, draped in a long dress trimmed with lace, edged with tresses and embraced in a wrap made of ornate cotton weave. Wisdom exuded from her eyes and her voice was smooth with the depth of years and experience. David looked up and down her, attempting to take in yet a mind-boggling transition. Smiling in the face of his confusion, she said, "I need to tell you this as the woman I was before I died. I need you to hear this from the woman I became."

She paused, took a breath and said, "What they know David is that this war is not over. What they know is terrible fear and terrifying uncertainty. These are the things that these people know," she said, turning and gazing at the disbursing mass of simple people. "But my dear David, my great-grandson" she said squeezing his hands with tears welling up in her eyes. "What I know is this… and what I want you to know is this… there is always hope. Even here, with this terrible war raging on out there, there remains hope. Death, death of the vilest sort was in this place, here," she said pointing in a slow circular sweep. "All around us. But now, now hope is all around us."

Catching her breath, she looked intently into David's eyes and said, "Even with the terrible war raging within you, there is hope... and it's all around you. And David, in the world that you will soon return to, a world that's turned sour and stale, a world with roads divided and all but ruined, there is still hope. Forgive yourself and forgive those who have hurt you. Forgive David and what is torn completely in two can come back together again as if it had never been torn at all. And those things that have been so badly torn can go on and be healed so thoroughly that they cannot ever remember being torn. That's what hope and forgiveness can do David."

Taking the Bible from David's hands, she pulled out the fourth page. Handing it to him, she said, "Read this." Scanning the page, he looked back at his great-grandmother who again pointed to the page and said, "Read."

The script was somewhat educated, but simple nonetheless. David began to read:

"The Army chaplain came six days ago. Right then and there I knew what that meant, especially during these times of war. It was fate coming to my door. I fell to my knees before he got to the door because right there everything went out of me. He was a kindly man, helping me to my feet and getting me to a chair. I haven't gotten it all straight in my head yet, but Billy's gone. The kind of gone that has to wait for eternity's reunion.

"So I'm sitting in this store and can't figure out how to go on. Too much has been taken to go on. Thought about selling out and doing something less difficult. Get a job that I can do on my own without all the demands of running this place.

"But then I started thinking, as I sometimes do on these kinds of occasions, that I got everything that I need to make this work. I got the store, and the stock, and the customers, but most important I got the memories of Billy. Started realizing that with hope you can always go on regardless of how much you have to go on without. Don't need to consider what I lost. Hope doesn't keep that kind of tally because hope by itself is more than I'll ever need. Hope says no loss is too big that hope can't handily replace it. Hope just says that it can be done when you don't think it can. I'm beginning to think I can. So starting today, I'm believing it can be done. Right now I'm building this store and my future on hope because that's enough.

Mabel Bauman

June 20th, 1944"

"Never forget the words of our most admirable President. Never forget what happened here," she said pointing out to the thinning masses of people. "Never forgot the words you just read. I love you my precious grandson. I so do love you."

"I love you too," David responded with a voice breaking and tears streaming.

With that, she took David's hand, turned it palm down and said, "Goodbye David, many are countin' on you. I'm countin' you." With that she pressed David's palm to the paper.

Chapter 15
A General Store
Giving Hope to Oneself

Among life's many oddities, one is the simple reality that what we can readily extend to others we have great difficulty extending to ourselves. We can be fully convinced of something on the behalf of another but have no conviction that it applies to us or that we are deserving of whatever it might be. Others are seen as worthy recipients of life's best, yet we do not place ourselves in the same category; settling it seems for rotting pabulum and life's discarded scraps. What can be for others isn't necessarily something that can be for us.

Of these many things that we easily extend to others, hope seems predominant. There always seems to be ample room to extend a spirited hope to others. Yet, hope is a precious jewel that we ourselves are unworthy to hold and entirely too incompetent to integrate into the dank hopelessness of our own existence. There are many things that we can believe for others, but far less that we can believe for ourselves. In the scheme of life, believing in hope for ourselves is the second most difficult to believe in. The first is yet to come.

Just as it had happened upon his arrival, his great-grandmother and the scattered masses of people began to dissipate much like smoke in a listless breeze, sweetly succumbing to the winds of time passing. Groupings here and there evaporated in like manner until the entire mass of people evaporated into history, leaving the landscape entirely clear and completely intact.

The voices disseminated in just the same way, the background noise of the crowd growing dim long after the people disappeared, leaving a few scant and scattered conversations until they too dissipated into silence. All that was left were the sounds of nature, being the same here on this November day in 1863 as they were in the 21st century along a road of Indians, horse and heavy wagon. It reminded David that while time may pass, and while both culture and technology may change in ways unthinkable, the strivings and longings of the human drama remain entirely unchanged in the changing.

In the span of a few moments nothing was left except an empty field with skeletal trees embroidering the landscape. As he watched, the landscape slowly transformed itself, with rolling hills leveling out a bit and distant trees gradually bearing the leaves of summer instead of the stark nakedness of November. A few trees filled in here and there. A forest found its place to his distant left with a split rail fence edging it to the horizon. The sky warmed to a lustrous blue with a few cottony clouds bathing in the warmth of a golden, morning sun.

As the scene took shape, David once again wondered if this would be his trip back to the farmhouse. He had previously presumed that he had fully learned what these events were attempting to teach him, assuming that the lessons of history were complete and that he would be deposited back in his time with lessons well in hand. Yet, he had also learned that when we presume to know something, we likely only know the barest essence of that thing even though we presume the fullest understanding. Arrogance is far too rogue and presumptuous, while humility is wise and cautious. And so while the landscape became mysteriously familiar, it was not the farmhouse.

The sound of birds moved in with the whisper of a summer's breeze playfully calling from the canopies of giant oaks, broad ashes and muscular maples. Several fields unhurriedly came into view, each rolling off to forested edges. Each were slowly etched with precise furrows cut in the thick loamy soil, gradually filling in with the greenery of hearty young crops of corn and beans stretching themselves awake in the mid-western sun. Within a moment it was all sharp and stunningly clear.

Suddenly, behind him, the sound of a slow and monotonous dinging met his ears… calling out over and over and over. It was the one sound that had not been replicated anywhere else in his life. Some things find a place in many places. And then there are those most rare things that find their place in only one place. Turning, David realized that somehow, someway he was at the back of aunt Mabel's old general store. Past or present, he wasn't sure for it never changed much even after aunt Mabel sold it so many years ago. Yet, the sound of the old gas pump around the front filling the tractors and trucks of common folk caused his heart to leap and his spirit to soar in ways long forgotten, yet never forsaken.

Despite the inexpressible spectacle of them, David had become strangely familiar with these mindboggling leaps in time. Some things are so implausibly grand that they handily wrestle our unbelief, easily pinning it to the mat of belief. One of the greatest goals of all is to recognize the commonality of the grand that only appears uncommon because it is missed by the ignorance of our souls turned

281

sour. And it is to understand that the grand things in life do not extend invitations only to the privileged few who hold some elevated status, but that all are privileged.

It is not that these things had taken on something of a diminishing commonness for David. Rather, grandness will not in any way be weakened by time or exposure or anything else that renders all lesser things quickly mediocre and instantly bland. In fact, things grand can only be diminished by our attitude of them. Even in such sad places they are not in fact diminished at all, as it is only our appreciation of them that is diminished.

If we wish to identify the truly great things in life, we can identify them by the fact that no matter how much we are exposed to them or how often we're privileged to engage them, they remain great despite what our perception of them might do to them. Such things are great solely of their own accord and not because of any status we might grant them or any element we might errantly believe ourselves able to add to them. This distinction became ever clearer to David, helping him see that many things are good, but only a handful are great. Yet something inordinately deep within him suggested that at more times than we realize 'good' might actually be 'great' in disguise.

He stood for a moment, soaking up the scene in the miracle of a man gone young again. Closing his eyes tight and inhaling the dense sweetness of summer afoot, he went back to a place he had always wished he'd never left, reclaiming something that in reality had never left him even though he had thought it had. It represented everything that he had rigorously and rather feverishly attempted to replicate along the road of his life. Yet, replicating suggested that he had lost it. He hadn't... at all. Rather, he had believed it burned to smoky ash among the cinders of a soul brunt to the ground. As he was yet to learn, hope is fire-proof.

Something indefinable gained a steady momentum and then swelled with him, rising and then blowing out the soul of himself. Suddenly he was ruptured awake; wide awake in a way that gives being awake an entirely new definition. David's eyes shot open and with a fascination borne of a longing too long disappointed he realized that he was in fact here, in this place of deep sanctuary and priceless memory. This was no longer cherished memory. This was hard reality. And maybe this time, he need not ever leave it or it leave him.

David turned in fascinated circles, drawing in the whole of everything around him like some child caught in the arms of a summer's day. Old wooden soda containers, deeply weathered by time and use were stacked in less than perfect piles around back, scrawled with fading print reading Pepsi, Coke-a-Cola, Fanta, and Sprite. Their contents likely filled the old fifteen cent soda machine that was sitting inside, if indeed this was David's past. The Babcock dairy sign with the familiar smiling cow graced the front corner of the building. Out front, a metal Sinclair gas sign hung on a study metal frame, gently swinging in a slight Michigan breeze. The old light fixture hung from the corner of the building, securely fastened to the peeling clapboard corner of the store. For some reason it was always painted a drab, olive green. It's expansive round metal cover was slightly canted, shielding a single, bare light bulb from the Michigan weather.

The scene began set itself more firmly in time. What looked to be a 1958 Chevy pick-up with it's distinctively short bed and bulbous wheel-wells gingerly rolled out of the store's gravel drive and bounced off down the dirt road leaving a trailing wisp of thinning dust in it's wake. It gradually disappeared as the road rolled out of the reach of farm fields and meandered into the distant woods. Parked just around the front of the store, the rear of a 1961 Ford Falcon Station wagon with it's wide-eyed tail lights was just visible from where David had found himself. Its passengers apparently about the business of buying groceries or renewing friendships inside the store.

This was, as David increasingly suspected, the store of his youth. Of any place that time had transported him, this was the childhood place liberally sprinkled with magic and doused heavy with fathomless mystery. He knew that he could spend forever in this place without even so much as an ounce of regret in missing anything that staying here might cause him to miss. At times we find ourselves altogether willing to forsake our futures if we could trade them for some cherished place in our pasts. What we forget is that the past is not a place to live. Rather, it is the place that gives us what we need to live more robustly in a present that will become an even more magical past if we let it be so.

David hadn't run in years. However, something boyish came over him, as if being here returned him to that romping child of so many years ago. Running around the clapboard side of the building, he suddenly caught a glimpse of the front of the store. Stepping back, he saw it all exactly the way he had as a boy. It was all there; the sight, the smells, the sounds, the aroma of soft earth and forest scents combining in a glorious bouquet intermingled with the slight smell of gasoline and a wisp of dust stirred up from the road. The storefront was littered with handmade signs and the décor of a culture that was much more concerned with being a community and much less concerned with turning a dollar. It was his favorite place of childhood; the place of warm and misty memory that was everything magical and all things good.

Some magical force had physically transported David to this place. Except for the old farmhouse, which in retrospect was really the one before the fire, all the other places had been places within which none of his own history existed. He had no connection to Normandy or

Gettysburg. He'd never been there, except maybe through lineage and genealogy or a handful of cloudy photos. His history had not been penned in the cramped confines of a barracks awaiting an invasion, or on the sprawling expanse of those November fields. The pages upon which to write the story of his life had not even existed in those places. The footprints of his journey did not litter those roads.

But this time, his history in this place was profusely penned and his footprints were to be found everywhere. Unlike the other three times, it seemed that something more of his soul had been transported here as well. Sure, his soul was in those other places. Of course. But this was a coming home to the home that rested at the very center of his heart both then and now. This was not the history of someone else that he was to intersect for the first time, although that was not entirely true. This was David intersecting his own history a second time. Here again! This was David going back to himself in a colossal loop that would bring him face to face with himself at the time that he was at most a peace with himself; most of the time anyway.

Standing there, watching the Michigan summer listlessly dance in the fields, here he was swept up in an unparalleled excitement. Holding out both arms as if to draw the whole of it into himself, he realized this is what he had lost. This is what the scourge and pain of life had ripped away. This is what the scarring had told him didn't really exist; that in the carnage of life, all of this that surrounded him was the muse of childhood and the hope of the ignorant. That when pain beset us, it would become the resident evil that no amount of energy or prayer or determination of the most determined sort could ever hope to cast out.

Betrayal had stared David in the face and shouted in words cold, cynical and bellicose that life was a marriage destroyed and children stolen. Nothing more. Nothing more ever. "What did you expect?" betrayal seemed to shout.

Shrilly snickering at him, betrayal dared him to be so foolish as to believe in Michigan landscapes. The chill of its corrosive breath demanded that he bend the muse of childhood in order to accept the reality that the bloodied landscape in his heart was all that there ever was, and all that would ever be. How many times he had sat in his office, staring out at a dispirited maze of concrete and asphalt, asking himself if this place of soft fields and sturdy forests was ever really real.

But, here it was. Here it was! The general store and the old dirt road that tenderly knit field, forest and rural folks together. Somehow David knew, or began to know that the road in his heart could likewise be knit back together. No road is ever so destroyed that it is lost to the journey of those who walk in hope. Scanning the old dirt road up and down, David became entirely absorbed in the embrace of such wonderful feelings. For all practical purposes, David never wanted to leave it again. Ever. Yet, the things that are within you are things that are always within you whether or not you remain in the place that put them there.

Suddenly, something of his past, or what would be his future grabbed him. Pain would not easily surrender to gentle Michigan summers. Quite unexpectedly David was met with a frigid trepidation that seemed entirely out of place, especially in this place. Something rushed up beside him and whispered, "What if the voice of betrayal is right," it said. "What if it's true? What if all of this doesn't matter? What if it's all going to end badly because we don't have the power to have it end any other way? What if there is no hope, even here?" David froze. Treads of pain suddenly began knitting a despondent patchwork of discouragement in and through him.

His mind wandered, stepping away from the hope bound tight in the fields, farms and a clapboard general store. *What if the memories of this place were really my imagination?* he thought. *What if, what if I was just a kid who really didn't understand what life was about, so this, all of this looked magical when it wasn't?* Turning and running a trembling hand over the clapboard side of the general store, he pondered, *what if I made this out in my head to be something that I wanted it to be because I didn't know any better? I was just a kid. What if this is not what I've always counted on it being?* Stepping away from the store and scanning the sweeping fields of corn and beans he began to panic and thought, *Please. No. Oh no! What am I going to do if this, if this is more imagination than anything else? How do I live... how will I live without this?*

This marvelous place of sweet refuge had so often held David fast against the tyranny of betrayal. In the midst of a present that repeatedly assaulted him bloodied and black he returned to a past that repeatedly nurtured him healed and whole. This place told him what life could be when the life David was living was everything it shouldn't be. It grounded him. It said that death of a marriage or a family or anything else was just the end of something making space for the beginning of something else. Even though David had never recognized it, such was the essence of hope. Such was the essence of this place.

Up to this point in his life, David was able to relish the past at will without having to challenge the accuracy of it simply because he couldn't come back here as an adult to determine what it really was. It remained tenderly preserved with the jaded acumen of adulthood held at bay... until now. Until this moment he had been at complete liberty to edit the past with lines of sweet prose that never had to be challenged because he was not here as an adult to do that. He could make it whatever he needed it to be to offset a present that was killing him. It had become his sole place of refuge all of those many times when the roads of adulthood had offered him none.

And now that precious past, that singular place of desperately needed refuge might succumb to the horribly divesting scrutiny of adulthood. It was pure magic to be here. But being here now might forever jeopardize his ability to ever retreat to it again. Until now, this had been his one safe place in a world that was not. And now, standing in the middle of the place that had painted those assuring memories across the canvas of his soul, the whole of it fell into jeopardy. The whole of it.

Yet, there are those moments when what we stand to lose is greater than the pain that threatens to take it. There are those critical crossroads when we find ourselves standing facing certain surrender only being certain that we must refuse such a surrender. Much like that critical moment in the basement some days ago when David stepped beyond the confines of the finite to embrace the infinite, we say "no" to what demands a "yes." And here, for the second time, David reached down into that bit of the infinite within him and said "no."

David believed in what he was in this place so many years ago. Once again seizing the strength that it had given him over and over during terribly dark days in those terribly dark places, he forced his belief. He breathed it alive. He believed, becoming wildly enamored in believing. He believed in dreams and in all that is good. He believed in dirt roads and in the warmth of rural farm folk tilling the soil until their hands were blessed by a harvest and their tables filled with all things good.

He believed that uncle Bill died embracing hope, and that Lincoln walked it out to the end of a war and the end of his life. He believed that his grandfather found hope after a fire, and his great-grandmother held onto it even as a war brushed by her front porch. He believed to the point that anything but belief was simply not possible.

And in embracing the belief reborn of childhood and gentle Michigan summers, David realized that what he was feeling was nothing of childhood at all; at least what we attribute childhood as being. Whatever this was, it was something much, much more. This wasn't naiveté, or immaturity, or a soul yet unseasoned by life. This wasn't the muse of story-tellers spinning fanciful tales of places both magical and mystical. This wasn't bedtime stories or being tucked in bed by loving hands. Not at all. Childhood was, in fact, a place with eyes marvelously unsoiled by the assaults of a world gone mad. Therefore, they can see what adult eyes cannot. And because we as adults cannot see what children see, we are quick to write off their descriptions to the play of muse and imagination, when in reality what they see is real beyond our imagination.

This wasn't immaturity. This was iridescent lucidity. This wasn't life uninformed. This was life that was supposed to inform. This was the essential essence of childhood. And this precious essence was intentionally crafted by a brilliant God for the sole purpose of importing it into our lives as adults so that the arduous rigors of adulthood might be handily overcome by the hope granted of childhood. Yet, we leave this gift behind because we errantly assume that the task adulthood is to leave childhood. We could not be more wrong.

Suddenly at some indefinable level he realized that was why he was here. Only a moment ago he came so close to missing this realization. But the child within him had done what that part of ourselves is designed to do. It had reached out and pulled him back from the edge of such a devastating choice. Rather than leave childhood in the pursuit of adulthood, he was to bring all of this, every part of this... the store, the fields, the forests, the rural farm folk with their folksy tales... every piece was to come with him into his future. He had brought parts of it before, thank God. And those parts had saved him more times than he could count. But now, now that he was actually here, he could bring the whole of it back. Imagine what doing that would do! Imagine how that would change his life! Imagine everything being different, because that's what would happen. Imagine the hope birthed of such a choice!

Shaking, with tears rolling down his cheeks he held out his arms and shouted, "Thank you, dear God, thank you for bringing me here... twice! Thank you!"

David suddenly became everything that he had lost so long ago. Instantly. He was everything he had become over the years, now shaped and reshaped by everything he had been in this place. Too often we lose what we cannot afford to lose because it wasn't deemed real in the first place. Therefore, we foolishly let it go. And sometimes, in these most rare and magical moments its not that the roads of our lives are repaired when we take those things back. It's that we're repaired sufficiently to take those roads up again despite the nature of them.

David breathed deeply, smiled even more deeply, and let all that was this place consume all that he was. In doing so, it was about to give him all that he is.

After a moment of reflection, David turned and looked at the old general store; scanning it up and down. He found himself afraid to go into it, fearing that it might not be the way he remembered it, or that he might fall so wonderfully in love with it all over again that leaving it for another leap in time would simply be too much for him to ever bear again. There are those places in our lives that we'd gladly go back to, and in the going we would forever forfeit ever leaving them again despite whatever we might be leaving in our present. Of course, none of us would understand what it would be like to consider such a choice, except that is, for David. The fact of the matter is; he did not understand such a choice either. Not fully.

Despite the pain and loss in life, despite the betrayal and caustic realities of people willing to sacrifice others for their own sordid gains, despite a world deteriorating and cheering its own toxicity daily under some legitimizing banner of progressive thinking; despite it all, this place never lost any wonder and never fell to any of those vices. This place remained insulated when everything else and everyone else did not. Quite the opposite, the more that the world betrayed him the more sacred and safe this place of his childhood became. And now here he was. Believe it or not, here he was.

"Got yer soda and mint candy," came a familiar voice.

David jumped as his mind raced, triggered into some sort of dizzying emotional freefall by the all too familiar voice.

Pausing as if waiting for an answer, the voice said, "Well, are ya comin' in or not?"

Turning and looking up, it was aunt Mabel. Not the aunt Mabel of dementia and nursing homes. Not the aunt Mabel of wildly bizarre phone calls and irritatingly weird comments. Not the aunt Mabel that everyone was waiting to die out of a sense that she would be freed from her dementia, and the remaining family would be freed from the effects of her dementia. Not that aunt Mabel at all.

What stood before him was the aunt Mabel of strength, vigor and uncanny country wisdom. Standing before him was the gristle-like woman shaped by country living, hardened by great loss, chiseled by determination, yet blended soft by an unparalleled appreciation for life. Her powder-blue checkered dress was partly hidden by a full length white bib-apron draped around her neck and tied firmly around her waist. Enough of the dress extended below the apron to be gingerly caught by a slight breeze that caused the hem of the dress to flutter around her stocky knees. Somewhat short, but husky in a manner that didn't diminish her femininity, it all granted her a compelling vitality.

Holding a frosty vanilla soda and an assortment of mint candies was the aunt Mabel with that flair of dry humor, quiet wisdom, fathomless patience and endless energy. She had grown deep through the death of uncle Bill twenty-five years earlier, and she had grown broad by running the general store to meet her meager needs and keep a close-knit community close-knit.

David desperately attempted to correlate who she was in his time verses who she was standing holding on old screen door open with soda and candy in hand. It was another person, but it was the same person all at the same paradoxical time.

"Come on boy," she said, "I'm lettin' all the flies in."

With that David stepped forward, cast a long and rather perplexed glance at her, took hold of the screen door and watched aunt Mabel as she sauntered into the old general store. She casually walked behind the counter and plopped the soda and candy down.

It was as if his relationship with her, in this time, had never stopped at all. David had been thrust back and forth over centuries of time with the abruptness being startling and entirely unfathomable. Yet, this time it all seemed seamless, as if he was picking up right where he left off without losing a single step in the process. Sometimes we become so identified with a time in our lives that that time becomes timeless. Sometimes time cannot sweep wonderful places and people into the backwater of our own histories because the preciousness of those places and those people refuses to be swept away. In places like this, the road of life is not defined by demarcations. Rather, it's entirely fluid and connected. Such was this place and this time.

"I'm, like, I live in the future. I'm guessing you know that... like everyone else knew that," David said with some degree of confidence that still had an element of confusion stitched in and around it.

"I know what I know," she said, "which is just shy of what I don't need to know." She turned and leaned on the counter.

"Okay," David replied in a somewhat quizzical tone. "You still have the best comebacks, don't you?" he said with a smile.

"Nothin' like a comeback for someone who's 'come back'," she said while shaking her head in amusement at herself.

David found the connection with aunt Mabel as immediate. She had always been a part of his life for the whole of his life. Those listless summer days as a kid here at the store. Christmas and other family gatherings where the adults would go about the rather serious business of playing cards and talking politics while aunt Mabel would sneak off to play with the kids. Her thick cut pumpkin pies and deep scalloped potato casseroles. The cards that came every birthday with ten dollars lovingly tucked in them. Her kisses on the cheek which marked both her arrival and departure every time she would visit. Such was aunt Mabel.

"Look the same?" aunt Mabel said with an inflection that already knew the answer even before the question was asked. Standing up and wiping her hands on her apron, she stared up with a wily grin of knowing anticipation.

"What?... ah, yeah... yeah... actually it does. It looks exactly the same," David replied. "Exactly... the same. Thank God it does. Thank God."

"I thank God everyday," aunt Mabel replied. "Everyday. Mornin' and night. Weren't for Him, this place wouldn't be here," she said with a tone rich with thankfulness.

At that most magical moment, he found talking to be entirely too cumbersome and far too intrusive. His mind was flooded with sweet memory and magical wonder. He continued to turn in rotating circles, taking in the whole of the store; every nook and cranny, every counter and sign.

"It's exactly the same," he said again, reaching out and touching the old soda machine as some old friend.

"Well, that's 'cause it is," aunt Mabel said wiping a counter again and moving sordid items around, "Jest the same. Jest the same 'cause no time's passed for it to change into anything other than what it is. Thought about doin' some upgrades and such, but sometimes improvements are really detractions. Sometimes goin' forward is really goin' backwards, although most people don't see it that way."

David knew that. For him, the clock had been abruptly thrown back some four decades and more. But for this place, the second hand of time had methodically ticked off the seconds of time without any such alteration of time. It was entirely the same because it had never changed.

David slowly moved through the tiny aisles, stopping to look at items long-gone in the 21st century. Candy and gum long relegated to the dusty archives of history sat in neat stacks. Sugar Mama's Candy Bars. Beechnut Gum. Butternut Candy Bars. There were soaps and canned goods and various cereals that had been carelessly lost in the culture's pell-mell race into an ill-defined future of processed foods and processed thinking. Sugar Pops. Crispy Critters. Nabisco Ginger Snaps.

The old soda machine sported glass bottles that were pulled out of a glass door once a meager fifteen cents had been inserted. Coca-Cola. Sparkling Orange Soda. Veep. Fanta.

"Don't have that where you came from, do ya?" aunt Mabel said.

"Ah, no, not anymore," David mumbled as he held a loaf of Wonder Bread realizing how cool it was to have something without a 'best when used by' date on it.

"Sad as it is, seems that the good always goes and gets replaced by something a whole lot less than good," Aunt Mabel replied as she rearranged items in the old glass case. "Just seems we discard too much good in tryin' to make things better. Maybe we should just enjoy what we got without always thinkin' about what we don't."

Walking over to the glass case behind which aunt Mabel stood, he asked, "So, how much do you know about where I came from?"

"Nothin'," she replied while continuing to arrange various boxes and articles of goods. "Nothin' at all. Not mine to know. Don't want to know. Hasn't happened yet so we'll jest let it happen in its own sweet time." Pausing while continuing to work, she said, "All I know is that yer here 'cause there's something you need to get here 'cause its needed in yer time. Don't necessarily understand how all this works, but I found out a long time ago that it ain't worth questioning great things."

David found her statements odd. Grandpa, uncle Bill and great-grandmother Donna all had some knowledge of their future. But not aunt Mabel. Maybe it was hidden from aunt Mabel because seeing a future of dementia and nursing homes would be too much. Or knowing that the general store would be squeezed out of existence by the larger chain stores that would eventually bring the demise of these precious places of commerce and community. Or knowing that she would outlive most of the family, which means she'd be attending more funerals than any one person should ever have to attend. And that when it was all said and done, she'd be largely alone.

Maybe, David pondered, *That's why we don't know our futures. Maybe if we knew what was coming we'd mess with our lives so much that the very thing that life is calling us to do is the very thing we'd screw up.*

The sultry Michigan breeze floated in through the screen door, wafted about the general store and waltzed out the back door at the rear of aunt Mabel's small attached home, keeping everything fresh and entirely alive in the warm wash of summer. In his mind, David went back to his own childhood, finding himself experiencing the wonder of it all both as part of his past and now part of his present; something like double the wonder.

Next to the cash register he spied the calendar. It was turned over to June, 1969.

"I was ten" David muttered to himself. "I was ten. Aunt Mabel…" he began to say as several customers walked in.

"Howdy fellas," she said.

"Howdy Mabel" they replied with great vigor and energy.

"Be right there," she said. The customers strolled through the store apparently oblivious to David, which by this time he had become quite accustomed to but nonetheless amazed by.

A weathered farmer embellished with the sweet smell of soil and earth and worn overhauls strolled up to David and looked directly at him, giving David the sense that for some reason this was one of those people who actually might see him. The farmer then extended a calloused hand that effortlessly slipped through David's left arm and retrieved a pack of gum from the counter.

"Nope," Aunt Mabel quipped, "He doesn't see you 'cause for him you ain't here."

"What?" The earthy farmer replied as he moved to the back of the store.

"Oh, nothin' Fred. Just a talkin'. I got new stock of flour," she said pointing him to the back of the store. "Yer wife was awaitin' for that."

"Thanks," he said, meandering down the aisle. "She'll be glad to git that. Get some good baking done, she will."

Behind David, out a window framed of darkened oak and wavy glass, the head of a young boy went by, heading toward the back of the house. The crunch of bicycle tires on gravel loam came to a stop.

"Guess what," aunt Mabel whispered to David, motioning him with her finger. "There's someone who's here and who's on the back steps waitin' to meet you." With a wily wink, she motioned David to the back. Walking into her tiny attached home aunt Mabel turned to David and said, "Sometimes we're the hardest people to convince; ourselves I mean. It's easy to spout all kinds of good things to others and tellin' 'em that it's true and all. But the hardest person to convince is us. Specially when it comes to hope," aunt Mabel said while picking up an item here and placing something there. "It's downright easy to tell others that there's always hope, but we don't hear that for ourselves... kinda goes in one ear and out the other. It'd do us a world of good to listen to ourselves."

David listened intently but somewhat haphazardly, trying to make sense of whatever this was, realizing by now that it made sense, but that he didn't quite get it anyway. Then, out of the corner of his consciousness he heard a cough and detected a slight movement. Turning to look out the back of the small house to the screen door at the very back, he spied the back of a small boy dressed in a faded striped shirt. Sitting on the weathered back steps, he seemed to have his legs drawn up and was holding them tight to a tiny chest. His hair was cropped short. The striped shirt was draped over a small pair of shoulders not having yet borne the adversities of life. Boney arms emerged from short sleeves, wrapping themselves around his legs and drawing them tightly to his chest. His attention seemed to be out in the fields and forest that rolled out back behind the general store.

"Who's the kid?" David asked. Sometimes the greatest things escape us at the very point when it seems impossible that they should be able to do so.

Completely side-stepping the question, aunt Mabel said, "Well, that's part of why yer here. That boy there, that boy out there..." she said pointing, "you need to go tell that boy about hope. That ten-year-old don't know much about hope right now. It's certain he needs some in his life here and how, but later on in that little life he's really gonna need it." Reflectively she said, "He's strugglin' a bit with pain that you might know somethin' about. So you git on out there and give that youngin' a reason to hope." As she passed through the door back into the general store, she turned and said, "And he'll see, he'll see you right to the heart. That's how he'll see you. So show him somethin' real. Be genuine, if you know what I mean."

"I'm not a kid counselor," David said.

"You are today," aunt Mabel shot back over her shoulder as she wiped her hand on her apron and walked back out into the store.

Suddenly, David was left entirely alone in aunt Mabel's small house. Some scrawny kid on the back steps. Having to talk about hope to some farm kid. That was odd. *Weird*, David thought.

Then the scent of history living in the moment swirled all around him. Faded black and white photos of other bygone days littered the walls, hanging canted as if they were warmly comfortable with themselves; inviting the casual passerby who decided that they no longer wanted to live life casually.

Suddenly drawn in, his attention was irresistibly moved away from the boy to the photos. *They're the same,* he thought. *Exactly the same.* The same but different. Walking up to them, he scanned the potpourri of photographs, finding himself drawn to the rather large photo that he immediately recognized. Squinting, contorting his face and canting his head, he pointed and mumbled, "That's Gettysburg."

"Yup," came the voice of aunt Mabel who had somehow slipped back into the room and stood just over his left shoulder. "Must be real odd to be lookin' at a picture that's pert-near a hundred years old, give or take a year, and realizing that you just came from there."

Immediately turning to aunt Mabel, David said, "How'd you know that?"

"Past is past," she said. "It's written and all. Future's not."

Marginally satisfied, David turned back to the photos. "You have no idea how this feels… nobody has any idea, I'm not sure I have an idea." David said under his breath. "That's just how it looked," he said. "Just like that. Exactly like that. In fact, I stood right, over, there," he said pointing to a place near the stage. "Right there."

Scanning the wall of photos as if looking for something of inestimable worth, he stumbled upon a photo of a young soldier standing at attention, yet radiating a warm smile that could only come from the fields and forest of Michigan.

"Uncle Bill," David gasped leaning into the photo and running his fingers around its frame. "Uncle Bill… Uncle Bill."

After a long pause of scanning the floor and then looking back up at the photo and scanning the floor again, he abruptly turned to aunt Mabel and said, "I know how he…"

Before he could get another word out, she placed a soft finger over his lips, drew close to David and said, "Not mine to know David. Not mine to know. Not now anyway… sometimes we're not supposed to know 'cause life's got another plan in it all."

At times we know that something's right even though we don't necessarily know it's right. This was one of those times. And so, David let it go even though he was desperate to tell her. "I understand," he replied.

"What's this?" David asked, pointing to a faded bookmark sandwiched into the frame that held uncle Bill's photograph. Stitched into its cloth backing in small but sweeping letters it read, "When all other hope fails, hope in God never fails."

"He carried that onto Normandy with him," she said, "Which kinda speaks to what it says… if ya know what I mean." She paused to collect her thoughts and then continued. "I always kinda thought that whatever mankind hopes in other than God is gonna fail ya sooner or later. Even such a great cause as the war, 'cause it was a great cause; even though it might fail the people who believed in it the most. We won the war, but tyranny goes on; always will. But yer uncle Bill, that man believed in God in a way that makes my belief look pretty small sometimes. Outright tiny."

With tears welling the corners of his eyes, David said, "I saw that in him. I saw something in him that I wished I had; that thing that makes you a remarkable person. I mean, in everything he said. I didn't recognize it until you just explained that. But now I see it." Pausing, he turned toward aunt Mable and said, "That's the key right? An invasion of hope is what he said."

Caught in thought, he continued, "Of course. An invasion that's of God can't be stopped by anything." Pausing and holding the bookmark, David said, "That's the key to a remarkable person, you know, the kind of person that can live above the world and all the stuff that's going on in the world, even all the stuff's that going on right in front of him."

"Even right inside of him," aunt Mabel chimed in.

Suddenly, as if embracing some priceless truth that might slip away through the folds of his soul, he held his head in his hands, he said, "An invasion of God is an invasion of hope... I gotta remember that, I gotta remember that."

Sometimes in life we're given a life-altering vision; the kind of insight that changes everything that we know in a manner that everything we knew is entirely supplanted in some grand sweep of some kind. But, sometimes before that happens, it just kind of needs to percolate a bit because integrating too much right away might keep us from really understanding just how big that insight is. And sometimes life has a few more things to add to that insight to make it as grand as it really is, or maybe even grander. And so, right there, life turned David away for a moment to ponder that message so that it might ponder him. Carefully, he placed the bookmark back in the picture frame.

Turning back to the wall he scanned the clustered conglomeration of photos. Instantly he spied a picture of the old farmhouse with a bright young man and a tidy young woman standing astride the gaping front porch.

"Grandpa," David gasped. "Grandpa! I met him. He looked just, just like that. Exactly. Same clothes, I think," he said as he pointed at the photo and turned back to aunt Mabel. "Just like that! I heard grandma's voice, but I didn't meet her. That voice that I heard, that voice looks exactly like her… I mean if a voice had a face that would be hers… that would totally be hers."

"Remember what he told you David?" said aunt Mabel softly and a bit reflectively.

"Remember?" Falling inside of himself for a moment David attempted to collect himself, nodded his head and said, "Yeah, yeah I do."

"Well David," aunt Mabel replied, "that's what that boy out on the back steps needs to hear right about now. Same thing. Same exact thing right there. You're holdin' inside yourself what that child needs right now, and what he'll need four decades from now." Turning, taking a step and casting a glance out to the back steps, aunt Mabel drew down inside of herself and said, "He needs it right now, but he'll need it a whole bunch more when he's all grown up. So git out there and give him hope."

Chapter 16
A General Store
Giving Yourself Yourself

Life doesn't afford us the opportunity to step back into time and tell ourselves all of the things that we've learned over time. It seems that that sort of thing would be a priceless privilege. It would be marvelous to be able to grace our younger selves with all of the wisdom and experience that we garnered from the years we've lived before we actually live those years. In fact, that wisdom and experience might have served us better back then than how it serves us now only because our younger selves were in greater need of it. Therefore, we might have appreciated it more. On the flip side however, we may have well rejected it because we didn't have the maturity to embrace it. Regardless, bringing all of that back around to ourselves so that we can tread the path of our lives a second time blessed with those magnificent insights would be rich beyond measure.

Yet facing ourselves in that way, or in any way really, may in reality be the most daunting thing that we could ever do. To do that in a worthy manner, we would of necessity find ourselves forced to confess to ourselves all of our pathetic failures, the sordid details of our selfish exploits, the degradation and shame of our foolish and sometimes cavalier choices, and all of the things we've done that have irreparably wasted so many years of our lives. For, if we're really going to give ourselves the best of ourselves, we have to be honest with the worst of ourselves. And the one thing of many that we would likely have to confess was that somewhere along the way we abandoned hope at the very place and time when we shouldn't have.

Aunt Mabel had gone back into the store to respond to a handful of customers that had meandered up the sleepy road and passed through the old screen door. The animated conversation floated in from the tight aisles and from his past all at the amazing same time. David became lost in the memories of this place. Since having been transported here, he had not had sufficient time to stop, reflect and immerse himself in this most cherished place.

How many times had he longed to come back here? How many times had he sat at his desk somewhere in the 21st century, decades in the future from where he now stood, and found himself lost in the memories of this very place? How many times had he walked its well stocked aisles, run out to pump gas for a friendly farmer, constructed forts out of the empty soda containers, and walked the hedgerows of the adjacent wooded wonderland? How many times had he flushed pheasants and tracked deer? How many times did he grieve over the feeling that such times were forever lost to both him and the country itself? How many times?

Standing inside of aunt Mabel's small clapboard home, with the sweet sounds of simple people celebrating life by exchanging their lives filtering in from the front of store, with the tepid breeze of a Michigan summer floating out of the back, the memories that he always thought were so clear became ever clearer. For every second that passed the memories became strikingly cleaner, wildly richer and increasingly more robust to the point that David was living that time as a child again. He was back here, back in this exact place, not as an adult etching off the hash marks of his late fifties on distant river-rock fence. But as a child visiting something as if he had never left that place in the first place.

It's one thing to have memories as we all have reams of them. It's one thing to have memories, but it's another thing altogether to revisit those memories and in the revisiting actually return to live in the very places and with the very people from which those memories were birthed. It is a gift indeed to seize the sweetness of memories cherished, particularly those deemed forever lost to the backwaters of time, and have them surge to life after they were thought to be irreparably drown in those same backwaters. It's an entirely different thing to have those memories refreshed to a vivid vitality that far exceeds the original memory simply because we're privileged to live it again with the keener eyes of maturity combined with a previous recollection that inexplicably embellishes the experience of it the second time around.

Slowly, David realized that out back on those wooden steps, the young boy was talking. It was one of those leisurely realizations where we unconsciously know that we're not hurried, that whatever's asking for our attention is patient enough to wait for it; that time is going to taking nothing from us in the waiting. Sometimes we need to pace the road of life a bit rather than feeling that everything is always something of the urgent.

The boy's voice was low and muffled, hovering somewhere between the high pitch of a child, but edging close to adolescence. Suddenly David was instantly reminded of the back porch and the young boy who sat there hunched and solemn.

"Come here," aunt Mabel said. She had mysteriously reappeared again, much like she did back home with her mysterious calls that had that uncanny timing to them. There he found it all an irritant. Here, it was magic.

Looking at her with a slight smile, David said, "You're going to have a lot of fun with cell phones."

Entirely undaunted by the comment, she motioned David back out through the general store and out the screen door at the front. Turning to the right, she glanced up and said, "look there," while pointing a confident finger.

Out of the corner of his eye he spied an old, red Western Flyer bicycle quietly leaning against the front of the store directly underneath the old Sinclair sign. It was a rich metallic red with chromed fenders slightly rusted in spots. It sported a worn leather seat with two thick springs firmly underneath it. It's thick white-walled tires had grayed a bit, lending it a sense of miles ridden and adventures had. It had a metal mesh basket on the front that was slightly bent and speckled with brownish spots of rust.

David walked toward it, his eyes never leaving it. "This," he said, "This can't be my old bike… can it? Is it?" Pausing at its side, he reached out tentatively as if it might not exist and that he would be horribly disappointed in the reaching. Gently, he touched the leather seat, then lifted his hand and ran it across the rich red frame much like he did the river rock fence several weeks ago in what was yet the future. Then suddenly, as if struck by the full force of a lightening bolt thrown from those one of those ferocious Michigan storms, he had a thought far more terrifying but far more wonderful than any other he had had on these travels through time. "If my bike is here, is it… is it possible that I'm here? Is this… my bike?"

A silence fell over him. It seemed that David and aunt Mabel both needed a moment to prepare to say what was about to be said next. Sometimes in life we need to sit with things for a minute, maybe on the fringe of things, not only to savor the wealth of the moment, but take a moment to figure out how to respectfully engage it.

A voice finally broke the silence.

"David," aunt Mabel said softly. "David, you know who that is a sittin' out there, on those back steps?"

David bowed his head, wiped tears from his eyes and said, "It's me, isn't it? I know. It's me. I mean, I don't know how… but I know it's me."

Shaking his head, he stammered, "It's me. It's me," trying to somehow make the realization solid enough to grab it sufficiently. David began babbling, "I'm not the best with kids in first place, but a kid that's me. I mean… how do you talk to yourself? No one does that… I mean at least with their past self… if you know what I mean. I don't know what I mean!"

Sometimes minutes seem like hours, even in a place where time has been turned inside out. After a few eternal moments, he stopped his pacing, turned to aunt Mabel and said, "Okay. Okay. Yeah… I would have never guessed that talking to myself would be hardest person I could ever talk to." He paused again, looking up and down the old dirt road. "It's strange, but I'm scared to death to talk to me. Shouldn't I be the easiest person to talk to?"

Resuming his pacing around the front of the store with his hands still tightly clenched in front of himself he said, "What am I supposed to say… to me? I mean, what… what am I supposed to say?"

Stepping in front of him and clasping David's face in her country calloused hands, aunt Mabel said, "Tell that boy out there what the pictures on that wall in there are tellin' you. What your grandpa told ya. What my husband told ya. What Lincoln told ya. What your great-grandma told ya. You tell him that. You go right out there and tell him that. That's what ya tell 'em."

Backing away with a soft smile, she shooed David and said, "Now get along and I'll have some soda and mints for both of you when yer done."

David smiled, stepped forward and gave aunt Mabel an enveloping hug. As he did he felt the guilt of finding such a remarkable woman as such an irritant in his time. It would be different when he got back. "In the future, I promise aunt Mabel, I promise that I will treat you so much better than I have," he said.

"Shush," she replied. "Told ya, future's not mine to know. Now get along."

David smiled, paused and quietly said, "You're as stubborn now as you are in the future."

"That's disappointin'," she casually replied with a tilt of her head. "Thought I'd get better at is as I aged." Turning to head back into the store, she said, "Get on about the business that brought ya here."

Abruptly, David stepped toward a retreating aunt Mabel, lifted his hands and in a pleading voice said, "What brought me here? Why am I here?" Gesturing skyward he said, "Every other place I've gone, I've been told why I'm there. Someone made sense of what in the world was happening and why it was happening and what was supposed to happen." By this time, aunt Mabel had turned, stepped back at the screen door of the store and stood with a rapt, but quietly knowing attention.

Thinking about the faded photos handing canted on the wall, David said, "I've been to a lot of those places in those photos over the past, past, I don't know how long." Fighting for words, he said, "I don't even know what's happening. Half the time I really feel like I'm in those places, and the other half of the time I'm just hoping to wake up from some dream that I really don't want to wake up from."

He said, "I know, I know that it's about hope... that there's always hope somewhere, even, even when you can't see any. God's invasion of hope." Pausing, David said, "You know, he died. uncle Bill died, he died twice... so did all of these other people. And I, I'm not certain at all about how all of this works, or, or why people who choose to do that... but I talked to him the night before he died."

Stammering into some sort of reflection David said, "And he was so young, you know. So young. I don't know how he faced it all. I mean, if I were his age I couldn't have done that. No way could I have done that."

Pausing and pointing, he said, "And then there was grandpa, and great-grandma, and Lincoln, as hard as that is to believe. And now, now there's you, who's kinda the person I know in, well in the future, which is my present, which... I don't even know where time is or what time is anymore." Turning and staring into the ground he said, "I don't know what this is all about. I'm mean, it's about hope, I know. I know that. That whatever life burns up hope can rebuild. That hope can invade anything. That things torn in two can be made whole again. What else? Oh yeah, that hope is enough even when we lose everything."

Beginning to speak out of fear, David said, "But I think I'm worried that I'm going to miss whatever it is that all of this is about. Not miss it. That's not what I meant. What I mean is that I won't get it like I need to get it." Shaking his head, he said, "For some reason this happened to *me* and I think if it was going to happen, it should've happened to someone else someplace else who would really be able to get it all and do with it whatever was supposed to be done with. I'm afraid I won't get it like I should get... you know, get it in a way that really makes a difference for whoever this is supposed to make a difference for."

Staring at aunt Mabel, David said, "I'm afraid aunt Mabel! I'm afraid that I'm not going to understand it like I should. I'm afraid I'm going to blow it for this kid, I mean for the 'me' that's sitting back there," he said pointing to the back of the store. "I know that it's all about hope, and I, I know that all of these people chose to come back or I've gone back, however all of that's done or how in the world that happened, and they've died twice to get this message of hope to me."

With tears welling up in his eyes, he said, "And I'm afraid I'll miss it. Or maybe even worse than that, I'll get it but I won't believe it. And if that happens, these people, all of these people died, died twice for nothing!" Standing with his hands in the air, David said, "What if I don't get like I'm supposed to, or what if I don't believe it which is probably the worst thing of all, and they all died for nothing!"

Having stepped back up to him, with a voice firm but soft she placed a hand on his shoulder and said, "Davie B. I'm not all that certain, but sometimes I think that it's harder to watch people sacrifice than actually be the one doin' the sacrificing. I mean, we're not doing it, the sacrificin' I mean, but sometimes I think watchin' it and wishin' that we could do something about it, but findin' out that we can't is worse than goin' through it ourselves. Or maybe wantin' to do the sacrificin' so they don't have to well... well, that's hard.

"But ya know, I mean, I'm just a simple woman who runs a simple general store for farmers and country-folk that live in these parts. But because ya kinda live out on the edges of life doesn't mean that ya don't understand it. In fact, I sometimes think that life happens most out on the edges ya know. Out here," she said gesturing out to the Michigan landscape of farm and fields, "'cause it ain't tainted by all the fake stuff and the movin' too fast and all the things that cause us to miss life while we're livin' it. Seems to me that real living happens out here on the fringes 'cause it ain't all dirtied by the rush and all the greed that causes most of the rush."

After a long pause, aunt Mabel continued, "Some time ago I got a letter from a private who bunked with yer uncle Bill. Probably came five, maybe six years after the end of the war. I figured that he probably waited so long 'cause of the war, and then how life after the war got in his way, and maybe his own need to get some space from it all."

"Wrote me a letter sayin' how much he appreciated Billy." Sighing heavily, with tears welling up in her own eyes, she said, "He wrote and said that Billy was talkin' out loud to himself the night before the invasion… kinda like he was talkin' to someone about sacrifice and hope and dying twice and such." Canting her head, she said, "He told me he couldn't have got up that next morning if it weren't for Billy. More particular, for that conversation he overhead. Said it made him think about life and what's important and that sacrificin' is kind of like the ultimate calling and all. Changed his life, he said. Said he saw Billy go down and figured that the way it happened, he didn't feel no pain. Went on, he said, to become a pastor 'cause that was the way to live out what he heard Billy say that night; that he wanted to invade the world with hope. So, he gave his life over to that callin.'"

"I remember that guy," David said with a voice of authority. "I remember him. He, he asked uncle Bill what he was saying because, because uncle Bill was talking to me but the other guy couldn't see me, which has been the case in all of these situations." Pausing out of the gradual and dawning realization that aunt Mabel knew how uncle Bill died, he said, "He died twice, just like these other people died twice for me to get this message. I mean it's about hope… right? That's what that red-headed kid got ahold of… that's what he took away from the conversation." Turning and canting his head, David said, "Man, that changed everything for him didn't it? Everything. But, it's got to be more than that, right? It has to be."

"David," aunt Mabel said, "It's about hope, you got that right. But it's about understandin' that we can hope by ourselves, like create our own hope by talkin' ourselves into things or doin' things with our lives. That kinda hope ain't lastin'. It ain't. The only kinda hope that lasts is the kind that someone else gives us. Someone a whole lot bigger than us. I mean, a whole lot bigger. Ya know, someone who doesn't bounce around in time like you have. But someone who's bigger than time so He's in all of time all the time. 'Cause if you think about it for a minute, I mean really ponder it, it makes a whole lot of sense that real hope, you know, hope that doesn't get stomped on by life 'cause life will stomp on us ya know, that kinda hope has to come from someplace that's bigger than life, that's, well, over life, maybe even created life. Holds life in His hand so it doesn't hold him."

Pausing as if to knit the whole of it together, she said, "Then ya got to live that kind of hope out, kinda talk it out, not just in what ya say 'cause that's way too limited. Too cheap, ya know. But live it out in what ya do. Like Billy did that night. Talked it out he did… with you. With you, David. And that young man heard it all… most of it anyway. And then he saw it lived out that next day on that beach. Seein' it made it real and less some nice idea. Changed his life, it did. Forever. And that change in his life changed the lives of others, how many I don't know. Only God knows. But it changed 'em. Certainly didn't stop with him cause hopes too big to settle in jest one place.

"Well, just think on that a bit Davie B. You changed a life once without even knowin' it, 'till right now. You changed a life. That life changed others. Lots of others. Well, it's time to do it again. Now, there's a boy out back who's kinda lost in life right now. He ain't got much hope fer a ten-year-old, so I reckon that yer the person who's goin' to give it to him 'cause ya remember those times back then, right? Remember? He needs hope that'll get him through the years ahead, 'cause that sweet boy is gonna run right into things that are gonna cause him to need somethin' a whole lot bigger than you to give him hope. But fer now, go on out there and talk some hope into his life."

With a smile, David reached out, hugged aunt Mabel with one of those deep hugs that are all too rare. Smiling and stepping back, she said, "You want to make certain that you really understand all about hope? Well, no better way to ground it in yer heart than sayin' it to yerself."

Smiling, David turned to go out to the back porch. From behind him, aunt Mabel said, "By the way, remember what yer gonna say to yerself out there, 'cause there's someone else that's gonna need to hear pretty much the same thing real soon. Once ya say it to them I can guarantee ya that you'll understand what everyone's been tellin' ya."

Puzzled yet again by events turning on some grand stage, David smiled and walked down the side of the clapboard store to the back. "Someone else…" he pondered. "Who?"

As David approached the corner of the store, he glanced around to a catch of glimpse of himself at ten sitting there. Sure, David expected it to be difficult in some way that he wouldn't be able to explain to himself or anyone else for that matter. Yet, the abruptly visceral shock of seeing himself was startlingly intense. A rush of incomprehensible emotions erupted from some subterranean place within him with a force that threw him backwards. Tripping, he fell against the side of the clapboard store, bracing himself against the impossible sitting just around the corner. Attempting to catch his breath and slow a racing heart, he stared into the listless blue sky as if seeking something bigger than himself to help himself.

David's head spun. He emotions gyrated to near nausea. David had not been much for philosophical thinking, or doting on ethereal ideas as the exercise of imagination had done nothing more than render him acutely

313

vulnerable to pain. The impossible was just that…
impossible. Therefore, life had been stripped down to a raw
practicality that may have killed the wonder of it, but
without question it made it safe. Yet, his recent travels
through time or imagination or whatever this was had
begun to realign him back to what he had been as that boy
sitting on those steps. Maybe the impossible was
impossible only because we thought it to be so. Maybe the
impossible was not based on how life actually worked, but
on how we constricted life through our bluntly stunted
vision and all the other abhorrent things that we did to keep
it safe.

He suddenly realized that that boy 'David', that ten-
year-old was experiencing the events that allowed David to
experience the memories that had sustained him through so
much of life's darkness. That boy was rooting in his heart
and his mind the very memories that David would draw
from decades later. That kid, that tender child was creating
what David already had in his head. That young
Midwestern boy had no idea about the world David lived
in. Yet, by the simple act of living he was creating the man,
this man who would live in that very world. That boy was
living what David would cherish. That boy was creating the
gift that would gift David through the abandonment and
loss that, from where he now stood, loomed decades ahead.
This boy… this boy was precious.

David suddenly found himself pacing back and
forth in front of the store, having no idea how he had gotten
back there. Several people had entered and left the store,
with David passing through them without a thought of it
all, his pacing set to the cadence of a mind lost in itself.

Turning, David entered the store through the flimsy
screen door, seeking its solace in the midst of his turmoil.
The store had become entirely empty. Utterly vacant.
Sometimes we must take the most important journey's in
isolation; alone except for the experience itself. Sometimes

314

the things that we reach for to help us will only be the distractions that hurt us. If we don't journey alone, that journey might be diluted in ways hopelessly irreparable. Without a doubt, this was one of those moments.

David pensively walked to the back door of the small, clapboard house. A worn screen door that was held closed by a single spring screwed to the doorframe kept the hoard of Michigan insects outside where they belonged. Taking hold of the handle, he casually glanced up to see a small sign hanging over the door. It was nothing more than a small, embroidered picture mounted in a simple oak frame. It read, "'Silent night, holy night.' This is where hope began."

"Hmm," David mumbled, "Has that always been there?" Wondering why he had missed it until now; unless 'now' was the moment for the message.

He quickly turned his attention back to the small boy now a few feet away; the decades between who he was today and who he was then being now measured in mere feet. Yesterday and tomorrow about to meet in the moment of the now. Drawing a deep breath, he opened the door. Putting a hand on the door frame to steady him as he stepped out, David felt a deep pitting on the frame. Pulling his hand away he suddenly saw a series of worn hash-marks vertically etched down the door frame. A date written beside each one.

Every summer aunt Mabel chronicled his growth on this doorframe. Every summer. No sooner had his Mom walked him into the store, checked his suitcase for the millionth time to make certain that he had everything, given him one of those magically enveloping hugs and then headed out the door that aunt Mabel would say, "Well, let's see how much ya've grown since last summer." Off to the backdoor they would go with pocketknife in hand to record life on the move.

David was instantaneously slammed with the realization that the etching of his life had begun here, on this doorframe, in this store, when he was who he was as the little boy sitting now just a few feet away. *I forgot about these,* he thought. *I totally forgot.* In the mushing of a mind pounded raw he wondered how many other things he had forgotten in the scandalous rush of a life down a road to nowhere. The river-rock fence was nothing more than an extension of what had started here, on this tottering doorframe.

Gently running his hand down the hash-marks, David thought, *Maybe, maybe this is my moment to change all the things the mark my life.* For if we've enough faith and if we're courageous enough to possess the courage born of that faith, the future is ours to change. *It's going to be different,* he thought. *It will be different.* David paused, withdrew his hand, glanced at the hash marks one final time, turned, opened the door and stepped out.

"Hi," David said descending the stairs, his voice a bit shaky.

"Hi," the boy replied. Staring at the young boy, David's mind was lost in remembering everything who he once was and everything he forgot about who he was.

It is interesting how we shape memory either to forget what we don't want to remember, or recreate what we remember in a way that it's easier to remember. We arrogantly take license with the past, whether that means we attempt to erase it, or we rigorously edit it, rewrite it or, in some cases, leave it just the way that it is if that best suits us. But whatever we do, and for whatever reason that we do it, it's typically not the way it really was. Suddenly, David was entirely aware of that reality. Standing next to this young boy who he once was, his mind was wildly gyrating in its attempts to re-program the entirety of his memories at all once.

Shaking himself free, he cleared his throat and said, "Hi, I'm… David."

The young boy said, "My names David too!"

"Really?" David replied. "How's that for a coincidence?"

"But you know, my aunt Mabel calls me Davie B." the young boy said, handily moving into the conversation. "She's the only one that does that. That's like a baby name or something." David himself had thought that a time or two.

"Oh, I don't know about that," David said as he took a seat next to himself. Finding himself much more at ease with himself than he anticipated, he said, "I understand that. I really do, but that's just her lovin' on you. You know," he continued while staring out across the field and into the woods, and then returning his gaze to the boy, "When you get older, kind of like me," he said pointing at himself, "those kind of names mean something, so I'd hold onto that if I were you."

"You in the Army?" little David asked abruptly.

Having totally forgotten that he was still wearing uncle Bill's military jacket, he said, "Ah, no. I just know someone who was."

"So, where you from?" little David said.

"Oh," David replied, "from around here. Actually, more from Ohio, but I come here, or came here… a lot when I was a kid."

"Okay," little David said. Pausing, little David continued, "I'm from Ohio too. So when did you come here?"

"Oh, when I was about your age. Way back in the 60's and 70's." Pausing and realizing what he had just said, David continued, "I know. Kind of confusing." Redirecting himself, he said, "a long time ago."

"Yeah," said the little boy, not really considering what David had said but attempting to be polite nonetheless.

There was an immediate and wholly comprehensive connection between the two of them. Unexpected but wholly welcomed. It was entirely beyond some conscious recognition or play of social graces that would have formally connected the two of them. They were 'two', but they were 'one' at the selfsame time over all of time. There was no meeting of souls for there was no separation. There had never been an introduction because there had never been a parting of the ways that would require a joining of the hearts. Rather there was what had always been. David. Then or now, it was David.

With that immense comfort enveloping the whole of him, little ten-year-old David looked up and stared out across the field and into the woods just like David had done; one-in-the-same becoming ever more obvious.

Then he said, "I'm finding out that life is kind of confusing sometimes." Pausing and looking back down, he said, "I don't want to grow up. I think that's why I like coming here and workin' the store with aunt Mabel because I don't have to grow up like I do at home." Looking up at David, little David said, "That probably doesn't make much sense to you, being an adult and all." Looking back down, he rather sullenly said, "I just don't want to grow up."

Drawing a deep breath, David said, "Well, actually that makes a lot of sense. A whole lot of sense. I've often thought the very same thing. In fact, I've thought that lots of times." Pulling out a single stalk of Indian Grass growing along the side of the steps, David turned its stem between his fingers, spinning the head at the end of the stalk. "It should be simpler, shouldn't it?" David said.

"My dad died," little David abruptly said shrugging his shoulders. "I don't know if aunt Mabel told you. It wasn't his fault. It was cancer they said. But I had to grow up 'cause he wasn't there no more. I mean, Mom couldn't do everything on her own now. She needed my help," he said with a pause in his voice. "So I helped, you know. My friends, well they'd be out playing baseball or riding their bikes," he said gesturing with his hand. "I could go sometimes, but lots of time I had work to do. Mom, she's kinda sick sometimes so she couldn't do everything. But I'm okay with helping. It's okay," he said. "aunt Mabel and I have talked about it a lot and that helps."

Running his hand over the strands of Indian grass alongside the steps, little David paused and said, "But aunt Mabel's a girl."

"Yeah…" David replied somewhat inquisitively as the conversation appeared to move in an entirely different direction. "That would be so."

Reaching down and picking his own stalk of Indian grass and twisting it just like David, he continued, "Well, she's a girl. But not really. I mean, she's my aunt and all. That makes it all real different."

David realized that his younger self was looking for an older self to talk to. A man to talk about 'man' things with. He had largely forgotten the hole left by his father. He had been left to figure out most of his life without that father-figure to shape him or tell him what everything was about from the perspective of an older male. While it was arduous, he had done it fairly well. And now, he was in a very strange way asked to be his own father-figure. Somehow it was odd, but it seemed oddly appropriate.

I'll bet this is about Amy, David suddenly thought to himself out of nowhere. He, he wants to talk about girls and he needs a guy to do it. *Ten years old. Fourth grade. Mrs. Kolbeck's class. Yup. It has to be,* David thought. Amy broke his heart real bad, or so it seemed when he was ten. Devastated him. The fact of the matter was, David never really pursued her because, at ten, he didn't have the slightest idea of how to do that. She was nice to him and even did things that suggested she liked him as well. But he was ten and it was all puppy love.

"It's a girl, right?" David asked somewhat slyly. "Let me guess," he continued finding this somewhat amusing. With a bit of showmanship, David said, "She's got medium brown hair, about down to her shoulders, right about here" he said gesturing around his neck. "She always wears these white, fluffy blouses and has Frito's with her lunches. She runs faster than all the other girls at recess. And in your class she sits just to the right of you, up two rows next to Mike Blair, who kind of likes her too."

"You talked to aunt Mabel didn't you?" little David said with a deeply sad tone. The tone caught David and spun his conscious sideways. Instantaneously he realized that he was placating his own self by writing the emotions of this ten-year-old off as some trivial event of childhood. But, this wasn't puppy love for his ten-year-old self. He remembered it now. It came to him as he went back to the boy he sat next to on those rickety steps. He'd forgotten. Completely. It was painful. Horribly painful for at that time. Many nights it left him with an aching pit in his stomach that his yellow stuffed dog couldn't take away... sobbing under the sheets well into the night.

Suddenly, David's pain from the divorce was joined with this previous pain he had altogether forgotten. And in this juncture he realized that he had too often written off the pain of the divorce or he had somehow attempted to placate it. It suddenly came to him that he had done that with most of the pain in his life. And that doesn't create any space to heal from the pain, whatever it might be.

Taking a deep breath, David replied, "No, aunt Mabel didn't tell me. Some things... you just know." Looking out at the woods again, David said, "I kinda went through what you're going through. Kind of the same thing… really a lot like the same thing." Staring back down at the piece of field grass that he was twisting between his fingers, David said, "Yeah, I kinda went through that when I was just about your age, and, come to think of it, I kinda went through something like that when I was an adult too."

"Yeah?" said little David with excitement. "What happened to you? I thought that bad stuff only happened to kids 'cause adults can figure that stuff out, can't they? I mean, adults know what to do, right?"

Smiling, David replied, "Well, adults don't always figure it out. Actually, I think that adults create a lot of that stuff, sad to say. I mean, they create a lot of their own problems. Kids don't do that as much. Most times kids are, well, they're victims more than anything else."

Having picked another stalk of Indian grass and twisting it between his fingers, little David went on, "You just can't count on people, can you? You just can't have much hope in 'em." Pausing, he continued, "Dad didn't mean to leave, I mean he couldn't do nothin' about it. And Amy, I mean she's better than me anyway so she doesn't hang around. A lot of my friends don't understand me, so I don't see 'em much. All except aunt Mabel. She's good. She's special! She loves being with me," he said spinning the stalk of Indian grass this way and that.

David was struck by the words coming from his young heart and mind. His head started rummaging through his own life experience and his divorce. He sorted through the words of wisdom aunt Mabel has just passed on to him. He began pulling from his grandfather, and uncle Bill, and his great-grandmother, and Lincoln, and now aunt Mabel all at once. Yet, his amazement with the fact he was having a conversation with himself had not abated sufficiently to be able to even begin to think through everything that they had said.

Pulling more weeds and spinning them through his fingers, David attempted to draw it all together in order to know what to say to himself. Somehow what he heard his young self say was so true and so powerful that he had to have an answer. Sure, more times than he could remember he grappled with what to tell himself as an adult. But, he never cared enough to really pursue an answer until now. Rather, he had always stuffed the questions and ran from the answers. But not now.

Looking into who he was as a child, he realized that this tender ten year old needed an answer. Not some cheesy or shallow answer. Not something to pacify this young boy and make him feel better today but leave him open to pain tomorrow. Not some trite saying that would help this kid buck up only to get knocked down. The world was full of that kind of stuff because few people want real answers. Most people just want to be pacified. People don't want to know about hope because hope demands belief, and belief demands that we step up and step outside of ourselves. And who wants to do that? David realized that this kid had his whole life ahead of him and he needed something that would be sturdy enough to navigate that life.

Sitting there, David's mind ran wild with all of the things that this kid, this young boy who was himself, would face in the years ahead. A rather impoverished life. A single Mom eking out a living. Teasing at school because of hand-me-down clothing and ill-fitting glasses. Of challenges getting through high school and putting himself through college. Of falling in love, and of having the one that he loved betray him and cost him his family and his life. These things were the big things, the things that wrenched David's heart and sliced his soul to pieces, not to mention all of the other things that would scar him as well. This kid, this young man needed something real because all of that stuff was coming at him. It was all sitting just over the horizon of his future.

"You know what I've learned?" David asked clearing his throat yet again. "People can give us some hope. But, they're people, which doesn't make them bad, it just makes them people." Pausing and scanning the landscape for a moment, he turned back to little David and with a subdued voice said, "You just have to have hope in something bigger than people, that's all. You have to have hope in something that's so big that if everything you've got is taken from you, you'll always have more than what was taken."

"So… what would that be?" little David asked in a quizzical way. "I mean, what else is there other than people 'cause I can't think of anything else. You mean like this store, or nature or something like that?"

"I don't know," David replied. "Maybe that's God or something, 'cause that would be bigger wouldn't it?"

As the words leapt out of his mouth they made all of the sense that he wished they hadn't made. It was exactly what the bookmark had said. It runs against a man's grain to think that he needs something bigger than himself. That kind of thinking takes a big bite out of a man's pride. If life were the way it should be, it would be a journey where a man's confidence in his ability to chart a course and walk it to completion would grow stronger over his lifespan. Life shouldn't be about the gradual realization that we can't pull off the impossible much less most of the stuff that's possible. And that to chart any course that really matters we need something bigger than ourselves to pull it off. That feels like growing more into weakness than strength, but that's where life goes.

David couldn't believe the words he said next. Yet, he said them. "Never stop hoping, David. Never, okay. Promise me. Promise me."

"I promise," little David said, "I'll try real hard."

David continued, "God is bigger than all the things in your life that have hurt you," he said pointing at little David's heart. "He's never smaller than any of that stuff in there. God can invade all the bad stuff with hope that's bigger than all the bad stuff combined."

"Really," little David said something quizzical but excited nonetheless. "Really," David replied. "Really."

Sitting on those creaking back steps, his gaze then drifted off to the distant forests with his mind having drifted even further. He went back, or in this case forward to a wife's abandonment, the scandalous lies that cost him his children and decimated his family, aunt Mabel's deterioration, the incessant challenges of his job, the fire of 1928, an uncle dying on a foreign beach and all of it. It seemed that life cruelly set him up so he couldn't do it alone. If life would leave him alone he'd be fine. But then he thought, *if it did all alone, I'd be lonely. So, good or bad, there's something I'm needing.*

All of sudden aunt Mabel's voice rung out. Somehow, she was standing right in front of him. "God?" she said. "Of course there's a God 'cause if you think on it long enough ya realize life doesn't make any sense without Him," she continued, raising her hands and gesturing toward the sky. "You can try and figure God out of life, but when you do that, there's nothin' left. You think there is, but that's only you foolin' yerself." Smiling, and pointing a serious finger at both David and little David, she said, "Come to think of it, it's the only sense that life makes. Look around you. Think about everything that's ever been or ever will be. How's that all work without a God in it? God's the great 'because' that puts all this here and makes it all work."

With a long mile, she pulled two bottles out of the pockets in her apron and held out a ginger ale to David and a vanilla soda to little David.

"You know I don't care for ginger ale," older David said, being somewhat disappointed that aunt Mabel apparently didn't remember that obvious fact.

"I know ya don't," she replied curtly and with a touch of anticipation. "But there's someone who does, and it ain't this little guy over here," she said winking toward little David. The meaning of the statement was entirely unclear for David, leaving a starkly quizzical look on his face.

Bringing the conversation back to where it had left off, little David said, "Thanks mister."

"For what?" David asked, feeling he had added little to his younger self.

Little David continued, "Not many people, except aunt Mabel here, know the right things to say to me. It's kinda like you've known me a long time or something. But thanks for talking 'cause I'll never forget it."

At that moment the very conversation that David had with his young self elicited a memory that he had with an older man, on these very steps, on this day. He'd never recalled remembering that moment in his life before. But now it was there; fitted in with all the other memories of this place. Fuzzy like most memory, but steadfastly there. And in the remembering, it took on the aura of a special moment… almost a pivotal one. One where hope it seemed had dawned then and had dawned now, all at once.

"You're rememberin' aren't ya?" aunt Mabel whispered. "Ya just gave yourself what you needed for the rest of yer lives," she said as she pointed back and forth between them. "It's in there now. And now it's part of yer memory."

Turning to little David, aunt Mabel said, "I put out lunch fer you on the counter up front. Why don't you take your soda and get along and go eat. I'll be along shortly."

"Okay," little David said, jumping up and bounding up the steps to the old screen door. Stopping, he turned around and said, "It was really nice to meet you mister. Maybe we can talk again sometime. Oh, and I'll work hard to keep my promise about hoping and all."

Turning and standing, David said, "Oh, you can bet that we'll share a whole bunch of conversations."

Reaching out to shake little David's hand, he suddenly reached out embraced his ten-year-old self with a firm hug that seemed to be a million hugs all in one.

With emotions welling up within him, he choked back impending tears and said, "Now get along and eat." David stood and watched his young self skip through the small clapboard house and disappear into the store. Tenderly watching his ten-year-old self disappear into the general store, he said, "That's it? That's all? Did I… did I give him what he needed?"

With a flair of country wisdom, aunt Mabel said, "The greatest things are said in the poverty of a few words. Yup. He's good."

Turning and sitting down, David looked out at the forest and the fields and said, "I love this place. I always did. It's too bad that the world isn't like this."

Pulling up an empty soda container and sitting it up on its end right in front of him, aunt Mabel sat on the top of it at direct eye level with David.

"Davie B," she said. "My situations a bit different than everyone else's. You know, all by themselves they decided to come back to give ya this message. That was their decision, and it was a whole lot bigger than mine, 'cause I don't have to die twice. I'm gonna die for certain, 'cause we all do. But only once for me. And I'll be waitin' fer ya before I do."

"I thought you didn't know the future. I don't even know that future," David replied.

"Well," aunt Mabel replied thoughtfully, "That hasn't happened fer either of us yet, but I'm thinkin' it will happen to benefit both of us. I guess it's a little piece of the future that I'm supposed to know so we'll both recognize it when it gets here."

With a bit of trembling she placed her hand on David's knee and continued. "What I had to decide to do," she said choking back pending tears, "was to relive this here place with all that I love about it, and be reminded what it was like not to have dementia, 'cause when you're in that state Davie B, you don't know exactly who you are or who other people are. You're just kinda locked into some prison in your head that you're not even sure's a prison most of the time. It's kinda like dying twice, if ya know what I mean." Pausing and gathering herself, she said, "So for me, it was a whole lot easier to come back here than it was for all of those other folks. I been spared a full memory 'cause I reckon it's gonna be a tough time for me. But I been told enough to get you what you need."

"Aunt Mabel, I don't know..." David began.

"Shush boy," aunt Mabel said. "We can have that conversation at some future time...'cause we will."

David stood. "One thing," he said. "I want you to have this," carefully taking off uncle Bill's jacket. Taking it in her hand, she caringly laid it across her lap and stroked it as if it were something impossibly precious.

"I miss him," she said. "I sure miss him. That's okay though, 'cause sometimes it's good to hold onto a little pain so that you don't forget things that ya'd be remiss forgetting."

Then, taking the Bible in her hands, she pulled out the fourth page. Handing it to him, she said, "Read it to me David, read it to me."

By now David knew what that meant. "I don't know if I want to read it," he said. "I'd rather stay right here. I don't want to go! I could just stay here forever." Pausing and looking around one final time, he said, "But, I know I've got to go. As much as I'd love to, I know I can't stay," he said with a sigh that went all the way to the bottom of his soul.

Picking up the page, the script was in tall, bold letters, written by the hand of a child on wide ruled paper. It was innocent and tender. Holding it firm in a slight Michigan breeze, he read:

"Dear God:

I know that Santa comes in a few days and I think you know him. Maybe. Could you please tell Santa this year I don't want no presents. I hope that does not make him feel bad. I am sorry if it does. Please could you tell Santa at the North Pole that all I want is if he could help my Mom and Dad not fight and for my Dad not to drink anymore. That is all I need. In case you don't know, I have a house and good clothes and even my own bed. In my room I even have some dolls and a toy box in the corner by the window. In the summer I have a bike I ride too! It is pink and white. All I want is for Mom and Dad to love each other because that would be enough for Christmas. God I hope that you have a Merry Christmas up there in heaven. Love, Kristin."

"There's the faith of a child, David," aunt Mabel said reflectively. "I've learned that the faith of a child is the greatest faith of all. None like it. It's somethin' we easily lose 'cause we think it's too small to face an adult world, and it's somethin' we have to work hard to get back once we finally figure out that it's bigger than the adult world. I've also learned that if ya've got faith, ya got hope all the same. David, hope is born in simple places to simple hearts that have enough space for a miracle to happen. Most folks don't have any room in their hearts for hope anymore. It's all full so hope has to find room someplace else. Just keep the childlike faith David. Make room in your life for it," she said, pointing at his heart. "Just keep it."

"I love you," aunt Mabel said as she reached out her hand, took David's in hers and held it over the page. "I won't be able to tell you that again, but next ya see me, look for it in my face. It'll be there for certain."

As she began to press his hand against the page, David felt something on the page itself. Peering down he saw the bookmark that had been sandwiched in the picture of Uncle Bill.

Looking back up, he said, "How did this…" only to be stopped short by aunt Mabel.

"You and I, we'll see this old bookmark again. You and me. I love ya and I'll see ya soon," she said as David fell backwards into steps as if they were never there. He immediately hit the ground, finding himself lying in deep snow, with a gray sky overhead and the laughter of a little girl filling the frigid air.

Chapter 17
A Christmas Eve Swing Set
Giving Hope to the Betrayer

One might think that facing oneself would be the most difficult task imaginable. To look into the face of innocence and realize that even though that face was once yours, you ended up living out a life that was less than the innocence once reflected in it. They say that forgiving yourself is the most difficult person to forgive. Indeed, there may be more truth in that statement than we can effectively overcome despite our most rigorous efforts. After all, forgiveness is divine.

In fact, however, there may be one other person who is more difficult to face. One person who betrayed us in ways incomprehensible; in ways that left us profusely bleeding, systematically scarred, alone and with the forever pain that we learn to tolerate because it never heals. To meet 'that person' is unthinkably difficult, but to meet them years before their souls were ever tainted and the actions ever taken, that is a stupefying conundrum indeed. To speak into their lives before they hurled reckless toxins and unspeakable carnage into yours... that is possibly the most difficult thing one can conceivably do.

And so, David lay on his back in the snow, looking up into a gray sky of drifting snowflakes with the giggles of a little girl pirouetting hand-in-hand with the falling snow.

Sometimes life puts us in places that we had never could have envisioned even in our most inventive moments. Therefore, we have no means of preparation or any sense of forewarning. And when we arrive in those unexpected places, we have to squint through the windows of our souls and wipe clean the eyes of our hearts, for in our blinding routines and mediocre plots we had not anticipated the need of doing so.

It might be quite wise to say that the only way that we can truly reach things remarkable is to place the inflexible walls of the rational mind aside at times and journey outside the confines of those walls. For you see, wonder and majesty and things both great and marvelous typically lay many miles outside of those kinds of walls. But, there are also those times wherein they lay only a step or two outside of them. If you dare think about it, that's where the roads of hope run. For David, stepping outside of those familiar walls had been forced upon him because somewhere in his once jaded mind, things great and marvelous simple did not exist. The ability to hope in this manner did not exist either. And while these trips through time had opened that up, now…

"You're supposed to land on your feet," came a sweet and listless voice wrapped in a mixture of laughter and concern. "You got to put your legs down, you know," came the voice again. "You do that before you come off the end!"

The sky had turned a thick, cottony gray; the kind that he knew on those dreary mid-Western winter days. The sun itself, as mighty as it was, was held at bay, casting a gray and flatly diminished light. Looking around, the trees were tall and skeletal; having long been in winter's slumber. The muscular bows of both scotch and white pines sagged under the weight of winter's snowy dressing. Snow fell lightly in thick flakes that floated like an infinite number of kisses from some magical place far above. It was all a far cry from the Michigan summer that he had sat immersed in only seconds ago.

Sitting up and shaking himself free of a mental blur, David found himself holding the Bible in one hand and a bottle of ginger ale in the other. Across a small parking lot, a massive church of rich red brick held itself tall and proud. It was ornamentally studded with three pairs of large, stained glass windows running the length of the building from front to back. The building itself was tastefully framed both on top and the bottom with massive blocks of smooth granite that created a rich edging to the endless red brick. Casting his eyes upward, the steeple was a modest brick box topped by a simple white cross. It seemed odd to him that such a massive and ornate building would be graced by such a simple cross. "Maybe," David pondered, "Maybe that's what it's about… simplicity."

The expansive parking lot was vacant, it's inhabitants having taken the lessons of faith back to their respective homes. Down around the corner of the brick church, David spied a black 1970 Chevelle parked in front of a double-glass door. Two spaces to it's left a 1968 Ford Bronco sat at a bit of angle, it's driver appearing to have paid less attention to the lines of the parking space and more attention to whatever else was occupying his mind. With snow covering much of the lot, the error was certainly excusable. Out beyond the largely vacant lot, what appeared to be a rather large road ran sporadically with various cars that had marked David's teen years.

"Where is this?" David muttered.

"Like I said mister, you've got to put your legs down," the voice came again, sprinkled with laughter and a touch of giggling.

Turning, David saw a little girl nearly lost in a thick coat, a massive white scarf within which her neck was completely consumed, a white woolen hat whose ties draped half of her tiny frame, and a pair of worn mittens. A pair of ill-fitting boots swallowed her thin legs in their sizable expanse. Her appearance was rather impoverished in nature. However, her joy was anything but.

"It was kinda funny though," she said. "You're a funny man."

Brushing himself off, David stood, turned, and looked at the snow expecting to see an imprint left by his backside. There was none. David canted his head out of curiosity thinking, "Am I here or not?" That, of course, was not a new question.

Directing her attention away from the fact that there was no print, even though such was not her focus, he said, "Yeah. I need to put my legs down. I don't know, I just kinda ended up there."

"Well," said the petite little girl pointing to the slide, "When you came down the slide it was like you weren't paying attention. I don't even know how you got there because I thought I was all alone, but all of a sudden down you came, right on your rear. You're funny!"

Suddenly, the bell of the massive church began to toll. Turning, David said, "What, is this Sunday or something?"

"Nope," the little confidently replied. "It's Christmas Eve." Pointing a mittened finger to the lofty steeple high above the church she said, "The church rings the bells every hour on Christmas Eve until midnight when it's Christmas Day," she said with a childlike excitement under her breath. "That means we're one hour closer!"

Rubbing his forehead with his hand, David asked, "So... this is Christmas Eve?"

Perking up, the little girl said, "Is your head hurt mister, 'cause you keep rubbing it?"

Pausing, David said, "Ah, no. Sometimes it's just the thoughts that hurt."

"Well," said the little girl with an air of confidence, "rubbing your head isn't going to help with that! I know because I have some of those too. But I don't rub my head. It doesn't help."

"How old are you?" David said turning and brushing the snow off of himself.

"Nine!" she said proudly, suddenly standing erect and confident.

"And so," David replied continuing to wipe off the snow, "you know about thoughts that hurt, and you're only nine? You sure about that?" For some reason David's tone was more demeaning that empathetic. While the edge had been taken off him in his travels, it was clear that it still needed some polishing. And this encounter would do that.

"Well, when your Mama keeps leaving your Daddy, or she yells and screams at him, and your Daddy cries a lot and really doesn't know what to do, and Daddy's drinking all of the time, and Mama's out with some other man that's not my Daddy, that makes my head hurt sometimes. But I still don't rub it! Not like you do," she said pointing at David's head.

Immediately David felt awash in shame and filled with an indescribable pity for whoever this little girl was. "I'm, I'm sorry," he said. "I'm really sorry." In a turn of focus, David asked, "Ah… what time is it?"

"I don't know, sometime in the afternoon, that's all I know" she replied with a shrug of her tiny shoulders.

"Don't think this is a dumb question," David said gesturing with his hand that held the ginger ale, "but what year is this?"

"1973" came the immediate reply. "That's a one with a nine and a seven and a three behind it! I know my numbers!"

"1973," David mutter half out loud and half to himself, completely missing the response of the little girl. Attempting to find his place in time this time, he said,

"That means I came forward in time, what, four years, right?"

"What'd you say mister," the little girl said with a sprightly voice.

"Umm, nothing really," David said with his mind elsewhere. "Nothing really."

Collecting his thoughts and his mind, David began rapidly piecing everything together. This was a process he'd come to understand; this piecing together where he was and why he was here. But this was somehow different in a way that was pointedly unique. Unexplainable, but different.

"Okay," he said gesturing to the diminutive nine-year-old standing fascinated in front of him. "This is 1973… and it's Christmas Eve sometime in the afternoon, or late afternoon, or something like that."

"Yup!" came the animated reply. "Yup, yup, yup!"

"You're nine," David said with his eyes fixed on this little diminutive girl. "Just nine. So what are you doing out here, all alone… on Christmas Eve… in a snow storm? Aren't your parents worried, or aren't they looking for you?"

"Nope," replied the little girl, showing a marked shift to something strikingly sullen. Staring at her feet as she moved them back and forth in the snow, she said, "Mama started throwing things at Daddy and tipped over the Christmas tree. And then she got in the car and took off real fast down the street, the street right there," she said pointing. "She's still gone, I think." Then rubbing her mittens together, she said, "It's more like Christmas Eve being here in the snow at the church… this is more like Christmas than home right now. Jesus' home," she said pointing to the church, "is the best place to be on Christmas Eve 'cause it's His birthday you know." Pausing, she continued, "Besides, Daddy didn't want me walking around with all the broken ornaments on the carpet, so I came down here," said with a sweeping motion.

By now, David had forgotten the snow and the time and the place. He had seen more than any man had ever seen, as far as he knew anyway. Somehow he had found himself flung across the span of centuries and had encountered amazing people in the middle of amazing things that had long fallen into the chasm of history when maybe it shouldn't have. His life, for whatever amount of time he had been traveling time, had been the stuff of novels and likely the dreams of those adventurous hearts who penned those novels into the reality of their lives. Yet, he had actually been privileged to live out those dreams in a way that would handily transform the most stubborn of people. In whatever way it was all unfolding, somehow this moment and this little girl topped it all.

"Mama's not a bad person, just so you know," she said with both a boldness edged with a bit of sheepishness. "I'm not supposed to know that, so don't tell, but the doctor said Mama's got some mental problem. Something's wrong inside of her, I heard." Pausing and rubbing her mittens together again, she said, "But I know she can get better… I know she can do that 'cause she's my Mom. She can! Daddy's not bad either, he just drinks more than he should sometimes, or at least that's what Mom says. But I love them both a lot!"

Looking up, the little girl paused and said, "Mister, why are you crying?" At that point David had not realized that tears had traced wide lines down both of his cheeks. It didn't take much to piece this together. Not much at all. In these extraordinary travels through time David had struggled figuring out what the other places were and what they meant. But this one, this one was clear. Painfully clear.

Wiping his face with his sleeve, he said, "This is Swanton isn't it? And, well, you're Kristin… right?"

"Wow," exclaimed the little girl, "do you know my parents or something?"

David had only known Kristin's parent's after they had divorce. His entrance into her life was at a point that 1973 and lonely Christmas Eves were the stuff of distant history and fuzzy memory for her. For better or for worse, her parents had gone their separate ways and built separate lives, neither of which had worked out in any manner that might be described as meaningful. In the oddity which is life, Kristin's dad actually carried the scars of their marriage far longer than her mother had because alcohol can't heal scars. Rather, it perpetuates them. They each built separate lives that were always somehow diminished, somehow lacking something key and foundational that neither were able to fill, somehow never getting sufficient traction to feel like a real life. Each life seemed to have aching gaps, both large and small. Something about the impact of their marriage on both of them left each of them unable to fully recover. Such was their lives.

David remembered the first time he met them. He had heard of their history and these kinds of days, but they were the stuff of story. Now, standing in the rawness of this very history, which until this moment was only the stuff of story and lore, their deficits became glaringly obvious and the reason why they were to never overcome them became resoundingly clear.

The most tension he had seen between the two of them was at David and Kristin's wedding. The mix of the moment, the attempts by both to claim roles that the other felt that they had abandoned, the angst of simply seeing each other; all of that in combination had set a pitch of wildly intense proportions. How they had managed through the wedding, David never knew. Yet, the fact that they had became even more remarkable as he stared into the nine-year-old eyes of the young girl who, twenty-two years later would become his wife.

"Ya, I know your parents," David said. "I mean, not now, but I will... someday." David winched and said to himself, *I never get this stuff right*. With a sense of befuddlement nine-year-old Kristin canted her quizzical head and stared at David. "Never mind," David said, "I just know them."

"You want to swing?" Kristin blurted out, changing the direction of the conversation.

"Shouldn't you be going home?" David asked.

Skipping through the snow over to the swings she casually said, "Nope, there's not a home to go home to right now. It'll be better in a little while, then I can go home. Not now, but later."

Suddenly it made sense. This is the girl who would betray him. She would tell endless lies, she would engage in an affair that she denied even to this day or that day as the case might be, she would physically assault him and threaten to call the police claiming with great theatrics that she was the one being abused. For years on end, she would relentlessly utter an endless litany of cutting remarks, and she would ruthlessly work to destroy him in whatever way that she thought she could. Although David was a reasonable man in both thought and contemplation, her actions at times seemed diabolical; something of another force beyond the worst of our humanity.

At the end, she would cunningly concoct a devastating series of well-orchestrated lies to turn their two children against him and steal them away to another state. And in the courtroom of divorce, she would blacklist David and paint him in the darkest colors she could find to permanently remove him from the lives of their two children. She would do things that David deemed unthinkable and unfathomable; things that were the stuff of storylines that seemed inconceivable to pen even when a person might be at their worst. This little nine-year-old who wanted David to swing with her would be the very one who would carry out these horribly malevolent deeds.

"There's a swing right here," little Kristin said, grabbing the chain of the swing next to her. "See, I brushed the snow off of it for you!" Patting it, she said, "come swing!"

The grinding contradiction in his heart was who to respond to. Should he respond to who this innocent little nine-year-old was, or what she would become? David stood ankle deep in winter's soft snowfall with the unfathomable pain caused by this nine-year-old who hadn't caused anything yet, but most certainly would, tearing at his soul.

Should he be mad at her? Should he tell her now how important it would be to love the man that she would marry some day and hope that she would remember that for the next twenty-two years so that their marriage might be different? Or should he just give her what she needed at nine? With darkness beginning to fall, should he do the adult thing and walk her home? Or should he be the stand-in parent on this Christmas Eve and just swing? Inherently he knew, as would any of us. In keeping with the perfect timing that had marked these journeys, enough of this new man had taken hold within him for him to hold his heart still and swing. More of this new man was to come.

"Come on, Mister!" she said. "Come on! Let's swing!"

David walked over, but found that both of his hands were full. Looking at the ginger ale, he turned to Kristin and said, "Would you like a ginger ale?"

"Oh, that's my favorite," she responded, "my best favorite!"

"Your best favorite," David replied in a tone of ascending curiosity.

"Yup, yup, yup," she replied again.

Interesting, David thought. *How'd aunt Mabel know that?*

"But mister, you only have one. What are you going to drink?" she said.

"Oh, I, I just had a vanilla soda a couple of, ah, minutes ago, a couple of minutes ago," he responded shaking his head at himself. "This one's for you."

"Thank you!" she said excitedly.

Spun by time passing, David realized that the soda might be four years old, or it might not be. "What's the expiration date on this?" David said holding up the bottle in his hand.

"What's a 'spiration date?" she quickly replied.

"Oh yeah. That's kinda new," David mumbled. Handing the bottle to her, he said, "Someday that'll just be something else you'll have to pay attention to. Just let me know if it tastes okay."

Handing the soda to her, he gently placed the Bible at the foot of the slide, walked back to the swing, took hold of the chain and seated himself. "You know what my favorite thing is?" little Kristin said while opening the soda.

"Thinking about horses," David replied immediately.

"How'd you know that?" she said with a tone thick with curiosity.

"I'll bet you've got a room full of toy horses in your bedroom, right?" David said.

"Yep. And someday I'm going to get a real one!" she said with all the confidence in the world. "And I'm going to ride him wherever I want to go!"

"I believe that you will," David said with confidence.

His travels up until this time had been about hope. An invasion of hope. That hope could handily withstand the worst that life could throw at it. And the worst that life ever threw at David would be what this little nine-year-old would throw at him a little over two decades in the future. Everything else would be downhill from there. And so, the one thing that would kill his ability to hope would be her. Conversely, the one thing that would liberate his ability to hope would be her as well. And that would depend entirely upon him.

These trips through time. The messages from these wonderful people. All that he had seen and experienced and held... all of that would pivot on whether he would make this moment about his need to seek revenge, or about her need to be loved. Would he believe that pain is the soil within which joy finds its roots? Would he forgive knowing that not doing so would hold him hostage to history? Would he believe that hope makes the greatest losses places for the greatest gains? Much like that time he had fled up the basement steps only to grab that bit of the infinite within himself and return to that which he feared, would he do so yet again? What would be do? What choice would he make? These trips had worked their magic. His next words would say it all.

"Kristin," David said with her swinging next to him. "You're a good girl." Pausing, he went on. "A really good girl. And do you know that even when you do bad things, I still think that you're a good girl? A really good girl."

"I am a good girl, right?" she replied brightly.

"Yes you are, even if you don't always do good things." Bringing his swing to a stop and staring at her as she somehow continued to swing with soda in hand, he said, "I will always believe that you are a good girl. Always. I want you to know that no matter what happens. No matter what, I will always believe that you are a really good girl. I want you to believe that too."

"Okay," little Kristin replied not really understanding the moment or what had been spoken into it. How could she? The hope was that while she would not grasp his words, her memory would.

Collecting his thoughts and parsing them down from the thirty-one-year old he had married to the nine-year-old that swung next to him, he continued. "Can you do something for me Kristin," David said choking up.

"Sure," she replied in a sprightly tone.

"If someday you happen to hurt somebody who's really close to you, I mean somebody you really, really love…"

"You mean like my Mom or my Dad?" she interrupted. "Like them, you mean?"

"Yeah, yeah, somebody like that. Like that. Just like that. Just remember that if there's somebody you really love that you hurt someday, please, please remember that they still love you no matter what. They still love you. Can you remember that for me?"

"Okay," she replied. "I'll 'member. I will!"

Staring at little nine-year-old Kristin swinging, David drew a breath and said, "Can you remember one more thing for me that's really, really important."

"Okay," she said with a bright tone. "You want me to remember a lot!" she said with brightness and energy.

"I guess so," David replied. "Sorry about that. But could you remember that when you hurt that person who's really close to you that they forgive you, okay? Remember that they understand and that they really, really forgive you because they love you no matter what and they want the best for you even though you don't want to be with them."

"Why wouldn't I want to be with them if I love them?" she said with all of the innocence of a nine-year-old.

At that point, David knew that he had moved some place beyond the understanding of this adorable and innocent nine-year-old child. The future of which he spoke was nothing of her present. Nothing. She was not yet the woman who would betray him. That person had yet to coalesce from the tender heart of this little girl. David grappled to embrace the reality that this bright and adorable nine-year-old was nothing more than nine. Just nine. She had, or more appropriately, was watching her world spiral in the dysfunction that she did not create nor understand. She was wholly innocent in a world of toxic drama played out by two adults who could not manage their own dysfunction sufficiently to keep her from it.

"What is this moment about?" David muttered out loud.

"What?" she said. "What did you say?" she said as she continued to swing with energy and vitality.

"Oh, nothing" David replied.

"When I get married," she said out of nowhere, "I'm going to live happily ever-after you know, 'cause I saw that in Cinderella. I know it can happen because it happened to her! Like the prince and all." Caught entirely off guard, David stumbled over all of the words that he would want to say to the Kristin he had married, knowing that this little girl was but the first budding seed of that person. Yet, that seed was decades away from blossoming into that person. This person was two people for David, forcing him to parse out who she was throughout their marriage, from who she was innocently sitting on the swing next to him.

Once again forcing himself into the mindset of a nine-year-old, he said, "You know what?"

"What?" she blurted out with excitement.

"You can have that kind of marriage. And you know what else?" David said.

"What, what?" she retorted.

"I know that the man that you're going to marry will love you very much. I know that. You will get your prince. He won't be perfect, but you'll get him. I know it."

"I already know what he's going to be like. Do you want to know?" she asked with all the excitement of a heart yet untainted.

"I would love to know," David said with corresponding energy.

Bringing her swing to a stop she said, "He'll be smart, and he'll have a good job, and we'll live in a big farmhouse 'cause I always thought that would be fun and it would have a place for my horses, and we'll have two kids and really love each other!" With a huge smile on her tiny face, and with her swinging having resumed, she said, "that's what it'll be like!"

David shook inside with an immense joy for this little nine-year-old. Her dreams were of the sweetest sort, spun by innocence untainted and fresh. However, his joy was simultaneously offset by the excruciating pain of knowing that she will get exactly what she's dreamt of. Yet, she will choose to throw it away. To discard dreams is to kill the person who spun them. Sadly, she will hurt him, but she will kill her own soul in the killing. He had never quite thought of it that way before.

Clearing his head from the mass of swelling emotion, he said, "You know what? I believe that you're going to get that. In fact, I believe it so much that I know that you're going to get it! So do me a favor, okay?"

"Okay," she quickly replied.

"When you get that stuff," David said, "make sure that you really appreciate it, okay? That you thank God that you have it, that you hold onto it real tight, and that you make certain that you don't let anything take it away from you."

"Okay," she said. "I can do that! I can!"

David found that he wasn't really giving this little girl hope, although she was clearly encouraged. In an entirely unexpected turn of events, she was giving him hope. Glorious hope. She was helping him to see that underneath the apparent monster that his wife had become, deep on the inside, in her soul of souls there lay this wonderful nine-year-old. In the recesses of her nine-year-old eyes and in the lightness of her simple mannerisms there lay something authentically simple, something untainted and something wholly innocent.

In her simplicity she was simply wonderful. The trappings of the world and the sludge of life that would splash itself on her in the coming years would smudge and smear what he was seeing in her at that moment. While the sludge of several decades would hide this simple wonder, the magic of this little girl was far too deep to ever have it washed away. Yes, she had betrayed him in ways decadent beyond words. Yet, this little girl sitting on this swing on this wintery Christmas Eve sat off in some dark corner of it all. And maybe, just maybe as the years following the divorce rolled on, she would step back out into the light. Maybe. And it was in the power of this simple simplicity that hope could be mostly clearly seen.

Leaping off the swing she ran over the slide. David had left his Bible sitting at the bottom of the slide. Peeking out from the edge of the Bible was the ornate book mark that aunt Mabel had placed in it before she sent him here.

"Oh," little Kristin gasped. "That is such a pretty bookmark. Can I see it?" she said bouncing with childlike glee. Stepping over to the Bible and picking it up, David slid it out of the Bible, scanned it a moment himself, and then handed it to her. Once in her mittened hands, she held it as if it were a treasure of the most precious sort.

"Oh," she gasped. "It's so pretty. So pretty!"

"Yes it is," David replied. "My aunt gave it to me earlier today… I mean awhile ago… or… well, my aunt Mabel gave it to me." By this point he figured he'd never get the whole time thing figured out sufficiently to say it accurately. Somehow he was okay with that.

Cupping the bookmark in her hand she said, "We don't have many pretty things in our home. Dad says we don't have much money, and then my Mom's broken some of the pretty things Dad got so he doesn't get much anymore. Mom says we don't have stuff because Dad spends all our money on drinking."

"That's too bad," David said. "I feel sad for you. I'm sure that they didn't mean to do that stuff."

"I know," came the reply as she appeared lost in the bookmark.

"Can you read what it says?" David asked.

"Yup, I'm a good reader. My teacher says I read better than anybody in my class. She says I read like a fifth grader," she said proudly.

"I believe that you do," David replied.

Reading it slowly and laboriously, forming the words as she went, she said, "It says, 'When all other hope fails, hope in God never fails.'"

"Very good," David said, clapping his hands in applause. "Do you know what that means?" he continued.

"Yup," she said confidently. "It means that even when my Mom and Dad don't do everything that they should, God will do that for me instead."

With tears once again starting down his face, David said, "You are so right! Can you remember that?"

"I'll try," she said, cupping the bookmark in her hands.

Handing the bookmark back to David, he paused and said, "You know, maybe the best way for you to remember that is to keep the bookmark. What do you think?"

"Really, really?" she said jumping up and down in glee. "Really?"

"Really," David said.

This little nine-year-old Kristin unzipped her coat, pulled it open, and slid the bookmark into an interior pocket. Zipping her coat back up, she patted her coat and said, "It will be safe in there forever!"

With the snow continuing to fall and darkness starting to set in, the church bell rang again heralding the coming of Christmas Day. David realized that he had been privileged to be out on this sacred playground for an hour with this remarkable nine-year-old. *This may have been the best hour of my life,* he thought to himself.

"You know what?" David said.

"What?" she replied while continuing to be entirely captivated by the intricate bookmark that she had tucked in her coat.

"I think we should take you home. It's getting a little dark, and so maybe we should take you home."

"Okay," came the sprightly reply. Somehow having this treasure and embracing its message had transformed this little nine-year-old.

Taking her by the hand, David said, "Show me where you live."

As they walked off the playground onto a short parking lot that led to the street, David turned and looked back. Somehow this playground seemed like one from his own childhood, yet he knew that it could not be. He also noticed that he had left no footprints in the snow. Much like Gettysburg and every place else, he was there, but he was not. *I guess that some things are not be figured out, only enjoyed* he thought. *Come to think of it, that makes life a whole lot easier.* Catching himself he then thought, *That's quite a departure from the way I normally think. Who am I anyway?* For whoever he was becoming, he was quite pleased with it.

"Do you sing?" came that sprightly voice again.

Rather caught off guard, David said, "Well, umm… some. Let me guess," he continued, now becoming animated with this amused nine-year-old, "Your favorite Christmas song is 'Jingle Bells,' right?"

"You know everything Mister," she said.

"I'm learning. I'm finally learning" he replied.

And so they started to sing out loud with an energy so robust and electrically alive that it seemed as if all the wonder of the Christmas season had distilled the whole of it itself down into both of their hearts. Her home was little more than half a block away from the playground, a 'walk and skip' as they say. As they walked, they passed brightly decorated homes hung with a glorious array of brilliant Christmas lights, nativity scenes and plastic Santa's. Windows glowed golden as families tucked themselves indoors against the cold and into the warmth of family and an awaiting holiday. Walking and skipping, they sang down the road of her life.

Two doors down from Kristin's house there sat a home that had two, huge pine trees standing as sentries on each side of the concrete sidewalk in front of a light, green facade. The sidewalk began at a small cement porch and gently curved around to intersect the adjacent driveway. Each of the two pine trees were draped in a dazzling array of multi-colored Christmas lights that ascended all the way to their lofty peaks. Their light seemed to cascade from the trees, leaving multi-colored pools of color all about the fresh snow at their bases.

On the sidewalk, there stood a rather stout man in his mid-30's shoveling the newly fallen snow from the walkway. Looking up as David and Kristin walked by, he shouted out, "Hello Kristin!"

Stopping her singing she said, "Hello, Mr. Meyers," in a voice completely taken captive with cheer.

"You out here by yourself?" he asked with a tone of concern.

"Oh no!" came the swift reply. "I've got my friend here. We just had fun playing at the playground down at the church and now we're going home!"

Staring at her, Mr. Meyers saw no one but Kristin. David gave a rather silly smile and waved mostly to amuse himself. "Oh," Mr. Meyers said. "So, you're on your way home, right?" he continued.

"Yup. Going home for Christmas Eve."

"Okay," Mr. Meyers replied. "It's cold out here, so you better get going."

"I will," little Kristin replied. "Merry Christmas, Mr. Meyers," she said in a light and cheery voice.

"Merry Christmas," he replied waving a gloved hand.

"Merry Christmas," David said, smiling and waving frantically at Mr. Meyers as to take advantage of his invisibility.

Looking up at him and catching David by surprise, Kristen said, "Wow mister, you really like Christmas don't you?"

"More than ever," he said playfully rubbing her head. "More than ever."

Street lights highlighted the falling snow, layering the landscape in a magical dusting of winter and Christmas.

Before they had a chance to complete another chorus, she stopped and pointed, "That's my house." Pausing she said, "Looks like my Mom came back."

"Is that good?" David asked pensively.

"Oh, yeah," came the confident reply. "She's always better when she comes back. She'll be better now, I know."

"Well, then," David said. "I guess you better go."

"You want to come in?" little Kristin asked pulling on his hand.

"Umm, I better not," David replied. "I've got to get home myself."

"Where do you live?" came the energized yet quizzical voice. "Maybe I can come and visit you!"

"That would be nice," David replied, "but I live a long way from here."

"I have a bike and I can ride real fast," she replied.

"Well, I think it would take a long time on your bike."

"Maybe my parents could bring me?" she said.

"You know what, I think that someday you'll probably visit me and stay awhile… would that be good?"

"Oh yes," came the excited reply. "That would be good!"

"Okay," David said, "Let's wait until you visit me in the future, okay? In the meantime, you better go before they miss you."

"Okay," came the exciting reply. "Have a Merry Christmas!" she said, reaching over and giving David a hug full of everything a hug should be full of. Running halfway up the driveway she stopped, turned and said, "What's your name? You never told me your name."

"My name's David," David replied.

"I love you David" came a reply with all the wonder of a nine-year-old on Christmas Eve.

"I love you too," he shouted back. *I love you still,* he said to himself. And she was gone.

Darkness had largely fallen on this neighborhood cloaked in the wonder of Christmas Eve in 1973. David stood alone on the street, taking it all in. *This is where she came from*, he thought to himself. *This is the 'why' that I always figured was behind everything, but I never knew for sure. This is where the wounded-ness came from.* Shaking his head, a terrible sadness slowly engulfed him.

He stood there for a moment, soaking in the scene and allowing it to transform the anger that he held within himself. The bitterness and the hatred toward her fell from his heart in a way so thick and thorough that it seemed to fall at his feet and become consumed in the accumulating snow. He had forgiven in bits and pieces over time. Now, he was forgiving in something much larger. He felt a swelling hope that the woman that she was in his time was much more the little girl who he had just skipped and sang with. Whether the future stayed the same or not, David would be different.

He stood and did something that he rarely did anymore; he prayed out loud… very out loud it seemed; talking to God in the waning hours of Christmas Eve, 1973. Praying into a future that was yet to be, believing that God was in that future just as much as he was where David was at that moment. He prayed that in that future she would find that little girl within herself, that she would embrace that nine-year-old, and that she would never let her go.

For David, his hope and the prayer that spoke his hope out loud did arise out of the desire that she would return to him or that somehow this would change the future as he knew it, for he realized the unforgivable selfishness of such a thought. Rather, he simply wanted her to be what God had designed her to be. To be this innocent and wonderful nine-year-old once again and forever, whether she be with him or not.

Pulling out his Bible, he pulled out the final piece of paper. *I suppose that I should read this one as well*, he said to himself. *Apparently I'm on my own this time.*

Turning and tilting the page toward an adjacent streetlight, the script was cursive and beautiful. It was precise and ornate. Slowly he read:

"Been thinking about hope lately. I've become convinced that hope is not of this world because hope says that no matter what happens in this world we can overcome it. Big things too, like war or people dying or farms destroyed or all kinds of tragedy. Hope says that we can overcome all of that. I don't suppose I know how hope can do that if it didn't come from something else. Someplace that's bigger than this place. Maybe that's why the world out there's always inventing something new, thinking that these contraptions are going to be the things that stop the wars and the dying and the tragedies. I don't think we can think up any invention that can stop tragedy or make hope.

"I think that hope comes from someplace bigger than here. I would reckon that it comes from God, otherwise it would never be big enough because this world's got some right big problems. We might have a hard time finding it sometimes, or maybe believing in it, but I think it's there anyway just like God's there. I tend to think that God puts it right in front of us but we don't see it because we're looking at other things. Kind of like being captivated by things that don't matter much.

"Hope is the greatest gift given to us. I think we are hopeless to construct it. We can only follow its light, kind of chase after it and receive it with thanks when we find it. And when I think like that, nothing much scares me anymore. Don't need to be scared. It a right peaceful place to be.

Nellie Morris

December 10th, 1928"

"My grandmother," he gasped. "It's my grandmother!" Somehow he knew that this was the one person he would never meet. He had heard her voice, but a visit was not permitted. As to why, he didn't know. By this time David had come to understand that great journey's down the road of life are dictated by something far bigger than us, and it is this thing that charts the journey to perfection… if we let it. Therefore, we need to believe that the journey's right even though we don't have the rationale to explain it all. David stared at the date.

"Two days before she died," he said to himself in a solemn tone. "Two days."

David looked up at the home to see little nine-year-old Kristin press her face against a frosty window to try and see him. Once she spotted him, she waved with all the electricity that he had fallen in love with… that he still loved.

Standing warm in loves embrace as held against the cold of December's winter, he was unexpectedly reminded of the road of Indian, horse and heavy wagon. He thought of the seasoned split-rail fence that somehow bridged both the meadow and the road, creating a unifying point of connection that allowed each to live in perfect harmony with the other while granting themselves latitude to cultivate the fullest appreciation of the other. It was something of the most perfect kind of harmony one can envision, where things deemed as mutually exclusive were seamlessly interwoven into a life-giving and life-blessing camaraderie.

Although his marriage had been decimated and any connection whatsoever had fallen entirely irreconcilable, at that moment it was immediately unified in ways he had deemed impossible. And just as impossibly, the wounds were, somehow, someway gone. His sense was that this moment would not save his marriage. This would not change a future yet to be written. However, it would do something far better. It would save his heart.

Vigorously waving back, he slowly lowered his hand and pressed it to the page. The strength in his legs seemed to entirely evaporate. Falling on his knees in the snow, he leaned forward to place his hands in front of him to brace his fall and his palms hit concrete.

Chapter 18
Back to 1928 and a Lesson
The Last Leg Home

Life is circular it seems, causing us to leave something only to find ourselves back at that same place as if time had never budged an inch. Sometimes we arrive back shortly after we had departed, our return reflecting a sense that whatever we departed from it should in some way remain part of our lives for the rest of our lives. Therefore, the occasional return is embraced and even welcomed. These returns represent a sort of soft reminiscence that soothes us against the rigors of whatever our lives are.

Sometimes however, the route away from those places is decades long. The miles are mapped in intervals of time so broad that the route itself has long fallen off the map of our lives. The point of origin itself is entirely forgotten or deemed irrelevant in the forgetting. We unexpectedly find ourselves back at some place long departed from, wondering why we're here while trying to remember what 'here' is. In whatever time frame we come back, we come back as a result of some mystically circular event that is far more blessing than curse. But whatever the case, time is secondary to the fact that the journey happened. And the greatest journeys of all appear to be circular.

David found himself back in the root cellar, prone on his knees; his palms flat on cold concrete. Before him was the chest, just as he had left it. In his hands the old family Bible with all six pages now aged and brittle. No time had passed, or so it seemed. He had gone to 1928, then 1944, then back 1863, and to 1969 and then forward to

1973; crossing centuries of time in either real time or shadow and coming right back to where it all began at the precise moment that it all began. It was December 11th, but what year?

The silence around him was suddenly shattered.

"David," a rather listless female voice called from the basement door. Suddenly, upstairs he could hear the soft sound of someone walking. "Who you takin' to?" came a voice from upstairs.

"Just talking to myself Nel," the young man shouted at the basement ceiling, "you know full well that I do that quite a bit."

"Well, pumps froze again," said a delicate but strong female voice. "Can't do supper without water," she continued.

"Things do tend to get froze in December, don't they?" the young man replied, casting a winking eye toward David. "Be right up," he said, projecting his voice toward the stairway. It was his grandfather.

Returning his attention to David, his grandfather said, "Welcome back. Ya don't look all that worse for wear," he said smiling. "So, how was yer trip? Kinda wish I was the one that was able to do that. I mean, I'm not all that certain 'bout where ya went, but I know that it was the life changin' kinda stuff that few folks get to do," he said while pulling a wrinkled handkerchief out of his worn overalls.

"Where am I?" David asked.

"Back where ya started," his grandfather replied with a slight flair, "Well sorta. That's kinda how life works ya know," he said with the deep drawl of wisdom. "We seem to end up back where we started even though we thought we'd gotten a fer piece away from all of that," he said tucking his handkerchief back in his overalls and burying his hands deep in his pockets. "In comin' back we bring with us all of the things that we learned along the trip," he said, shaking his head in some sort of reflective approval. Continuing, he said, "Kinda seems to me that we go away to learn about life and then come back to where we first came from so we can make it just that much better. No sense learnin' things that you can't use, right? That's a sad waste."

David continued to sit on the floor. Slowly he pulled his legs up into his chest, laid his head on the top of his legs and attempted to collect himself; working hard to somehow correlate all that had happened and everything that his grandfather just said.

"It's gonna take time to get it all sorted in yer head David," his grandfather spoke into the silence. "Sometimes a man's exposed to so many things that he's gotta step back and get it all figured out. To line it up in yer head. Make sense of it, kinda."

With increasing energy and a tad of buoyance, he continued, "But see, that's when ya know you've been blessed. Things that you understand right away, well, I'm not altogether certain that's a blessing 'cause it's just too easy. It's just simple things, like everyday thoughts and such. But the things that are grand, those things, well those ya got to ponder for a spell. And David, ya been blessed more than most, so I know full well that ya got some ponderin' to do. But I know that you will, and you'll fer sure take it all back to where ya started."

Leaning against the old sink, his grandfather rubbed his hand on the underside of his chin as if contemplating some deep thought and said, "Like I said, if yer in a place where ya gotta let it all soak in, that's those times of blessin' David, that's those times when life's kinda pulls back the curtain and lets ya see what most folks never see in the whole of their lives. It's quite a burden fer sure, but sometimes our biggest burdens are our biggest blessin's. Yer in a time of great blessing David."

David was listening, for now he had a platform or a grid of sorts where all of this fit perfectly and made impeccable sense. Everything his grandfather was saying fit precisely into everything else and everyone else he had encountered. His grandfather's simple, earthy words pulled the pieces together with an ease that seemed entirely opposed to the magnitude of what he had just done and what he had just seen. And yet, they fell together in a seamless sort of manner, uniting into a completely unanticipated whole.

Sometimes it seems that we choose to see the 'parts' of our lives as the 'whole' of our lives. Parts are far less frightening, for if we were sufficiently daring to piece them together with all the other assorted parts of our life, the 'whole' of them might become bigger than the 'whole' of us. And that is frightening indeed. Sadly, in our ignorant stubbornness, we've yet to understand that if something is not bigger than us, it's not worth the life of 'us.'

And then, in those rarest of moments when we're actually daring enough to put the pieces together, we typically try to force-fit them. We ram our agendas into ill-fitting spaces in order to make the 'whole' something that serves us rather than abandoning ourselves to the service of it. We might recognize that there's a larger 'whole' in all of this, but it has to be our 'whole.' And that kind of 'whole' always leaves a gaping 'hole' in us.

It seemed that his grandfather was simply tying many of the scattered thoughts together and cinching them tight into some sort of marvelous puzzle. It was simple and clean, but tenderly ornate and beautiful in its simplicity. His voice was the voice of all of the others, just consolidated into one. There was the grand summation unfolding right in front of him. Maybe 'the' grand summation. Maybe this was last chapter that tied all of the others into some comprehensive whole. And this unassuming, earthy man educated by nothing other than hard work and a tough faith was tasked with this marvelous responsibility.

Pausing, his grandfather continued, "David, nobody in history's ever done what ya just did. Nobody, no how, 'cept maybe God Himself 'cause He can do that. But you son, you, yer special. Bible says many are called but few are chosen. And you, you were chosen."

Glancing out of the basement window to the fields that swept away to the horizon, his grandfather said, "I don't know everything that ya just saw 'cause when it comes to this life that God made, there's a lot to see out there, a whole lot. Beyond our imagination fer sure. I ain't got that kind of imagination. But I know enough to know that a whole passel of folks chose to come back, live their lives all over again and die again so that you'd get that message. I think ya know what I'm talking about."

Taking a deep breath, he said, "That message. It was on the bookmark that ya gave that nine-year-old girl. Nine years old. That's all she was and she understood it." Wiping a bit of smudge off the window, he said, "It's funny how a life-changing message, a message that's really a message for all time can fit in the space of a simple bookmark or find space in the heart of a little girl." With a knowing smile and a shake of his head, he said, "That's quite amazin' indeed. Although I'm just a simple farmer, I would reckon that's why people miss it, because it seems too simple and not near big enough to face the problems in that world out there. Or so they think."

Stepping away from the window and rubbing a hand on the timbered ceiling as if loving the house for the last time, he said, "I suppose it's even funnier that a nine-year-old understands that message better than most grown-ups. See David, we need to heart of a child sometimes. Maybe most of the time. You, David, somewhere ya gave that heart of yers away. You didn't lose it. That's too simple.

Nope. Ya gave it away… that's what ya did. And ya gave it away because you thought it was far, far too painful to hold onto it. What I think ya learned is that holding onto to it can be painful beyond words to explain. But giving it away jest to get away from the pain… well that there's even more painful… ain't it?"

Turning back to the window, he said, "Yep, giving your heart away can be painful if it's fer the wrong reasons. Outright painful if pain's what yer running from. If that's why you do it. But if ya think on it long enough, ponder if fer a piece, givin' it away ain't nearly as painful if I'm givin' it away 'cause it heals someone else. If someone needs my heart to heal theirs, then givin' it away… well that's good. That givin' is good. Real good. And if my hope's in God, I mean really in God, I can't do nothin' but give it away 'cause He gave His heart away fer me. Started that on Christmas, He did. So David, give yer heart away, not to run from it like ya have. But to heal people, like ya did with that nine-year-old. Like ya will with all those people standing out in yer future."

Lifting up his head, David's face was washed with bewilderment, thinking he shouldn't have given the bookmark away, questioning his decision with some sort of wild panic. Reading his mind as wisdom can so easily do, his grandfather walked over to him, stooped in front of David, put his arms on his knees and said, "Ya did the right thing David, givin' that to her I mean." Looking David in the eye, he said, "This here's 1928, so she ain't born yet, but she will be and I know enough about the power of that there message, that she'll carry it with her forever. Just like all them other folks ya met, that'll ride high in her heart. In the end it'll save her. I want ya to know that. No matter what kind of choices she makes David, she'll for certain come back to that message. She will."

Getting up and walking back to door of the root cellar, his grandfather said, "Look son, it ain't the pages in that book that have the power. Some mighty things were written on those pages. But it ain't them that's got the power. It's the book, David, it's the message in the book," he said pointing to the Bible that David was holding. "It's that book."

"Hope in God is hope that ya can't beat David. Nothin' can be beat it. Nothin'. A farmhouse up in flames and a wife lost can't beat it. Jest can't. A world war can't beat it. Carryin' the weight of a nation ripped in two by a civil war can't beat it. Havin' to carve out a life fer yerself 'cause the person ya married died defendin' that country can't beat it. Living as a scared, helpless little girl in home torn by fighin' parents can't beat it. Divorce and betrayal of the worst sort can't beat it. Jest can't."

Taking a step toward David who by this time had stood to his feet, his grandfather stared with the sternness of truth and the unstoppable power of conviction said, "Divorce and bein' betrayed can't beat it David. You mind what I'm tellin' ya? 'Cause in the end, God is bigger than all that. May not seem so at the time, but He is." Pointing directly at David, he said, "and ya've seen people, stared 'em in the face, talked to 'em even, and they came right on back to this side of their pain to tell ya what it was like on the other side. And over there, after all of it was over, God was bigger. He is a forever kind of bigger. No pain comes close to matchin' this God and what He'll do fer ya. That's why I've got hope," he said with a growing passion and accelerating conviction.

Turning and walking to the window over the washbasin, his grandfather again reflectively stared at the farm fields that rolled away to the edge of the woods and said, "That woman upstairs is gonna burn in this house tomorrow. December 12th it's gonna happen. Makes ya wish ya could stop time, just halt it right here forever. Enjoy her here for all of eternity right here. I'd farm those fields forever if that'd keep her. That'd be fine by me. But," he paused, "it don't work like that."

Taking a long breath, he continued, "She don't know about the fire and all, but I do. And I thought that, when that happened, when the flames just consumed the house here and I couldn't get to her," he paused, "I thought that hope had burned up for sure. Fact is, it made me wonder if hope's real at all, and if it was how could it get burnt up like everythin' else? Took me pert-near ten years, give or take a month, to realize that hope didn't get killed at all, although I coulda sworn it did. Coulda sworn by everything I knew. Just like you, I gave hope away fearin' that hopin' was too painful. But I learned, like ya did."

Turning to David he said, "I just chose to believe that there weren't no hope no more 'cause I thought somethin' had happened to me that was bigger than God. David," his grandfather said with a steeled conviction, "Life is gonna do things to ya, or let things a happen to ya that strike ya so hard that ya swear that there's no hope nowhere. Yer gonna be convinced that it's all a cruel joke and that hope, whatever that is, is jest some fanciful story made up so we have somethin' to hold onto in a world where there's nothin' to hold onto. And let me tell ya, if ya lose hope David, if somehow ya let that go, well, if ya let yourself believe there's no hope, then life's just not tolerable. Ya can't live without hope David. The beauty is, ya don't need to."

Turning and walking back to the window, his grandfather paused and said, "They said that the smoke, from the fire I mean, the smoke could be seen over in the next county. I really can't recall, or maybe I don't want to," he said shrugging his shoulders. "Sometimes I wonder if that wasn't her way of sayin' goodbye in a way everyone could see it." Pausing and lifting a sleeve to wipe away the tears that had begun to roll down his cheeks, he said, "What I fergot was that nothin's bigger than God… ever. Seems like it sometimes, but it's not. No fire, whether that's a house burnin' or a marriage burnin' or a family burning or a nation burnin'. Don't matter. Nothin' in this life is bigger than God no matter how big it might seem. And 'cause that's true, there's always a place for hope... always."

Shifting his weight and looking out the window, David had no idea what to say. Sometimes it seems that saying nothing is the best thing that we can say. At times there's nothing we can add to anything and to do so would only diminish the magnitude of the moment. And without a doubt, this was one of those moments for David.

"Yer goin' back home David," his grandpa said as he turned to face David. "And when you do, yer never gonna travel again, I mean not like this. All that's closed to ya. Journey's done. Ya might say that the doors of history are gonna be closed again, and they ain't never gonna be opened to you again. They'll open again, but not to you."

Pausing he said, "Ya know why that is David? Do ya know? It's 'cause ya've got what ya need. Ya don't need this anymore," he said gesturing around the basement. "Ya got a message that you, and the world that you came from needs more than anything else. Ya just got to go see it in yer own time. Tell people in yer time. Let 'em know. Let 'em know in a way they won't ferget."

David leaned toward his grandfather and said, "but I don't know that I've got it, at least like I need to. The first couple of times I traveled through, through whatever this was, I thought I got it. I hate to admit it, but that arrogant attitude just grabs me sometimes, and I'm ashamed of that. But now," he said, "Now that you tell me I've got it, I'm not sure that I do. I'm not certain at all. Yeah, hope and all... I got that, and I'm glad I do. But I'm not certain that I've got it enough to warrant what those people did, and the decisions that they made to live it all over again, and die all over again."

Incessantly pacing back and forth, David rung his hands and said, "It's too big for me, it's too big of a responsibility. This, this should have been given someone else, someone else better. Maybe this time thing should be rearranged so that I never did this and that somebody else could. I mean, time could do that. I'm just not the guy for this."

Walking face to face with David, his grandfather said, "Of course ya don't have it. Not all of it anyways. 'Cause that's a life journey. We learn a little at a time, David. But that's part of the adventure, knowin' we don't have it all but being brave enough to go on out there anyway. To build on what we do know. To look the world in the face everyday that ya live and say, 'I'm not done and yer not goin' stop me from bein' done! The man who waits to know everythin' is the man who never does anythin' David. But ya got enough," he said pointing at David's heart. "Right here, ya got enough. Now ya just build it up and ya build it out."

Pausing, he said, "but I got one more thing for ya. Just hold here for a minute." Turning, David's grandfather walked up the rough-hewn oak basement stairs. He heard some muted conversation and footsteps on the floor above. What David wouldn't have given to go up there. To see his grandmother, face to face… even for just a moment. That's all… just a moment. To see the house as it was before it fell to the flames and the spin of stories handed down over card games and family barbecues. To go out and walk the fields. To meander out to the road of Indian, horse and heavy wagon as it was when it was ninety years closer to the time when those sturdy pioneers had walked it themselves. To touch the river-rock fence, if it's been built yet, at the precise place where the harsh marks of his life would be made so many decades later. If only…

However, some things in our journey are withheld from us for reasons we don't understand, but reasons we have to place faith in. Some incredible things are withheld. But in the withholding we must believe that something even more incredible transpires in the withholding itself. For, if we tread where we should not, we may kill what should have been. And so, we bow to things greater than ourselves. This was one of those moments.

Within a minute or two, David's grandfather came back down the basement steps. He steps were cautious and light. In his arms he held a small bundle, gently caressing it as if it were some priceless treasure. He walked up to David and paused. Standing before David, his grandfather looked up and with an elongated pause he said, "David, meet yer mother."

The introduction was abrupt, without the formality or preparation that would have given David a moment to ready himself for what this was.

"My what... my mother?" David said stepping back. This was opposite of how life was supposed to be, or should be. This was a reversal of the grandest sort. This was life rammed in reverse so that David might live it better forward.

Sure, in all his travels logic had loosened it grip and freed David. It had made room for the impossible. But it had 'loosened.' This was the place where the security of logic collapsed entirely, utterly imploding and leaving David reorienting the impossible in his head without any constraints to restrain it. And that is the very place that God must bring each of us, for the restraints of man will do nothing less than become the constraints of our faith. At some point those restraints must implode in upon themselves so that faith can explode within us. And in the wild juxtaposition of time reversed, this was that moment for David. This was the final step in an impossible journey of impossible impossibilities.

Trembling, David tentatively peered into the generous wrap of blankets. A tiny, bulbous face stared back.

"Barely six months old," his grandfather said. "My first, and my only with Nellie. She's it. All I'll ever have. Couldn't imagine having another child with anyone else. Ya know, sometimes life robs us blind. Sure does. But we know that in whatever plan that's workin' itself out in all of that, it's not about reclaiming somethin' or tryin' to get somethin' back. It's about havin' faith in it all, it's about joinin' the plan, whatever it is, and goin' forward with it. And it's hope David, it's hope that helps us do that."

Pausing, he looked up at David and said, "David, tomorrow she'll lose her Ma. She's only six months old, so she'll never understand all that, thank goodness. But, she'll lose her Ma tomorrow. She'll meet 'er in eternity, but that's some time away. Until then, she'll only know her through pictures and stories and such.

Pausing in the realization of the momentous nature of the moment, his grandfather said, "David, I want ya to hold her. I want ya to hold her before she loses her Ma. I want her to kinda have another connection before this one's gone. And next to me, yer the closest connection she's got."

"I can't," David shot back immediately. Stumbling, he said, "I can't. I just can't. I, I don't want to hurt her." Wrapped in confusion of the most confusing sort, he said, "I mean, she's my Mom. I know she's my Mom, but I don't know how she's my Mom. But she's my Mom. I can't hold my Mom. It doesn't work that way. None of this works that way."

"Hold her," his grandfather said firmly, extending her out to David. "Hold her. She needs you to hold her before her Ma can't."

Looking at his grandfather and then back at his mother and then back at his grandfather, he drew a calming breath which didn't do much to calm him. With trembling arms, he stepped up on shaking legs and pensively took her in his arms. It had been a long time since he held a baby. Years actually. He drew her close to him and gently coddled her in his arms, instantly finding a camaraderie of connectivity. In some way bizarre yet wholly beautiful, her warmth passed into him and he into her; not just a physical warmth, but one of deep soul and enlivened spirit. He fell into everything that she was, remembering everything that she would be. He could not take his eyes off of her; her smile, her tiny hands, every facial feature… all of it.

"Mom," he said, half laughing at it all. "Mom, mom." Starting to cry, he continued, "I wish, I wish I could have done more for you. I wish, I wish so much."

His grandfather stepped back, interrupted and said, "She'll go on and pick tomatoes in her teen years. The Brock's, good people they are, the Brock's have a tomato farm about two miles up the road. She'll pick for them for a lot of years. Old man Brock always told me that she was the best hand that he had on the farm. Said she handily outworked all the men." Pausing, with a smile and a touch of laughter he said, "Never had so many tomatoes in all my life. She'd bring 'em home by the bushel. Kinda developed an aversion to 'em, if ya know what I mean."

Continuing he said, "She'll go to secretary school and get herself one of those certificates. Then she'll work as a secretary in town. She'll actually have a couple of jobs with promotions and all. That last job at The Scale Company, at that job she'll meet your Dad. She was datin' someone else at the time, some whiney guy that was always complainin' 'bout somethin' she said. He didn't treat her well at all. Not at all. I told her that I don't how many times. Kinda scolded her 'bout that.

"Then yer Dad came along." Pausing, he said, "She loved that man. So did I. There's a depression comin' and he'll lose his Dad to alcohol and other women right in the middle of it. His ma will support him and his three siblings working a passel of odd jobs. Sad. But, he'll serve in the war, World War II, I mean. Enlisted at nineteen. Jest a boy. Won't see combat, thank God. He'll be fixin' radios on B-17 and B-24's. Mighty big planes. But he'll serve.

"Yer Dad worked hard, designing things for companies, but never getting' the credit. I know that made him right frustrated at times. They said that when ya design a machine ya have to build something called a prototype to work out any problems 'cause there's certain to be some. But yer Dad, yer Dad didn't need no prototypes 'cause he built 'em right the first time. Sure did. But that cancer thing. That got the better of 'em. You were nigh about eight when he passed. I'm guessin' ya remember that quite well," he continued.

Drawing a deep breath, he continued, "And so, yer Mom here will deal with her pain by herself so that you don't see it; kinda protectin' ya 'cause she was a Mama bear for certain. She'll raise ya pretty much on nothin' 'cause that's all she had. She worked hard, did some work on the farm fer me and the Brock's down the road. She'll do some secretary work, typing and answering phones and such. And she'll pick up some part-time work in the University bookstore in town. She'll pull her pennies together and give ya a home. Not a house, but a home 'cause there's a world of difference 'tween those two."

Pulling back the blankets enough to see her face, he continued, "She'll give it all to ya David, just like she should. Everything… she'll give ya that. Kinda like her Mom. But it'll catch up to her and all. She was always a little frail. She got a touch of the tuberculosis her friend Millie had. Jest a touch, that's all. But, it scarred those lungs of her's real bad. Yup. Sad to say. But, she'll hang on until yer through college and well into yer career. I know ya took care of her after that, and I know that ya wish ya would have done it sooner and all. But you did fine David. Ya did really fine."

He continued, "That little baby girl right there, I was able to get through the flames to get her. It was easy. She was right there in the front room, right by the door, just a sleepin'. Didn't even know what was happenin'. I'll do that again tomorrow. And just like I went through the flames for her, she'll do the same and go through the flames fer you. Different kind, but there's all kinds of flames David. All kinds. And now David, now it's yer turn to go through the flames fer her. I know you'll do that 'cause ya loved her... still do I know."

Turning his gaze from David's mom and fixing it on David, he said, "So take the message to them, David. Fer your Mom. Fer yourself. Fer everyone. It's like plantin' the fields out there," he said pointing outside. "Go sow this precious seed that you've been given. Sow it, plant it in people's hearts I mean. Plant it deep 'cause hope sown deep can't be uprooted by nothin'.

Collecting some thoughts, he continued, "I don't know what people need in yer time, but I'm prone to think that they need what we need, but they probably need it a whole lot worse. Human nature, well that jest kinda stays the same no matter what time yer in. Jest my guess. All these people ya met came back because God Almighty knew that the world ya came from needs that message." Pausing, he said, "Heck, we all need it, but our time's over. Yours ain't."

"Grandpa," David said with his thoughts all ajar, disjointed and suddenly heading off in another direction. "If there's one thing I can ask, why the river-rock fence? I don't even know if it's out there yet... I don't know when you built it. But, whenever you did, why? Why? What's it mean?"

His grandfather smiled, nodded with his eyes welling up with tears while stroking his daughter's tiny head. Collecting some great thought that seemed to be welling up from his heart, he said, "David, I, I built that after I rebuilt this house in '38. You know, farmers in these parts had pulled those boulders out of these farm field's years before. And, well they was just sittin' there, in different places up and down the road, in various piles and such. They seemed real disjointed, like they was just waitin' to be used for some grand purpose. So I collected 'em. Jest collected... lots of 'em. And, I started buildin' it."

Drawing down into himself as if he was pulling up something wonderfully deep, he continued, "I reckon I fully didn't recognize what I was doin' until I had built about, oh forty or so feet of fence. Maybe more," he said. "If ye look real hard, you'll notice there's a place down the road a piece where the boulders in the fence all line up. Well David, that's where I stopped. I stopped right there, until I realized what I was doin'. I was tryin' to visualize eternity, David. That eternity's immovable; rock hard and impenetrable and all, like the wall. This here house burnt. That wall won't ever burn. Can't. Jest like eternity."

Continuing, he said, "When that struck me, I set about buildin' it so it ran outta sight in both directions, right over the ridges at both ends. 'Cause, ya see David, it took me over a decade to figure out that ya can't stop life. It just keeps right on goin' on regardless of what happens to us while we're a livin' it. It never pulls up and stops... ever.'

Pointing in the direction of the old road, he said, "I jest had to put those boulders together to see it, to bring 'em together like yer bringing all of these experiences together to see that life out there never stops. It's all connected with no beginnin' and no end at all. Some

370

tragedy of some kind might make us think it stops, like it pulls up forever. But it don't. That gives me a heap of hope." Pausing, he said, "That there, that right there is why I built it. And after I built I'd go out there and jest look at it to remind me, to remind me of hope eternal. That's why I built it."

After a collective pause, David said, "Thank you. Thank you. 'Cause that wall has become a big part…"

His grandfather broke in, "Of yer life. Yup. And the questions people had about it that ya've always pondered. And I'm glad that it's been part of yer life. Go on and keep marking yer life by it David, mark yer life by eternity 'cause that's where yer gonna end up no matter what happens to ya. That gives a whole lot of hope."

David leaned down and kissed his mother on her six-month old cheek. She gurgled slightly as David pulled the blankets over her and handed her back. "She beautiful," he said.

"Sure is," his grandfather replied. "Cause everythin' God makes is beautiful 'cause it can't be otherwise."

Holding David's mother tightly, his grandfather grabbed a stray piece of paper and a pencil. He then stepped over to a small table designed for folding laundry and scrawled a few lines on the page. Handing the page to David, he said "Read that there sentence, that one right there."

Clearing his throat, David looked at his grandfather as he held his mother, and then looked down at the page and with trembling hands he read, "When all other hope fails, hope in God never fails."

"Read it again, David, read it again, real loud" his grandfather said with a clear and commanding voice.

Drawing a breath, he read, "When all other hope fails, hope in God never fails."

"There ya have it," his grandfather said, placing his hand on David's shoulder. "That kept me alive when she died," he said pointing upstairs. "And it'll keep me alive again. That right there is what allowed the people ya've met to face things that were impossible to face, but they did it anyway. That right there caused people to get back up when they'd been knocked to their knees like aunt Mabel when word come that Billy had died in battle. Real hope says that ya never have to stand alone even when ya feel alone 'cause ya never are. Everythin' else in life is gonna fall short and fail at some time 'er another. There's only thing that never does that, and that's God."

Collecting his thoughts, he took a firm hold of David's shoulder and said, "I'm just a farmer, that's all. Never been anything more and never will be other than that. That's the fact of it. I plow and I plant and I harvest. That's what I was born and bred to do. Now mind ya, upstairs," he said pointing upward again, "that woman, yer grandmother Nellie, she's just a sweet and innocent farm girl from the next county over. Sweet as the day is long. Seems her dying is as wrong as wrong can get. She's too good and wholesome. But hope says that life goes on to somethin' better despite how bad it all is. Can you remember that?"

Smiling, David replied, "How could I forget it?"

With a choked voice, David continued, "How, how can I thank all of those people? How can I... how can I..." David stammered.

"That's simple David, real simple," his grandfather answered. "I'm a simple man so I like simple things. They work for me. Jest live out this message the rest of the years that the good Lord gives ya. Live it out boy, right smack dab in front of people everywhere. Right along the fence of yer life. That road yer on. That's thanks enough."

372

"David," the thin female voice called from the basement door. "David, do I need to come down there; who you talkin' to?"

"Be right up," he replied.

"Ya said that ten minutes back," she replied. "It'll be nightfall before ya get up here."

"I know, be right there sweetheart," he said with a softness woven by love of the greatest sort.

"Gotta go son," his grandfather said. "I want to spend as much time with that sweet girl as I can before... well, before I can't."

"I so wish I could stay here," David replied.

With a sigh, his grandfather said, "This ain't your life to live, David. Ya got your own life to live and it's waitin' for ya, so ya better get busy livin' it."

After an extended pause, his grandfather drew a breath and said, "Remember that I love ya, David. And remember that all the people that ya met love ya too. They respect ya. They believe in ya. We all do. Yer Mom here, she'll believe in ya like ya yerself can't believe. Ya got a whole bunch of great people who believe in ya." With an authority in voice, he said, "And I believe in ya."

"I'll never forget you," David replied in a voice choked in emotion. "I couldn't if I tried, and I don't want to try."

"I don't reckon I'll forget you either. That would be shame for certain," his grandfather replied with a somber and solemn tone.

Taking David's hand, he looked into David's eyes and said, "When all other hope fails, hope in God never fails."

Before he could speak the last words his grandfather and his mother were gone; vanished into thin air in an instance. Shocked and perplexed, David quickly looked around and he had not moved an inch, but his grandfather had disappeared entirely.

Chapter 19

Christmas with History in Tow

There are those gingerly exuberate times where we find ourselves oddly open to the miraculous. Sometimes we do so voluntarily; pressed to the precarious edges of the 'possible,' finding ourselves tentatively peeking over into the adjacent realm of the 'impossible.' At other times, we are open to the impossible because hope, in its unrelenting pursuit of us, has fatigued us sufficiently that we have no alternative but to surrender to it.

At these moments, we are vexed with the reality that we will most certainly live inexcusably diminished lives if our stubborn refusal to surrender wins out. Then there are times when we feel that the relentless concourse of events has pried us open through the sheer force of their impact, leaving us no recourse but to surrender wholesale to the impossible. Whatever it may be and in whatever manner it might come, we are now open to the miraculous and to hope, which may be one of the most miraculous things of all.

His grandfather had vanished... without a sound. Suddenly, he was not there, as if he had never been there at all. The instantaneous nature of his disappearance left David wondering where the line between imagination born of silently raging hope, and reality born of intellectual prudence was drawn. Things in life seldom simply vanish. More often than not there is a transition of some sort, whether something is transitioning into our lives or out of them. There are 'hellos' and 'goodbyes' of all assorted types that formalize the beginning and the end of our encounters. But this was not the case at all, as if it were neither a 'hello' or 'goodbye' to ground the moment in.

Nor was this like the other transitions across time. It was abruptly different. It was immediate, as if it had picked up some sort of arresting pen and straightaway put some sort of period on everything.

In an odd sort of way previously unimagined, David had gotten used to these journeys; comfortable even. True to his nature, he had unconsciously assigned them a pattern of sorts. David preferred patterns and routines as that made things predictable. They granted him a sense of control even though that sense was entirely illusionary. In fact, it was little more than the cyclic rumination of his fears. And so, in the midst of such radical and incomprehensible jaunts across history, he had ascribed some patterns to the manner in which he had traveled. Yet, when we assign the miraculous some sort of pattern or sense the need to make it rotely predictable, it is then that the miraculous does something miraculous so that it remains exactly that. And it did so to David.

He stood there in a basement suddenly dispirited and lonely; wrapped in a fog of dizzying befuddlement wondering, "What happened?" There was here some finality unexplained; some conclusion that was less than glorious and anything but moving. There was the sense of an ending unarticulated except the lingering sense of it. We are often positioned in our own mind's-eye for the next step that we've convincingly determined as the next step. But then life turns in a manner sharp and undetected. At these frequent junctures we are left stumbling on what we thought was a certain path, only to realize the uncertainty of our own calculations as held against the certainty of God's. Mundane roads never turn in such fashion as they go nowhere of any importance. However, roads to marvelous destinations will turn in just such a manner. Marvelous roads to hope.

As David began to sort out the hand of the miraculous and how it had unexpectedly moved, his thoughts slowly drifted over to, "Now what?" There were no pages left to transport him. All six had been used. He opened the old family Bible and pulled them out. Sorting through them, each had now aged with their use. Flipping through the Bible he wondered if one had been missed or somehow inserted in a manner hidden in its pages or tucked in its margins.

The very message of hope that he had seen lived out and compellingly spoken of in so many lives began to erode around the edges. We want to believe that some principle has been sufficiently rooted within us in a manner so elaborate and deep that we are able to stand against any force that might assail us. Yet, when we find ourselves alone on one of life's innumerable battlefields our courage wanes and our faith melts as wax in summer's sun. And it is not the discouragement in our faith that vexes us, although we often lay the guilt in that place. Rather, it is our discouragement in our ability to hold to our faith that torments us.

A panic that gnawed at the edges of this new found hope began to overtake him as he wondered if he was somehow, for some reason trapped in 1928. He had wanted to stay here, but when faced with that very reality he realized how terribly bad he wanted to be back in his time, in his home, living his life out with this new sense of revitalized hope. How he wanted to recalibrate the whole of his life with this hope. How it could make so many things so unimaginably different for so many people. How he could tell aunt Mabel before she passed; to close the loop that started in the general store. How he could handily seize the magic of Christmas lost in the barbarism of a divorce, and reclaim the sense of this colossal intervention of God in the very span of human history within which David had traveled. But how could he if he was trapped here, ninety years away from all of that? But hope disappointed is not hope gone.

As his head began to emerge from the panicked mix of thoughts, entangled emotions and dispirited exuberance, something seemed to reach out and catch his attention; something he had not noticed. Looking immediately behind where his grandfather had stood only moments ago, he noticed the old, sturdy sump pump, standing at the ready to hold the line against transgressing water. David leaned forward and squinted to make certain that what he was seeing was what he was seeing, for after all, given recent events the aberrant shortfall of his own vision had been made clear. It is odd that the mind always has to catch up with the heart, for the heart is exuberantly free from the stiff encumbrances of the norms to which the mind is enslaved. Hence our limited vision.

Scanning the basement, to the left of the sump pump the washer and dryer silently stood, awaiting the soiled garments of a 21st century careening off to unknown destinations. Spinning around he saw the furnace and the cable wires running through the ceiling. Looking up, the plumbing that ran this way and that peeled off to their various destinations.

Rushing and stumbling to the basement window he raised a sleeve, wiped away the frost and peered out. There stood the old garage…again. Parked in front was his car silently sitting in the driveway, dusted with a waifish layer of fresh, white snow. Suddenly, with a mix of wild elation and sordid grief he realized that he was home… home in the 21st century. In the space of a nanosecond he had crossed the span of ninety years and he was, gloriously and thankfully, home.

The old chest sat directly in front of him, precisely in the same place as it had been whenever this had all started, however long ago it had all started. However, it was aged as it had been for all the years he had remembered it. Stepping up to it, he dropped to his knees. Reverently lifting the lid and teasing it open, it was as it had been; as it had always been. Assorted mismatched jewelry, yellowed papers rendered brittle by time, a pair of gloves worn thin on the palms, a tattered scarf, a stack of letters bound by a faded red ribbon, several novels whose stories had grown old in the telling of their stories, a tattered photo album, and several scattered glass bottles that had long forgotten what ointment or perfume or liquid they had once held. It was all there.

David affectionately touched the chest, running thoughtful hands over its aged edges and teasing fingertips over it's ornate metal edging. There was now an impassioned comradery of time shared with the things in the chest. David had visited the very places where these things had lived right at the very time that they were living them. Each had a shared the self-same history, entirely different in the manner of the journey, but unmistakably the same in the experience. History was now David's story which rendered it something less of history, and something more of his very existence.

There's the etching of history in the objects that history leaves behind as it marches across the span of time; things such as worn dress gloves that delicately held tender hands on some grand occasion. Emptied apothecary bottles that once lent sweet scents of the most fascinating kind to holiday gatherings and other special moments. Mismatched jewelry that at one time graced supple necks swept up on those magical engagements that were the stuff of dream and enchantment. Yellowed papers where a caged heart finally found a needed place of release in the craft of supple penmanship. Novels that carried someone to charmed places filled with adventure that laid far beyond candle lit evenings and the warmth of hearth and home.

We compile these faint etchings sufficiently to construct a hazy and rather disjointed account of wherever it was that they came from. This dim account is so indistinct that it is more of story and less of the reality of

379

lives lived out in an existence as strikingly tangible as the very one that we're living. Sadly, our reach is too short and our vision too jaded to lift history to a point parallel to the present. And so, we lose the treasures of the past to the scourge of an imagination hamstrung by apathy.

But for David, all of that, every bit of it had entirely vanished as he did not need those pieces and their faint etchings, for he now held those etchings within the soul of himself. And therefore, these pieces transformed from conveyors of the past to cherished companions in a journey mutually shared in the past.

Standing, he ran to the root cellar doorway, stepped in and looked at all of the boxes. Tears filled his eyes as he looked at one after the other, after the other, caressing them with a fondness of preciousness once hidden and now seen. The root cellar was exactly the same, but now it was forever different. Whatever this journey was, he began to realize that it was completed. Whatever that meant for his life from this point forward… that part was yet to occur.

He took the Bible in hand and in the moments of preceding panic (or elation) he had not even noticed that it had also aged again. It had returned to what he had remembered it being for all of his life. There had been an incredible circular journey with this book. Unimaginably, it had been handed to him out of an old chest filled with a past that held a more relevant message for the present than the present itself could ever fabricate. It had been his companion, his compass and his key to places that no other book had ever taken anyone. And more than taking him to places, it had taken him to people in those places who embraced an authenticity free all the contaminating things that so many find their lives soiled by. And through the whole of the journey, the single message delivered to him by resilient people living in desperate times was a message of abiding hope. Steeled hope. Authentic hope. Imperishable hope. Hope in God and of God.

He thought, *All of these people, these remarkable people, all of them talked about hope. That hope could get them through anything. And the first thing I do when I'm dropped back here is lose hope.* Walking back over to the old chest, he said out loud, "Why can't I hope like they did?"

As he pondered that thought, a cavalcade of memories deluged his mind in a tsunami of variant emotions. His grandfather; David's namesake. A sturdy young man hardened strong by the rigors of farming and a young nation raising itself up in the early days of the 20th century. He was a transparently simple man, yet correspondingly deep and wise. Indeed, he was grounded in a way that makes a man a man in a manner beyond words or possibly beyond understanding at all. He was everything of the mixture that David himself yearned for as he attempted to become a man of men. A man who found hope after the flames when there seemed to be nothing to draw hope from. A man who drew himself out of a decade long depression to raise a house and build a fence. A man who seized hope when others would have surrendered to the cold gray of stilled ashes. Maybe it was that very character and strength for which his grandfather was chosen, if great things are chosen, to be the bookends of this most remarkable journey.

Then there was uncle Bill. This incredibly young man sitting hunched on a thin bunk in a crowded barracks packed full of anxious men who, within hours, would face the slaughter of Normandy. In the horror of its beaches they would come to understand the true price of freedom. The magnitude of what they were about to do, or more accurately what was now done, would not be fully understood until after the carnage. For many, it would be long after as it seems that the size of great things requires ample time for them to be understood. Sadly, there would be those who would never understand. David desperately

hoped that uncle Bill had been able to grasp the enormity of
the hope that had allowed him to make the ultimate
sacrifice. That no darkness, regardless of how thick or how
deep or how intimidating was able to hold back an invasion
of hope.

That would, David pondered, *make the loss of his
life the exclamation point behind hope.*

His great-grandmother dressed in a fine blue dress
with white trim; simple but orderly. Her diminutive
mannerisms and unfathomable wisdom, all of which had
been packaged into the tiny eight-year old frame within
which she had come to him, or he to her. Her wisdom had
been tediously crafted by a war that had rolled right by her
doorstep and had violently collided with her life. While she
had never mentioned it, David had heard through various
stories that several family members had fallen in the great
campaign known as the Civil War. Their bodies were never
identified. Therefore, closure was never achieved, for the
bodies were never retrieved so that one might have a point
from which to grieve more fully. Her staunch belief that
hope could seamlessly mend anything that could be torn.
Her defiance of all things bad. Hers was a steady defiance
born out of the conviction that all things bad were always
inferior to all things good. That's the message of hope.
What a privilege to meet her and what an honor to be her
descendant.

Then, amazingly... Lincoln. This towering figure of
history and presence that had clasped David's hand with a
hand so broad that David's hand was entirely lost in the
calloused span of his. That chiseled face, pockmarked with
the inconsolable grief of a nation ripping itself apart in a
war of brother against brother. To hear him speak of hope,
to even be able to utter the word while finding himself
worn thin leading the nation through the grip of a bloody
Civil War. It was a war that seemed to perpetuate itself,
feeding in some sort of frenzy on the deaths that were given

over in the effort to stop it. Seeing that etched in Lincoln's face was sufficient evidence that a hope durable enough to endure all that life could ever throw at him existed with a determination that nothing could diminish.

Then, sweet aunt Mabel. She was soft and warm, yet tough like gristle and filled with an improbable energy. She had lived out most of her life in a simple, one-bedroom white clapboard home that was attached to the back of a small general store set deep in the warm embrace of Michigan farm and forest. Of all the people that he had encountered, she was the single one that had been a part of his life, all of his life. His heart filled with grief around how he had treated her in her later years; how he had carelessly let the dementia define her when she was so much more. Throughout her life she had demonstrated the commanding reality that you can have everything taken away, but if you have hope you have the kind of 'everything' that nothing can take away. And it was that woman brilliantly caught in a siege of hope that walked the aisles of that general store, and moved through the tiny clapboard house as if it were a mansion with a bottle of vanilla soda in one hand and love in the other.

Then himself. That ten-year-old boy with his sturdy Western Flyer bicycle teasing out the mysteries of life on the back porch of a back-road store along the back-road of history. In those younger years he had seen himself as horribly inadequate; a direct off-spring of irrelevancy and a first cousin to all things meaningless. A Dad dies when you're eight and you errantly think it's because you weren't good enough for him to stick around. Yet, aunt Mabel had given him value through her easy embrace and simple wisdom. The unassuming farm folk of those meandering Michigan back roads had imbedded in him a sense that what he saw in himself was but the thin edge of a deeper greatness gaining strength within. Yet, David saw in his ten-year-old self a sturdy greatness that begged someone to believe in it so that it might be unleashed. And here David realized that maybe the scrawling's on the old river-rock fence that had begun on the tottering doorframe were, in some hopeful way, the hope that by the time the next one was etched, that greatness would have been unleashed.

And finally, little Kristin. This most innocent little girl relegated to a lonely playground in the waning hours of a snowy Christmas Eve. How her young life would impact her life as adult, and how unfair such an arrangement seemed to be. He was able to see her life at both ends now, to listen to her stories as a tiny nine-year-old and then watch her as a wife, decades later. To touch the very place that she came from and to understand with uncanny acumen where that ultimately took her… and where it ultimately took him. How he wished he could have done something to change her life at nine, in that encounter on that empty playground. Yet, David was certain that that was not the reason he had been able to warp through time to that most delicate moment. The thought of her waving to him from the window of her house on that snowy Christmas Eve in 1973 brought both a warming joy and a deep ache. It is amazing indeed how innocence has the eyes to see hope when no one else has such vision.

Sorting through the pages, these people of family, of time and of history moved in and out of his mind, interweaving warm thoughts and with golden threads of rich memory. David found himself having lived what had been stored in the old root cellar for decades. The treasure of lives lived is too easily lost to the foggy years of history now gone. Of decades rolling off discarded calendars that checked off the centuries as they rolled off the distant horizon of time. History's messages become faded, or are deemed altogether irrelevant. In the greatest disservice of all, they too often roll off the distant horizons of the past, becoming altogether lost to the bane of progressive thinking.

Yet he, this sharply jaded man had been granted the inestimable privilege of going back there, over those horizons long gone, and stand face to face with the people of those horizons. And in doing so it dawned on him that the past sets the stage for the future, and in doing so, is in fact the future. What happens in the past is not confined to the past, nor will it adhere to horizons, although in our feeble minds we think it to be so. In fact, the past is the place where the present is birthed and the future is charted. Therefore, we would be abhorrently foolish to ignore it, and we'd be ignorantly naïve to relegate it only to the place in which it occurred. In doing that, we cram ourselves into the one-dimensional confines of the present, forfeiting the endless dimensions of the past as they fold and repeatedly enfold in and upon themselves over time.

In the wild wonder of recollection, David slowly began to recognize himself to be different; extraordinarily different beyond words. He had not considered the impact of events upon him as he had been entirely enraptured by the events themselves. Standing once again in the 21st century, grounded in the basement from which this indescribable journey had begun, he had changed without knowing it had happened at all. There is the sense of change, which in fact is little more than an inkling born of a much greater upheaval roiling deep inside of us. Often we are so completely caught up in what we've been privileged to encounter that we have not fully contemplated its effect upon us nor even noticed the enormity of it. Yet, we are different sometimes without seeing that we are different. And it may well be that the greatest differences are so great that we are unable to detect the fullness of them.

David was not transformed necessarily as a result of some sort of mystical encounter that's more like the magic of cheap dime novels, or story-tellers bent on spinning thin tales to spur a momentary emotion. This was not a transformation based on embracing some new concept, or finally "seeing the light" of whatever it was that was presumed to be the light. It was not about falling in love with some compelling story-line that swept him away.

He had been transformed by real people who lived real lives in a real history that for them was nothing of history, but everything of their lives as lived in each moment. David began to realize that we are profoundly changed by that which is real, and we are only superficially altered by that which is imagined. For that which is imagined might provide us some reprieve or give us momentary hope in a fabricated fantasy, but it will fade. Real change comes only through engaging real life. The more 'real' the thing that we're engaging, the deeper the change goes.

These people that embodied this history lived raw and authentic lives because their times and the demands of their circumstances would permit nothing less. Sometimes greatness is demanded of us, and in those most harrowing of moments we become great because the demand awakens the greatness slumbering within us. And in their experiences, David saw himself… for the very first time.

David's transformation was more something like discovering himself when all along he had refused to take a single step in order to really find himself; for finding oneself is often the most frightening thing we can find. It was the realization that inherent within him were great things that were not deftly placed there through a series of marvelous events or pasted in by some cosmic benefactor as a fitting addition. Rather, they had been there all along. Through all the years and all the hash marks. Yet, he had refused to be real enough to see them because being real meant being vulnerable, and that had come at too great a cost.

Standing in that basement, he began coming to himself… to his full self, recognizing that within himself

God had woven in so much more than he had ever recognized. He began to understand that life was not about the addition of things as much as it was about the discovery of what already exists within oneself that then sets the stage for additions. He realized that we live out pale identities that we create to forcefully minimize risk, and that we play unquestioningly obedient roles in the pursuit of selfish agendas. We become something of our own pathetic design, a design forged of cancerous insecurities and fed fat by fear.

He saw that events didn't 'add' as much as they 'revealed.' That intersecting the lives of others who are living out the rawness of their lives with uncompromising vulnerability creates an environment to intersect ourselves in a collision of the most liberating sort. To have the fathomlessness of our own depths rocked and then plumbed by our encounters with the kinds of people who are doing nothing more than living out the drama of their times with the boldness of their hearts changes our lives for the whole of our lives. It's the oddity of the human existence that we find ourselves in finding others, and we meet ourselves in meeting them.

Yet, adventure does not posit a firm destination that is abruptly final. How could it, for that is not the nature of adventure. Adventure is adventure because it does not end, which always leaves the question of "what is next" a question. The roads designed by God are thick with the joy of the journey itself, they are incessantly energized by the celebration of the arrival, and forever imbued with the anticipation of the 'next.' And in any adventure, the 'next' can never be thwarted by an end because there's no end to thwart it. If the journey on the roads of our lives were anything other than this, they would succumb to the rot of predictability and therefore be nothing of adventure but more the stumbling of mediocrity.

Once we move beyond the panic of resistance born of mediocrity, we often become engrossed or more possibly mesmerized by the course of life when it thrusts us up and out. Yet, life is more than simply events that challenge us, inspire us, sooth us, captivate us or somehow inflict pain upon us in its passion to inject growth into our soul of souls. Life is meticulously intentional, and we would be foolishly foolish to think otherwise. Worse yet, we would be terribly foolish to believe otherwise, for belief of this nature is faith in nothing. God is no fool. Quite the opposite, He is a most meticulous genius, threading life to wonderfully impossible outcomes.

But the one thing that holds the power to kill all of that is the loss of hope. Souls have become terminally anemic for lack of it, and lives have perished because of its absence. Indescribable achievements and mind-boggling advancements were forfeited because somewhere along the way hope was lost. Possibilities were abandoned, relationships were shattered, dreams fell to cold cinders and gray ash, roads vanished, and entire lives were lost because hope was lost. People die because they lose hope, and all that they are die with them.

As we journey through life or time we sometimes assume that what we have experienced somehow represents the sum total of the journey as we cannot fathom that anything else that could possibly be a part of it all. We feel we've learned the lessons. Yet, we errantly forget that adventure is of necessity defined by our inability to sufficiently define the course of it and that we are forever unable to chart its path. Otherwise, it would merely be a plan, and a plan is never an adventure. Nor is it a lesson.

David had not fully learned that particular lesson, as that destination would be miles ahead along his own journey through his own time. However, the rumbling in the recesses of his soul was that the destination would never be reached for the journey was far too marvelous to end. Despite the enormity of his journey and the riches unearthed within him, he had missed likely the most crucial part; or more rightly, it had been carefully withheld. For to have hope is one thing. To unleash it is to test our grasp of it. That was but a phone call away.

A buzzing emanated from his pocket, suddenly interrupting his thoughts. His cell phone was back in his pocket! He had looked for it the first time that he had met his grandfather. He recalled his anxious rummaging through every pocket in a foraging attempt to locate it. His grandfather had said that David "didn't have any such contraption" because David didn't exist yet, which was the first of many comments that David had to figure out and make sense of.

Pulling his phone out of his pocket, he squinted at the screen.

The caller ID read, "aunt Mabel." The date read, December 11th. With a deep gasp, David held the phone at a distance and then put it right in front of his face and then held it at a distance again.

"I'm right back where I started," he blurted out. "I'm right back where this all began. Not a minute has passed, not a minute. Not a second even. How... how could that be?" Pausing, he said to himself, *Of course. It had to come full-circle to go full-forward.* But then thinking with a bit more levity, he said, "But it's kind of cool not getting used to it."

It dawned on David that he had left aunt Mabel entirely out of the events of recent weeks. He saw her as only being able to participate from a far distance; her dementia relegating her to some remote point around it all, but not in it all. She was entirely ancillary to these events; a key part whose mental health would not permit her to play a key role.

"Got yer soda and mint candy." The voice came right back into his head as if she were speaking right then and there. "Well, are ya comin' in?" The words were there again. It was not the aunt Mabel of dementia and nursing homes. Not the aunt Mabel of wildly bizarre phone calls and irritatingly weird comments. Not the aunt Mabel that everyone was waiting to die out of a sense that she would be freed from her dementia, and the remaining family would be freed from the effects of her dementia. Not that aunt Mabel at all.

What had stood before him had been the aunt Mabel of strength, vigor and uncanny country wisdom. Standing before him had been the gristle-like woman shaped by country living, hardened by great loss, chiseled by determination, yet blended soft by an unparalleled appreciation for life. Holding a frosty vanilla soda and an assortment of mint candies was the aunt Mabel with that flair of dry humor, quiet wisdom, fathomless patience and endless energy. That was the aunt Mabel of times gone by. Although the years had taken their toll, the aunt Mabel of Michigan farmlands was still the aunt Mabel who was calling at that very moment. It was impossible that the richness of such character could have been lost to anything.

Reaching for the phone, he said, "aunt Mabel?"

There was a pause of dead-air. "Is this David Morris?" an unfamiliar voice asked.

"Yes, yes this is he." he replied slowly.

"Mr. Morris, my name is Rachel Higgins. Sir, I'm the charge nurse here at Spring Meadows. We have attempted to contact you several times. I'm sorry to disturb you."

"No, no, that's fine," David replied in a voice mixed with business, confusion and concern.

"Sir," the nurse continued, "We wanted to inform you that your aunt Mabel has fallen into a coma. We would suggest that you, as well as any other family members might want to get here as quickly as possible as we're uncertain regarding her condition."

There was another long pause. David had just been thrown across the span of a century in a nanosecond. His journey had afforded him little time to make sense of the journey. And now, this call.

"Uncertain," David stammered. "What exactly do you mean by uncertain?" although the meaning was obvious.

"Mr. Morris," the nurse replied with a bit of empathy overlying a slightly sterile medical tone, "Her vitals are weak. We think she may be passing."

David had gone through a series of events where people had come back to life, or he had somehow gone back to their lives, or something that was still not entirely clear. His journey, if you would call it that, was about gaining, or in some instances regaining these people. This phone call was a sharp and jarring departure. Here he was on the precipice of losing someone; someone he had just met again in her prime. He had just spoken to this vigorous woman what seemed only moments ago. He had rejoined her only now to lose her. Time had fast-forwarded some five plus decades, and she was dying in the forwarding.

"How late are you open, ah… what time is it anyway?" David mumbled.

"Sir, we accept visitors in these situations twenty-four hours a day," the nurse replied. "I would encourage you to…"

"I'll be right there," David jumped in. *These situations?* David thought. It was clear what the nurse had meant.

Without waiting for a reply he hung up, grabbed the Bible, scanned the pages to make certain that they were all there, ran his hand across the lid of the old chest, stuck his head inside the root cellar to hurriedly turn off the bear bulb and then raced up the old rough-hewn oak stairs. Pausing at the top of the stairs, he had gathered himself enough to embrace what had just been given to him in light of what was apparently about to be taken away. Too often when we are about to lose something, all that we have been given is suddenly forgotten. And so loss becomes much bigger than the single thing that we are about to lose.

David turned and ran back down the stairs. Hurrying back to the root cellar, he turned on the light, stepped in and extended his hand to the boxes. This time, felt no loss of balance or sense of something being there. This time he ran his hand over them. Standing there he choked back tears, and said, "Thank you." Collecting himself and clearing his throat he said, "Thank all of you. Thank all of you," hoping that somehow his "thanks" would be transported across time to these people as he had visited them. Pausing, he fell into a bit of thought, looked up and then continued, "Dear God, help me, please, to… to take a bit of this to aunt Mabel today. Grandpa Dave, uncle Bill, great-grandma Donna, Mr. Lincoln, Kristen… if you, you are somehow, in some way able to help me, please, please help. Help me take this to her."

And then pausing, he drew a breath that went to the soul of himself, closed his eyes, held the Bible firmly to his chest and said, "Dear God, above all, above all these wonderful people, please, I'm asking you to help. Keep her alive until I get there, and then give me the words I don't have, because I don't have them. I'm not a man of words… not those kinds of words. Please…"

Exhaling, he turned, ascended the steps with Bible in hand, walked through the kitchen, went out the back door and leapt into the car. Turning the car around, he headed down the long driveway framed by meadows grasses and the split-rail fence. Despite a driveway seemingly hidden by fresh snow, the car confidently found its way, perfectly following the muted pair of tracks that David had made on his way to the farmhouse just moments ago. It gently wound through sweeping pastures intermittently bordered by aged split rail sentries, some of whom had fallen under the weight of time and duty. It was picturesque; creating a tin-type yearning for another distant, innocent time that was in reality that very time.

Reaching the end of the driveway that adjoined the road of Indians, wagons and heavy horse, Dad brought the car to a sudden stop. Throwing open the car door, he trudged through the snow to the real estate sign that stood alongside the road.

Taking hold of it he pulled it out of the ground, looked directly into its metal face, and spoke to it as if it was alive. "Thanks, but we won't be needing you anymore," David said with the conviction of a man redeeming himself. "I *hope* you don't feel rejected" he said with a bit of his own sarcasm. With that said, he hurled it across the road into the deep woods, laughed heartedly, shouted "yeah baby!" (which was a bit odd), got into the car and drove off to engage history in the making.

Chapter 20
A Nursing Home and Aunt Mabel

Often in life, we draw conclusions and reflexively take action based on what we see; which in the majority of situations is achingly insignificant or just plain wrong. We assume that whatever stands before us is the sum total of whatever it is that stands before us. We have fallen into a miserable naiveté where we engage life based solely on what our senses can ascertain. And such a lamentable acumen is less than a scant sliver of the massive whole which, in fact, stands in front of us. Errantly assuming there to be no more, we ourselves are certain to be diminished by our crippling lack of insight. As a consequence, we are doomed to marginalize that which we're engaging because our lack of vision suppresses our engaging in the first place.

Few of us have come to understand that what we see, albeit whatever that might be, is only a miniscule fraction of the whole. We walk, or more likely we stumble through this journey that we call life, permitting ourselves less than a fleeting moment to give the things around us a passing glance. The skin of life is but a slightly lean wrap under which beats the fuller heart of life. Yet, we see skin as the whole of it all. We gather up a few thin blades of meadow grass and call them the meadow, when the meadow itself rolls off to horizons that escape our view. And from these most fleeting and scant observations, we serendipitously draw life-altering conclusions.

David had come to learn, or I suppose was learning, that life is a process not an event. He was coming to understand that there was far more to life than he could ever hope to fathom. Therefore, the journey is more taken and less understood in the taking. The riches in life don't exist at skin level or within a few scant blades of meadow grass. No. In fact, the majority life, whether it is good or bad doesn't lay there.

As David was discovering, real riches lay deep. In fact, they lay so passionately deep that this dreadfully brief life will simply not permit us sufficient time to unearth anything but a nearly negligible handful of them. Worse yet, sometimes in our hurriedness and jaded attitudes we unearth none of them. These riches lay down roads foolishly abandoned. They're nestled deep in vacated root cellars. They find themselves stored in antique chests. And on those special moments, they're penned on yellowed pages tucked in forsaken Bibles.

Turning out to the road of Indians, horse and heavy wagon, he came to the river-rock fence. Suddenly, he somewhat reflexively spun the car onto the berm. Stepping out into brisk December air, he made his way to the hash marks with the soft crunch of snow sounding out with each step. By this time, the hash marks were covered in December's kiss of white. Clearing the snow away with his bare hand in a manner thoughtful and reverent, they slowly revealed themselves. He stooped and blew the remaining snow away. David wondered if they might have been changed by his travels through time. Yet, they remained unchanged. As one might imagine in such a situation, a brief tinge a sadness ran though David. However, as he pondered it he found that he preferred the fact that they were unchanged. Indeed, he actually saw it as entirely fitting. He realized that he stood between a past that had shaped these marvelous travels through time, and a future that would be shaped by them. Therefore, to change his own history would be to throw all of that askew. And such an action might destroy the whole of it.

These marks had defined the span of his life, speaking of successes, but mostly speaking to failures. They had encased his life in the telling. He had come each Thanksgiving to add another harsh mark to the story.

Reflectively he ran his finger-tips over each one, recalling the doorframe at the back of the old General Store; committing in some yet undefined but wholly committed way that the marks from here forward would be forever different. For was that not the purpose of his journey, and the purpose of ours?

Somehow, they no longer measured time or checked off life lost. Scanning up and down the river-rock fence he began to see the cluster of hash marks as a tiny recounting etched out on a fence infinite at each end. That life was more like the river-rock fence. It was not defined by the hash marks etched upon it. Life was exceedingly vaster than any mark or collection of marks. It ran off the horizon of time in each direction as his grandfather had said, and while we inhabit only the smallest part of it, the whole of it is ours as well.

"It's all connected with no beginnin' and no end at all. Some tragedy of some kind might make us think it stops, like it pulls up forever. But it don't. That gives me a heap of hope," his grandfather had said.

"Gives me hope too," David said while pressing his hand to the fence. David now knew that because it all goes on forever, there is every reason to hope because in the span of existence there will always be a tomorrow to look forward to and a past to draw from. "Thanks for the fence Grandpa," he muttered. Turning and scanning the length of it, he said, "Thank you."

David turned to walk back to the car. In light of the call from the nursing home, a sense of uncertainty and urgency began to swell within him. Yet, despite the strength of it, a thought suddenly laid its firm hands upon his shoulders and spun him around in the snow. Quickly turning, he scanned the fence to find the place where the rocks lined up; that place where it finally dawned on his grandfather why he was constructing the fence in the first place. That place where his grandfather realized that life doesn't end at a tragedy and that hope is eternal, that fires don't end life and that roads never have a terminus.

He'd never noticed it before, somehow completely missing it for all of those years. Sometimes we won't see things until we're ready to see them, or they're ready for us to see them. Instantly his eyes landed on the very spot as if instinctively he knew precisely where it was... for he did. It was here, at this very point that he had carved those hash marks for all those years. He'd never seen, for maybe it hadn't been the time to see it. But it was right here. Right here where his Grandfather had closed down his life only to open it up yet again.

Sometimes the 'obvious' is cleverly hidden simply because the power of the obvious 'hidden' and then abruptly released is so indescribably potent that only a power of this magnitude possesses the force to throw back our ignorance and throw open our minds. Otherwise, the wonder of what stands before us would fall to the death of ignorance, and we then would fall to the death of ourselves.

Walking over to it, he realized that here, at the point of years now marked by hash marks, the construction of the fence had halted... and it was here that it had begun again. Here, at this precise spot his grandfather had felt life to be tragically short, having been brought to an abrupt halt by December fires and relationships fallen into cinder and ash. Here everything about life instantaneously terminated, stripping life down to the wretchedly single task of awaiting the arrival of death.

But it was at this exact spot, in this very place that his grandfather realized that nothing in life stops despite the unrelenting feeling born of fires and ash that would scream in billowing smoke that it does. That life is a road rolling from a forever past into a forever future. That no event or series of events despite the gravity of them has the force to stop that progression, or kill the promise of that progression, or lay waste to the road upon which it all progresses. Life and death in whatever form they come and in whatever manner they might assail us are part of something that is beyond both and eclipses both. And all of that had transpired at this precise spot. David had been etching those marks for all of those years without even seeing that those marks had been made at this very point in the wall. He had been marking the years of his life off at the very place where his grandfather realized that you can't mark off something that doesn't end. Standing at that sacred spot that so defined his life, David realized what his grandfather had realized so many years ago… it never ends. And we are invited, or more appropriately, we are privileged to participate in the endlessness of it.

This was David's moment now. His grandfather's moment had happened at this point in the fence, and now his had as well. Hope was born for both of them at the very same point.

Smiling at the wonder of it all while shaking his head, he said, *It's not over. My life, this life's not over at all. In fact, it hasn't even really begun has it?* he thought. *It's only now beginning, and it's a beginning without an ending*, he pondered. Looking to his right and scanning the wall until it rolled out of sight, he thought, *how can you not hope in something that never ends? How can you not hope?* And then…

Suddenly he heard something, something indefinable. He turned, stepped up on soft gravel berm. He was certain, in a manner that leaves no room for doubt, that he had heard something coming down the road; something of a yearning but not a reality. Stepping around the front of the car, he stepped onto the road's gravel bed to scan the road beyond the trees that edged it and the horizon that hemmed it in. Whatever the sound was it was so compelling that he expected to see something or someone.

It was now familiar; a voice of history visited calling to him. It seemed more something like a multitude of sounds layered on and over and in each other rather than some single sound that would identify whatever it was. It was like a cacophony of voices so blended together and stacked upon each other that you simply could not tease out the threads of the individual voices. Yet, he knew them nonetheless.

Yes, they were voices. Generations of them, it seemed, raised in a single moment. A joyous confluence of centuries no longer barred from one another by time. Voices that now included his own. With the voices ebbing and flowing, David stepped further out into the road and vigorously scanned it up and down. Yet, the road was vacant. Looking yet again, he stepped into the middle of the road, determined that he would not again miss history afoot.

Then, a scant wind oddly warm caressed him, spinning several leaves around his feet and then sending them cavorting down the road in some secret waltz. The same breeze then brushed the tall grasses bordering its dirt edge on its way out to wherever it was going. It seemed that there were voices woven in the breeze, ebbing and flowing, not clear and distinct as if to understand what they were saying. It seemed that they weren't meant to be understood. They seemed to be words with just enough clarity to evidence that they were words of a history thanking David for having visited them, while simultaneously encouraging him into and onto the road of hope now in front of him. It seemed a message uncloaked and unleashed. Then, all fell silent and all fell still.

Exhilarated beyond containment, David yelled "thank you!" into the winter sky. "Thank you, thank you, thank you!"

Nodding his head and wiping the tears away, he was again reminded of aunt Mabel.

"Sir," the nurse had said, "We wanted to inform you that your aunt Mabel has fallen into a coma. We would suggest that you, as well as any other family members might want to get here as quickly as possible as we're uncertain regarding her condition."

David leapt into the car and sped down the road of Indian, horse and heavy wagon with the spirits of history past cheering him into a future unfolding.

The drive to the nursing home was a mix of dread stirred heavy with the thoughts of his journey, the road of Indian, horse and heavy wagon and the river rock fence. David realized that the repercussions of this unexplainable event had only begun to set in. He certainly was not the same, but he was not exactly certain in what way he was not the same other than he was not. Neither did he understand how much he was yet to be changed, although he knew that it would likely be rather drastic in a good sort of way. Time would unfold it all.

Typically, life wants to hand us a simple message along the river-rocks fences of our lives and the pages strewn along our way. But it's along unpretentious fences and upon simple pages that life's greatest messages are penned. And the messages were being read and re-read into David's soul as some soothing story of great wonder.

The drive to the nursing home took nearly an hour. That was the reason David seldom took the trek. Typically, he dreaded the drive, coursing his way down a mix of country roads and concrete freeways out of a jaded sense of obligation. It was an entirely contradictory endeavor every time he took the drive, as he lived desperately wanting not to be obligated to anything. Obligation after all, makes one vulnerable and David had lived a life where vulnerability had cost him dearly.

But today it was indescribably different. It might be better expressed as being entirely otherworldly; so distinctly different that he had no point of reference from which to understand it, or from which he might diminish it. It was something like being someone else entirely and trying to figure out who this new person was.

As field and forest and city rolled by the car, David found himself trying to figure out himself. It was not something like being panicked or lost, as much as it was a wonderful adventure of glorious self-discovery. It was more like finding yourself for the first time and feeling an electrifying mix of elation finally having found your true self, while feeling a tinge of grief that it hadn't happened long ago. Sometimes when we finally find ourselves, we end up caught in the angst of why it took so long, rather than celebrating the fact that it finally happened. And somewhere along the drive, for the first time in his life he said "hello" to himself.

Finally, David arrived at the nursing home. A sense of hurriedness was quickly replaced with a foreboding sense of trepidation. He was torn by the need to rush into the nursing home which was entirely tempered by a colossal fear of what he would encounter inside. Death never sat well with David. And this place was full of it. Parking the car, he found his hands frozen to the steering wheel. Inside himself he was irreconcilably torn.

He had just seen aunt Mabel in the old grocery store in Michigan as this robust, wise and witty woman who carved a living from the indescribable pain of her loss. As a kid she has spoken more into her life than most anyone else. As an adult she spoke into his life in a way that built upon what she had previously constructed there. Then the specter of dementia had turned it all sour and dark. It seemed that he had seen her just hours ago, at best, as this vibrant person. And in the incomprehensible journey that he had somehow taken, five decades had elapsed in the span of those few hours and now she was aged, consumed in the muddle of dementia and hotly pursued by death.

Shaking himself free, he said to himself, "When all other hope fails, hope in God never fails. Well," David said clutching his hands over his mouth, "If that's true, if that's really true, I need it to be true right now."

The nursing home was a bit colonial in structure and style, lending something austere to those waiting upon death. It was a proud place, embracing those who had run the race of life and were closing in on its finish. It sat surrounded by an enclave of muscular maples and oaks that stood back sufficiently enough to permit a sizeable pond. A red-brick pathway encircled the pond, each brick etched with the names of those who has passed in this place. Carefully tended gardens in the back and on both sides of the building had fallen into the brown of winter's slumber. The home was tastefully edged in several strings of brilliant Christmas lights that ran the length of the building and wrapped their strands around the two evergreen bushes that framed the front doors.

It was modern, clean and especially tidy. It carried within it the constant smell of disinfectants as is wholly typical of nursing homes. However, the scent was not overly commandeering. The fact that it was minimal appeared to be a product of a loving atmosphere that seemed to have a sweet scent all of its own, somehow offsetting any odor that might be offensive.

Winter had laid claim to the nursing home, as it had the surrounding woods. It seemed that it had quietly laid down a thick, white blanket and had tucked the nursing home in on all four corners of its brick expanse. The lofty pines seemed to be dressed in the regal robe of winter as they stood as sentries on each end of the building. A handful of courageous waterfowl milled about the pond in the back, deciding to forgo warmer climates for the company of the nursing home. They swam sufficiently to keep a small part of the pond ice-free, refusing to permit winter to lay claim to the entire pond. Standing on its banks, they watched winter be as glorious as it was on this day.

Drawing a deep breath, he opened the car door and the chill of a December day spilled into the car as the chill of the phone call had spilled into his heart. Wrapping his coat around him, he cinched it tight as if he were attempting hold himself together by having his coat hold him. With the crunch of snow beneath his feet, he made his way to the double doors that marked the entrance to the colonial style nursing home. Stepping up to the doors, he looked in, knowing what awaited him. He had seen this before on previous visits. This one however had a vivid sense of finality to it; a feeling of something in front of him about to close behind him.

Sometimes we have to step through doors knowing that what awaits us on the other side will change everything on this side once we step through them. Sometimes there is no going back and there is no option in not going forward. There are those times that the whole of our lives and the entire ascent of our histories will pivot in ways irreconcilable. There is a cessation of what we've known in a forced trade for the unknown. Yet, the roads of our lives and the river-rock fences that run alongside of them grant us confidence in the certainty of both a road and a destination.

Oddly, David's attention was drawn back out to the Christmas lights that sparkled from the two evergreen bushes that edged the front door. He followed their lights as they ran upward and edged the roofline of the building in both directions, rolling out of sight around their respective corners at each end. Simultaneously it reminded him of the river rock fence, while drawing him back to the fact that Christmas was but a mere two weeks away.

Christmas was God stepping through a door that would change everything, David thought. *And there was no going back for Him.* Indeed, it was a thought he had never had before that moment, at least with that intensity or clarity or both. It was a thought he never wanted to lose.

We know that life will not allow us to side-step these doors. Sometimes the doors that we face present us with no option other than going through the doors, knowing that once they close behind us, what we were on the other side will never be again. This was one of those doors for David. Christmas was that door for God. Exhaling in the kind of sigh that acknowledges the closing of the past for the unknown of the future, David took hold of the doorknob, pulled the door open, and stepped out of the present into a very different future. It was likely the same kind of sigh God took on Christmas Eve as he took hold of the doorknob of history, pulled the door open, and stepped into a manger.

Its linoleum hallways ran as empty corridors washed cold in the flat glow of fluorescent lights. Air tainted with the slight scent of urine and disinfectant hung in thin layers, held in check by disinfectants lovingly applied. Here in a world of aging wheelchairs, stained bedpans, and death's familiar face the celebration of a birth two thousand years and half a world removed was all but nonexistent. It seemed to be half-heartedly played out in an empty display of a plastic Christmas tree and twinkling lights that blinked to a nonexistent rhythm.

The emptiness of the nursing home engulfed David as soon as he passed through the double glass doors. Amid murmuring televisions echoing down barren hallways and plaintive moans of discomfort coming from rooms beyond his view, he stood wondering why the final hours of so many should be so terribly empty.

Why should it end here, like this? David thought. Life boiled down to single, morbid task of anticipating death. *Jesus was born anticipating death*, he thought as if some long forgotten Sunday school lesson unexpectedly resurfaced in his soul. "This is a beginning," came a commanding voice in his head. The voice possessed a power, an authority and an acumen above and beyond David. He reflexively turned, trying to determine the origin of the voice only to realize that it was a voice. Whatever its source, it said, "Jesus was born to build the ultimate river rock fence. He did. And this is now a beginning." David stood swept into in the paralysis of the thought.

"Mr. Morris?" a voice rang out. Her words drew him up out of the depths of his thought and dropped him in front of a tidy nurse. "Are you Mr. Morris?" she said again.

Stumbling, David said, "Yes… I'm sorry, my minds not here right now." Shaking himself out of thought, he continued, "My mind's been in the past. Way in the past," he said with a smile.

Pausing and finding his comments a bit humorous, he said, "I guess you see a lot of that."

"Yes we do," came the polite reply. "People tend to spend a lot of time thinking about the past when a loved one is passing away," she continued.

"It's one thing to think about it," David said. "It's another thing to have just been there," he said looking up and down the hallway.

"Excuse me?" replied the nurse.

"No. Sorry. Nothing really" David responded. Drawing a deep breath, he said, "I'm sorry, yes I'm Mr. Morris. Where's my aunt?"

"Right this way," she replied.

Walking down the sterilized hallway, David was attempting to correlate the incredible highs of his journey through time with the incredible low that he was now awash in. Of God coming through doors and of river rock fences. Of roads that don't end. The nurse walked beside him, carefully and rather meticulously explaining aunt Mabel's condition as if aunt Mabel was a favored patient. Yet her words were muddled and terribly distant as if she were speaking from many miles away.

It seemed that a single human mind simply did not possess the capacity to embrace the extremes that David had just experienced. When life opens up in all of its grandeur we are deluged in the immensity of it all, finding ourselves swept away in beautiful torrents that we'd gladly drown in. Yet few of us are willing to permit belief, or faith, or whatever we might call it to open up life in this manner. Therefore, we become asphyxiated and confined to a few scant hash marks etched in the expanse of eternity.

His soul and his heart felt entirely overwhelmed as if he himself might collapse in this linoleum causeway. But maybe that's where hope really was anyway. Maybe hope rested in the fact that we can't do this thing that we call life on our own. Not real life. Not river rock fence lives. Not the life of eternal roads. We can settle for mediocrity and settle ourselves in some sort of pathetic compromise out of some kind of surrender and call it life. But surrender of that kind was hope abandoned, and that was no longer possible for David.

What David began to realize walking that hall and looking into each room as he passed by them was that life is too big for any of us. Forever too big. Looking into the rooms of aged people with long histories now behind them and eternity sprawling out at their doorstep, he saw river rock fences in flesh and blood. Seeing it in room after room, it struck him that life is bigger than the whole collection of us combined. But that was the whole idea wasn't it? If life's bigger than any of us individually or all of us collectively, then there must be something bigger than us to walk us through it. More than just walking through it much like he was walking this hallway, there must be something bigger than us that gives us what we need to embrace it, experience it, and savor it for life is bigger than any resource we have to do that.

We can only grasp slight parts of it in a manner that any collection of these slight parts, no matter now vast, remains only a slight part. Because, what's the sense of the journey for just the sake of a few scant pieces and parts of the journey? What's the sense of just "doing" part of life, if you can't "live" the whole of life? There is no sense to that at all.

And because it's far too big for us to live on our own, most people just do miniscule pieces of life because they don't want to acknowledge that they need something bigger than themselves to seize the whole of it. Hope rests in the fact that the whole of life is available to us. That we're not restricted to a few hash marks, but that the whole of the river rock fence is ours. That our roads run without an ending. That what is burnt down will be raised up. And because the whole of life is, we have the whole of it to walk knowing with unexplainable confidence that nothing in life will ever bring us to a point where fences end, roads stop, buildings lay in ash and we end with them. That's hope. And that hope is handed to us because God stepped through a door of no return on Christmas Eve.

"Here we are," a voice came rushing into his head. Nodding his head, David looked at the room number and peer slightly inside to see a tiny bathroom and a small closet.

"Mr. Morris, do you need someone to be with you?" the nurse questioned.

"Ah, no." Turning to her and smiling he said, "That's very kind of you, but I think I just need to be alone with her." Placing his hand on her shoulder, he said, "This is only an end that is really a beginning. It's really the beginning of an endless series of beginnings. Believe me, I learned that in ways you can't imagine."

Smiling, the nurse replied, "When all other hope fails, hope in God never fails."

Canting his head and looking intently at the nurse David said, "How'd you know that?"

"Well," replied the nurse, "Your aunt Mabel told me that over and over. She even repeats it in her sleep." Pausing, she glanced into the room and said, "That… well Mr. Morris, that changed my life. She's special," the nurse said pointing into the room.

She smiled, and then nodded as if more words would only diminish the moment. Thanking her while trying to correlate what she just said with all the thoughts that had just deluged him, she walked away down the linoleum corridor.

Collecting himself, he prayed, "Dear God, I have no hope of my own that's big enough for this. Make hope in You a hope that never fails. Make that so right now. Please." Drawing a breath, he turned and walked into the room.

The room was sparsely filled with photographs pinned on a small cork bulletin board and taped on walls. Many of them were the pictures that had hung on the wall in her small clapboard board house behind the old general store. It seemed that someone had tried to recreate that place here for her now.

While scanning the photos, David pulled a chair up to aunt Mabel's bedside. He gently laid the old family Bible on her end table and turned toward her. The blankets etched out the skeletal shape of a feeble woman. Her cheeks were sunken and falling into an ashen gray. Her hair had thinned into weak curls that fell scattered and helpless on her pillow. Her breathing was labored and somewhat shallow. Reaching under the blanket, he took hold of her emaciated hand. Holding it in his, he rubbed it, somehow hoping that this might infuse life back into her body.

How he longed to talk with her, to share the experiences of his recent journey, especially his time with her. He wondered, would she remember it herself as she had lived it in her time? It was only hours old for him but decades old for her, but would she somehow, in the fog of dementia, would she someway recall it? How he wished he could talk about his journey with her. Especially uncle Bill. Tears welled up in his eyes as he thought about how he could tell her about uncle Bill's last day, what he said; the man that he was on that fateful day.

Lost in thought, David pondered, *what can I give her? At the end like this, what can I give this remarkable woman?*

His mind was drawn back to the old general store on that summer day in rural Michigan. A worn screen door that was held closed by a single spring screwed to the doorframe kept the hoard of Michigan insects out where they belonged. On its frame those first hash marks were etched, recalling those early years and the milestones of a simple child. Over that simple door hung a small, embroidered picture cradled in a simple oak frame. It had read, "'Silent night, holy night.' This is where hope began." David had completely forgotten about it… again. Abruptly he sat up and thought, *why hadn't that struck me before?*

He tried to rehearse the verses of that simple song in his mind, collecting pieces of them but not the whole. For the life of him, he could not remember the verses, in any kind of order anyway. Each time he rehearsed them in his head he could only come up with frustrating snippets and disconnected shards. He had left their stanzas behind as life had jaded him, causing him to leave things like hope and songs of redemption behind him as well.

Increasingly exasperated, he mumbled, "I'll just sing it and we'll see where this goes." Clearing his throat, in low tones he sang hoping that the verses would come. "Silent night, holy night. All is calm, all is bright…"

The song came back to him in its entirety as if he'd been singing it every day for all of his life. Sometimes what we've presumed lost to us is not lost, rather it's just forgotten through out inattentiveness or lax living. Rubbing her hand and staring into her face, he continued to sing, over and over; louder and louder. It seemed that his words and the broken melodies bounced off her and became absorbed into the antiseptic air as quickly as they were sung. Despite the desperation of any moment, a song can go deeper than just about anything else. Words caught in the warm wrap of melodies can deliver those words with a potency unimagined. Particularly a song about hope. And so he sang about where hope started… over and over and over.

David had bowed his head and was singing the carol over and over, for how long he was unsure, although it was for some time. Suddenly the nurse was standing at the foot of the bed, a few feet from him.

Looking up startled, David said, "I'm sorry, I didn't see you."

"No you didn't," the nurse responded. Pointing, she said, "But she did."

Turning toward aunt Mabel, her eyes were opened; slight and tentatively, but they were open. Her mouth moved in a struggle to say something. Shocked and perplexed, David leaned over her and put his ear close to her mouth. "Pray for me, please pray for me," she uttered so low that David barely heard her. Her hand began to tighten around his in a moment of wholly sacred connection. Clasping her hand with both of his, David tried to collect himself in the midst of an aunt in a coma now awakened.

Aunt Mabel was suddenly awake, and she was irreparably dying all at the same disorienting time. Death only affords us the slimmest amount of time as life ticks off the few final seconds. And in those terribly confining parameters we must be able to say something that will close out the entirely of their life in a handful of words. That is likely one of the most difficult tasks in all of life, but it is also one of great privilege. For David, it created great fear.

Caught in the torrent of a head spinning, he said, "Yes. Yes, I would love to pray." Pausing, he said, "It's been a long time aunt Mabel, since I prayed I mean." Shaking his head in disappointment, he said, "I kind of forget how. I mean, I left God behind because I thought He'd left me behind… but now I know," he said pausing. "But yes, of course. Let's pray."

He squeezed her hand, bowed his head and searched for words to say. There are times when we suddenly wish we were something we aren't, wondering how we let this part of ourselves or this aspect of life escape us. This was David's moment. He grabbed at a few scant words and began to pray. Frustratingly, the words escaped him. But then he thought of the kid at the general store and asked himself, *How would he pray?* Shifting away from the adult he was to the kid sitting on the back steps of the old general store, he prayed the way he did as a kid; the kid he was in that general store, the kid of Michigan woodlands, farm fields and a Western Flyer bicycle. That precious part of himself that he was back then; that part of himself he had lost as an adult. He found himself fumbling, but that child took his hands, seized his heart, shaped the words and prayed with elegance.

The words "Amen," brought the prayer to a close. Looking up at aunt Mabel, tears rolled down each of her cheeks. She was far too weak to smile, but it was written all across her face nonetheless. We don't need the face to tell us what's transpiring in the soul. Slowly she gestured with her eyes toward a simple night stand. Raising a weak arm, she attempted to point but her arm fell useless.

Stammering and not knowing what aunt Mabel meant, David turned the conversation and said, "Let me show you something." Reaching over to the end table, he grabbed the old family Bible. Trembling as he turned and laid it on her bed, he said, "Here, here are the pages' aunt Mabel. I finally found them… or, it's probably more accurate to say that they found me." A slight smile spread itself across her graying face.

David continued, as if trying to pull the whole of the incredible events together with a few simple words, "I know that the family always talked about them, but I always thought they were myth or something like that. Crazy stuff, you know?" he said. "And you… well if I were to be honest, and I guess that this is the time to be honest, when you talked about them I thought you were crazy too. I mean, I don't want you to think bad about me or anything, but you know how crazy that talk about pages sounded like… right?" Aunt Mabel's eyes had become brighter, more attentive and filled with that improbable energy once again.

"Here," he said, pulling them from the pages of the Bible. "Here." Laying them carefully on her bed as if they were priceless sacred parchments, he picked up her limp hand and placed them squarely on all six pages. "There they are, aunt Mabel. There they are. Finally. All six of them… every one of them. You don't need to worry anymore. They're right here. Right here."

David went on to read each one, one at a time, beginning with the letter written by uncle Bill that started his remarkable journey. Gently, with both the tone and inflexion of each letter's author, he read. Having met them, he had some general idea how each one would read them, and so he did; bringing something of their essence into the room. One by one David read the pages, and in doing so relived the marvelous journey again.

Reading the final one and tucking it under her hand, he said, "There's the pages, aunt Mabel. There they are." And with his words she seemed to relax as if the final page of her life had now been completed in the reading of those six pages. Yet, one thing remained.

The nurse had returned to the room and stepped to the bed to check aunt Mabel's vitals.

"Oh yes," the nurse stated as if forgetting some event. "Someone dropped something by that she wanted your Aunt to have. It's over here, I believe." Going around to aunt Mabel's beside and rummaging through a small stack of assorted papers and envelopes, she found one and said, "Ah ha. I believe this is it." Taking it over to aunt Mabel and holding it in front of her, the nurse said, "Is this the right letter?" With the slightest nod that seemed in and of itself to be exhausting the nurse handed it to David.

"Is this what you were trying to point to?" David asked. A slight nod of her head let David know that whatever this was, this was the item.

It was an envelope addressed to aunt Mabel. Inside was a letter. Taking the envelope, David slowly removed the letter, laying the envelope aside. As David gently opened the letter, a bookmark fell from the crevices of the letter, landing directly on aunt Mabel's bed. Reaching down, David picked it up and turned it over. On the bookmark, it read "When all other hope fails, hope in God never fails."

Stunned, David looked at the bookmark and then back at aunt Mabel and then back at the bookmark. Immediately paralyzed, he placed a hand on his forehead in utter disbelief and stared out the door and into the vast space of his own ascending emotions.

He realized that this was the very bookmark that aunt Mabel had slipped into his Bible back in the general store. And it was the bookmark, the self-same bookmark, the very same one that he had handed to his nine-year-old future wife on that snowy Christmas Eve in 1973. Amazingly, it was the very same one, and now it had come back to him for whatever reason it had come back.

Looking at aunt Mabel and then back at the bookmark, David realized that no explanation was needed. It was painted across the whole of her face. She knew. Just like she said back at the store. Sitting on those back steps she had said, "You and I, we'll see this old bookmark again." She knew, for the past five decades she lived each moment of her life knowing that this moment would come.

David turned to the nurse and began to ask who delivered the bookmark. Before he could say anything, the nurse said, "I believe that a woman named Kristin, or something like that came by earlier today and dropped this off. She seemed quite distressed herself. She didn't stay long, but she said that she had decided not to mail it, but bring it by herself. She left this letter for your Aunt."

"Has she read it?" David asked.

"No sir," the nurse replied. "Not that I know of. Each time we pulled it out she made us put it back in the envelope. Maybe she was waiting for you."

Turning to aunt Mabel, he said, "Do you want me to read it to you?"

She registered the slightest nod, causing David to feel an anxiety that he had not felt before. This was from the woman who had betrayed him so deeply. Of course the other letters had impacted him. But this one, well this one eclipsed all the rest to a point of a nearly violent fear. It was easy to read the other pages, in fact they were something of joy and adventure. They were about other people in other places far removed from him and his life. But this one, this person had marked his violent departure away from hope and thrust his life into a jaded darkness he had only now climbed out of. This letter spoke of a road he had thought devastated beyond hope of navigation. This was from the woman of lies, betrayal and thievery. He had no idea what the nature of the letter might be; good or ill. Taking the letter in trembling hands, he carefully opened it, scanned the sweeping script, drew a breath and began to read it out loud:

"Dear Aunt Mabel:

A long time ago on Christmas Eve a stranger gave this bookmark to me. I don't remember him well. I remember though that this person showed some real concern for me at a time when no one else really did. That has always stuck with me. Over the years I sometimes thought about him, particularly when I was lonely and things were hard. But one thing still stands out that I remember. He told me to just remember that if there's somebody you really love that you hurt someday, remember that they still love you no matter what. Of course, I was only an imaginative child, but that stuck with me. I've always kept this bookmark in a drawer with the little trinkets that I've kept over the years.

"Years later I married David. During our marriage I really never thought about David and that nice stranger from so long ago. Sadly, I think that sometimes we think of things when it's too late. And when it's too late, all that's left is regret. So I want to tell you that I regret so much what I've done and the hurt it caused David, because I know it hurt you as well.

"I've made some bad choices in my life. Looking back, leaving David was probably one of the worst decision I've ever made, even though I hate to admit it. Sometimes your greed gets the best of your heart. And I let that happen. I've done too much to ever be able to go back, and so I live with the regret that I've denied for so long. But when I heard about your condition, I had to come.

"The bookmark that I enclosed gave me hope all of those years through my childhood and adolescence with the kind of family that I grew up with. I kind of left God behind, but I always had this bookmark in whatever book I was reading at the time. It kept my place in all of those books, and somehow it's helped me find my place in life again. I'd love to find that stranger and thank him, but I know that's impossible.

"So, in your time of need I wanted you to have this. I know I hurt you when I hurt David, so in remembering the words of that stranger on that Christmas Eve I just want to say I'm sorry. I hope that this bookmark does for you what it has done for me.

Remember, "When all other hope fails, hope in God never fails."

Sincerely,

Kristin"

"This, this is the seventh page," David shouted with utter conviction. "This is the last page isn't it?"

Aunt Mabel gently squeezed his hand, managed a slight smile and nodded, "Yes."

Chapter 21
The Eighth Page

Death looks different when you know that death is not an end; when we realize that death is a passage of really the most glorious kind. When we grasp hope and river rocks fences and roads and carnage rebuilt and God stepping through the door of history, everything looks inexplicably different. In the grays and blacks that so often define this world of ours, hope is a rare and often non-existent commodity. It splashes everything with color. It is ever-present but seldom recognized. Hope is something that we wish for, and in the wishing we have relegated hope to a fantasy rather than a reality, for if hope is really a reality, we shouldn't need to hope for it. Yet, we only hope for it because we're too faithless to see it.

One lifetime is not long enough to embrace the whole of life. David had found himself living several lives it seemed. He had found himself mired along a road buckled by the pain of loss and pitted by the anger of betrayal. He saw no other life from the vantage point that his pain afforded him. His life was marked by a handful of hash marks which were mostly painful and largely frustrating. Yet, in a totally indescribable turn of events, he had been flung across time. And in the flinging, he began to realize that life was made up of more than anyone could see from any one vantage point. Yet, from the vantage point of heaven you can see everything.

Aunt Mabel was still conscious, but had little strength left to respond to David. Those few words about an eighth page had exhausted the whole of her. It left the whole of David sitting with a handful of words that suggested that a journey he had assumed completed was not. At all. Inherently he knew that aunt Mabel did not have the energy nor likely the insights to tell him what this 'eighth page' was. Whatever remained of a journey assumed concluded was something he would walk alone, for now the weight of it rested on him. Oddly, it all seemed right and proper… a calling of sorts for which one has been amply prepared.

The nurse had stepped out of the room, leaving the two of them alone. And in the space of their time together, David told her all about his travels. He had recited them to her many times by now, telling and retelling to the joy and emotional elation of them both. It was all part of tying her life together, and part the telling of sweet stories to a mind closing out her life. She seemed to relish hearing them over and over. She never tired of them it seemed. David found that whatever aunt Mabel had given him those many summers in the General Store was being returned by the telling of those wonderful stories in a simple nursing home that tenderly held aunt Mabel until she would be swept into eternity.

Yet, David was hesitant to speak of uncle Bill, so he focused on his meetings with his grandfather in the cellar of the old farmhouse and what a great man he was. He told her of his great-grandmother and the indescribable excitement of meeting with Lincoln and what Gettysburg was really like. He spoke of his time with her in 1969, and Christmas Eve with little Kristen in 1973.

Having recited all of his encounters and conversations in detail, he was left with one unspoken. One that became increasingly absent in the telling of all the other stories. Sometimes the things that are missing in our lives are highlighted by the holes that they leave. Such were the stories of uncle Bill.

Holding her hand, after having recited all the stories again, he cast his glance downward, exhaled a deep breath and said, "Do you want to hear about uncle Bill?" He let the question sit for a moment as great questions sometimes just need to sit a bit. Glancing up and into her eyes, he saw a pain mingled with something not concluded. Some end not tied up. A space that was saved for one more story in a life abounding with them. A spaced saved for *this* story.

She ever so slightly nodded her head "Yes."

"Okay. Well," he began, "I should probably start by saying that he was… he was a remarkable man. I mean, not just because he was my uncle. No, he was remarkable." Pausing, he continued, "I met him, or really kind of ended up in his barracks the night before the invasion, in a huge barracks full of soldiers," he said gesturing his arms wide. "There were so many men there, aunt Mabel. So many of them," David said as he became increasingly energized in the telling of the story. "And they were so young," he continued. "Just kids. I thought that they were too young for a task like that."

"And, well, if you looked around, it was kind of like they all knew something big was happening. They all knew. But from the way that they talked it made me wonder if they knew how big it really was." Pausing, he continued, "Anyway, I think the thing that struck me, now that I think about it, was how calm he was. I mean, I wouldn't be calm at all. Not at all. But he was. Just relaxed and calm. Just talking like it was another day. He was young you know," David continued. "But man, he was wise. He was so wise. So calm and wise and all."

He paused and continued, "He died on Omaha Beach, aunt Mabel." And the story unfolded in a manner that was heroic and somehow majestic. It seemed to fill in a gap for aunt Mabel. It was kind of like putting a period on the end of her life where the period had gone waiting for decades. It was the piece of the puzzle that would finish the puzzle. And unlike most puzzles, had this piece not been the last one, the grandeur of the puzzle would have somehow been less.

By the end of the story, aunt Mabel had grown calm. She had taken David's words and had fashioned multiple images in her head in order to traverse the span of years and somehow share those last moments with uncle Bill. She seemed moved but marvelously serene. Now, finally, the last page had been read, the last piece of the puzzle was set in place, and the book of her life could be closed.

Death done well is a life gathered at the edges, wrapped neatly and packaged to be unpackaged in eternity. It is a book with a period placed at the end of the final sentence of a grand novel. Such seemed her journey. And David was there as much as he could be to pen the pages with her. David had decorated for Christmas. Rather than just decorate, he rather lavishly bedecked the house for the first time in who knows how long. What had become a chore before, became a joy that he could not immerse himself in enough. For in some vague yet not entirely defined manner David had begun to realize two things: first, that hope existed and second, that it was born on Christmas. That God stepped through a very real door that He would never step back out of. His choice to be born into the human race was an eternally binding commitment that mankind would never again be left to live without hope. In fact, mankind would be provided a hope stubbornly undeterred by events or time or mankind itself. Such was the gift of Christmas.

Carefully placed on his fireplace mantel was the bookmark that read, "When all other hope fails, hope in God never fails." David had also had a sign needlepointed much like the one that had hung over aunt Mabel's back door at the general store. The old sign had vanished with time and several moves, but the message never left him.

So, David had it remade. Silently, the needlepointed words spoke the greatest words ever spoken, "Silent Night, Holy Night. This is where hope began."

On an antique oak coffee table there laid the old family Bible with six, weathered and worn pages, charting this most remarkable journey that had been his. He had gently tucked the seventh page from Kristin on top of the other six. He had read the page's numerous times since his journey, finding previously undiscovered richness with each reading. Each time he sat with them, they somehow in some inexplicable way expanded on an already impossibly wide journey.

Friends called, a handful of family members visited, and Christmas cards arrived. Snow fell and the world took on all the wonder of Christmas. As Christmas Eve descended, David found himself in his favorite chair with a fire blazing in the yawning rock fireplace. The Christmas tree shown with more magic than he had ever seen, or thought he'd ever seen. The lights and decorations seemed alive as if living in that moment was living more than any other moment he had ever lived in.

Back on Thanksgiving Day, on the road of Indian, horse and heavy wagon David had thought that he had heard something roll down the old road. At times like those, the line between mystery and imagination is an exceedingly thin one indeed. Mystery too often falls victim to imagination as David had attributed things of great wonder to the irresponsible musings of his mind. On that day, standing in the center of a road of Indians, horse and heavy wagon, David's mind had teetered between the two and then fell to imagination. As he did, the veneer remnants of Indians, horse and heavy wagons looked back over evaporating shoulders as they spun down the road in the waltz of a warm breeze. They had danced by David and touched him with the warmth of hope. But back on Thanksgiving, he had not embraced it. Nor could he.

Now, his travels through time had been more than enough for him to be able to not only believe these voices of time, but to know them intimately. Indeed, he had walked with them in their own history-in the-making. He had been there right along side of them while history was being written right along with them. He and they were fixed comrades, having been united by a mutual undertaking of history at the very moment that history was being undertaken.

Sitting deep in the warmth and embrace of his living room; with winter spinning the glory of the season outside, suddenly and quite unexpectedly the voices passed by him yet again. They came just like they had done that Thanksgiving morning, and on the day he had driven to the nursing home. Indeed, they were identical. The same in fact. But clearer. Much clearer this time. Strikingly clearer. David shot up in his chair.

Somewhere in their whisperings he heard something different. Something like an addendum to what they had said before. A sort of continuation that had built upon itself, so it seemed. Something he'd never heard or recalled hearing, for he most certainly would have remembered it. Something out of place but in perfect place. Sitting on chairs' edge, he listened with startled intent.

Something said, "Write the eighth page." It was slight, but clear enough. "Write the eighth page." Yes, David was certain that that's what the voice said. Leaning forward in his chair, it said again, "write the eighth page."

There was no eighth page. There never had been one. No one had ever mentioned an eighth page. It was seven and out… at least according to aunt Mabel. Six in the Bible. One from Kristin. A total of seven and the story's over. Close the book, so to speak. The voices faded, their message having been delivered.

Teetering on the edge of his chair, his mind moved in and amongst the flames of the fire directly to his left. Confusion crept up on him. Strong as it was, it was not strong enough to take hold of his mind and throw it into disarray like it would have before his journey's. Rather, he pressed through it as it pressed upon him.

"The eighth page," he pondered. His mind went back to the fire of December, 1928. The words of his grandfather. The voice of his grandmother. The deep sadness of a pending fire. uncle Bill, his great-grandmother, Lincoln, aunt Mabel and Kristin. Yet, the idea of an eighth page made no sense nor did it seem to fit into any of that. At all.

As he attempted to push it aside and fall back into the warmth of the holiday, the voices of Indian, horse and heavy wagon returned as a single voice. Not the group of voices gathered from all of history in some sort of grand and glorious chorus of a road well-traveled. Not what he had heard in the early hours of that Thanksgiving morning or on his way to the nursing home. No. It was a single, solitary voice this time. It seemed a collective of voices, but it was single. And it seemed, as odd as it was, that this single voice held the collective message of all the other voices in its voice.

Again sitting up in his chair, David leaned forward again in an attempt to hear this single voice with clarity. There was a familiarity to it. Not a common voice that we might somehow deem it as familiar. But one heard enough to give it a sufficient thread of recognition. Leaning forward in his chair with the splendor of Christmas dripping all around him, he listened intently, begging in his mind that it would speak again. Sometimes things call out to us and we know them with total certainty. Yet, the certainty eludes us and we're left with the angst of the unknown regarding something that, in fact, we know.

And then it spoke again. Clearly. Softly. Lovingly. But with distinctly sharpened clarity. It came from David's left, somewhere in the room. David turned and listened, the whole of his being brought to sharp attention. It spoke again, and as it did David realized that it spoke from the fire which seemed all too improbable. But, he had seen stranger things. He waited. From the flames it came again. It didn't move in and through the living room as if passing by on some mystical errand to some place else. Instead, it came directly from the fire. To him. To David. It was more distinct than the other voices. Standing up he slowly walked to the fireplace, knelt in front of it and canted his head slightly. As he scanned the flames and listened, it spoke again. "Write the eighth page." It was the same message. Again. "Write the eighth page."

For some reason, David focused on identifying the person and less on embracing the message. It might have been that the messenger gave power to the message. Try as he might, he could not match the voice to a face. Inventorying his memory back into the farthest most recesses of his mind, no face emerged. No one came to light. No features or expressions of anyone were provoked. He knew the voice (so he thought), but there was simply no match. Falling ever deeper into an investigative search of sorts, his mind played itself out with no match forthcoming, leaving him kneeling in front of the fireplace utterly perplexed. Both the message and the person who granted it power were frustratingly mysterious.

There are times in life when our efforts have played themselves out and our confusion remains entirely unabated. At these times, our confusion is compounded. We relent and give up hope, only to find that our confusion suddenly clears without our having had a hand in it at all. Sometimes the biggest thing that we can do is to get out of God's way so that He can show us the way.

In doing that quite by accident, David was suddenly struck with the realization that this was the one person he did not get to meet. He had heard her footsteps above him, and listened to her voice float down the basement steps. For some reason, he had never really considered why a meeting with her had been withheld from him, or had even considered that it had. He had just seen it as a part of journey he couldn't explain and had to accept. It was the woman who had perished in the fire of December 12th, 1928. Unbelievably, it was his grandmother.

She was there somehow, her role now coming to fruition long after everyone else's had ceased. It was a calm voice, speaking in soothing tones out the very flames that had killed her. It was soft but direct, seeming to seize the very thing that had ended her life in order to help another begin theirs. It was exactly as he had heard it before, ninety years ago. It was the flames back in 1928 that had killed her. And now she was speaking from them, having mastered what had mastered her in the manner in which hope always does. Hope takes the very things that would destroy us and in the greatest twist of victory it uses them to build us instead. Hope takes that which is evil and turns it to our good.

But quite unexpectedly she was playing a role that pulled together everyone else's role in the grand drama David had lived. Unbeknownst to David, she was tying together a host of marvelous threads into a timeless cord that would change David's life. A rather simple cord indeed.

The old photo that had mysteriously aged had come to a halt sometime in David's journey. He had actually forgotten about it until he had sat down with the old family Bible and opened it to the Christmas story a week or so ago. Somehow, it had sandwiched itself right at the first page of Luke chapter 2. For some reason it had disappeared throughout the course of his journey. Seemingly, it had been introduced at the beginning of his travels and then held to the end of them.

When he had seen it again, David had been shocked to see that the teen that he had last seen in the photo had aged into his grandfather now standing by a tractor. Leaning against it soiled and seemingly sweaty, there had been an air of indomitable pride etched across his face. The photo seemed to possess a life, as if it were actually living and breathing and moving within its stilled confines. The photo had spoken a million words that brought that still-life moment to life for David. The photo seemed to symbolize the start of his journey, rendering the beginning of that great journey captured in the stillness of black and white imagery.

Sometimes we do rather strange things. As odd and ridiculous as it might have seemed, David leapt up, went to the old family Bible, pulled out the photo, turned it and held it in front of the fire as if to let his grandmother see his grandfather yet again. But far more than that, it was David having both of them there, at the same place, together in that single moment. For those briefest of seconds, they were there together again. They were there with David like they were in 1928. An image and a voice. Just like then.

Kneeling in front of the fire, his grandmother's voice made David realize that things were not quite complete. Sometimes there's that unexplainable check in our spirit that says something's not quite done. That a piece remains absent. That something's not concluded; not quite. Sometimes this sense strikes us at the very point that we've assumed something to be concluded, leaving us confused in the paradox. And because we've assumed it completed, we've moved on to whatever our next challenge might be. But sometimes we have to assume something is concluded to truly understand how much it's not.

Unexpectedly, his grandmother spoke out of the fire to complete them. She said, "Write the eighth page." That was all she said. "Write the eighth page." On the heels of that collection of voices she said it twice, enough for David to be clear regarding what she said and to understand the apparent importance of it. And with the message delivered, the voice was gone. The flames feel silent. Indeed, sometimes it is the death of something, despite how tragic that death might have been, that gives desperately needed meaning to a journey that would languish without it. And his grandmother's death nine decades ago granted David greater meaning than he had yet to imagine. For a road without hope is a road without meaning. However, a road of hope is never concluded for hope is eternal, and that renders everything meaningful.

David had thought his journey to have been concluded. He had thought that the threads have been woven. He had settled into life as a changed man, reshaping the entirety of his life and walking aunt Mabel through the remainder of hers. He had gone back to work the two weeks before Christmas a changed man, so much so that his boss and friend Steven was both amazed and blessed. He had called the real estate agent who, despite her few encounters with David herself marveled at his transformation and was more than pleased to remove the farmhouse from the market. He had reignited relationships with family and restored friendships and returned to church and become a man of deep prayer and uncontainable faith. He had already begun the process of restoring the old farmhouse and had a handful of contractors set to begin the process of restoration the first week of January.

But great journeys are never concluded… not really. Like the river-rock fence, the road of life, of Indians, horse and heavy wagon goes on forever. Nothing is concluded for in any conclusion things are only beginning.

"Write the eighth page," she had said. He thought he had heard her correctly, but because it didn't make sense he was left to ponder what that meant and what that was. So, he sat there and waited for the voice again. It did not come. It never would. Taking the poker, he gently prodded the burning logs as he had prodded the contents of the old chest with a broom stick. Sparks leapt up from the flames and curled in lively dancing wisps up the chimney and out of sight.

"The eighth page," he said to himself. "The eighth page."

No wonder aunt Mabel hadn't mentioned it. It was the only page that was not a page of history. It hadn't been written because it couldn't have been. She wouldn't have known… couldn't have known. It wasn't there to be known. It was the compilation of history visited that spoke into a future waiting. It would be the single page that would have the gargantuan task of bridging the past with the future. It was the summation that couldn't have been written until the events had played themselves out so that they could be summarized. It would be monumental because it could be nothing less.

"What would an eighth page even say?" David pondered kneeling in front of the fire. "What else can be said?"

Turning back to the old oak table, he picked up the old family Bible, set back in his lounge chair and placed the photo back at the beginning of the Christmas story. Half glancing at it, David abruptly turned. It had changed again, or so it seemed. Grabbing his reading glasses and pulling the photo close to himself David realized it had changed… again. There were now two people in the photo. Squinting in disbelief and holding the photo at a distance, his grandmother had now joined his grandfather. There they were. No longer by a tractor, but in the old basement. Standing arm in arm with smiles of pure joy drawn across each of their faces. Right where David had met with his grandfather.

Sometimes it seems that a photo is anything but still. Sometimes photos seem to have a voice; to be alive in the stillness of their own image. And such was the case with this photo. Despite the cessation of his travels through time some two weeks' prior, the photo gave David some yet undefined closure to his encounters with his grandfather; for what had always felt somehow incomplete was now complete. As odd as it might have been, it seemed to have given them closure as well. All was now done... except the eighth page.

In some way undefined, it set the stage for the writing of the eighth page, whatever that would be. The settled look on their faces, the ease of their stances, their gentle embrace... there was a peace about it all that suggested a journey well done and a lesson learned in the journey. But what were the words that would explain all of that? How could that be articulated so that others might understand it so as not to miss it? How do you put words to things beyond words? That task seemed impossible. Indeed, there was nothing new in that.

Staring into the photo, the last words of his grandfather suddenly found their way to David once again.

"Remember that I love ya, David," he had said. "And remember that all the people that ya met love ya too. They respect ya. They believe in ya. We all do. Yer Mom here, she'll believe in ya like ya yerself can't believe. Ya got a whole bunch of great people who believe in ya." With an authority in voice, he said, "And I believe in ya."

Pausing, David drew the photo close and said, "Thank you, thank you for believing in me. Both of you."

Standing the photo up against the old family Bible so that his grandparents could watch him take his most important step, David pulled out the seven pages and read each one again, seeing if he could extract from them whatever the eighth page might mean or what it might be. They had seemed to have aged even more than when his journey had been completed. There was a sense that they were now catching up with the age that they always were.

"Well," he said out loud, "I suppose that when she said, 'Write the eighth page,' I should probably write the eighth page. But, write what? What?" Turning to the photo, he said, "What do you want me to write," as foolish as talking to a photo seemed to be. The photo remained still and the fire remained quiet except for the occasional crackling of wood rubbing the house warm. Standing up from his chair and walking to the fire, David took the poker and moved the logs this way and that, trying to ignite his imagination as much as he was trying to heighten the fire.

Rearranging the logs, David sent sparks pirouetting up the chimney. Standing up, he placed the poker on its stand and wiped his hands. Turning, David walked to an old oak roll-top desk in an adjacent study. Opening a drawer, he pulled out a white sheet of paper and an ornamental pen.

"Well, let's see where this goes, or doesn't go," David mumbled to himself.

Settling back into his lounge chair, he likewise settled deep into thought. Minutes passed, stretching out in a manner that seemed like hours; for they were. No thought seemed to fit or work. Nothing clicked. He wondered how he could write anything that would somehow match all the other pages, for his life was not reflective of any of those kinds of journeys. A fresh cup of hot coffee, standing and staring out into winter's royal white, running questioning fingers over the ornaments on the tree, and even prayers of petition to God for a handful of words yielded nothing except nothing.

After several hours of futile thinking, a thought began to massage itself into his heart and move into his mind. As some sort of sunrise granting a whisper of light to a new day, he realized that he was attempting to assemble some sort of great thought that would match the greatness of the people he had met and the grandness of their times.

In doing so he had completely missed the lesson in it all. It didn't matter if it was his grandfather or uncle Bill or Lincoln or his great-grandmother or aunt Mabel or Kristin any of them. This wasn't the summarizing of their lives in some grand tale of epic proportions. Although it had ample merit to be that, this eighth page wasn't supposed to be a recalling of great moments in history as a compilation that would help people face the challenges of the present.

It was a message of hope. Hope. That was all, and that was enough. The simple message of hope had been precisely the same for every person and every place. Sure, hope had been held up against unimaginably different challenges and obstacles from dying in the flames to a nation ripped in two by Civil War and beyond.

But in it all, hope was the single thing they all had in common. Obviously. Things either monstrously large or indiscriminately small could be navigated and overturned by this single and sole thing called hope. God's hope. It wasn't about any event. It was about hope rooted in the event. So simple was hope that it could seize everything and be repelled by nothing. Hope was the common thread that had the tenacity to be woven through any crisis either monumental or miniscule, bringing to everything both the possibility and promise of better things. The thought felt far too simple, seeming to cheapen everything David had experienced. Staring into the fire, his vision was suddenly lifted to the manger scene neatly displayed on the sweeping oak mantel. His mind moved in and among the characters, placing himself amidst them and attempting to somehow travel back in time to that event as he had through the pages lodged in the old family Bible. Who were these people in their time? What were the circumstances of their situation and their lives? What did they actually live out that night in that place? Not the stories spun over the centuries, but what was it really like? Real people toiling in the rigors of that moment. How he would have loved to have gone back there. To that night. To that place of all places. One more trip if he could. To live the reality that the figurines only spoke of in storybook form. But this time, his mind would have to take him there.

This infant child had been born in a manger to two impoverished teenagers in a town far off the pages of politics and commerce. He was born into poverty with all the superficial trappings of life wholly absent. He had been relegated to a barn in an overcrowded town that was being taxed to economic death by an oppressive regime. The past was precarious for them and the future uncertain. They lived a story yet untold, moving ahead into a foreboding future that seemed as dim as their present. Yet, how could it have been any simpler? How can anyone write a story any less adorned? How is it that the eternal and infinite God of the cosmos would pen the most transformational story of all time in such a few simple lines? How could it have ever been any more intentional? Why had God chosen to enter the world in a manner so unobtrusive and so far removed from anything resembling royalty? A makeshift barn. Two anxious teenagers. A random pile of swaddling cloths. A handful of backwoods shepherds meandering about. A bunch of domestic animals jostling for space in terribly cramped quarters. Simple. Beautifully simple.

The message of hope born that night was a simple message delivered in simplicity. God's greatest message was told in the few impoverished words of a manger, obscurity, two frightened teenagers, and a handful of societally rejected shepherds. Of course.

Could it be that the eighth page was to be simple too? Could it be that simple? Could that be why he had missed it through the handful of hours that he'd just spent rolling it over and over in his mind? Slowly reflecting on it all, he realized that in this journey of his there had been two simple messages. He turned and pulled the bookmark out of the old family Bible and read, "When all other hope fails, hope in God never fails." "There's one," he said.

But that began... David thought. His eyes scanned upward to the needlepointed sign above the mantel. It read, "Silent Night, Holy Night. This is where hope began." Then, in deeply reflective tones, David said, "What all other hope fails, hope in God never fails. And that hope began on this Silent Night." A deep pause fell over him; a connecting of two thoughts; more a beautiful collision of two thoughts that had always been with him but thoughts he had never knitted together. "What all other hope fails, hope in God never fails. And that hope began on this Silent Night!"

"Of course," he said out loud. "Of course! That's all it is. That's all it has to be." David turned, looked into the fire and thought to himself, *we see simple as naïve. We see it as shallow and weak and unintelligent. But God turns all of that logic around. That's why we don't find it. Simple is not enough so we're looking for something else.* Stopping for a moment, he said, "But if you think about it, what is simple is what is great in disguise."

David returned to his chair, settled in and fell deeper into thought. Talking to himself, he said, "We miss the simplicity of hope, but we can't find anything else to replace it with because we need something. So what do we do? You know what we do? We wrap a bunch of cheap traditions around it to give it some sort of form or shape or meaning. Something we can hold onto. We make it about wrappings and tinsel and ribbons and colorful myths. We've made it into office parties and white elephant gift exchanges and elfish characters and a barrage of marketing so it's something other than nothing."

Pondering further, he thought, *no wonder we've missed it. We missed it and then unknowingly we buried it under all of that stuff. We buried hope under all of that because all that stuff became all that there is. No wonder we're a society without hope.* Continuing, he said, "But I did that. I'm no better, I buried hope. I buried it… for all of those years I buried it." And then with a markedly more reflective tone, he said, "And then I rejected the stuff I buried it under." Pausing, he wove everything together and thought, *and that leaves a man more alone than you thought you could ever be. Oh man…*

Shifting, he said, "But grandpa, and uncle Bill, and great-grandmother, and Lincoln, and aunt Mabel, and Kristin, and now grandma… they stood out because they took it for what it was." With accelerating energy, he said, "They let it be simple so that it could be powerful. They let it alone… to be what it was. And it worked. It actually worked."

Quite unexpectedly, his thoughts leapt out beyond Christmas to a cross erected on a desolate hill some thirty-three years later. Of a rough hewn tomb, a stones throw away. While the city swelled with hoards of people reveling in the Passover celebrations, this baby turned Savior was executed in obscurity much in the same way that He was born into it. His body was placed in a borrowed tomb by a handful of followers much like he had been born in a borrowed barn surrounded by a few shepherds. It was the same at both ends. And He would rise because hope is simple and hope can't be buried on either side of this existence.

"Or course," he said. "That's why there was a resurrection. There had to be. If you bury hope, it's going rise up anyway. Let it be what it is and it will rise… every time. By its very nature, it's just going to."

The images of his trips through time were still fresh and vivid as such images are. The voices, the faces, the words, the obstacles that loomed ahead of them and over them… they all coursed in front of his mind in some fast-forward momentum that took the whole of them and condensed them down to this single, simple thought.

By this time David had settled into his chair and was leaning forward, letting his head run with the life-changing insights that swept over him. Quickly taking the piece of paper and pen hand, he began to write:

"In the span of life, both that of mine and others, I have learned the transformation message that *'when all other hope fails, hope in God never fails.'* And I've discovered exactly when that hope was born. *Silent Night, Holy Night. This is where hope began.* It's truly that simple. It's my hope that no one misses this because of its simplicity! This is the hope that the roads of our lives are paved with. If anyone holds onto these two truths, and if we guard them with our lives, and if we refused to let them be buried because we missed them in thinking that they weren't enough, and in doing so if we live them out with all of our being, hope will be our constant companion down the road of Indian, horse and heavy wagon. Life is a river-rock fence and hope says it will always be ours to etch hash marks on for all of eternity. We can know that whatever falls to cinders and ash will rise to something greater than that to which it fell.

"With hope, we might be broken, but we will never be beaten. With hope, a mountain is nothing more than a road in the making. With hope, I am invincible. With hope I have hope. And I would surmise that those who changed history did so because they held fast to hope even when their worlds were fast falling apart around them. They let it be what God made it to be. And it worked! This is the power of God's hope! May we, despite the nature of our journey, never think otherwise.

David B. Morris (Davie B.)
December 23th, 2018"

Taking the letter in hand, he read it over and over. Placing it aside, he leaned back in his chair and for the first time he could remember, he felt truly whole.

The next day David drove to the nursing home. Aunt Mabel was slowly fading, but she seemed to be committed to living out to Christmas Day. And now it was Christmas Eve.

Arriving at the nursing home, David passed through the double front doors and turned down the hallway to aunt Mabel's room.

Passing the nursing station, he turned to Rachel and with a perky voice said, "Merry Christmas."

By now, he had developed a friendship with several of the nurses. However, because Rachel had been the first one to call him when aunt Mabel had begun to deteriorate, there was something a bit more special in their exchanges.

"Merry Christmas," came her lively reply.

"So, how's my favorite old lady?" he quipped with a bit of levity in his voice.

"She's stable," Rachel said. "I think she's hanging on for Christmas. I'll bet that's what she's doing."

Going into her room, she was fast asleep. Walking around her bed, he pulled a chair up to her bedside. He had visited her daily for the past two weeks and had become familiar with this place and these people. It had become, in a sense, a second home of sorts.

Having been roused, aunt Mabel looked up through eyes of age and fatigue. Seeing him, a sudden glint found a place in them. The rest of her face was desperately aged, but her eyes seemed to suddenly have a youthful vitality about them. They had not changed since those glorious days at the general store.

"It's good to see you," he said. "It's really good." Taking the letter he had written and placing it on the bed, he said, "You're the only one who'll understand this, believe me. I was sitting by the fire last night and, well, grandma talked to me out of the flames. Crazy right?" Pausing, he said, "Yeah, I think we both know how all of this works. In fact, I think we're the only two on the face of the earth that understand how this works," he said in a rather amused manner. "So don't tell anyone or they'll think we're both crazy." A slight smile etched itself across aunt Mabel's face.

Taking on a tone of seriousness, he continued, "But what she told me, what she said," David said while holding the letter in his hand, "She told me to write an eighth page." Pausing and shaking his head, he continued, "I never expected that. I thought this was all done, you know, that the lessons had been learned. But it seems that there's always the next lesson."

"So, I wanted to bring this and read it to you. I really want to know what you think," he said knowing that she couldn't respond other than a slight smile or the words that only eyes can speak. "I didn't know what to write... it kind of caught me off guard. I guess really off guard." Pausing, he said, "This whole experience has caught me off guard. But I think I understand what I'm supposed to write and I want to know what you think." And so he began to read. Slowly and with great heart, he read the eighth page. All of the pages had had a tremendous impact on him. But he had been given the privilege of pulling all of them together and distilling out of them the greatest message of all time. Of any time. This simple man who had been jaded rigid by life and had lived a life of anger and simmering hatred had been granted the unfathomable privilege of passing through time and meeting these people. This man of seething fury and bubbling rage had been granted this opportunity, for sometimes the most calloused of us are the very ones who can save the most desperate of us.

Meeting these people of history would have been enough for anyone. More than enough really. It had been a miraculous privilege. But as impossible as it all sounded, now he had been given the even greater privilege to sum it all up. Into his hands was trusted the greatest message of all time, and into his hands was trusted the ability to speak it into his life, the life of aunt Mabel, and the life of all mankind.

Slowing and with great depth he read each word. It was short and simple, as was hope. As was a manger. As was a cross. As was the general store and those Michigan farm fields. Completing it, he laid it on aunt Mabel's bed, placed her hand on the page and looked into her face. Tears streamed down each of her cheeks. She took several deep breaths and worked to call up a final bit of strength.

With great effort, she uttered the words, "Jesus is hope." She hadn't been able to say anything all of these weeks. But in a moment that consolidated the magic and mystery of the pages, she found the strength and she uttered the words. Drawing another few breathes, she said, "Jesus is the only hope." Her words exhausted her, causing her to lean back in bed. Yet the words brought a wide smile to her face and it enlivened eyes that seemed to have a life laid out behind them and an eternity set in front of them.

Taking her hand in his, David said, "I know. I finally know."

As he uttered those words he looked down at the page and was shocked to see that it too had aged just like all the others. It was suddenly brittle and yellowed as well, tattered around the edges and crinkled at its corners. David took it and held it, feeling the stiffness that age had somehow granted it. Holding it, he knew he had gotten it right. His page had come to join in the message of other pages. He had understood the message of the pages.

Aunt Mabel passed away the day after Christmas. A nursing home is acclimated to death. Death is a constant visitor in ways that it doesn't visit any place else. However, when aunt Mabel passed there was a grieving in that place unlike any other time. Yet, laced with this heavy loss there was an entirely offsetting feeling of hope. Aunt Mabel had transformed the staff and changed the visitation of death to the advent of life. The nursing home was never the same.

Her funeral was transforming as well. While he spoke a brief eulogy, David had not yet conceptualized everything in a manner that he could speak it into the lives of the handful of people who had gathered to say goodbye to this marvelous woman. Neither would they believe the journey that Davie B. had taken and aunt Mabel's role in it. He made no mention of it at her funeral for such a tale would cause those gathered there to question his sanity and wonder if his grieving had driven him mad. Clearly, he and aunt Mabel were alone in this. Now, he was alone in this. It seemed that aunt Mabel's death was the sign that David was ready to be alone in this; to take this message to a world desperate for hope. To live out the eighth page.

David spent the remainder of his life formulating the message of hope. He would speak it into the lives of those he encountered as a fellow sojourner down the road of life. Not in some forceful manner. But as each moment made space for it. His own demeanor was transformed by it and saturated in it. He would spend the remainder of his life in the old farmhouse, restoring it to what it was before the fire of 1928. Despite the massive restoration, he never touched the old root cellar. He frequented it often, but he wanted it to remain just as it was the first day he met his grandfather. It remained entirely the same right up to his own death.

Over the years his children had come back to him. Kristin forever remained at a distance, living out her life in some diminished capacity that was always painful for

David to hear of. Since receiving the bookmark from aunt Mabel in the old general store his anger toward Kristin had been completely replaced by his sorrow for her. He had prayed for her daily ever since, hoping that her heart would be softened, her eyes would permit her to see, and that she would be returned to the innocence of the nine-year-old that he had played with on that Christmas Eve in 1973. David went to his grave never certain what changes, if any, Kristin had made. He found that we can hope for others with a longing indescribable, but they must hope for themselves.

His children, Cheyenne and Corey were willed the old farmhouse. History was freely handed to them as it was to David. His daughter Cheyenne had entertained ideas of working in the limelight of media and entertainment, mingling with those who spun stories that were not even the slightest shadow of the realities that her father had lived. She decided to choose a simpler life and moved into the farmhouse, working with media remotely at a distance through the expanse of the internet. Corey built a business shaped of the acumen and abilities he had seen in his father.

Two weeks after their father's death, both Cheyenne and Corey went to the old farmhouse and began going through the house that their Dad had meticulously restored. One of the last places they went was the old root cellar. Forgotten boxes proliferated. Seemingly stacked without real regard for the fact that in whatever manner they were stacked, they would remain so for decades. It was as if someone had stacked them thinking that they would be back to retrieve them shortly. And yet, 'shortly' never came, rendering the boxes captive to the abyss of time and the tragedy of forgetfulness. And so they both scanned the scrawling's on the boxes, gathered their strength and randomly reached for them, breaking the bonds of time and self by sorting and moving the brittle boxes.

As they moved time packed in brittle boxes, in the deeply graying and cobwebbed shadows of a far corner Cheyenne spied the old chest. She blithely turned her glance away from it and continued parting the sea of brittle boxes. Then something inaudible met their ears, sounding as if it arose from some great and inestimable distance, drawing toward both of them and lodging in the chest itself. It filled the chest so completely and entirely that it was almost as if the chest had called out to them, as if it had a single voice that was in reality many voices melded together beckoned her. This voice of many voices was entirely silent but sufficiently loud and altogether familiar. Both of them reflexively jerked back, realizing that they had heard something, but that they had not; that something audible had spoken to their souls or their hearts or something that doesn't hear in words, but hears in the far more convincing and compelling language of the soul.

Both of them reached back and pulled out of the old chest. Carrying it out into the basement, they set it down, opened its creaking lid, scanned the contents and reached in.

Made in the USA
Coppell, TX
08 February 2020

15607425R00259